BEGGARS & CHOOSERS

NANCY KRESS

A TOM DOHERTY ASSOCIATES BOOK
NEW YORK

BEGGARS & CHOOSERS

Copyright © 1994 by Nancy Kress

This book is printed on acid-free paper.

Edited by David G. Hartwell

A Tor Book
Published by Tom Doherty Associates, Inc.
175 Fifth Avenue
New York, N.Y. 10010

Tor® is a registered trademark of Tom Doherty Associates, Inc.

Design by Lynn Newmark

ISBN 0-312-85749-7 (hardcover)

Printed in the United States of America

To
Miriam Grace Monfredo
and
Mary Stanton

without whose friendship in a bad time
this book would not have been finished.

Prologue

2106

The clanging of the priority-one override alarm ripped through the cavernous backstage dressing room. Drew Arlen, the only occupant, jerked his head toward the holo-terminal beside his dressing table. The screen registered his retina scan and Leisha Camden's face appeared.

"Drew! Have you heard?"

The man in the powerchair, upper body fanatically muscled above his crippled legs, turned back to putting on his eye makeup. He leaned into the dressing table mirror. "Heard what?"

"Did you see the six o'clock *Times?*"

"Leisha, I go on stage in fifteen minutes. I haven't listened to anything." He heard the thickening in his own voice, and hoped she didn't. Even after all this time. Even at just the sight of her holo.

"Miranda and the Supers . . . Miranda . . . Drew, they've built an entire *island*. Off the coast of Mexico. Using nanotech and the atoms in seawater, and almost overnight!"

"An island," Drew repeated. He frowned into the mirror, rubbed at his makeup, applied more.

"Not a floating construct. An actual island, that goes all the way down to the continental shelf. Did you know about this?"

"Leisha, I have a concert in fifteen minutes . . ."

"You did, didn't you. You knew what Miranda was doing. Why didn't you *tell* me?"

Drew turned his powerchair to face Leisha's golden hair, green eyes, genemod perfect skin. She looked thirty-five. She was ninety-eight years old.

He said, "Why didn't Miranda tell you?"

Leisha's expression quieted. "You're right. It was Miranda's place to tell me. And she didn't. There's a lot she doesn't tell me, isn't there, Drew?"

A long moment passed before Drew said softly, "It isn't easy being on the outside for a change, is it, Leisha?"

She said, equally softly, "You've waited a long time to be able to say that to me, haven't you, Drew?"

He looked away. In the corner of the huge silent room something rustled: a mouse, or a defective 'bot.

Leisha said, "Are they moving to this new island? All twenty-seven Supers?"

"Yes."

"No one in the scientific community even knew nanotech had reached that capability."

"Nobody else's nanotech has."

Leisha said, "They're not going to let me on that island, are they? At all?"

He listened to the complex undertones in her voice. Leisha's generation of Sleepless, the first generation, could never hide their feelings. Unlike Miranda's generation, who could hide anything.

"No," Drew said. "They're not."

"They'll shield the island with something that Terry Mwakambe invents, and you'll be the only non-Super ever allowed to know what they're doing there."

He didn't answer. A technician stuck his head diffidently in the door. "Ten minutes, Mr. Arlen, sir."

"Yes. I'm coming."

"Huge crowd tonight, sir. All pumped up."

"Yes. Thank you." The tech's head disappeared.

"Drew," Leisha said, her voice splintering. "She's as much a daughter to me as you were a son . . . what is Miranda planning out on that island?"

"I don't know," Drew said, and it was both a lie and not a lie, in ways that Leisha could never understand. "Leisha, I have to be on stage in nine minutes."

"Yes," Leisha said wearily. "I know. You're the Lucid Dreamer."

Drew stared again at her holo-image: the lovely curve of cheek, the unaging Sleepless skin, the suspicion of water in the green eyes. She had been the most important person in his world, and in the larger public world. And now, although she didn't know it yet, she was obsolete.

"Yes," he said. "That's right. I'm the Lucid Dreamer."

The holostage blanked, and he went back to his makeup for the stage.

I

JULY 2114

Concern for man himself and his fate
must always form the chief interest of all
technical endeavors, concern for the great
unsolved problems of the organization of
labor and the distribution of goods—in
order that the creations of our mind shall be
a blessing and not a curse to mankind.

**—Albert Einstein, address to California
Institute of Technology, 1931**

One

For some of us, of course, nothing would be enough.
That sentence can be taken two ways, can't it? But I don't
mean that having nothing would ever be satisfactory to us.
It isn't even satisfactory to Livers, no matter what pathetic claims
they lay to an "aristo life of leisure." Yes. Right. There isn't a
single one of us that doesn't know better. We donkeys could always
recognize seething dissatisfaction. We saw it daily in the mirror.

My IQ wasn't boosted as high as Paul's.

My parents couldn't afford all the genemods Aaron got.

My company hasn't made it as big as Karen's.

My skin isn't as small-pored as Gina's.

*My constituency is more demanding than Luke's. Do the blood-
sucking voters think I'm made of money?*

My dog is less cutting-edge genemod than Stephanie's dog.

It was, in fact, Stephanie's dog that made me decide to change
my life. I know how that sounds. There's nothing about the start
of my service with the Genetic Standards Enforcement Agency
that doesn't sound ridiculous. Why not start with Stephanie's dog?
It brings a certain satiric panache to the story. I could dine out
on it for months.

If, of course, anyone were ever going to dine out again.

Panache is such a perishable quality.

Stephanie brought her dog to my apartment in the Bayview
Security Enclave on a Sunday morning in July. The day before,
I'd bought pots of new flowers from BioForms in Oakland and
they cascaded over the terrace railing, a riot of blues much more
varied than the colors of San Francisco Bay, six stories below.

Cobalt, robin's egg, aquamarine, azure, cyan, turquoise, cerulean. I lay on my terrace chaise, eating anise cookies and studying my flowers. The gene geniuses had shaped each blossom into a soft fluttery tube with a domed end. The blossoms were quite long. Essentially, my terrace frothed with flaccid, blue, vegetable penises. David had moved out a week ago.

"Diana," Stephanie said, through the Y-energy shield spanning the space between my open French doors. "Knock knock."

"How'd you get into the apartment?" I said, mildly annoyed. I hadn't given Stephanie my security code. I didn't like her enough.

"Your code's broken. It's on the police net. Thought you'd like to know." Stephanie was a cop. Not with the district police, which was rough and dirty work down among the Livers. Not our Stephanie. She owned a company that furnished patrol 'bots for enclave security. She designed the 'bots herself. Her firm, which was spectacularly successful, held contracts with a sizable number of San Francisco enclaves, although not with mine. Telling me my code was on the 'bot net was her ungraceful way of needling me because my enclave used a different police force.

I lounged back on my chaise and reached for my drink. The closest blue flowers yearned toward my hand.

"You're giving them an erection," Stephanie said, walking through the French doors. "Oh, anise cookies! Mind if I give one to Katous?"

The dog followed her from the cool dimness of my apartment and stood blinking and sniffing in the bright sunshine. It was clearly, aggressively, illegally genemod. The Genetic Standards Enforcement Agency may allow fanciful tinkering with flowers, but not with animal phyla higher than fish. The rules are very clear, backed up by court cases whose harsh financial penalties make them even clearer. No genemods that cause pain. No genemods that create weaponry, in its broadest definition. No genemods that "alter external appearance or basic internal functioning such that a creature deviates significantly from other members of not only its species but also its breed." A collie may pace and single-foot, but it better still look like Lassie.

And never, never, never any genemod that is inheritable. Nobody wants another fiasco like the Sleepless. Even my penile flowers were sterile. And genemod human beings, we donkeys, were all individually handcrafted, in vitro one-of-a-kind collector's items. Such is order maintained in our orderly world. So saith Supreme Court Chief Justice Richard J. Milano, writing the majority opinion for *Linbecker* v. *Genetic Standards Enforcement Agency*. Humanity must not be altered past recognition, lest we lose what it means to be human. Two hands, one head, two eyes, two legs, a functioning heart, the necessity to breathe and eat and shit, this is humanity in perpetuity. We are *the* human beings.

Or, in this case, *the* dogs. And yet here was Stephanie, theoretically an officer of the law, standing on my terrace flanked by a prison-sentence GSEA violation in pink fur. Katous had four adorable pink ears, identically cocked, aural Rockettes. It had an adorable pink fur rabbit's tail. It had huge brown eyes, three times the size of any dog's eyes Justice Milano would approve, giving it a soulful, sorrowing look. It was so adorable and vulnerable-looking I wanted to kick it.

Which might have been the point. Although that, too, might be construed as illegal. No modifications that cause pain.

"I heard that David moved out," Stephanie said, crouching to feed an anise cookie to the quivering pink fur. Oh so casual—just a girl and her dog, my illegal genemod pet, I live on the edge like this all the time, doncha know. I wondered if Stephanie knew that "Katous" was Arabic for "cat." Of course she did.

"David moved out," I agreed. "We came to the place where the road forked."

"And who's next on your road?"

"Nobody." I sipped my drink without offering Stephanie one. "I thought I'd live alone for a while."

"Really." She touched an aquamarine flower; it wrapped its soft tubular petal around her finger. Stephanie grinned. "*Quel dommage.* What about that German software dealer you talked to such a long time at Paul's party?"

"What about your dog?" I said pointedly. "Isn't he pretty illegal for a cop's pet?"

"But so cute. Katous, say hello to Diana."

"Hello," Katous said.

Slowly I lowered my glass from my mouth.

Dogs couldn't talk. The vocal equipment didn't allow it, the law didn't allow it, the canine IQ didn't allow it. Yet Katous's growled "hello" was perfectly clear. Katous could talk.

Stephanie lounged against the French doors, enjoying the

effect of her bombshell. I would have given anything to be able to ignore it, to go on with a neutral, uninterested conversation. I could not manage that.

"Katous," I said, "how old are you?"

The dog gazed at me from enormous sorrowful eyes.

"Where do you live, Katous?"

No answer.

"Are you genemod?"

No answer.

"Is Katous a dog?"

Was there a shade of sad puzzlement in its brown eyes?

"Katous, are you happy?"

Stephanie said, "His vocabulary is only twenty-two words. Although he understands more than that."

"Katous, would you like a cookie? Cookie, Katous?"

He wagged his ridiculous tail and pranced in place. There were no claws on his toes. "Cookie! Please!"

I held out a cookie, which was from the Proust's Madelines franchise and were wonderful: crunchy, fragrant with anise, rich with butter. Katous took it with toothless pink gums. "Thank you, lady!"

I looked at Stephanie. "He can't defend himself. And he's a mental cripple, smart enough to talk but not smart enough to understand his world. What's the point?"

"What's the point of your spermatic flowers? God, they're salacious. Did David give them to you? They're wonderful."

"David didn't give them to me."

"You bought them yourself? After he left, I would guess. A replacement?"

"A reminder of male fallibility."

Stephanie laughed. She knew I was lying, of course. David was never fallible in that department. Or any other. His leaving was my fault. I am not an easy person to live with. I needle, pry, argue, search compulsively for weaknesses to match my own. Worse, I only admit this well after the fact. I looked away from Stephanie and gazed through a gap in the flowers at San Francisco Bay, my drink frosty in my hand.

It is, I suppose, a serious flaw in my character that I can't stand to be in the same room for ten minutes with people like Stephanie. She's intelligent, successful, funny, daring. Men fall all over her, and not just for her genemod looks, red hair and violet eyes and legs a yard and a half long. Not even for her enhanced intelligence. No, she has the ultimate attraction for jaded males: no heart. She's a perpetual challenge, an infinite variety that custom doesn't stale because the tariff is always about to be revoked. She can't really be loved, and can't really be hurt, because she doesn't care. Indifference, coupled with those legs, is irresistible. Every man thinks he'll be different for her, but he never is. Her face launched a thousand ships? Big deal. There's always another fleet. If pheromone genemods weren't illegal, I'd swear Stephanie had them.

Jealousy, David always said, corrodes the soul.

I'd always answered that Stephanie was soulless. She was twenty-eight, seven years my junior, which meant seven years more advancement in the allowable technological evolution of *Homo sapiens.* They had been a fertile seven years. Her father was Harve Brunell, of Brunell Power. For his only daughter he had bought every genemod on the market, and some of that hadn't quite arrived there, legally. Stephanie Brunell represented the penultimate achievement of American science, power, and values.

Right behind Katous.

She plucked a penile blue flower and turned it idly in her hands. She was making me choke on my curiosity about Katous. "So it's really over with you and David. Incidentally, I glimpsed him last night at Anna's water fete. From a great distance. He was out on the lily pads."

I asked casually, "Oh? With whom?"

"Quite alone. And looking very handsome. I think he had his hair replaced again. It's curly and blond now."

I stretched and yawned. The muscles in my neck felt hard as duragem chains. "Stephanie, if you want David, go after him. *I* don't care."

"Don't you? Do you mind if I send your rather primitive house 'bot for another pitcher? You seem to have drunk this whole one without me. At least your 'bot works—the breakdown rate on the cop 'bots has accelerated yet *again.* I'd think the parts franchises were all owned by crooks, if they weren't owned by some of my best friends. What's your 'bot's name?"

"Hudson," I said, "another pitcher."

It floated off. Katous watched it fearfully, backing into a corner of the terrace. The dog's absurd tail brushed a hanging flower.

Immediately the flower wrapped itself around the tail, and Katous yelped and jumped forward, quivering.

I said, "A genemod dog with some self-awareness but afraid of a flower? Isn't that a little cruel?"

"It's supposed to be an ultra-pampered beastie. Actually, Katous is a beta-test prototype for the foreign market. Allowable under the Special Exemption Act for Economic Recovery, Section 14-c. Non-Agricultural Domestic Animals for Export."

"I thought the President hasn't signed the Special Exemption Act." Congress had been wrangling over it for weeks. Economic crisis, unfavorable balance of trade, strict GSEA controls, threat to life as we know it. All the usual.

"He'll sign it next week," Stephanie said. I wondered which of her lovers had influence on the Hill. "We can't afford not to. The genemod lobby gets more powerful every month. Think of all those Chinese and EC and South American rich old ladies who will just love a nauseatingly cute, helpless, unthreateningly sentient, short-lived, very expensive lapdog with no teeth."

"Short-lived? No teeth? GSEA breed specifications—"

"Will be waived for export animals. Meanwhile I'm just beta-testing for a friend. Ah, here's Hudson."

The 'bot floated through the French doors with a fresh pitcher of vodka scorpions. Katous scrambled away, his four ears quivering. His scramble brought him sideways against a bank of flowers, all of which tried to wrap themselves around him. One long flaccid petal settled softly over his eyes. Katous yelped and pulled loose, his eyes wild. He shot across the terrace.

"Help!" he cried. "Help Katous!"

On that side of the terrace I had planted moondust in shallow boxes between the palings, to make a low border that wouldn't obstruct the view of the Bay. Katous's frightened flight barreled him into the moondust's sensor field. It released a cloud of sweet-smelling blue fibers, fine as milkweed. The dog breathed them in, and yelped again. The moondust cloud was momentarily translucent, a fragrant fog around those enormous terrified eyes. Katous ran in a ragged circle, then leaped blindly. He hurled between the wide-set palings and over the edge of the terrace.

The sound of his body hitting the pavement below made Hudson turn its sensors.

Stephanie and I ran to the railing. At our feet the moondust released another cloud of fibers. Katous lay smashed on the sidewalk six stories down.

"Damn!" Stephanie cried. "That prototype cost a quarter million in R&D!"

Hudson said, "There was an unregistered sound from the lower entranceway. Shall I alert security?"

"What am I going to tell Norman? I promised to baby-sit the thing and keep it safe!"

"Repeat. There was an unregistered sound from the lower entranceway. Shall I alert security?"

"No, Hudson," I said. "No action." I looked at the mass of bloody pink fur. Sorrow and disgust swept through me: sorrow for Katous's fear, disgust for Stephanie and myself.

"Ah, well," Stephanie said. Her perfect lips twitched. "Maybe the IQ *did* need enhancing. Can't you just see the Liver tabloid headlines? DUMB DOG DIVES TO DEATH. PANICKED BY PENILE POSY." She threw back her head and laughed, the red hair swinging in the breeze.

Mercurial, David had once said of Stephanie. *She has intriguingly mercurial moods.*

Personally, I've never found Liver tabloid headlines as funny as everyone else seems to. And I'd bet that neither "penile" nor "posy" was in the Liver vocabulary.

Stephanie shrugged and turned away from the railing. "I guess Norman will just have to make another one. With the R&D already done, it probably won't bankrupt them. Maybe they can even take a tax write-off. Did you hear that Jean-Claude rammed his write-off through the IRS, for the embryos he and Lisa decided not to implant in a surrogate after all? He discarded them and wrote off the embryo storage for seven years as a business depreciation on the grounds that an heir was part of long-term strategic planning, and the IRS auditor actually allowed it. Nine fertilized embryos, all with expensive genemods. And then he and Lisa decide they don't want kids after all."

I gazed at the throwaway pile of pink fur on the sidewalk, and then out at the wide blue Bay, and I made my decision. In that moment. As quickly and irrationally as that.

Like most of the rest of my life.

"Do you know Colin Kowalski?" I asked Stephanie.

She thought briefly. She had eidetic recall. "Yes, I think so.

Sarah Goldman introduced us at some theater a few years ago. Tall, with wavy brown hair? Minimal genemod, right? I don't remember him as handsome. Why? Is he your replacement for David?"

"No."

"Wait a minute—isn't he with the GSEA?"

"Yes."

"I think I already mentioned," Stephanie said stiffly, "that Norman's company had a special beta-test permit for Katous?"

"No. You didn't."

Stephanie chewed on her flawless lower lip. Actually, the permit is pending. Diana—"

"Don't worry, Stephanie. I'm not going to report your dead violation. I just thought you might know Colin. He's giving an extravagant Fourth of July party. I could get you an invitation." I was enjoying her discomfort.

"I don't think I'd be interested in a party hosted by a Purity Squad agent. They're always so stuffy. Guys who wrap up genetic rigidity in the old red-white-and-blue and never see that the result looks like a national prick. Or a nightstick, beating down innovation in the name of fake patriotism. No thanks."

"You think the idealism is fake?"

"Most patriotism is. Either that or Liver sentimentality. God, the only thing bearable about this country comes from genemod technology. Most Livers look like shit and behave worse—you yourself said you can't stand to be around them."

I had said that, yes. There were a lot of people I couldn't stand to be around.

Stephanie was on a political roll, the kind that never made it to campaign holovids. "Without the genemod brains in the security enclaves, this would be a country of marching morons, incapable of even basic survival. Personally, I think the best act of 'patriotism' would be a lethal genemod virus that wiped out everybody but donkeys. Livers contribute nothing and drain off everything."

I said carefully, "Did I ever tell you that my mother was a Liver? Who was killed fighting for the United States in the China Conflict? She was a master sergeant."

Actually, my mother had died when I was two; I barely remembered her. But Stephanie had the grace to look embarrassed. "No. And you should have, before you let me give that tirade.

But it doesn't change anything. *You're* a donkey. You're genemod. You do useful work."

This last was either generous or bitchy. I have done a variety of work, none of it persistently useful. I have a theory about people who end up with strings of short-term careers. It is, incidentally, the same theory I have about people who end up with strings of short-term lovers. With each one you inevitably hit a low point, not only within the purported "love" affair or fresh occupation, but also within yourself. This is because each new lover/job reveals fresh internal inadequacy. With one you discover your capacity to be lazy; with another, to be shrewish; with a third, to engage in frenzied hungry ambition that appalls you with its pathetic neediness. The sum of too many careers or too many lovers, then, is the same: a composite of personal low points, a performance scattergram sinking inevitably to the bottom right quadrant. All your weaknesses stand revealed. What one lover or occupation missed, the next one will draw forth.

In the last ten years, I have worked in security, in entertainment holovids, in county politics, in furniture manufacture franchises (more than one), in 'bot law, in catering, in education, in applied syncography, in sanitation. Nothing ventured, nothing lost. And yet David, who was after Russell who was after Anthony who was after Paul who was after Rex who was after Eugene who was after Claude, never called *me* "mercurial." Which is certainly indicative of something.

I hadn't reacted to Stephanie's jibe, so she repeated it, smiling solicitously. "*You're* a donkey, Diana. You do useful work."

"I'm about to," I said.

She poured herself another drink. "Will David be at this Colin Kowalski's party?"

"No. I'm sure not. But he'll be at Sarah's campaign fund-raiser on Saturday. We both accepted weeks ago."

"And are you going?"

"I don't think so."

"I understand. But if David and you are really finished with each other—"

"Go after him, Stephanie." I didn't look at her face. Since David moved out, I'd lost seven pounds and three friends.

So—say I joined the GSEA because I was jilted. Say I was jealous. Say I was disgusted with Stephanie and everything she represented. Say I was bored with my life at that extremely boring moment. Say I was just looking for a new thrill. Say I was impulsive.

"I'm going to be out of town for a while," I said.

"Oh? Where are you going?"

"I'm not sure yet. It depends." I gave a last look over the railing at the smashed, semi-sentient, pathetic and expensive dog. The ultimate in American technology and values.

Say I was a patriot.

The next morning I flew down to Colin Kowalski's office in a government complex west of the city. From the air, buildings and generous landing lots formed a geometric design, surrounded by free-form swaths of bright trees bearing yellow flowers. I guessed the trees were genemod to bloom all year. Trees and lawn stopped abruptly at the perimeter of the Y-field security bubble. Outside that charmed circle the land reverted to scrub, dotted by some Livers holding a scooter race.

From my aircar I could see the entire track, a glowing yellow line of Y-energy about a meter wide and five twisting miles long. A platform scooter shot out of the starting pod, straddled by a figure in red jacks that, at its speed and my height, was no more than a blur. I had been to scooter races. The scooter's gravs were programmed to stay exactly six inches above the track. Y-cones on the bottom of the platform determined the speed; the sharper the tilt away from the energy track, the faster the thing could go, and the harder it became to control. The driver was allowed only a single handhold, plus a pommel around which he could wrap one knee. It must be like riding sidesaddle at sixty miles per hour—not that any Liver would ever have heard of a sidesaddle. Livers don't read history. Or anything else.

Spectators perched on flimsy benches along the scooter track. They cheered and screamed. The driver was halfway through the course when a second scooter shot out of the pod. My car had been cleared by the governmet security field, which locked onto my controls and guided me in. I twisted in my seat to keep the scooter track in view. At this lower altitude I could see the first driver more clearly. He increased the tilt of his scooter, even though this part of the track was rough, snaking over rocks and depressions and piles of cut brush. I wondered how he knew the second scooter was gaining on him.

I saw the first driver race toward a half-buried boulder. The yellow line of track snaked over it. The driver threw his weight toward center, trying to slow himself down. He'd waited too long. The scooter bucked, lost its orientation toward the track, and flipped. The driver was flung to the ground. His head hit the edge of the boulder at over a mile a minute.

A moment later the second scooter raced over the body, its energy cones a perfect six inches above the crushed skull.

My car descended below the treetops and landed between two beds of bright genemod flowers.

Colin Kowalski met me in the lobby, a severe neo-Wrightian atrium in a depressing gray. "My God, Diana, you look pale. What is it?"

"Nothing," I said. Scooter deaths happen all the time. Nobody tries to regulate scooter races, least of all the politicians who pay for them in exchange for votes. What would be the point? Livers choose that stupid death, just as they choose to take sunshine or drink themselves to oblivion or waste their little lives destroying the countryside marginally faster than the 'bots can clean it up. Envirobots used to be able to keep up, when there was enough money. Stephanie was right about one thing: I don't care what Livers do. Why should I? Whatever my mother might have done forty years ago, today Livers are politically and economically negligible. Ubiquitous, but negligible. It was just that I had never seen a scooter death that close before. The crushed skull had looked no more substantial than a flower.

"You need fresh air," Colin said. "Let's go for a walk?"

"A what?" I said, startled. I'd just had fresh air. What I wanted was to sit down.

"Didn't the doctor recommend easy walks? In your condition?" Colin took my arm, and this time I knew better than to say *My what?* The old training returns fast. Colin was afraid the building wasn't secure.

How could a government complex under a maximum-security Y-field not be secure? The place would be multishielded, jammed, swept constantly. There was only one group of people who could even remotely be suspected of developing monitors so radically undetectable—

I was surprised at myself. My heart actually skipped a beat. Apparently I could still feel an interest in something besides myself.

Colin walked me past a lovely meditation garden out to an expanse of open lawn. We walked slowly, as befitted someone with my condition, whatever it was.

"Colin, darling, am I pregnant?"

"You have Gravison's disease. Diagnosed just two weeks ago, at the John C. Frémont Medical Enclave, from your repeated complaints of dizziness."

"There's no complaint files in my medical records."

"There are now. Three complaints over the last four months. One misdiagnosis of multiple sclerosis. Your medical problems are one reason David Madison left you."

Despite myself, I flinched at the sound of David's name. Some locales are full of gleaming skyscrapers built on infertile, treacherously shifting ground. Japan, for instance. And then there are places like the Garden of Eden—lush, warm, vibrant with color—where only bitterness is built. Whose fault? The Garden dwellers, obviously. They certainly couldn't claim deprived childhoods.

Nothing is more bitter than to know you could have had Eden, but turned it into Hiroshima. All by your two unaided selves.

Colin and I walked a little farther. The weather under the dome was mild and fresh smelling, without wind. Colin's hand on my arm felt pleasant. Stephanie was wrong; he was handsome, even if his looks weren't genemod. Thick brown hair, high cheekbones, a strong body. Too bad he was such a prig. Religious reverence for one's own job, even if the job is worth doing, is a sexual turnoff. I could picture Colin inspecting his naked lovers for GSEA violations. And then turning them in.

I said, "You're rushing ahead, darling. Why the medical record changes? I haven't even said I'm willing to play."

"We need you, Diana. You couldn't have contacted me at a better time. Washington has cut our funds again, a ten percent drop from—"

"Spare me the political lecture, Col. What do you need me for?"

He looked slighty offended. A prig. But of course his funds had been cut. Everybody's funds had been cut. Washington is a binary system; money can only go in and out. More was going out than was coming in. Lots more: supporting a nation of Livers was expensive when the U.S.A no longer held the only world patents for the cheap Y-energy that had made it possible in the first place. Plus, aging industrial machinery, long kept underrepaired, was breaking down at an accelerating rate. Even Stephanie, with all her money, had complained about that. The public sector must feel it even more. And deficit spending had been illegal for nearly a century. Didn't Colin think I knew all that?

He said stiffly, "I didn't mean to lecture. I need you for surveillance. You're trained, you're clean, nobody will be tracking your moves electronically. And if they do come to anybody's attention, Gravison's disease is the perfect cover."

This was true, as far as it went. I was "trained" because fifteen years ago I'd taken part in an unrecorded training program so secret its agents had never actually been used for anything. Or at least I hadn't, but, then, I'd dropped out before the end. Claude had come along. Or maybe it had been somebody else. Colin Kowalski had also been in that program, which marked the start of his government career. I was clean because nothing about the program appeared in anybody's data banks, anywhere.

But there was something Colin wasn't telling me, something slightly wrong in his manner. I said, "Who, specifically, is it that I won't come to the attention of?" but I think I already knew.

"Sleepless. Neither Sanctuary nor that group on Huevos Verdes. La Isla, I mean."

Huevos Verdes. Green Eggs. I bent over and pretended to adjust my sandal, to hide my grin. I'd never heard that Sleepless had a sense of humor.

I said, through rising excitement, "Why does Gravison's disease provide the perfect cover? What *is* Gravison's disease?"

"A brain disorder. It causes extreme restlessness and agitation."

"And immediately you thought of me. Thank you, darling."

He looked annoyed. "It often leads to aimless travel. Diana, this isn't a joking matter. You're the last of the underground agents who we're positive doesn't show up on any electronic record anywhere before Sanctuary cultured these so-called SuperSleepless on their protected orbital. Well, it's not protected anymore. We've got it crawling with GSEA personnel. The labs we dismantled completely; Sanctuary will never pull those dangerous genemod tricks again. And that treasonous Jennifer Sharifi and her revolutionary cell will never get out of jail."

Colin's words struck me as understatement: a peculiarly gray-toned, governmental sort of understatement. What he'd called Jennifer Sharifi's "dangerous genemod tricks" had been a terrorist attempt to use lethal, altered viruses to hold five cities hostage. This incredible, daring, insane terrorism had been an attempt to coerce the United States into letting Sanctuary secede. The only reason Sanctuary hadn't succeeded was that Jennifer Sharifi's granddaughter Miranda, from God-knows-what twisted family politics, had betrayed the terrorists to the feds. This had all happened thirteen years ago. Miranda Sharifi had been sixteen years old. She and the other twenty-six children in on the betrayal had supposedly been so genetically altered they don't even think like human beings anymore. A different species.

Exactly what the GSEA was supposed to prevent.

Yet here the twenty-seven SuperSleepless were, walking around alive, a fait accompli. And not even "here"—a few years ago the Supers had all moved to an island they'd built off the coast of Yucatán. That was the word: "built." One month it was international ocean, no "there" there, the next month there existed a genuine island. It wasn't a floating construct, like the Artificial Islands, but rock that went all the way down to the continental shelf, which was not especially shallow at that point. Luckily. Nobody knew how the Sleepless had developed the nanotechnology to do it. A lot of people passionately wanted to know. Nanotechnology was still in its infancy. Mostly, nanoscientists could take things apart, but not build them. This was apparently not true on La Isla.

An island, says international law, which predates the existence of people who can create one, is a natural feature. Unlike a ship or an orbital, it doesn't fall under the Artificial Construct Tax Reform Law of 2050, and it doesn't have to be chartered under a national flag. It can be claimed by, or for, a given country, or can be assigned to it as a protectorate by the UN. The twenty-seven Supers plus hangers-on settled on their island, which was shaped roughly like two interlocking ovals. The United States claimed La Isla; the potential taxes on SuperSleepless corporate businesses were enormous. However, the UN assigned the island to Mexico, twenty miles away. The UN was collectively unhappy with Americans, in one of those downward cycles of international opinion. Mexico, which had been getting fucked over by the United States regularly for several centuries, was happy to receive whatever monies La Isla paid to leave the inhabitants strictly alone.

The Supers built their compound under cover of the most sophisticated energy fields in existence. Impenetrable. Apparently the Supers, with their unimaginably boosted brainpower, weren't geniuses at only genemodification; they included among their number geniuses at everything. Y-energy. Electronics. Grav tech. From their island, officially if unimaginatively named La Isla, they have sold patents throughout a world market on which the U.S. can offer only the same tired recycled products at inflated prices. The U.S. has 120 million nonproductive Livers to support; La Isla has none. I'd never before heard it called Huevos Verdes. Which translated as "green eggs" but in Spanish slang meant "green testicles." Fertile and puissant balls. Did Colin know this?

I stooped to pick a blade of very green, genemod grass. "Colin, don't you think that if the Supers wanted Jennifer Sharifi and their other grandparents out of prison, they'd get them out? Obviously the successful counterrevolutionaries want the senior gang right where you've got them."

He looked even more annoyed. "Diana, the SuperSleepless are not gods. They can't control everything. They're just human beings."

"I thought the GSEA says they're not."

He ignored this. Or maybe not. "You told me yesterday you believed in stopping illegal genemod experiments. Experiments that could irrevocably change humanity as we know it."

I pictured Katous lying smashed on the sidewalk, Stephanie laughing above. *Cookie! Please!* I had indeed told Colin that I believed in stopping genetic engineering, but not for reasons as simple as his. It wasn't that I objected to irrevocable changes to humanity; in fact, that frequently seemed to me like a good idea. Humanity didn't strike me as so wonderful that it should be forever beyond change. However, I had no faith in the kinds of alterations that would be picked. I doubted the choosers, not the fact of choice. We'd already gone far enough in the direction of Stephanie, who considered sentient life-forms as disposable as toilet paper. A dog today, expensive and nonproductive Livers tomorrow, who the next day? I suspected Stephanie was capable of genocide, if it served her purposes. I suspected many donkeys were. There were times I'd thought it of myself, although not when I genuinely thought. The nonthought appalled me. I doubted Colin could understand all this.

"That's right," I agreed. "I want to help stop illegal genemod experiments."

"And I want you to know that I know that under that flip manner of yours, there's a serious and loyal American citizen."

Oh, Colin. Not even boosted IQ let him see the world other than binary. Acceptable/not acceptable. Good/bad. On/off. The reality was so much more complicated. And not only that, he was lying to me.

I'm good at detecting lies. Far better than Colin at implying them. He wasn't going to trust me with anything important in this project, whatever it was. I was too hastily recruited, too flip, too unreliable. That I *had* left my training before its completion was de facto unreliability, disloyalty, unacceptability for anything important. That's the way government types think. Maybe they're right.

Whatever surveillance Colin gave me would be strictly backup, triple redundancy. There was a theory for this in surveillance work: cheap, limited, and out of control. It started as a robot-engineering theory but pretty soon carried over into police work. If there are a lot of investigators with limited tasks, they won't cohere into a single premature viewpoint about what they're looking for. That way, they might turn up something totally unexpected. Colin wanted me for the equivalent of a wild card.

I didn't mind. At least it would get me out of San Francisco.

Colin said, "For the last two years the Supers have been entering the United States, in ones and twos, heavily disguised both cosmetically and electronically. They travel around to various Liver towns or donkey enclaves, and then go home, to La Isla. We want to know why."

I murmured, "Maybe they have Gravison's disease."

"I'm sorry, what did you say?"

"I said, have you made any progress penetrating Huevos Verdes?"

"No," he said, but then he wouldn't have told me if they have. The sexual innuendo he missed completely.

"And who will I be keeping under surveillance?" The excitement was a little bubble in my throat now, still surprising. It had been a long time since anything had excited me. Except David, of coure, who had taken his sexy shoulders and verbal charm and sense of superiority to hold in readiness for plunking down temporarily in the middle of some other woman's life.

He said, "You'll be following Miranda Sharifi."

"Ah."

"I have full ID information and kit for you in a locker at the gravrail station. You'll pass as a Liver."

This was a slight insult; Colin was implying my looks weren't spectacular enough to absolutely mark them as genemod. I let it pass.

Colin said, "She's only made one trip off the island herself. We think. When the next one happens, you go with her."

"How will you be sure it's her? If they're using both cosmetic and electronic disguises, she could have different features, hair, even brain-scan projection all masking her own."

"True. But their heads are slightly misshapen, slighty too big. That's hard to disguise."

I knew that, of course. Everybody did. Thirteen years ago, when the Supers had first come down from Sanctuary, their big heads had given rise to a lot of bad jokes. The actuality was that their revved-up metabolism and altered brain chemistry had caused other abnormalities, the human genemod being a very complex thing. Supers are not, I remembered, an especially handsome people.

I said, "Their heads aren't *that* big, Colin. In some lights it's even hard to tell at all."

"Also, their infrared body scans are on file. From the trial. You can't move the position of your liver, or mask the digestive rate in your duodenum."

Which are both pretty generic anyway. Infrared scans aren't even admissible in court as identity markers. They're too unreliable. Still, it was better than nothing.

All of this was better than the nothing with David. The nothing of Stephanie. The something of Katous. *Thank you, lady.*

Colin said, "The trips off Huevos Verdes are increasing. They're planning something. We need to find out what."

"Si, señor," I said. He wasn't amused.

We'd walked nearly to the perimeter of the security bubble.

Beyond its faint shimmer, a body pod had arrived for the dead scooter racer. I could just see some Livers loading him into the pod, at the very edge of my range of genemod-enhanced vision. The Livers were crying. They got the body into the pod, and the pod started down the track. After fifteen feet there was a sudden grinding sound and the pod stopped. Livers pushed. The pod didn't move. The funeral machinery, like so much other more important machinery lately, had apparently broken down.

The Livers stood staring at it, bewildered and helpless.

I walked with Colin inside Building G-14 looking dizzy, as a victim of Gravison's disease occasionally should.

Two

W hen I found out, me, about the rabid raccoon, first thing I did was run straight down to the café to tell Annie Francy. I ran all the way, me. That ain't so easy no more. All I could think was maybe Lizzie was already safe, her, with Annie in the kitchen, maybe Lizzie wasn't in the woods. Maybe.

"Run, old man! Run, old fuck!" a kid yelled from the alley between the hotel and the warehouse. They stood there, the stomps, when the weather was nice. The weather was nice. I forgot, me, that they'd be there, or I'd of gone around the long way, by the river. But this afternoon they was too lazy, them, or too splintered, to chase me. I didn't tell them shit about the raccoon.

At the servoentrance to the café, where only 'bots supposed to go, I pounded, me, as hard as I could and the hell with who heard. "Annie Francy! Let me in!"

The bushes to my right rustled and I almost keeled over, me. The coons come there for the stuff that drops off the delivery 'bots. But it was only a snake. "Annie! It's me—Billy! Let me in!"

The low door swung open. I crawled through on hands and knees. It was Lizzie, her, who figured out how to get the servoentrance to open without no 'bot signal. Annie could no more do that than grow leaves.

They were both there. Annie was peeling apples and Lizzie was tinkering with the 'bot that was supposed to peel apples. Which ain't worked in a month. Not that Lizzie could fix it. She was smart, her, but she was still only eleven years old.

"Billy Washington!" Annie said. "You're shaking, you! What happened?"

"Rabid raccoons," I gasped. My heart was going, it, like a waterfall. "Four of them. Reported on the area monitor. By the river, where Lizzie . . . Lizzie goes to play . . ."

"Ssshhhh," Annie said. "SSShhhh, dear heart. Lizzie's here now. She's safe, her."

Annie put her arms around me where I sat panting on the floor like some humping bear. Lizzie watched, her, with her big black eyes wide and sparkly. She probably thought a rabid raccoon was interesting. She ain't never seen one, her. I have.

Annie was big and soft, a chocolate-colored woman with breasts like pillows. She wouldn't tell me, her, how old she was, but of course all I had to do was ask the terminals at the café or the hotel. She was thirty-five. Lizzie didn't look nothing like her mother. She was light-skinned and skinny, her, with reddish hair in tight braids. She didn't have no hips or breasts yet. What she had was brains. Annie worried about that a lot. She couldn't remember, her, a time when we was just people, not Livers. I could remember, me. At sixty-eight, you can remember a lot. I could remember, me, a time when Annie might of been proud of Lizzie's brains.

I could remember a time when being held by a woman like Annie would of meant more than panting from a bad heart.

"You all right, dear heart?" Annie said. She took her arms away and right away I missed them. I'm an old fool, me. "Now tell us again, real slow."

I had my breath back. "Four rabid raccoons. The area monitor was wailing like death. They must of come down, them, from the mountains. The monitor showed them by the river, moving toward town. The biowarnings was flashing deep red. Then the monitor quit again and this time nothing couldn't get it started again. Jack Sawicki kicked it, him, and so did I. Them coons could be anywhere."

"Did the warden 'bot get sent to kill them, it, before the monitor quit?"

"The warden 'bot's broke too."

"Shit." Annie made a face. "Next time I'm voting, me, against Samuelson."

"You think it'll make any difference? They're all alike. But you keep Lizzie inside, you, until somebody does something about them coons. Lizzie, you stay inside, you, hear me?"

Lizzie nodded. Then, being Lizzie, she argued. "But who, Billy?"

"Who what?"

"Who will do something about them raccoons? If the warden 'bot's broke?"

Nobody answered. Annie picked up her knife, her, and went back to peeling apples. I settled myself more comfortable against the wall. No chairs, of course—nobody's supposed to be in the café kitchen except 'bots. Annie broke in, her, for the first time last September. She didn't bother the 'bots while they prepared food for the foodbelt. She just took a bit of sugar here, some soysynth there, some of the fresh fruit from the servobin shipments, and cooked up things. Delicious things—nobody could cook like Annie. Fruit cobblers that made your mouth fill with sweet water just to look at them. Meat loaf hot and spicy. Biscuits like air.

She added them, her, right onto the foodbelt cubbies going out into the café, to be clicked off on people's meal chips. Fools probably didn't even notice, them, how much better her dishes tasted than the usual stuff going round and round on the belt day and night. And of course with the holoterminal going full blast, and the dance music playing all the time, nobody would of heard her and Lizzie back here even if they was blowing up the whole damn kitchen.

Annie liked to cook, she said. Liked to keep busy. I sometimes thought, me, that for somebody trying so hard to bring up Lizzie to be a good Liver, Annie herself was more than a little bit donkey. Of course I didn't say that, me, to Annie. I wanted to keep my head.

Annie started to hum, her, while she peeled apples. But Lizzie don't give up on questions. She said again, "*Who* will do something about them raccoons?"

Annie frowned. "Maybe somebody'll come to fix the warden 'bot."

Lizzie's big black eyes didn't blink. It's spooky, sometimes, how she can stare so hard without never blinking. "Nobody came to fix the peeler 'bot. Nobody came to fix the cleaner 'bot in the café. You said yesterday, you, that you didn't think the donkeys would send nobody even if the mainline soysynth 'bot broke."

"Well, I didn't mean it, me," Annie said. She peeled faster. "*That* breaks and nobody in this town eats!"

"They could share, them. Share the food that people took off the foodbelt before it broke."

Annie and I looked at each other. Once I saw a town, me, where a café broke down. Six people ended up killed. And that was when the gravrail worked regular, so people could leave, them, for another town in the district.

"Yes, dear heart," Annie said. "People could share, them."

"But you and Billy don't think they would, them."

Annie didn't answer. She don't like to lie to Lizzie, her. I said, "No, Lizzie. A lot of people wouldn't share, them."

Lizzie turned her bright black eyes on me. "Why wouldn't they share?"

I said, " 'Cause people out of the habit of sharing, them. They expect stuff now. They got a right to stuff—that's why they elect politicians. The donkey politicians pay their taxes, them, and the taxes are the cafés and warehouses and medunits and baths that let Livers get on with serious living."

Lizzie said, "But people shared more, them, when you was young, Billy? They shared more then?"

"Sometimes. Mostly they worked, them, for what they wanted."

"That's enough," Annie said sharply. "Don't you go filling her head with what's past, Billy Washington. She's a Liver. Don't go talking, you, like you was a donkey yourself! And you, Lizzie, don't you talk about it no more."

But nobody can't stop Lizzie when she's started. She's like a gravrail. Like a gravrail used to be, before this last year. "School says I'm lucky, me, to be a Liver. I get to live like an aristo while the donkeys got to do all the work, them. Donkeys serve Livers, Livers hold the power, us, by votes. But if we hold the power, us, how come we can't get the cleaner 'bot and the peeler 'bot and the warden 'bot fixed?"

"Since when you been at school?" I joked, trying to derail Lizzie, trying to keep Annie from getting madder. "I thought you just played, you, down by the river with Susie Mastro and Carlena Terrell. You're an agro Liver, you!"

She looked at me, her, like I was a broken 'bot myself.

Annie said shortly, "You *are* lucky, you to be a Liver. And you say so if anybody asks you."

"Like who?"

"*Anybody.* You shouldn't go to school so much anyway. You don't never see the other children, you, going so much. Do you want to be a freak?" She scowled.

Lizzie turned to me. "Billy, who's going to do something about them rabid raccoons if nobody fixes the warden 'bot?"

I glanced at Annie. I got to my feet, me, puffing. "I don't know, Lizzie. Just stay inside, you, all right?"

Lizzie said, "But what if one of them raccoons bites somebody?"

I had the sense, me, to stay quiet. Finally Annie said, "The medunit still works."

"But what if it breaks?"

"It won't break."

"But what if it *does?*"

"It won't!"

"How do you *know?*" Lizzie said, and I finally saw, me, that this was some sort of private scooter race between mother and daughter. I didn't understand it, me, but I could see Lizzie was ahead. She said again, "How do you know, you, that the medunit won't break too?"

"Because if it did, Congresswoman Land would send somebody, her, to fix it. The medunit is part of her taxes."

"She didn't send nobody to fix the cleaning 'bot. Or the peeler 'bot. Or the—"

"The medunit's different!" Annie snapped. She hacked at an apple so hard that pulp flew off the table I stole for her from the café.

Lizzie said, "Why is the medunit so different?"

"Because it just is! If the medunit breaks, people could die, them. No politician is going to let Livers die. They'd never get elected again!"

Lizzie considered this. I thought, me, that the scooter race was over, and I breathed more easy. Lately it seemed like they fought all the time. Lizzie was growing up, her, and I hated it. It made it harder to keep her safe.

She said, "But people could die from rabid raccoons, too. So how come you said District Supervisor Samuelson probably won't send nobody to fix the warden 'bot, but Congresswoman Land would send somebody to fix the medunit 'bot?"

I laughed. I couldn't help it—she was so smart, her. Annie scowled at me and right away I was sorry I laughed. Annie snapped, "So maybe I was wrong, me! Maybe somebody'll fix the warden 'bot! Maybe I don't know nothing, me!"

Lizzie said calmly, "Billy said too, him, that nobody would fix it. Billy, how come you—"

I said, "Because even donkeys don't got the money, them, that they used to have to pay taxes with. And too much stuff gets broke nowadays. They got to make choices, them, about what to fix."

Lizzie said, "But why do the donkey politicians got less money for taxes, them? And how come more stuff gets broke?"

Annie flung her peeled apples into a belt dish and dumped dough on them like it was mud.

"Because other countries make cheap Y-energy now. Twenty years ago we was the only ones, us, who could make it, and now we're not. But the stuff breaking—"

Annie burst out, "You believe them lies politicians say on the grids? Land and Samuelson and Drinkwater? Pisswater! All lies, every time one of them opens their mouth, them, it's lies—they just want to get out of paying their rightful taxes! The taxes we earned, us, with our votes! And I told you not to fill up the child's head with them secondhand donkey lies, Billy Washington!"

"Ain't lies," I said, but I hated having Annie mad at me worse than I hated having her mad at Lizzie. It hurt my heart. Old fool.

Lizzie saw it. She was like that, her: all pushing and pushing one minute, all sweetness the next. She put her arms around me. "It's all right, Billy. She ain't mad, her, at you. Nobody's mad at *you*. We love you, us."

I held her, me. It was like holding a bird—thin bones and fluttery heart in your hand. She smelled of apples.

My dead wife Rosie and me never wanted kids. I don't know, me, what we was thinking.

But all I said out loud was, "You don't go outside, you, until them rabid raccoons are killed by somebody."

Annie shot me a look. It took me a minute to figure out she was afraid, her, that Lizzie was just going to start all over again:

killed by who, Billy? But Lizzie didn't start. She just said, sweet as berries, "I won't, me. I'll stay inside."

But now it was Annie who couldn't let it go. I don't understand mothers, me. Annie said, "And you stay away from school for a while, too, Lizzie. You ain't no donkey, you."

Lizzie didn't answer.

Annie only wanted what was best for Lizzie. I knew that, me. Lizzie had to live in East Oleanta, join a lodge, go to scooter races, hang around the café, choose her lovers here, have her babies here. Annie wanted Lizzie to belong. Like an agro Liver, not some weird fake-donkey freak nobody would want. Any mother would. Annie might sneak, her, into the kitchen of the Congresswoman Janet Carol Land Café to do some cooking, but she was still all Liver, all the way through.

And Lizzie wasn't.

A long time ago, when I was in school myself, me, and the country was different, I learned something. It's fuzzy now, but it keeps hanging in my head. It was from before donkeys and Livers. Before cafés and warehouses. Before politicians paid taxes to us, instead of the other way around. It was from back when they were still making Sleepless, and you could read about them in newspapers. When there *was* newspapers. This thing was a word about genemod, but it meant something that wasn't genemod. Was natural. Lizzie learns at school that donkeys are inferior, them, because donkeys have to be made genemod so they can be put to work providing all the things Livers need. But this word wasn't about the kind of natural that makes us Livers superior to donkeys. It was about a different kind of natural, a kind that happens by itself but makes you different from other natural Livers around you. The word explained why Lizzie asked so many donkey questions, her, when she wasn't no donkey and didn't have no donkey genemods, although the word was in her genes. How could that be? Like I said, I was fuzzy, me, about the word, and about how it worked. But I remembered it.

The word was *throwback.*

I watched Lizzie watch her mother put the apple dish on the foodbelt. It went under the flash heater and out through the wall into the café. Somebody would choose it, them, on their Senator Mark Todd Ingalls meal chip. Annie went on to cooking something else. Lizzie sat on the floor, her, with the pieces of the broken peeler 'bot. When her mother wasn't looking she studied each one, her, figuring out how it might go together, and when she grinned at me, her black eyes sparkled and darted, shiny as stars.

That night we had a meeting, us, in the café, to talk about the rabid raccoons. Forty people, not counting kids. Paulie Cenverno actually seen one of the sick raccoons, hind legs twitching like it was splintered, mouth foaming, down near the State Senator James Richard Langton Scooter Track on the other side of town from the river. Somebody said, them, that we should put chairs in a circle to make a real meeting, but nobody did. At the other end of the café the holoterminal played and the dance music blasted. Nobody danced but the holos, life-sized smiling dolls made of light, pretty enough to be donkeys. I don't like them, me. Never did. You can see right through the edges.

"Turn down that music so we can hear ourselves talk, us!" Paulie bawled. People slouching at the tables near the foodbelt didn't even look up, them. Probably all doing sunshine. Paulie walked over, him, and turned down the noise.

"Well," Jack Sawicki said, "what are we going to do, us, about these sick coons?"

Only a few people snickered, them, and they were the dumbest ones. Like Annie said: somebody has to serve at meetings, even if serving is donkey work. Jack is mayor, him. He can't help it. East Oleanta ain't big enough to have a regular donkey mayor— no donkeys live here and we don't want none. So we elected Jack, us, and he does what he has to do.

Somebody said, "Call County Legislator Drinkwater on the official terminal."

"Yeah, call Pisswater!"

"District Supervisor Samuelson's got the warden franchise, him."

"Then call Samuelson!"

"Yeah, and while you're at it, you, make another town protest that the goddamn warehouse don't distribute, it, but once a week now!" That was Celie Kane. I ain't never seen her not angry.

"Yeah. Rutger's Corners, they still got distrib, them, twice a week."

"I had to wear these jacks two days in a row!"

"I got sick, me, and missed a distrib, and we run out of toilet paper!"

Next election, District Supervisor Aaron Simon Samuelson was a squashed spider. But Jack Sawicki, he knew, him, how to serve a meeting.

"Okay, people, shut up now. This is about the sick coons, not about warehouse distrib. I'm going, me, to just call up our donkeys."

He unlocked the official terminal. It sits way in the corner of the café. Jack pulled his chair, him, right up close to it, so his belly almost rested on his knees. A few stomps from the alley gang swaggered into the café, carrying their wooden clubs. They headed, them, for the foodbelt, laughing and smacking each other, drunk on sunshine. Nobody told them to shut up. Nobody dared.

"Terminal activate," Jack said. He didn't mind, him, talking donkey in front of us. None of this fake shit about *I don't carry out orders I give them I'm an agro Liver, me.* Jack was a good mayor.

But I'm careful, me, not to tell him so.

"Terminal activated," the terminal said. For the first time I wondered what we'd do if the thing was as broke as Annie's apple-peeler 'bot.

Jack said, "Message for District Supervisor Aaron Simon Samuelson, copy to County Legislator Thomas Scott Drinkwater, copy to State Senator James Richard Langton, copy to State Representative Claire Amelia Forrester, copy to Congresswoman Janet Carol Land." Jack licked his lips. "Priority Two."

"One!" Celie Kane shouted. "Make it a one, you bastard!"

"I can't, Celie," Jack said. He was patient, him. "One is for disasters like attack or fire or flood at the Y-plant." That was supposed to make us smile. A Y-plant can't catch fire, can't break down no way with its donkey shields. Can't nothing get in, and only energy can get out. But Celie Kane don't know how to smile, her. Her daddy, old Doug Kane, is my best friend, but he can't do nothing with her neither. Never could, not even when she was a child.

"This *is* a disater, you shithead! One of them coons kills a kid of mine, and I'll tear you apart myself, Jack Sawicki!"

"Hey, stay together, Celie," Paulie Cenverno said. Somebody muttered "Bitch." The door opened and Annie came in, her, holding Lizzie's hand. The stomps at the foodbelt were still shouting and shoving.

The terminal said, "Please hold. Linking with District Supervisor Samuelson's mobile unit." A minute later the holo appeared, not life-sized like on the HT, but a tiny, eight-inch-high Samuelson seated at his desk and dressed in a blue uniform. He looked, him, about forty, but of course with donkey genemods you can't never tell. He had thick gray hair and big shoulders and crinkly blue eyes—handsome, like all of them. A few people shuffled their feet, them. If voters don't watch the donkey channels, then the only people they ever see not dressed in jacks are Samuelson's techs at the warehouse distrib twice a week. Once a week, now.

Suddenly I wondered, me, if that *was* Samuelson. Maybe the holo was just a tape. Maybe the real Samuelson was someplace dressed up for a party, or in jacks—if donkeys ever wore jacks, them—or even naked, him, taking a shit. It was weird to think about.

"Yes, Mayor Sawicki?" Samuelson said. "How can I serve you, sir?"

"There's at least four rabid raccoons in East Oleanta, Supervisor. Maybe more. The area monitor picked them up, it, before it broke. We seen the coons, right in town. They're dangerous. I told you, me, two weeks ago that the game warden 'bot broke."

Samuelson said, "Game warden duties have been franchised to the Sellica Corporation. I notified them, sir, as soon as you notified me."

But Jack wasn't taking any of that shit. Like I said, me, he was a good mayor. "We don't care, us, who's supposed to do the job! It's your responsibility that it gets done, Supervisor. That's why we elected you, us."

Samuelson didn't change expression. That's when I decided, me, that he was a tape. "I'm sorry, mayor, you're quite right. It is my responsibility. I'll take care of it right away, sir."

"That's what you said two weeks ago. When the warden first broke, it."

"Yes, sir. Funding has been—yes, you're quite right, sir. I *am* sorry. It won't be neglected again, sir."

People nodded at each other: *damn right*. Behind me Paulie Cenverno muttered, "Got to be firm, us, with donkeys. Remind 'em who pays the votes."

Jack said, "Thank you, Supervisor. And one more thing—"

"Hey!" a stomp screamed at the other end of the café, "The foodbelt stopped, it!"

Dead silence fell.

The holo of Samuelson said sharply, "What is it? What's the problem?" For a minute he almost sounded, him, like a person.

The stomp screamed again, "Fucking thing just stopped, it! Ate my meal chip and stopped! The food cubbies don't open, them!" He yanked at all the plasticlear cubby doors, and none budged, but of course they don't never budge, them, unless you put your chip in the slot. The stomp slammed on them with his club, and that didn't help neither. Plasticlear don't break.

Jack ran, him, across the café, his belly bouncing under his red jacks. He stuck his own meal chip into the slot and pressed a cubby button. The chip disappeared, it, and the cubby didn't open. Jack ran back to the terminal.

"It's broke, Supervisor. The goddamn foodbelt's broke, it— eating chips and not giving out no food. You got to do something real quick. This can't go no two weeks!"

"Of course not, Mayor. As you know, the café isn't part of my taxes—it's funded and maintained by Congresswoman Land. But I'll notify her myself, immediately, and a technician will be there from Albany within the hour. Nobody will starve within an hour, Mayor Sawicki. Keep your constituents calm, sir."

Celie Kane shrilled, "Fixed like the warden 'bot, you mean? If my kids go hungry even a day, you mule bastard—"

"Shut up," Paulie Cenverno told her, murderously low. Paulie don't like to see donkeys abused to their faces. He says, him, that they got feelings too.

"Within one hour," Jack said. "Thank you for your help, Supervisor. Dialogue over."

"Dialogue over," Samuelson said. He smiled at us, him, the same smile like on his election holos, chin up and crinkly eyes bright. The holo pushed a button on his desk. The picture disappeared. But something must of gone wrong because the voice didn't disappear, it, only it sounded all different. Samuelson still, but no Samuelson we never seen or heard campaigning, us: "Christ—what *next!* These morons and imbeciles—I'm tempted to just—oh!" The terminal yelped and went dead.

A woman at a far table screamed. The stomp with the biggest

wooden club had grabbed her food, him, and was eating it. Jack and Paulie and Norm Frazier charged over, them, and jumped the kid. His buddies jumped back. Tables crashed over and people started running. Somebody had just changed HT channels, and a scooter race in Alabama roared by, life-size. I grabbed Annie and Lizzie and shoved them to the door. "Get out! Get out!"

Outside, the Y-lights made Main Street bright as day. I could feel my heart banging but I didn't slow up, me. Angry people got no sense. Anything could happen. I panted, me, alongside Annie, she running with those big breasts bouncing, Lizzie running quick and quiet as a deer.

In Annie's apartment on Jay Street I collapsed, me, on a sofa. It wasn't none too comfortable, not like sofas I remembered from when I was young, the soft ones you kept around long enough to take the shape of a person's body.

But on the other hand, plastisynth don't never get vermin.

Lizzie said, her eyes bright, "Do you think a donkey will come, them, to fix the foodbelt in an hour?"

I gasped, "Lizzie . . . hush, you."

"But what if in an hour no donkey don't come to—"

Annie said, "You be quiet, Lizzie, or you'll wish them donkeys will come to fix *you!* Billy, you better stay here, you, for tonight. No telling what them fools at the café might do."

She brought me a blanket, one of those she'd embroidered, her, with bright yarns from the warehouse. More embroideries hung on the wall, woven with bits of pop can the young girls make jewelry out of, with torn-up jacks, with any other bright thing Annie could find. All the Jay Street apartments look alike. They was all built at the same time about ten years ago, when some senator came up from way behind and needed a big campaign boost. Small rooms, foamcast walls, plastisynth furniture from a warehouse distrib, but Annie's is one of the few that looks to me like a home.

Annie made Lizzie go to bed. Then she came, her, and sat on a chair close by my sofa.

"Billy—did you see, you, that woman in the café?"

"What woman?" It was nice, her sitting so close.

"The one standing, her, off by the back wall. Wearing green jacks. She don't live, her, in East Oleanta."

"So?" I snuggled under Annie's pretty blanket. We get travelers sometimes, us, though not as many as we used to, now that the gravrail don't work so regular. Meal chips are good anyplace in the state, they come from United States senators, and it didn't used to be hard to get an interstate exchange chip. Maybe it still ain't. I don't travel much.

"She looked different," Annie said.

"Different how?"

Annie pressed her lips tight together, thinking. Her lips were dark and shiny as blackberries, them, the lower one so full that pressing them together only made it look juicier. I had to look away, me.

She said slowly, "Different like a donkey."

I sat up on the sofa. The blanket slid off. "You mean genemod? I didn't see, me, nobody like that."

"Well, she wasn't genemod pretty. Short, with squinchy features and low eyebrows and a head a little too big. But she was a donkey, her. I *know* it. Billy—you think she's a FBI spy?"

"In East Oleanta? We ain't got no underground organizations, us. All we got is rotten stomps that want to spoil ilfe for the rest of us."

Annie kept on pressing her lips together. County Legislator Thomas Scott Drinkwater runs our police franchise. He contracts, him, with an outfit that has both 'bots and donkey officers. We don't see them much. They don't keep the peace on the streets, and they don't bother, them, about thefts because there's always more in the warehouse. But when we have an assault, us, or a murder, or a rape, they're there. Just last year Ed Jensen was genefingered for killing the oldest Flagg girl when a lodge dance got too rough. Jensen got took, him, up to Albany, for twenty-five-to-life. On the other hand, nobody never stood trial for the bow-shooting of Sam Taggart out in the woods two years ago. But I think we had a different franchise, us, back then.

FBI is a whole other thing. All them federal outfits are. They don't come to Livers unless something donkey is threatened, and once they come, them, they don't let go.

"Well," Annie said stubbornly, "all I know, me, is that she was a donkey. I can smell them."

I didn't want to argue, me. But I didn't want her to worry,

neither. "Annie—ain't no reason for FBI to be in East Oleanta. And donkeys don't have big heads and squinchy features, them—they don't let their kids get born that way."

"Well, I hope you're right, you. We don't need no visiting donkeys in East Oleanta. Let them stay, them, in their places, and us in ours."

I couldn't help it. I said, real soft, "Annie—you ever hear of Eden?"

She knew, her, that I didn't mean the Bible. Not in that voice. She snapped, "No. I never heard of it, me."

"Yes, you did. I can tell, me, by your voice. You heard of Eden."

"And what if I did? It's garbage."

I couldn't let it go, me. "Why's it garbage?"

"*Why?* Billy—think, you. How could there be a place, even in the mountains, that donkeys don't know about? Donkeys serve everything, them, including mountains. They got aircars and planes to see everything. Anyway, why would a place without donkeys ever come to be? Who would do the work?"

" 'Bots," I said.

"Who would make the 'bots?"

"Maybe us?"

"Livers work? But *why,* in God's name? We don't got to work, us—we got donkeys to do all that for us. We got a right to be served by donkeys and their 'bots—we elect them! Why would we want to go, us, to some place without public servants?"

She was too young, her. Annie don't remember a time before the voting came on HT and the franchises made cheap 'bots and the Mission for Holy Living was all over the place, them, contributing lots of money to all the churches and explaining about the lilies of the field and the sacredness of joy and the favor of God to Mary over Martha. Annie don't remember, her, all the groups for all the kinds of democracy, each showing us how in a democracy the common man was the real aristo and master of his public servants. Schools for democracy. Irish-Americans for Democracy. Hoosiers for Democracy. Blacks for Democracy. I don't know, me. The 'bots took over the hard work, and we were happy, us, to give it to them. The politicians started talking, them, about bread and circuses, and calling voters "sir" and "ma'am" and building the cafés and warehouses and scooter tracks and lodge buildings. Annie don't remember, her. She likes to cook and sew and she don't spend all her time at races and brainie parties and lodge dances and lovers, like some, but she still ain't never held an ax in her hand and swung it, or a hoe or a hatchet or a hammer. She don't remember.

And then suddenly I knew, me, what an old fool I really was, and how wrong. Because I *did* swing heavy tools, me, on road crews in Georgia, when I was just a few years older than Lizzie. And when I wasn't being an ass I could remember, me, how my back ached like it was going to break, and my skin blistered under the sun, and the blackflies bit, them, on the open sores where they'd bit before, and at night I was so tired and hurting, me, I'd cry for my mother into my pillow, where the older men couldn't hear me. That's the work we did, us, not some quiet clean assembling of donkey 'bots. I remembered the fear of losing that lousy job when there wasn't no Congresswoman Janet Carol Land Café, no Senator Mark Todd Ingalls meal chip, no Senator Calvin Guy Winthop Jay Street Apartment Block. The fear was like a knife behind your eyes when the foreman come over, him, on a Friday to say, "That's it, Washington. You through," and all you wanted to do was take that knife out from behind your eyes and drive it hard through his heart because now how you going to eat, pay the rent, stay alive. I remembered, me, how it was, all in a second after I opened my big mouth to Annie.

"You're right," I said, not looking at her. "There ain't no Eden for us. I should go home now, me."

"Stay," Annie said kindly. "Please, Billy. In case there's trouble at the café."

Like anybody could break into a foamcast apartment. Or like a broke-down old man could be any real help to her or Lizzie. But I stayed.

In the darkness I could hear, me, how Annie and Lizzie moved in their bedrooms. Walking around, laying down, turning and settling into sleep. Sometime in the night the temperature must of dropped because I heard the Y-energy heater come on. I listened, me, to their breathing, a woman and a child, and pretty soon I slept.

But I dreamed about dangerous raccoons, sick and full of death.

Three

I never get used to the way other people don't see colors and shapes.

No. That's not right. They see them. They just don't *see* them, in the mind, where it matters. Other people can't feel colors and shapes. Can't become colors and shapes. Can't see through the colors and shapes to the trueness of the world, as I do, in the shapes it makes in my mind.

That's not it either.

Words are hard for me.

I think words were hard even before the operation that made me the Lucid Dreamer.

But the pictures are clear.

I can see myself as a dirty, dumb, hungry ten-year-old, traveling alone halfway across the country to Leisha Camden, the most famous Sleepless in the world. I can see her face as I ask her to make me "be somebody, me." I can see her eyes when I boasted, "Someday, me, I'm gonna *own* Sanctuary."

Sanctuary, the orbital where all the Sleepless except Leisha Camden and Kevin Baker had exiled themselves. My grandfather, a dumb laborer, had died building Sanctuary. And I thought, in my pathetic ten-year-old arrogance, that I could own it. I thought that if I learned to talk like donkeys and Sleepless, learned to behave like them, learned to think like them, I could have what they had. Money. Power. Choices.

When I picture that child now, the shapes in my mind are sharp and small, as if seen through the wrong end of a telescope. The shapes are the pale lost gold of remembered summer twilight.

Miranda Sharifi will inherit a controlling interest in Sanctuary stock. When her parents, Sleepless, eventually die. If they ever do. "What belongs to me belongs to you, Drew," Miranda said. She has said it several times. Miranda, a SuperSleepless, often explains things to me several times. She is very patient.

But even with her explanations, I don't understand what Miri and the Supers are doing at Huevos Verdes. I thought I did eight years ago, when the island was created. But since then there have been a lot more words. I can repeat the words, but I can't feel their shapes. They're words without solid form: Auxotrophes. Allosteric interactions. Nanotechnology. Photophosphorylation. Lawson conversion formulas. Neo-Marxist assisted evolution. Most of the time I just nod and smile.

But I am the Lucid Dreamer. When I float onstage and put a raucous Liver crowd into the Lucid Dreaming trance, and the music and words and combination of shapes flow from my subconscious through my Super-designed hardware, I touch their minds in places they didn't know they had. They feel more deeply, exist more blissfully, become more whole.

For at least the length of the concert.

And when the concert's over, my audience is subtly changed. They might not realize it. The donkeys who pay for my performances, considering them bread-and-circus occult trash for the masses, don't realize it. Leisha doesn't realize it. But I know I've controlled my audience, and changed them, and that I am the only one in the world with that power. The only one.

I try to remember that, when I am with Miranda.

Leisha Camden sat across the table from me and said, "Drew— what are they doing at Huevos Verdes?"

I sipped my coffee. On a plate were fresh genemod grapes and berries, with small buttery cookies smelling of lemon and ginger. There was fresh cream for the coffee. The library in Leisha's New Mexico compound was airy and high-ceilinged, its light, earthy colors echoing the New Mexico desert beyond the big windows. Here and there among the monitors and bookshelves stood stark, graceful sculptures by artists I didn't know. Some sort of delicate, old-fashioned music played.

I said, "What's that music?"

"Claude de Courcy."

"Never heard of him."

"Her. A sixteenth-century composer for the lute." Leisha said this impatiently, which only showed how tense she was. Usually the shapes she made in my mind were all clean and hard-edged, rigid, glowing with iridescence.

"Drew, you're not answering me. What are Miri and the Supers doing at Huevos Verdes?"

"I've been answering you for eight years—I don't know."

"I still don't believe you."

I looked at her. Sometime in the last year she had cut her hair; maybe a woman got tired of caring for her hair after 106 years. She still looked thirty-five. Sleepless didn't age, and so far they didn't die, except through accidents or murder. Their bodies regenerated, an unexpected side effect of their bizarre genetic engineering. And the first generation of Sleepless, unlike Miranda's, hadn't been so complexly altered that physical appearance couldn't be controlled. Leisha would be beautiful until she died.

She had raised me. She had educated me, to the limits of my intelligence, which might once have been normal but could never compare to the genemod-boosted IQ of donkeys, let alone Sleepless. When I became crippled in a freak accident, at the age of ten, Leisha had bought me my first powerchair. Leisha had loved me when I was a child, and had declined to love me when I became a man, and had given me to Miranda. Or Miranda to me.

She put both palms flat on the table and leaned forward. I recognized what was coming. Leisha was a lawyer. "Drew—you never knew my father. He died when I was in law school. I adored him. He was the most stubborn human being I ever met. Until I met Miri, anyway."

The spiky pain-shapes again. When Miri came down from Sanctuary thirteen years ago, she came to Leisha Camden, the only Sleepless not financially or ethically bound to Miri's horror of a grandmother. Miri came to Leisha for help in starting a new life. Just as I once had.

Leisha said, "My father was stubborn, generous, convinced he was always right. He had boundless energy. He was capable of incredible discipline, manic reliance on will, complete obsessiveness when he wanted something. He was willing to bend any rules that stood in his way, but he wasn't a tyrant. He was just implacable.

Does that sound like anybody you know? Does that sound like Miri?"

"Yes," I said. Where do they get all these words, Leisha and Miri and the rest of them? But these particular words fit. "It sounds like Miranda."

"And another thing about my father," Leisha said, looking directly at me. "He wore people out. He wore out two wives, one daughter, four business partners, and, finally, his own heart. Just wore them out. He was capable of destroying what he passionately loved just by applying his own impossible standards toward improving it."

I put down my coffee cup. Leisha put her palms flat on the table and leaned toward me.

"Drew—I'm asking for the last time. What is Miri doing at Huevos Verdes? You have to understand—I'm scared for her. Miri's not like my father in one important way. She's not a loner. She's desperate for a community, growing up the way she did on Sanctuary, with Jennifer Sharifi for a grandmother . . . but that's not the point. Or maybe it is. She yearns to belong the way only an outsider can. And she doesn't. She knows that. She put her grandmother and that gang in jail, and so the Sleepless have rejected her. She's so superior to the donkeys they can't accept her on principle; she's too much of a threat. And the idea of her trying to find common ground communicating with Livers is ludicrous. There's no common language."

I looked carefully away, out the window, at the desert. You never see that clear crystalline light anywhere else. Like the air itself, the light is both solid and yet completely transparent.

Leisha says, "All Miri has, outside of you, is twenty-six other SuperSleepless. That's it. Do you know what makes a revolutionary, Drew? Being an outsider looking in, coupled with the idealistic desire to create the one true, just community, coupled with the belief that you *can*. Idealists on the inside don't become revolutionaries. They just become reformers. Like me. Reformers think that things need a little improvement, but the basic structure is sound. Revolutionaries think about wiping everything out and starting all over. Miri's a revolutionary. A revolutionary with Superintelligent followers, unimaginable technology, huge amounts of money, and passionate ideals. Do you wonder that I'm scared?

"What are they doing in Huevos Verdes?"

I couldn't meet Leisha's eyes. So many words pouring out of her, so much argument, so many complicated definitions. The shapes in my mind were dark, confused, angry, with dangerous trailing cables hard as steel. But they weren't Leisha's shapes. They were mine.

"Drew," Leisha said, softly now, the outsider pleading with me. "Please tell me what she's doing?"

"I don't know," I lied.

Two days later I sat in a skimmer speeding over the open sea toward Huevos Verdes. The sun on the Gulf of Mexico was blinding. My driver, a freckled kid of about fourteen whom I'd never seen before, was young enough to enjoy skimming water. He edged the gravboat's nose downward to just touch the ocean, and blue-white spray flew. The kid grinned. The second time he did it, he suddenly turned his head to make sure I wasn't getting wet, sitting in my powerchair in the back of the skimmer. Clearly he'd forgotten I was there. Sudden guilt and the new angle changed his face, and I recognized him. One of Kevin Baker's great-grandchildren.

"Not wet at all," I said, and the kid grinned again. A Sleepless, of course. I could see that now in the shape of him in my mind: compact and bright-colored and brisk-moving. Born owning the world. And, of course, no security risk for Huevos Verdes.

But with their defenses, Huevos Verdes wouldn't be risking security even if passengers were being ferried by the director of the Genetic Standards Enforcement Agency.

I had worked hard to understand the triple-shield security around Huevos Verdes.

The first shield, a translucent shimmer, rose from the sea a quarter mile out from the island. Spherical, the shield extended underwater, cutting through the rock of the island itself, an all-enveloping egg. Terry Mwakambe, the Supers' strangest genius, had invented the field. Nothing else like it existed anywhere in the world. It scanned DNA, and nothing not recorded in the data banks got through. Not dolphins, not navy frogmen, not seagulls, not drifting algae. Nada.

The second shield, a hundred yards beyond, stopped all non-living matter not accompanied by DNA that *was* stored in the data banks. No unmanned 'bot vessel carrying anything—sensors, bombs, spores—passed this field. No matter how small. If there wasn't a registered DNA code accompanying it, it didn't get through. We skimmed through the shield's faint blue shimmer as if through a soap bubble.

The third shield, at the docks, was manually controlled and visually monitored. The registered DNA had to be alive and talking. I don't know how they checked for a drugged state. Nothing touched us, at least nothing I felt. The design was Terry Mwakambe's. The monitoring was shared by everybody, in shifts. The paranoia was Miri's. Unlike her grandmother, she didn't want the Supers to secede permanently from the United States. But like her grandmother, she'd nonetheless constructed a defended refuge that government officials couldn't touch. A sanctuary. She'd just done it better than Jennifer Sharifi had.

"Permission to dock," the freckled kid said seriously. He gave a little half-mocking salute and grinned. This was still an adventure for him.

"Hi, Jason," Christy Demetrios said. "Hello, Drew. Come on in."

Jason Reynolds. That was the kid's name. I remembered now. Kevin's granddaughter Alexandra's son. Something about him tugged at my memory, a nervous quick shape like a string of beads I couldn't remember.

Jason docked the boat expertly—they all did everything expertly—and we went ashore, Jason with quick bounds and me in my powerchair.

A hundred feet of genemod greenery, flowers and bushes and trees, all of it part of the project. Plants grew right to the water's edge. When the sea threatened, a Y-shield switched on, capable of protecting even the most fragile genemod rose from a hurricane. Beyond the garden, the compound walls rose abruptly, thin as paper, stronger than diamonds. Miri told me they were only a dozen molecules thick, constructed by second-generation nanomachines that had themselves been made from nanomachines. In my mind I saw the walls' glossy whiteness, to which no dirt could adhere, as hot dark red motion, thick and unstoppable as lava.

Nothing here was stoppable.

"Drew!" Miri ran to meet me, wearing white shorts and a loose shirt, her masses of dark hair tied back with a red ribbon. She had put on red lipstick. She still looked more like sixteen than twenty-nine. She threw her arms around me in my chair, and I felt the quick beating of her heart against my cheek. Super metabolism is revved up a lot higher than ours. I kissed her.

She murmured into my hair, "This time was too long. Four months!"

"It was a good tour, Miri."

"I know. I watched sixteen performances on the grid, and the performance stats look good."

She nestled into my lap. Jason and Christy had discreetly vanished. We were alone in the bright, newly created garden. I stroked Miri's hair, not wanting to hear just yet about performance stats.

Miri said, "I love you."

"I love you, too."

I kissed her again, this time to keep from looking at her face. It would be blinding, white hot with love. It always was, when she saw me. Always. For thirteen years. *He was capable of complete obsessiveness,* Leisha had said about her father. *He just wore people out.*

"I miss you so much when you're away, Drew."

"I miss you, too." This was true.

"I wish you could stay longer than a week."

"Me, too." This was not true. But there were no words.

She looked at me, then, a long moment. Something shifted behind her eyes. Carefully, so as not to hurt my crippled legs, she climbed off my lap, held out her hands, and smiled. "Come see the lab work."

I recognized this for what it was: Miri offering me the best she had. The most valuable present in the world. The thing I desperately wanted to be part of, even though I wouldn't understand it, because not to be part of it was to be unimportant. Insignificant. She was offering me what I needed most.

I couldn't do less.

I pulled her back onto my lap, forced my hands to move over her breasts. "Later. Can we be alone first . . ."

Her face was the curving shape of joy, too bright to be any color at all.

Miri's bedroom, like every other bedroom at La Isla, was spartan. Bed, dresser, terminal, an oval green rug made of some soft material Sara Cerelli had invented. On the dresser was a green pottery vase of fragrant genemod flowers I didn't recognize. These people, who could command all luxury, rarely indulged in any. The only jewelry Miri ever wore was the ring I had given her, a slim gold band set with rubies. I had never seen the other Sleepless wear any jewelry at all. All their extravagances, Miri had told me once, were mental. Even the light was ordinary: flat, without shadows.

I thought of the library in Leisha's New Mexico house.

Miri unbuttoned her shirt. Her breasts looked the same as they had at sixteen: full, milky, tipped with pale brown aureoles. She pulled down her shorts. Her hips were full, her waist chunky. Her pubic hair was bushy and wiry and the same black as the hair on her head, where it was confined by a red ribbon. I reached up and pulled the ribbon free.

"Oh, Drew, I've missed you so much . . ."

I hoisted myself from my powerchair to her narrow bed, and then pulled her on top of me. Her breasts spread over my chest: soft on hard. On tour or not, I exercised my upper body fanatically, to make up for my crippled legs. Miri loved that. She liked to feel my arms crush her against me. She liked my thrusts to be hard, definite, even ramming. I tried to give her that, but this time I stayed soft.

She looked at me questioningly, brushing the wild black hair back from her face. I didn't meet her eyes. She reached down and took me in her hand, massaging gently.

This had happened only a few times, all of them recent. Miri massaged harder.

"Drew . . ."

"Give me a minute, love."

She smiled uncertainly. I tried to concentrate, and then not to concentrate.

"Drew . . ."

"Shhhh . . . just a minute."

The gray shapes of failure snapped their teeth in my mind.

I closed my eyes, pulled Miri closer, and thought of Leisha. Leisha in the New Mexico twilight, a dim golden shape against the sunset. Leisha singing me to sleep when I was ten years old. Leisha running across the desert, slim and swift, tripping in a kangaroo-rat hole and twisting her ankle. I had carried her back to the compound, her body light and sweet in my eighteen-year-old arms. Leisha at her sister's funeral, tears making her eyes reflect all light, naked to sorrow. Leisha naked, as I had never seen her . . .

"AAhhhhhh," Miri crooned triumphantly.

I rolled us both over, so that I was on top. Miri preferred it that way. I thrust hard, then harder. She liked it really rough. Eventually I felt her shudder under me, and I let myself go.

Afterward, I lay still, my eyes closed, Miri curled against me with her head on my shoulder. For a brief piercing moment I remembered how love was between us a decade ago, in the beginning, when just the touch of her hand could turn me shivery and hot. I tried not to think, not to feel any shapes at all.

But making a void in the mind is impossible. I suddenly remembered the thing that had tugged at my mind about Jason Reynolds, Kevin Baker's great-grandson. Last year, the kid had nearly drowned. He had taken a skimmer out on the Gulf straight into Hurricane Julio. Huevos Verdes had found him only because Terry Mwakambe had developed some esoteric homing devices, and Jason had been brought back from death only by using on him some part of the project that hadn't even been tested yet.

When he revived, Jason admitted knowing the hurricane was coming. He wasn't trying to commit suicide, he said earnestly. Everyone believed him; Sleepless don't commit suicide. They're too much in love with their own minds to end them. With all of them hanging over his bed, his parents and Kevin and Leisha and Miri and Christy and Terry, Jason had said in a small voice that he hadn't known the sea would get quite that rough quite that fast. He just wanted to feel the boat get pitched around a lot. He just wanted to watch the huge, angry sky, and feel the rain lash him. He, a Sleepless, just wanted to feel vulnerable.

Miranda whispered, "Nobody ever makes me feel like you do, Drew. Nobody."

I kept my eyes closed, pretending to sleep.

In the late afternoon we went to the labs. Sara Cerelli and Jonathan Markowitz were there, dressed in shorts, barefoot. One of the requirements of the project was that at no stage did anything need to be sterile.

"Hello, Drew," Jon said. Sara nodded. Their concentration on their work made closed, muddy shapes in my mind.

A blob of living tissue sat in a shallow open tray on a lab bench, connected to machines by slender tubes and even more slender cables. Dozens of display screens ringed the rooms. Nothing on any of them was comprehensible to me. The tissue in the tray was flesh-colored, a light dun, but no particular form. It looked as if it could change shape, oozing into something else. On my last visit, Miri had told me it couldn't do that. No Sleepless are squeamish. I'm not either, but the shapes that crawled in and out of my mind as I looked at the thing were pale and speckled and smelled of dampness, although diamond-precise on their edges. Like the nanobuilt walls of Huevos Verdes.

I said, stupidly, "It's alive."

Jon smiled. "Oh, yes. But not sentient. At least not . . ." He trailed off, and I knew he couldn't find the right words. It should have made a bond between us. It didn't. Jon couldn't find the right words because any words that he picked would be too easy, too incomplete, for his ideas—and still too hard for me to follow. Miri had told me that Jon, more than any of the others except Terry Mwakambe, thought in mathematics. But it was the same with all of them, even Miri: her speech was a quarter beat too slow. I had caught myself talking like that only a month ago. It had been to Kevin Baker's four-year-old great-grandson.

Miri tried. "The tissue is a macro-level organic computer, Drew, with limited organ-simulation programming, including nervous, cardiovascular, and gastrointestinal systems. We've added Strethers self-monitoring feedback loops and submolecular, self-reproducing, single-arm assemblers. It can . . . it can experience programmed biological processes and report on them minutely. But it has neither sentience nor volition."

"Oh," I said.

The thing moved a little in its tray. I looked away. Miri saw, of course. She sees everything.

She said quietly, "We're getting closer. That's what it means. Ever since the breakthrough with the bacteriorhodopsin, we're getting much closer."

I made myself look at the thing again. Faint capillaries pulsed below the surface. The pale, damp shapes in my mind crawled, like maggots over rock.

Miri said, "If we pour a nutrient mixture into the tray, Drew, it can select and absorb what it needs and break it down for energy."

"What kind of nutrient mixture?" I had learned enough on my last visit to be able to ask this question.

Miri made a face. "Glucose-protein, mostly. There's still a way to go."

"Have you solved the problem of getting nitrogen directly from the air?" I had memorized this question. It made a tinny, hollow shape in my mind. But Miri smiled her luminous smile.

"Yes and no. We've engineered the microorganisms, but tissue receptivity is still foundering on the Tollers-Hilbert factor, especially in the epidermal fibrils. And on the nitrogen receptor–mediated endocytosis problem—no progress."

"Oh," I said.

"We'll solve it," Miri said, a quarter beat too slow. "It's just a matter of designing the right enzymes."

Sara said, "We call the thing Galwat." She and Jon laughed.

Miri said quickly, "For Galatea, you know. And Erin Galway. And John Galt, that fictional character who wanted to stop the motor of the world. And, of course, Worthington's transference equations . . ."

"Of course," I said. I had never heard of Galatea or Erin Galway or John Galt or Worthington.

"Galatea's from a Greek myth. A sculptor—"

"Let me see my performance stats now," I said. Sara and Jon glanced at each other. I smiled and held out my hand to Miri. She grasped it hard, and I felt hers tremble.

(Quick, fluttery shapes filled my mind, fine as paper. A dozen molecular levels thick. They settled on a rock, rough and hard and old as the earth. The fluttering grew faster and faster, the fine light paper grew red hot, and the rock shattered. At its heart was frozen milky whiteness, pulsing with faint veins.)

Miri said, "Don't you want to see Nikos' and Allen's latest work on the Cell Cleaner? It's coming along much faster than this! And Christy and Toshio have had a real breakthrough in error-checking protein-assembler programming—"

I said, "Let me see the performance stats now."

She nodded once, twice, four times. "The stats look good, Drew. But there's a funny jag in the data in the second movement of your concert. Terry says you need to change direction there. It's rather complicated."

"Then you'll explain it to me," I said evenly.

Her smile was dazzling. Again Sara and Jon glanced at each other, and said nothing.

The first time Miri showed me how the Supers communicated with each other, I couldn't believe it. It was thirteen years ago, right after they came down from Sanctuary. She had led me into a room with twenty-seven holostages on twenty-seven terminal desks. Each had been programmed to "speak" a different language, based on English but modified to the thought strings of its owner. Miri, sixteen years old, had explained one of her own thought strings to me.

"Suppose you say a sentence to me. Any single sentence."

"You have beautiful breasts."

She blushed, a maroon mottling of her dark skin. She did have beautiful breasts, and beautiful hair. They offset a little the big head, knobby chin, awkward gait. She wasn't pretty, and she was too intelligent not to know it. I wanted to make her feel pretty.

She said, "Pick another sentence."

"No. Use that sentence."

She did. She spoke it to the computer, and the holostage began to form a three-dimensional shape of words, images, and symbols linked to each other by glowing green lines.

"See, it brings out the associations my mind makes, based on its store of past thought strings and on algorithms for the way I think. From just a few words it extrapolates, and predicts, and mirrors. The programming is called 'mind mirroring,' in fact. It captures about ninety-seven percent of my thoughts about ninety-two percent of the time, and then I can add the rest. And the best part is—"

"You think like this for every sentence? Every *single sentence?*" Some of the associations were obvious: "breasts" linked to a nursing baby, for instance. But why was the baby linked to something called "Hubble's constant," and why was the Sistine chapel in that string? And a name I didn't recognize: Chidiock Tichbourne?

"Yes," Miri said. "But the best part—"

"You all think this way? All the Supers?"

"Yes," she said quietly. "Although Terry and Jon and Ludie think mostly in mathematics. They're younger than the rest of us, you know—they represent the next cycle of IQ reengineering."

I looked at the complex pattern of Miri's thoughts and reactions. *"You have beautiful breasts."*

I would never know what my words actually meant to her, in all their layers. Not any of my words. Ever.

"Does this scare you, Drew?"

She looked levelly at me. I could feel her fear, and her resolution. The moment was important. It grew and grew in my mind, a looming white wall to which nothing could adhere, until I found the right answer.

"I think in shapes for every sentence."

Her smile changed her whole face, opening and lighting it. I had said the right thing. I looked at the glowing green complexity of the holostage, a slowly turning three-dimensional globe jammed with tiny images and equations and, most of all, words. So many complicated words.

"We're the same, then," Miri said joyfully. And I didn't correct her.

"The best part," Miri had burbled on, completely at ease now, "is that after the extrapolated thought string forms and is adjusted as necessary, the master program translates it into everybody else's thought patterns and it appears that way on their holostage. On all twenty-seven terminals simultaneously. So we can bypass words and get the full ideas we're each thinking across to each other more efficiently. Well, not the full ideas. There's always something lost in translation, especially to Terry and Jon and Ludie. But it's so much better than just speech, Drew. The way your concerts are better than just unassisted daydreaming."

Daydreaming. The only kind of dreaming SuperSleepless knew anything about. Until me.

When a Sleepless went into the lucid dreaming trance, the result was different from when a Liver did. Or even a donkey. Livers and donkeys can dream at night. They have that connection with their unconscious, and I direct and intensify it in ways that feel good to them: peaceful and stimulated both. While lucid dreaming, they feel—sometimes for the first time in their lives—whole. I take them farther along the road into their true selves, deeper behind the waking veil. And I direct the dreams to the sweetest of the many things waiting there.

But Sleepless don't have night dreams. Their road to the unconscious has been genetically severed. When Sleepless go into a lucid dreaming trance, Miri told me, they see "insights" they wouldn't have seen before. They climb around their endless jungle of words, and come out of the trance with intuitive solutions to intellectual problems. Geniuses have often done that during sleep, Miri said. She gave me examples of great scientists. I have forgotten the names.

Looking at the complex verbal design on her holostage, I could feel it in my mind. It made a shape like a featureless pale stone, cool with regret. Miri would never see this shape in my mind. Worse, she would never know she didn't see it. She thought, because we both saw differently from donkeys, that we were alike.

I had wanted to be part of what was happening at Huevos Verdes. Already, even then, I could see that the project would change the world. Anyone not an actor in the project could only be acted on.

"Yes, Miri," I said, smiling at her, "we're the same."

On a worktable in yet another lab, Miri spread out the performance stats from my concert tour. The hard copy was for me; Supers always analyzed directly from screens or holos. I wondered how much had been left out or simplified for my benefit. Terry Mwakambe, a small dark man with long wild hair, perched motionless on the open windowsill. Behind him the ocean sparkled deep blue in the waning light.

"See, here," Miri said, "midway during your performance of 'The Eagle.' The attention-level measurements rose, and the attitudinal changes right after the performance were pretty dramatic in the direction of risk taking. But then the follow-up stats show that by a week later, the subjects' attitudinal changes had eroded more than they did for your other performance pieces. And by a month later, almost all risk-taking changes have disappeared."

When I give a concert, they hook volunteer fans to machines that measure their brain wave changes, breathing, pupil variations—a lot of things. Before and after the concert the volunteers take virtual-reality tests to measure attitudes. The volunteers are paid. They don't know what the tests are for, or who wants them. Neither do the people who administer the tests. It's all done blind, through one of Kevin Baker's many software subsidiaries, which form an impenetrable legal tangle. The results are transmitted to the master computer at Huevos Verdes. When the stats say so, I change what and how I perform.

I have stopped calling myself an artist.

" 'The Eagle' just isn't working," Miri said. "Terry wants to know if you can compose a different piece that draws on subconscious risk-taking imagery. He wants it by your broadcast a week from Sunday."

"Maybe Terry should just write it for me."

"You know none of us can do that." Then her eyes sharpened and her mouth softened. "*You're* the Lucid Dreamer, Drew. None of us can do what you do. If we seem to be . . . directing you too much, it's only because the project requires it. The whole thing would be impossible without you."

I smiled at her. She looked so concerned, filled with so much passion for her work. So resolute. *Implacable,* Leisha had said of her father. *Willing to bend anything that stood in his way.*

She said, "You do believe that we know how important you are, Drew? Drew?"

I said, "I know, Miri."

Her face broke into shards of light, like swords in my mind. "Then you'll compose the new piece?"

"Risk taking," I said. "Presented as desirable, attractive, urgent. Right. By a week from Sunday."

"It's really necessary, Drew. We're still months away from a prototype in the lab, but the country . . ." She picked up another set of hard copy. "Look. Gravtrain breakdowns up eight percent over last month. Reports to the FCC of communications interruptions—up another three percent. Bankruptcies up five percent. Food movement—this is crucial—performing sixteen percent less efficiently. Industrial indicators falling at the same dismal rate. Voter confidence in the basement. And the duragem situation—"

For once her voice lost its quarter-beat-behind slowness. "Look at these graphs, Drew! We can't even locate the origin of the duragem breakdowns—there's no one epicenter. And when you run the data through the Lawson conversion formulas—"

"Yes," I said, to escape the Lawson conversion formulas. "I believe you. It's bad out there and getting worse.'

"Not just worse—apocalyptical."

My mind fills with crimson fire and navy thunder, surrounding a crystal rose behind an impenetrable shield. Miri grew up on Sanctuary. Necessities and comforts were a given. All the time, for everybody, without question or thought. Unlike me, Miranda never saw a baby die of neglect, a wife beaten by a despairing and drunk husband, a family existing on unflavored soysynth, a toilet that didn't work for days. She didn't know these things were survivable. How would she recognize an apocalypse?

I don't say this aloud.

Terry Mwakambe jumped down from the windowsill. He hadn't said a single word the whole time we'd been in the room. His thought strings, Miri said, consisted almost entirely of equations. But now he said, "Lunch?"

I laughed. I couldn't help it. Lunch! The one tie between Terry Mwakambe and Drew Arlen: food. Surely even Terry and Miri must see the joke, standing here in this room, this building, this project . . . Lunch!

Neither of them laughed. I felt the shape of their bewilderment. It was a rain of tiny, tear-shaped droplets, falling on everything, falling on the apocalypse in my mind, falling on me, light and cold and smothering as snow.

Four

One night in another lifetime Eugene, who came before Rex and after Claude, asked me what the United States reminded me of. That was the sort of question to which Gene was given: inviting metaphorical grandiosity, which in turn invited his scorn. I replied that the United States had always seemed to me like some powerful innocent beast, lushly beautiful, with the cranial capacity of a narrow-headed deer. Look how it stretches its sleek muscles in the sunlight. Look how it bounds high. Look how it runs gracefully straight into the path of the oncoming train. This answer had the virtue of being so inflatedly grandiose that to object to it on those grounds became superfluous. It was beside the point that the answer was also true.

Certainly from *my* gravrail I could see enough of the lush, mangled carcass. We'd come over the Rockies at quarter speed so the Liver passengers could enjoy the spectacular view. Purple mountain majesties and all that. Nobody else even glanced out the window. I stayed glued to it, savoring all the asinine superiority of genuine awe.

At Garden City, Kansas, I changed to a local, zipping through gorgeous countryside at 250 miles an hour, crawling through crappy little Liver towns at nothing an hour. "Why not just *fly* to Washington?" Colin Kowalski had said, incredulous. "You're not supposed to be pretending to be a Liver, after all." I'd told him I wanted to see the Liver towns whose integrity I was defending against potential artificial genetic corruption. He hadn't liked my answer any better than Gene had.

Well, now I was seeing them. The mangled carcass.

Each town looked the same. Streets fanning out from the grav-rail station. Houses and apartment blocks, some pure foamcast and some foamcast added onto older buildings of brick or even wood. The foamcast colors were garish, pink and marigold and cobalt and a very popular green like lobster guts. Aristocratic Liver leisure did not confer aristocratic taste.

Each town boasted a communal café the size of an airplane hangar, a warehouse for goods, various lodge buildings, a public bath, a hotel, sports fields, and a deserted-looking school. Everything was plastered with holosigns: Supervisor S. R. ElectMe Warehouse. Senator Frances Fay FamilyMoney Café. And beyond the town, barely visible from the gravrail, the Y-energy plant and shielded robofactories that kept it all going. And, of course, the scooter track, inevitable as death.

Somewhere in Kansas a family climbed onto the train and plunked themselves down on the seats across from me. Daddy, Mommy, three little Livers, two with runny noses, everybody in need of a diet and gym. Rolls of fat bounced under Mommy Liver's bright yellow jacks. Her glance brushed me, traveled on, reversed like radar.

"Hey," I said.

She scowled and nudged her mate. He looked at me and didn't scowl. The cubs gazed silently, the boy—he was about twelve—with a look like his daddy's.

Colin had warned me against even trying to pass for a Liver; he said there'd be no way I could fool Sleepless. I'd said I didn't want to fool Sleepless; I only wanted to blend into the local flora. He said I couldn't. Apparently he was right. Mommy Liver took one look at my genemod-long legs, engineered face, and Anne Boleyn neck that cost my father a little trust fund, and she knew. My poison-green jacks, soda-can jewelry (very popular; you made it yourself), and shit-brown contact lenses made not a bit of difference to her. Daddy & Son weren't so sure, but, then, they didn't really care. Breast size, not genescan, was on their mind.

"I'm Darla Jones, me," I said cheerfully. I had a lock-pocket full of various chips under various names, some of which the GSEA had provided, some of which they knew nothing about. It's a mistake to let the agency provide all of your cover. The time might come when you want cover from them. All of my identities were documented in federal databases, looking as if they had long pasts, thanks to a talented friend the GSEA also knew nothing about. "Going to Washington, me."

"Arnie Shaw," the man said eagerly. "The train, it break down yet?"

"Nah," I said. "Probably will, though, it."

"What can you do?"

"Nothing."

"Keeps things interesting."

"Arnie," Mommy Liver said sharply, interrupting this mild conversational excursion, "back here, us. There's more seats." She gave me a look that would scorch plastisynth.

"Plenty of seats up here, Dee."

"Arnie!"

" 'Bye," I said. They walked away, the woman muttering under her breath. Bitch. I should let the SuperSleepless turn her descendants into four-armed tailless guard dogs. Or whatever they had in mind. I leaned my head against the back of the seat and closed my eyes. We slowed down for another Liver town.

As soon as we left it, the littlest Shaw was back. A girl of about five, she crept along the aisle like a kitten. She had a pert little face and long dirty brown hair.

"You got a pretty bracelet, you." She looked longingly at the soda-can atrocity on my wrist, all curling jangles of some light-weight alloy bendable as warm wax. Some besotted voter had sent it and the matching earrings to David when he was running for state senator. He'd kept it as a joke.

I slipped the bracelet off my wrist. "You want it, you?"

"Really?" Her face shone. She snatched the bracelet from my outstretched fingers and scampered back down the aisle, blue shirt-tail flapping. I grinned. Too bad kittens inevitably grow up into cats.

A minute later Mommy Liver loomed. "Keep your bracelet, you. Desdemona, she got her own jewelry!"

Desdemona. Where do they ever hear these names? Shakespeare doesn't play at scooter tracks.

The woman looked at me from very hard eyes. "Look, you keep, you, to your kind, and we keep to ours. Better that way all around. You understand, you?"

"Yes, ma'am," I said, and popped out my lenses. My eyes are

an intense, genemod violet. I gazed at her calmly, hands folded on my lap.

She waddled away, muttering. I caught the words, "These people . . ."

"If I find I can't pass for a Liver," I'd told Colin, "I'll pass for a semi-crazy donkey trying to pass for a Liver. I wouldn't be the first donkey to go native. You know, the working-class person pathetically trying to pass for an aristo. Hide in plain sight."

Colin had shrugged. I'd thought he already regretted recruiting me, but then I realized that he hoped my antics would draw attention away from the real GSEA agents undoubtedly heading for Washington. The Federal Forum for Science and Technology, popularly known as the Science Court, was hearing Market Request no. 1892-A. What made this market request different from numbers 1 through 1891 was that it was being proposed by Huevos Verdes Corporation. For the first time in ten years, the Super-Sleepless were seeking government approval to market a patented genemod invention in the United States. They didn't have a fish's chance on the moon, of course, but it was still pretty interesting. Why now? What were they after? And would any of the twenty-seven show up personally at the Science Court hearing?

And if anybody did, would I be able to keep him or her under surveillance?

I gazed out the train window, at the robo-tended fields. Wheat, or maybe soy—I wasn't sure what either looked like, growing. In ten minutes, Desdemona was back. Her face appeared slowly between my outstretched legs; she'd crawled along the floor, under the seats, through the mud and spilled food and debris. Desdemona raised her little torso between my knees, balancing herself with one sticky hand on my seat. The other hand shot out and closed on my bracelet.

I unfastened it and gave it to her again. The front of her blue jacks was filthy. "No cleaning 'bot on this train?"

She clutched the bracelet and grinned. "It died, him."

I laughed. The next minute the gravrail broke down.

I was thrown to the floor, where I swayed on hands and knees, waiting to die. Under me machinery shrieked. The train shuddered to a stop but didn't tip over.

"Damn!" Desdemona's father shouted. "Not again!"

"Can we get some ice cream, us?" a child whined. "We're stopped now!"

"Third time this week! Fucking donkey train!"

"We never get no ice cream!"

Apparently the trains didn't tip over. Apparently I wasn't going to die. Apparently this shrieking machinery was routine. I followed everyone else off the train.

Into another world.

A fever wind blew across the miles of prairie: warm, whispering, intoxicating. I was staggered by the size of the sky. Endless bright blue sky above, endless bright golden fields below. And all of it caressed by that blood-warm wind, impregnated with sunlight, gravid with fragrance. I, a city lover to equal Sir Christoper Wren, had had no idea. No holo had ever prepared me. I resisted the mad idea to kick off my shoes and dig my toes into the dark earth.

Instead I followed the grumbling Livers along the tracks to the front of the train. They gathered around the holoprojection of an engineer, even though I could hear his canned speech being broadcast inside each car. The holo "stood" on the grass, looking authoritative and large. The franchise owner was a friend of mine; he believed that seven-foot-high swarthy-skinned males were the ideal projection to promote order.

"There is no need to be alarmed. This is a temporary malfunction. Please return to the comfort and safety of your car, and in a few moments complimentary food and drinks will be served. A repair technician is on the way from the railroad franchise. There is no need to be alarmed—"

Desdemona kicked the holo. Her foot passed through him and she smirked, a pointless saucy smile of triumph. The holo looked down at her. "Don't do that again, kid—you hear me, you?" Desdemona's eyes widened and she flew behind her mother's legs.

"Don't be so scaredy, you—it's just interactive," Mommy Liver snapped. "Let go, you, of my legs!"

I winked at Desdemona, who stared at me sullenly and then grinned, rattling our bracelet.

"—to the comfort and safety of your car, and in a few moments complimentary food—"

More people approached the engine, all but two complaining loudly. The first was an older woman: tall, plain-faced, and angled as a tesseract. She wore not jacks but a long tunic knitted of yarn in subtle, muted shades of green, too uneven to be machine-made. Her earrings were simple polished green stones. I had never before seen a Liver with taste.

The other anomaly was a short young man with silky red hair, pale skin, and a head slightly too large for his body.

The back of my neck tingled.

Inside the cars, server 'bots emerged from their storage compartments and offered trays of freshly synthesized soy snacks, various drinks, and sunshine in mild doses. "Compliments of State Senator Cecilia Elizabeth Dawes," it said over and over. "So nice to have you aboard." This diversion took half an hour. Then everyone went back outside and resumed complaining.

"The kind of service you get these days—"

"—vote next time, me, for somebody else—*anybody* else—"

"—a temporary malfunction. Please return to the comfort and safety of—"

I walked over the scrub grass to the edge of the closest field. The Sleepless-in-inadequate-disguise stood watching the crowd, observing as pseudocasually as I was. So far he had taken no special notice of me. The field was bounded by a low energy fence, presumably to keep the agrobots inside. They ambled slowly between the rows of golden wheat, doing whatever it was they did. I stepped over the fence and picked one up. It hummed softly, a dark sphere with flexible tentacles. On the bottom a label said CANCO ROBOTS/ LOS ANGELES. CanCo had been in the *Wall Street Journal On-Line* last week; they were in trouble. Their agrobots had suddenly begun to break down all over the country. The franchise was going under.

The warm wind whispered seductively through the sweet-scented wheat.

I sat on the ground, cross-legged, my back to the energy fence. Around me adults settled into games of cards or dice. Children raced around, screaming. A young couple brushed past me and disappeared into the wheat, sex in their eyes. The older woman sat by herself reading a book, an actual book. I couldn't imagine where she'd gotten it. And the big-headed Sleepless, if that's what he/she was, stretched out on the ground, closed his eyes, and pretended to sleep. I grimaced. I've never liked self-serving irony. Not in other people.

After two hours, the server 'bots again brought out food and drinks. "Compliments of State Senator Cecilia Elizabeth Dawes.

So nice to have you aboard." How much soysynth did a Liver gravrail carry? I had no idea.

The sun threw long shadows. I sauntered to the woman reading. "Good book?"

She looked up at me, measuring. If Colin had sent me to the Science Court in Washington, he probably had sent some legitimate agents as well. And if Big Head was a Sleepless, he might have his own personal tail. However, something in the reading woman's face convinced me it wasn't her. She wasn't genemod, but it wasn't that. You can find donkey families who refuse even permitted genemods, and then go on existing very solidly corporate but on the fringe socially. She wasn't that, either. She was something else.

"It's a novel," the woman said neutrally. "Jane Austen. Are you surprised there are still Livers who can read? Or want to?"

"Yes." I smiled conspiratorially, but she only gave me a level stare and went back to her book. A renegade donkey didn't arouse her contempt, or indignation, or fawning. I genuinely didn't interest her. I felt unwitting respect.

Apparently I didn't know as much about the variety of Livers as I'd thought.

The sunset ravished me. The sky turned lucid and vulnerable, then streaked with subtle colors. The colors grew aggressive, followed by wan and valedictory pastels. Then it grew cold and dark. An entire love affair, empyrean, in thirty minutes. Claude-Eugene-Rex-Paul-Anthony-Russell-David.

No repair technician appeared. The prairie cooled rapidly; we all climbed back onto the train, which turned on its lights and heat. I wondered what would have happened if those systems— or the server 'bots—had failed as well.

Someone said, not loudly and to no one in particular, "My meal chip, it came late from the capital last quarter."

Pause. I sat up straighter; this was a new tone. Not complaint. Something else.

"My town got no more jacks. The warehouse donkey says, him, that there's a national shortage."

Pause.

"We're going, us, on this train to get my old mother from Missouri. Heat blower in her building broke and nobody else took her in. She got no heat, her."

Pause.

Someone said, "Does anybody know, them, how far it is to the next town? Maybe we could walk, us."

"We ain't supposed to walk, us! They supposed to fix our fucking train!" Mommy Liver, exploding in rage and saliva.

The quiet tone was over. "That's right! We're voters, us!"

"My kids can't walk to no next town—"

"What are you, a fucking donkey?"

I saw the big-headed man gazing from face to face.

The holo of the tall swarthy engineer appeared suddenly inside the car, standing in the center aisle. "Ladies and Gentlemen, Morrison Gravrail apologizes once more for the delay in service. To make your wait more enjoyable, we are privileged to present a new entertainment production, one not yet released to the holo-grids, compliments of Congressman Wade Keith Finley. Drew Arlen, the Lucid Dreamer, in his brand-new concert 'The Warrior.' Please watch from the windows on the left side of the gravrail."

Livers looked at one another; instantly happy babble replaced rage. Evidently this was something new in breakdown diversions. I calculated the cost of a portable holoprojector capable of holos big enough to be seen from windows the length of a train, plus the cost of an unreleased vid from the country's hottest Liver entertainer. I compared the total to the cost of a competent repair team. Something was very wrong here. I knew nothing about Hollywood, but an unreleased concert from Drew Arlen must be worth millions. Why was a gravrail carrying it around as emergency diversion to keep the natives from getting too restless?

The big-headed man quietly watched his fellow travelers press their faces to the left windows.

A long rod snaked from the roof of the car behind ours, which sat in the center of the train. The rod rose at an obtuse angle to the ground and extended almost to the wheat field. Light fanned from the end of the rod downward, forming a pyramid. Everyone went "Ooooohhhhh!" Portable projectors never deliver the clarity of a good stationary unit, but I didn't think this audience would care. The holo of Drew Arlen appeared in the center of the pyramid, and everyone went "Oooooohhhhhh" again.

I slipped out of the train.

In the dark and up close, the holo looked even stranger: a fifteen-foot-high, fuzzy-edged man sitting in a powerchair, backed by miles of unlit prairie. Above, cold stars glittered, immensely high. I unfolded a plasticloth jacket from the pocket of my jacks.

The holo said, "I'm Drew Arlen. The Lucid Dreamer. Let your dreams be true."

I'd seen Arlen perform live once, in San Francisco, when I'd been slumming with friends. I was the only person in the Congressman Paul Jennings Messura Concert Hall not affected. Natural hypnotic resistance, my doctor said. Your brain just doesn't possess the necessary fine-tuned biochemistry. Do you dream at night?

I have never been able to recall a single one of my dreams.

The pyramidal light around Arlen changed somehow, flickered oddly. Subliminal patterns. The patterns coalesced slowly into intricate shapes and Arlen's voice, low and intimate, began a story.

"Once there was a man of great hopes and no power. When he was young, he wanted everything. He wanted strength, him, that would make all other men respect him. He wanted sex, him, that would make his bones melt with satisfaction. He wanted love. He wanted excitement. He wanted, him, for every day to be filled with challenges only he could meet. He wanted—"

Oh, please. Talk about crudely tapping into basic desires. And even some *donkeys* called this stomp an artist.

The shapes were compelling, though. They slid past Arlen's powerchair, folding and unfolding, some seemingly clear and some flickering at the very edge of conscious perception. I felt my blood flow more strongly in my veins, that sudden surge of life you sometimes get with spring, or sex, or challenge. I was not immune to subliminals. These must have been wicked.

I peered into the gravrail car. Livers stood motionless with their faces pressed to the glass. Desdemona watched with her mouth open, a small pink pocket. Even Mommy Liver's face hinted at the young girl she must have been on some forgotten Liver summer night decades ago.

I turned back to Arlen, still spinning his simple story. His voice was musical. The story was a sort of pseudo-folk tale without subtlety, without resonance, without detail, without irony, without art. The words were merely the bare bones over which the graphics shimmered, calling forth the real meaning from the watchers' hypnotized minds. I'd been told that each person experienced a Drew

Arlen concert differently, depending on the symbols freed and brought forward from whatever powerful childhood experiences stocked each mind. I'd been told that, but I hadn't believed it.

I walked along the outside of the train, in the dark, scanning the Liver faces behind the windows. Some were wet with tears. Whatever they were experiencing, it looked more intense than anything I had felt in the Sistine chapel, at Lewis Darrell's *King Lear,* during the San Francisco Philharmonic's Beethoven festival. It looked more intense than sunshine, or even nervewash. As intense as orgasm.

Nobody regulated Lucid Dreaming. Arlen had a host of shoddy imitators. They never lasted long. Whatever Drew Arlen was doing, he was the only person in the whole world who knew how to do it. Most donkeys ignored him: a manipulative con artist, having as much to do with real art as those holos of the Virgin Mary that suddenly "manifested" during religious festivals.

". . . leaving that home he loved," Arlen's low, musical voice said, "walking away alone, him, into a dark forest . . ."

Nobody regulated Lucid Dreaming. And Drew Arlen, as the whole world knew, was Miranda Sharifi's lover. He was the only Sleeper who went in and out of Huevos Verdes at will. The GSEA followed him constantly, of course, along with enough reporters to fill a small town. It was only his concerts they didn't take seriously.

I walked back along the gravrail and climbed into my car. The big-headed man was the only one not pressed to the windows. He lay stretched out on a deserted seat, sleeping. Or pretending to sleep. In order not to be hypnotized? In order to better observe the effects of Arlen's performance?

The concert wore on. The warrior took the usual risks, won the usual triumphs, exulted the usual exultations. Simplistic power-trip ideation. When it ended, people turned to each other with emotional hugs, laughing and crying, and then spilled out onto the cold prairie toward the holo of Drew Arlen. It sat, fifteen feet high, a handsome crippled man in a powerchair smiling gently down on his disciples. The surrounding shapes had vanished, unless they were flickering subliminally, which was possible. A few Livers stuck their hands into the holo, trying to touch what had no substance. Desdemona danced inside the pyramid and laid her head against the blanket over Arlen's knees.

Daddy Liver said abruptly, "I bet we could walk, us, to the next town."

"Well . . ." somebody said. Other voices chimed in.

If we follow the track, us, and stay together—"

"See if any of the roof lights are portable—"

"Some people should stay, them, with the old people."

The big-headed man watched carefully. That's the moment I was sure. The entire gravrail breakdown in this techno-forsaken place had been a setup, to gauge the effect of Arlen's concert.

How? By whom?

No. Those weren't the right questions. The right question was: What *was* the effect of Arlen's concert?

"You stay here, then, Eddie, with the old people. You, Cassie, tell the people in the other cars. See who wants, them, to go with us. Tasha—"

It took them ten minutes of arguing to get organized. They pried the roof lights off six cars; the lights were portable. People who stayed gave extra jackets to people who left. The first group was just starting down the rail when a light flashed in the sky. A second later I could hear the plane.

The Livers turned silent.

The plane held a single gravrail technician, flanked by two security 'bots, the no-fucking-around kind that both projected a personal safety shield and carried weapons. The crowd watched in silence. The tech's handsome, genemod face looked strained. Techs are a strained group anyway: genemod for appearance, but without the IQ and ability enhancements, which cost prospective parents a lot more money. You find them repairing machinery, running warehouse distribs, supervising nursing or child-care 'bots. Techs certainly aren't Livers, but although they live in the enclaves, they aren't exactly donkeys either. And they know it.

"Ladies and gentlemen," the tech said unhappily, "Morrison Gravrail, Incorporated, and Senator Cecilia Elizabeth Dawes apologize for the delay in repairing your train. Circumstances beyond our control—"

"And I'm a politician, me!" someone yelled bitterly.

"Why do we vote, us, for you scum?"

"Better tell the Senator she lost votes, her, on this here train!"

"The service we deserve—"

The tech walked resolutely toward the engine, eyes down,

paced by his 'bots. I caught the faint shimmer of a Y-energy field as he passed. But a few of the Livers—six or seven—glanced down the track, stretching away in the windy darkness, their eyes bright with what I would have sworn was regret.

It took the tech all of thirteen minutes to fix the gravrail. Nobody molested him. He left in his plane, and the train started up again. Livers played dice, grumbled, slept, tended their cranky children. I walked through all the cars, searching for the big-headed man. He had vanished while I was watching the Livers' reaction to the donkey tech. We must have left him behind, on the windy prairie, in the concealing dark.

Five

Every once in a while I need, me, to go off in the woods. I didn't used to tell nobody. But now when I go, two-three times a year, I tell Annie and she fixes me up some raw stuff from the kitchen, apples and potatoes and soysynth that ain't been made into dishes yet. I stay out there alone, me, for five or six days, away from all of it: the café and holodancers and blasting music and warehouse distribs and stomps with clubs and even the Y-energy. I build fires, me. Some people ain't left East Oleanta in twenty years except to go by gravrail to another town just like it. The deep woods might as well be in China. I think they're scared, them, of hearing themselves out there.

I was supposed to leave for the woods the morning after the café kitchen broke and we talked, us, to Supervisor Samuelson on the official terminal. But I sure wasn't leaving Annie and Lizzie without food, and I sure wasn't going no place, me, that had rabid raccoons and a broken warden 'bot.

Lizzie stood by my couch in her nightshirt, a bright pink blot on my morning sleep. "Billy, you think, you, that kitchen is fixed yet?"

Annie came out from her bedroom, yawning, still in her plasticloth nightdress. "Leave Billy alone, Lizzie. You hungry, you?"

Lizzie nodded. I sat up, me, on the sofa, with one arm shielding my eyes from the morning sun at the window. "Listen, Annie. I been thinking, me. If they do get that kitchen fixed, we should start taking all the food we can, us, and storing it here. In case it breaks again. We can take right up to the meal chip limit every day—Lizzie and you don't ever hardly do that and me neither, some days—and then raw stuff from the kitchen. Potatoes and apples and stuff."

Annie pressed her lips together. She ain't a morning person, her. But it felt so good to be waking up at Annie's place that I forgot that, me. She said, "The food would rot in just two-three days. I don't want, me, to have a lot of half-rotten stuff around here. It ain't clean."

"Then we'll throw it out, us, and get some more." I spoke gentle. Annie don't like things to be different than they've always been.

Lizzie said, "Billy, you think, you, that kitchen is fixed yet?"

I said, "I don't know, sweetheart. Let's go look, us. Better get dressed."

Annie said, "She got to go, her, to the baths first. She stinks. Me, too. You walk us, Billy?"

"Sure." What good did she think an old wreck like me'd be against rabid coons? But I'd of walked Annie past them demons she believes in.

Lizzie said, "Billy, you think, you, that kitchen is fixed yet?"

There wasn't no raccoons near the baths. The men's bath was empty except for Mr. Keller, who's so old I don't think even he remembers if he's got a first name, and two little boys who shouldn't of been there alone, them. But they were having themselves a wonderful splashing time. I liked watching them, me. They cheered up the morning.

Mr. Keller told me the café kitchen was fixed. I walked Annie and Lizzie, sweet-clean as berries in the dew, to get our breakfast. But the café was full, it, not just with Livers eating but of donkeys making a holo of Congresswoman Janet Carol Land.

It was her, all right. No tape. She stood in front of the foodbelt, which offered the usual soysynth eggs, bacon, cereals, and breads, plus some fresh genemod strawberries. I don't like genemod strawberries, me. They might keep for weeks, but they never taste like them little wild sweet berries that grow on the hillsides in June.

". . . serving her people with the best she has, no matter the need, no matter the hour, no matter the emergency," said a handsome donkey into a camera 'bot. "Janet Carol Land, on the spot to serve East Oleanta—on the spot to serve *you*. A politician who deserves those memorable words from the Bible: 'Well done, good and faithful servant'!"

Land smiled. She was a looker, her, the way donkey women are when they're not young: fine soft skin and pink lips and hair in pretty silver waves. Too skinny, though. Not like Annie. Who pressed her dark-berry lips together like she was going to squeeze cider with them.

Land said to the handsome man, "Thank you, Royce. As you know, the café is the heart of any aristo town. That's why when a café malfunctions, I move heaven and earth to get it operable again. As these good citizens of East Oleanta can attest."

"Let's talk to some of them," Royce said, showing all his teeth. He and Land walked to a table where Jack Sawicki sat, him, looking cornered. "Mayor Sawicki, what do you think of the service Congresswoman Land provided your town today?"

Paulie Cenverno looked up, him, from where he ate at the next table. With him was Celie Kane. Annie's lower lip trembled itself into a half-grin, half-wince.

Jack said miserably, "We're awful happy, us, that the foodbelt's fixed, and we—"

"When you fuckers gonna get them rabid raccoons killed?" Celie demanded.

Royce's face froze, it. "I don't think—"

"You better think, you, and think hard about them coons, or you and the Congresswoman gonna be thinking about new jobs!"

"Cut," Royce said. "Don't worry, Janet, we'll edit it." His smile looked like it was foamed onto his face, but I saw his eyes, me, and I looked away. My fighting days are over, unless I have to fight for Annie or Lizzie.

Royce took the Congresswoman's elbow, him, and steered her toward the door. Celie shrilled, "I mean it, me! It's been days now and you guys done shit! 'Public servants!' You ain't nothing but—"

"*Celie,*" Jack and Paulie both said.

Land broke free of Royce. She turned back, her, to Celie. "Your concern for your town's safety is natural, ma'am. The warden 'bot and any sick wildlife are not in my jurisdiction—they fall to District Supervisor Samuelson—but when I return to Albany I'll do everything in my power to see that the problem is solved." She looked straight into Celie's eyes, real steady, and it was Celie who looked away first, her.

Celie didn't say nothing. Land smiled, her, and turned to her crew. "I think we're done here, Royce. I'll meet you outside." She walked to the door, back straight, head high. And the only reason I ever saw anything different was because of where I stood, me, sideways to the door, between Annie and any trouble. Congresswoman Land reached the door and she was a smiling pretty cocksure politician, her. Then she went through the door and she was a woman with tired, tired eyes.

I glanced at Annie to see if she saw. But she was clucking at Celie Kane. Annie might of grinned, her, at Celie's balls, but deep down inside Annie don't approve of sassing public servants. *They can't help being donkeys.* I could almost hear her say it, me.

Lizzie said in her clear young voice, "That Congresswoman can't really help get the warden 'bot fixed in Albany, can she? She was just pretending, her."

"Oh hush," Annie said. "You never will learn, you, when to keep your mouth quiet and when not."

Two days later, two days of everybody staying inside, us, and no warden 'bot tech from Albany, we made a hunting party. It took hours of talk that went around and around in dizzies, but we made it. Livers ain't supposed to have no guns, us. No warehouses stock a District Supervisor Tara Eleanor Schmidt .22 rifle. No political campaigns give away a Senator Jason Howard Adams shotgun or a County Legislature Terry William Monaghan pistol. But we got them, us.

Paulie Cenverno dug up his granddaddy's shotgun, him, from a plastisynth box behind the school. Plastisynth keeps out damn near everything: dirt, damp, rust, bugs. Eddie Rollins and Jim Swikehardt and old Doug Kane had their daddies' rifles, them. Sue Rollins and her sister, Krystal Mandor, said they'd share a family Matlin; I didn't see, me, how that could work. Two men I didn't know had shotguns. Al Rauber had a pistol. Two of the teenage stomps showed up, grinning, not armed. Just what we needed, us. Altogether, we were twenty.

"Let's split, us, into pairs, and set out in ten straight lines from the café," Jack Sawicki said.

"You sound like a goddamn donkey," Eddie Rollins said in disgust. The stomps grinned.

"You got a better idea, you?" Jack said. He held his rifle real tight over his bulging green jacks.

"We're Livers," Krystal Mandor said, "let us go where we want, us."

Jack said, "And what if somebody gets shot, them? You want the police franchise down on us?"

Eddie said, "I want to hunt raccoons, me, like an aristo. Don't give me no orders, Jack."

"Fine," Jack said. "Go ahead, you. I'm not saying another goddamn word."

After ten minutes of arguing we set off in pairs, us, in ten straight lines.

I walked with Doug Kane, Celie's father. Two old men, us, slow and limping. But Doug still knew, him, how to walk quiet in the woods. Off to my right I heard somebody whooping and laughing. One of the stomps. After a while, the sound died away.

The woods were cool and sweet-smelling, so thick overhead that the floor wasn't much overgrown. We stepped, us, on pine needles that sent up their clean smell. White birches, slim as Lizzie, rustled. Under the trees moss grew dark green, and in the sunny patches there was daisies and buttercups and black-eyed Susans. A mourning dove called, the calmest sound in the whole world.

"Pretty," Doug said, so quiet that a rabbit upwind didn't even twitch its long ears.

Toward noon, the trees got skimpier and the underbrush thicker. I smelled blackberries somewheres, which made me think of Annie. I figured, me, that we come at least six hard miles from East Oleanta. All we seen was rabbits, a doe, and a mess of harmless snakes. No coons. And any rabid coons out this far, killing them wouldn't do the town no good anyway. It was time to turn back.

"Gotta . . . sit down, me," Doug said.

I looked at him, me, and my skin turned cold. He was pale as the birch bark, his eyelids fluttering like two hummingbirds. He dropped the rifle, him, and it went off—old fool had the safety off. The bullet buried itself in a tree trunk. Doug clutched his chest and fell over. I'd been so busy, me, enjoying air and flowers and I ain't even seen he was having a heart attack.

"Sit down! Sit down!" I eased him onto a patch of some kind of ground cover, all shiny green leaves. Doug lay on his side, him, breathing hard: *whoooo, whoooo*. His right hand batted the air but I knew, me, that his eyes didn't see nothing. They were wild.

"Lay quiet, Doug. Don't move, you! I'll go get help, me, I'll make them bring the medunit . . ."

Whoooo, whoooo, whoooo . . . then the breathing noises stopped.

I thought: *He's gone.* But his bony old chest still rose and fell, just shallow and quiet now. His eyes glazed.

"I'll bring the medunit!" I said again, turned, and nearly fell myself, me. Staring at me from not ten feet away was a rabid coon.

Once you seen a animal gone rabid, you don't never forget it. I could see, me, the separate specks of foam around the coon's mouth. Sunlight from between the trees sparkled on the specks like they was glass. The coon bared its teeth, it, and hissed at me, a sound like I never heard no coon make. Its hindquarters shook. It was near the end.

I raised Doug's rifle, me, knowing that if it come for me there was no way I was going to be fast enough.

The coon twitched and lunged. I jerked up the rifle, me, but I never even got it to shoulder height. A beam of light shot out from some place behind me, only it wasn't light but something else like light. And the coon flipped over backwards, it, in mid-lunge and crashed to the ground dead.

I turned around, me, very slow. And if I seen one of Annie's angels, I couldn't of been more surprised.

A girl stood there, her, a short girl with a big head and dark hair tied back with a red ribbon. She wore stupid clothes for the woods: white shorts, thin white shirt, open sandals, just like we didn't have no deer ticks or blackflies or snakes. The girl looked at me somber. After a minute she said, "Are you all right?"

"Y-yes, ma'am. But Doug Kane there—I think his heart . . ."

She walked over to Doug, her, knelt, and felt his pulse. She looked up at me. "I want you to do something, please. Drop this on the dead raccoon, right on top of the body." She handed me a smooth gray disk the size of a coin. I remember coins, me.

She kept on looking at me, not even blinking, and so I did it. I just turned my back, me, on her and Doug both, and did it. Why? Annie asked me later, and I didn't have no answer. Maybe it was the girl's eyes. Donkey, and not. No Janet Carol Land facing no camera with *well done good and faithful servant*.

The gray disk hit the coon's damp fur and stuck. It shimmered, it, and in a second that coon was cased in a clear shell that went right down to the ground and, it turned out, sliced through an inch underground. Maybe Y-energy, maybe not. A leaf blew against the shell and slid right off. I touched the shell. I don't know, me, where I got the nerve. The shell was hard as foamcast.

Made out of nothing.

When I turned back the girl was putting something, her, in her shorts pocket, and Doug's eyes were coming clear. He gasped, him.

"Don't move him yet," the girl said, still not smiling. She didn't look like she smiled much. "Go get help. He'll be safe until you get back."

"Who are you, ma'am?" It came out squeaky. "What did you do to him, you?"

"I gave him some medicine. The same injection the medunit would have given him. But he needs a stretcher to be carried back to your town. Go get help, Mr. Washington."

I took a step, me, right toward her. She stood up. She didn't seem afraid, her—just went on looking at me with those eyes with no smile. After seeing the coon, it came to me that she had a shell, too. Not hard like the coon's, and maybe not away from her body neither. Maybe close on it like a clear glove. But that was why she was out in the woods in shorts and flimsy sandals, and why she wasn't bit up, her, by no blackflies, and why she wasn't afraid of me.

I said, "You . . . you're from Eden, ain't you? It's really here someplace, in these woods, it's really here . . ."

She got a funny expression on her face. I didn't know, me, what it meant, and it came to me that I could better guess what a rabid coon was thinking than what this girl was.

"Go get help, Mr. Washington. Your friend needs it." She stopped, her. "And please tell the townspeople . . . as little as you feel you can."

"But, ma'am—"

"Uuuhhhmmmm," Doug moaned, not like he was in pain, him, but like he was dreaming.

I stumbled back to East Oleanta as fast as I could, me, puffing until I thought we'd have two heart attacks for the medunit. Just beyond the scooter track I met Jack Sawicki and Krystal Mandor, hot and sweaty, them, straggling back to town. I told them, me, about old man Kane's collapse. They had to make me start over twice. Jack set off, him, by the sun—he's maybe the only other good woodsman East Oleanta's got. Krystal ran, her, for the medunit and more help. I sat down, me, to catch my breath. The sun was hot and blinding on the open field, the lake sparkled down past town, and I couldn't find no balance no place in my mind.

Maybe I never did. Nothing ever looked the same to me after that day.

The medunit found Doug Kane easy enough, skimming above the brush on its gravsensors, smelling me and Doug's trail in the air. Four men followed, them, and they carried Kane home. He breathed easy. That night near everybody else in town gathered, us, in the café. There was dancing and accusing and yelling and a party. Nobody had shot no raccoons, but Eddie Rollins shot a deer and Ben Radisson shot Paulie Cenverno. Paulie wasn't hurt bad, him, just a graze on the arm, and the medunit fixed him right up. I went to see Doug Kane, me.

He didn't remember no girl in the woods. I asked him, me, while he lay on his plastisynth sleeping platform, propped up on extra pillows and covered with an embroidered blanket like the one Annie made for her sofa. Doug loved the attention, him. I asked him, me, real careful, not exactly saying there was a girl in the woods, just hinting around the edges of what happened. But he didn't remember nothing, him, after he collapsed, and nobody who went to bring him home mentioned finding any raccoon in a hard shell.

She must of just picked up the whole shell, her, safe as houses, and just walked off with it.

The only person I told, me, was Annie, and I made sure Lizzie was nowhere near. Annie didn't believe me, her. Not at first. Then she did, but only because she remembered the big-headed girl in green jacks in the café two nights before. This girl had a big head too, her, and somehow to Annie that meant all the rest of my story was true. I told Annie not to say nothing to nobody. And she never did, not even to me. Said it gave her the willies, her, to think of some weird outcast donkeys living in the woods with genemod machinery and calling it Eden. Blasphemous, almost. Eden was in the Bible and no place else. Annie didn't want to think about it, her.

But I thought about it, me. A lot. It got so for a while I couldn't hardly think about nothing else. Then I got a grip on myself, me, and went back to normal living. But the big-headed girl was still in my thoughts.

We didn't have no more trouble that whole summer and fall with rabid raccoons. They all just disappeared, them, for good.

But machines kept breaking.

AUGUST 2114

He that will not apply new remedies must
expect new evils; for time is the
greatest innovator.

—**Francis Bacon,** *Of Innovations*

Six

The first person I saw at Science Court, walking up the broad shallow white stone steps that were supposed to evoke Socrates and Aristotle, was Leisha Camden.

Paul, who came before Anthony and after Rex, and I used to enjoy intellectual arguments. He enjoyed them because he won; I enjoyed them because he won. This was, of course, before I understood how deeply rooted, like a cancer, was my desire to lose. At the time the arguments seemed amusing, even daring. The people Paul and I knew considered it rather bad form to debate abstract questions. We donkeys, with our genemod intelligence, were all so good at it—like showing off the fact that you could walk. No one wished to appear ridiculous. *Much* better to publicly enjoy body surfing. Or gardening. Or even, God help us, sensory deprivation tanks. Much better.

But one night Paul and I, daring nonconformists right up to our banal end, debated who should have the right to control radical new technology. The government? The technocrats, mostly scientists and engineers, who were the only ones who ever really understood it? The free market? The people? It was not a good night. Paul wanted to win more than usual. I, for reasons connected to a gold-eyed slut at a party the night before, was not quite as eager as usual to lose. Things got said, the kinds of embarrassing things that don't go away. Tempers ran high. My paternal grandfather's teak desk required a new panel, which never quite matched the others. Intellectual debate can be very hard on furniture.

In a subtle way, I blame the Sleepless for Paul's and my breakup. Not directly, but a *désastre inoffensif,* like the final small program that crashes an overloaded system. But, then, for the last hundred years, what haven't we blamed on the Sleepless?

They even caused the creation of the science courts: another *désastre inoffensif*. A hundred years ago, nobody ever made a decision that is was acceptable to engineer human embryos to be Sleepless. Genemod companies just did it, the way they did all those other embryonic genemods in the unregulated days before the GSEA. You want a kid who's seven feet tall, has purple hair, and is encoded with a predisposition for musical ability? Here—you got yourself a basketball-playing punk cellist. Mazel tov.

Then came the Sleepless. Rational, awake, smart. Too smart. And long-lived, a bonus surprise—nobody knew at first that sleep interfered with cell regeneration. Nobody liked it when they found out. Too many Darwinian advantages piling up in one corner.

So, this being the United States and not some sixteenth-century monarchy or twentieth-century totalitarian state, the government just didn't outlaw radical genetic modifications outright. Instead, they talked them to death.

The Federal Forum for Science and Technology follows due process. A jury composed of a panel of scientists, arguments and rebuttals, cross-examination, final written opinion with provision for dissenting opinions, the whole ROM. Science Court has no power. It can ony recommend, not make policy. Nobody on it can tell anybody to do or not do anything about any thing.

But no Congress, president, or GSEA board has ever acted contrary to a Science Court recommendation. Not once. Not ever.

So I had all the *force majeure* of the status quo on my side that furniture-wrecking night when I declared that the government should control human genetic modification. Paul wanted absolute control by scientists (he was one). We both were right, as far as actual practice. But of course practice didn't matter; neither did theory, really. What we'd really wanted was the fight.

Did Leisha Camden ever wreck furniture or put her fist through walls or hurl antique wineglasses? Watching her walk into the white-columned Forum building on Pennsylvania Avenue, I thought not. Washington in August is hot; Leisha wore a sleeveless white suit. Her bright blonde hair was cut in short, shining waves. She looked composed, beautiful, cool. She reminded me, probably unfairly, of Stephanie Brunell. All that was missing was the pink huge-eyed, doomed little dog.

* * *

"Oyez, oyez," the clerk called, as the technical panel filed in. And then they get huffy when the press calls it "science court." Washington is Washington, even when it's rising to its feet for Nobel laureates.

There were three of them this time, on an eight-person panel: heavy artillery. Barbara Poluikis, chemical biology, a diminutive woman with hyperalert eyes. Elias Maleck, medicine, who radiated worried integrity. Martin Davis Exford, molecular physics, looking more like an overage ballet dancer. Nobody, of course, in genetics. The United States hasn't won there in sixty years. The panelists had been agreed to by the advocates for both sides. Panelists were presumed to be impartial.

I sat in the press section, courtesy of credentials from Colin Kowalski, credentials so badly faked that anybody who checked them would have to conclude they'd been faked by me, the person incapacitated by Gravison's disease, and not by some competent agency. There was a lot of press, live and robotic. Science Court goes out on various donkey grids.

After the panel sat down, I stayed standing—very gauche— to scan the spectators for Livers. There might have been one or two in the gallery; the room was so big it was hard to tell. "Please sit down," my seat said to me in a reasonable voice, "others may have trouble seeing over you." That I could believe. In my bright purple jacks and soda-can-and-plastic jewelry I was one of a kind in the press box.

In the front of the chamber, behind a low antique-wood railing and an invisible high-security Y-shield, sat the advocates, expert testimony, panel, and VIPs. Leisha Camden sat next to amateur advocate Miranda Sharifi, who had suddenly appeared in Washington from God-knows-where. Not from Huevos Verdes. For days the press had been watching the island with the avidity of moonbase residents monitoring dome leaks. So from what geographical forehead had Miranda Sharifi sprung, helmeted to do battle for her corporation's product?

She had refused a professional lawyer to argue her case. She'd even refused Leisha Camden, which had caused much snickering in the press bar. Apparently they felt a SuperSleepless was inadequate to convincingly present the technology her own people had invented. I never ceased to be amazed at the stupidity of my fellow IQ-enhanced donkeys.

I studied Miranda carefully. Short, big-headed, low of brow. Thick unruly black hair tied back with a red ribbon. Despite the severe, expensive black suit, she looked like neither a Liver nor a donkey. I saw her furtively wipe the palms of her hands on her skirt; they must be damp. I'd seen pictures of the notorious Jennifer Sharifi, and Miranda had inherited none of her grandmother's coolness, height, or beauty. I wondered if she minded.

"We're here today," began moderator Dr. Senta Yongers, a grandmotherly type with the perfect teeth of a grid star, "to determine the facts concerning Case 1892-A. I would like to remind everyone in this chamber that the purpose of this inquiry is three-fold. First, to identify agreed-upon facts concerning this scientific claim, including but not limited to its nature, actions, and replicable physical effects.

"Second, to allow disagreements about this scientific claim to be discussed, debated, and recorded for later study.

"And third, to fulfill a joint request from the Congressional Committee on New Technology, the Federal Drug Administration, and the Genetic Standards Enforcement Agency to create a recommendation for the further study, for the licensing within the United States, or for the denial of Case 1892-A, which has already been awarded patent status. Further study, I may remind you, allows the patent's developers to solicit volunteers for beta testing of the patent. Licensing is virtually equivalent to federal permission to market." Yongers looked around the chamber gravely over the tops of her glasses—a currently fashionable affectation for donkeys with perfect vision—to emphasize the seriousness of this possibility. This is important, folks—you could get Case 1892-A dumped square in your laps. As if anybody here didn't already realize that.

I looked back at Miranda Sharifi, holding a thick printout bound in black covers. It was clear to me that the Sleepless are a different species from donkeys and Livers. I mention this only because of the large number of people to whom it is, inexplicably, not clear. Miranda undoubtedly understood everything in that stupendously complex printout, which was, after all, in her own field, and at least partly of her own devising. But she probably also understood everything important in my field (all my purported fields, pathetic kitchen gardens that they were). Plus everything important in art history, in law, in early-childhood education, in international economics, in paleolithic anthropology. To me, that added up to a different species. Donkeys have brains fully adapted to their needs, but then so did the stegosaurus. I was looking at a multi-adapted mammal.

Feeling spiny, I watched a grid journalist in front of me flick a finger to direct his robocam to zoom in on the legend carved across the chamber's impressive dome: THE PEOPLE MUST CONTROL SCIENCE AND TECHNOLOGY. A nice journalistic touch, that. I approve of irony.

"The chief advocate for Case 1892-A," continued Moderator Yongers, "is Miranda Sharifi, of Huevos Verdes Corporation, the patent holders. Chief opposition is Dr. Lee Chang, GSEA Senior Geneticist and holder of the Geoffrey Sprague Morling Chair in Genetics at Johns Hopkins. The following stipulations have already been agreed to by both sides—for details please consult the furnished hard copy, the master screen at the front of the chamber, or channel 1640FORURM on Govnet."

The "furnished hard copy" was four hundred pages of cell diagrams, equations, genenome tables, and chemical processes, all with numerous journal citations. But in front was a one-page list somebody had prepared for the press. I would bet my purple jacks that its simplifications had been paid for in hours of screaming by technical experts who didn't want their precious facts distorted just so they could be understood. But here the simplified distortions were, ready for the newsgrids. Washington is Washington.

"Pre-agreed upon by both sides," read Moderator Yongers, "are the following nine points:

"One—Case 1892-A describes a nanodevice designed to be injected into the human bloodstream. The device is made of genetically modified self-replicating proteins in very complex structures. The process which creates these structures is proprietary, belonging to Huevos Verdes Corporation. The device has been named by its creators the 'Cell Cleaner.' This name is a registered trademark, and must be indicated as such whenever used."

Always good to have your commercial bases covered. I scanned the faces of the Nobel laureates. They showed nothing.

"Two—Under laboratory conditions, the Cell Cleaner has demonstrated the capacity to leave the bloodstream and travel through human tissue, as do white blood cells. Under laboratory conditions, the Cell Cleaner also has demonstrated the capacity to penetrate a cell wall, as do viruses, with no damage to the cell."

No problem there—even I knew that the FDA had already licensed a batch of drugs that could do those things. I switched my contact lenses to zoom and saw Miranda Sharifi's hand steal into Leisha Camden's. Bad move—every grid journalist and on-line watcher could see it, too. Didn't Miranda know any better than to show signs of weakness to the enemy? How had she brought down the entire pseudo-government of Sanctuary, anyway?

"Three—Under laboratory conditions, the Cell Cleaner occupies less than one percent of a typical cell's volume. Under laboratory conditions, the Cell Cleaner has demonstrated the capacity to be powered by chemicals naturally present in cells."

Yongers paused and looked challengingly around the room; I didn't know why. Did she expect any of us to challenge what eight scientists had already stipulated? The Cell Cleaner could have been powered by gerbils on treadmills for all any of us laymen could prove. But only under laboratory conditions, of course.

It was already clear where the opposition would attack.

"Four—Under laboratory conditions, the Cell Cleaner has demonstrated the capacity to replicate at slightly slower than the rate at which bacteria replicate—about twenty minutes per complete division. Under laboratory conditions, this replication has demonstrated the capacity to occur for several hours using only those chemicals normally found in human tissue plus those chemicals contained in the fluid of the original injection. Under laboratory conditions, the Cell Cleaner has demonstrated the capacity to stop replicating after several hours, and to then replicate only to replace damaged units."

Go forth and multiply, but only to a predetermined point. Too bad the whole human race hadn't done that. The history of the previous century—and the cataclysmically Malthusian one before that—might have been entirely different. God forgot the "off" switch. Huevos Verdes didn't.

"Five—The Cell Cleaner contains a proprietary device referred to in Case 1892-A as 'biomechanical nanocomputing technology.' Under laboratory conditions, this technology has demonstrated the capacity to identify seven cells of the same functional type from a mass of cells of varying functional types, and to compare the DNA from these seven cells to determine what constitutes standard DNA coding for that type of cell. Furthermore, the Cell Cleaner is said to be able to enter subsequent cells and compare their DNA structure to its determined standard."

If that was true—and there was no way the opposition would have agreed to it if there were the slightest doubt—it was astounding. No other biotech firm on Earth could do that. But I noticed the careful wording: "is said to be able." Stipulations were supposed to be demonstrated fact. Why were mere claims by Huevos Verdes allowed in at this point? Unless they were necessary prerequisites to something that *had* been demonstrated.

"Six—Under laboratory conditions, the Cell Cleaner has demonstrated the capacity to destroy any cells whose DNA does not match what it has determined to be standard coding."

Bingo.

Even the journalists looked excited. In *Washington.*

"Seven—Under laboratory conditions, the Cell Cleaner has demonstrated the capacity to thus destroy each of the following types of abberrant cells: cancerous growths, precancerous dysplasia, deposits on arterial walls, viruses, infectious bacteria, toxic elements and compounds, and cells whose DNA has been altered by viral activity resulting in DNA splices. Furthermore, it has been demonstrated that under laboratory conditions, such dissembled cells can be handled by normal bodily-waste-removal mechanisms."

Cancer, arteriosclerosis, chicken pox, herpes, lead poisoning, tourista, cystitis, and the common cold. All gone, dissembled and washed away by your own team of customized internal cleaning ladies. I felt a little dizzy.

But what the hell could those "laboratory conditions" have been like?

The spectators buzzed loudly. Moderator Yongers glared at us until the room quieted.

"Eight—Under laboratory conditions, the Cell Cleaner has demonstrated the capacity to avoid destroying certain bacterial cells even though their 'genetic fingerprint' does not match the host tissue's DNA. These cells include, but are not limited to, bacteria normally found in the human digestive tract, vagina, and upper respiratory tract. It is noted for the record that Huevos

Verdes Corporation attributes this selectivity in dissembling non-standard DNA to 'preprogramming the protein nanocomputer to recognize symbiotic bacterial DNA.' "

Kill off the harmful, spare the useful. Huevos Verdes was offering the world's first immune-system enhancer with computerized Darwinian morality. Or maybe Arthurian morality: Replace 'Might makes right' with 'Right makes life.' I suddenly pictured legions of little Cell Cleaners in shining white armor, and I had to grin. The journalist in the next seat shot me an edgy look.

"Nine—No significant studies have been carried out concerning the Cell Cleaner's performance or effects inside whole, living, fully functional human beings."

There it was: the inevitable spoiler. Without long-term studies of its effects on real people, Huevos Verdes had no more chance of marketing Case 1892-A than of marketing powdered unicorn horn. Even if the Science Court permitted further study, I was not going to have my own private Cell Cleaner anytime soon.

I sat exploring how I felt about that.

Another buzz swept over the audience: disappointment? Satisfaction? Anger? It seemed to be all three.

"The *following points*," Moderator Yongers said, raising her voice, "*are in dispute*." The chamber quieted.

"One—The Cell Cleaner will cause ho harm to healthy human cells, tissues, or organs."

She stopped. That was it—one point in dispute. But that point, her face clearly said, was everything. Who wanted a cleaned, repaired, dead body?

"The first opening argument will be presented by the opposition. Dr. Lee?"

There was another printout to summarize Dr. Lee's points, which was fortunate because he couldn't. Every sentence came trailing clouds of evidence, qualifiers, and equations, all of which he clearly considered glory. The technical panel listened closely, taking notes. Everybody else consulted the printout. It summarized his windy points:

In dispute: "The Cell Cleaner will cause no harm to healthy human cells, tissues, or organs."

In rebuttal: There is no way to assure that the Cell Cleaner will not cause harm to healthy cells, organs, or tissues.

- Laboratory tests do not necessarily predict the effects of biosubstances on live, functional human beings. See CDC Hypertext File 68164.

- No partial-being studies have included the effect of the Cell Cleaner on the brain. Brain chemisty can behave much differently from grosser body tissue. See CDC Hypertext File 68732.

- The long-term effects submitted cover only two years. Many biosubstances reveal erratic side effects only after longer time periods. See CDC Hypertext File 88812.

- The list of so-called "pre-programmed symbiotic bacterial DNA" that the Cell Cleaner will not destroy may or may not be congruent with a complete list of useful foreign organisms in a living, functional human being. The human body includes some ten thousand billion billion protein parts interacting in intensely complex ways, including hundreds of thousands of different kinds of molecules, some only partially understood. The so-called "pre-programmed list" could leave out vital organisms which the Cell Cleaner would then destroy, possibly causing tremendous functional upset, including death.

- Over time, the Cell Cleaner itself might develop replication problems. Since it introduces what is in essence competing DNA into the body, it displays the potential to become an artificially induced cancer. See CDC Hypertext File 4536.

I wondered at the quirk in the printing program that had made the word "cancer" darker than the rest.

Dr. Lee took the entire rest of the morning for his opening argument, which seemed shut pretty tight to me. At no point did I question his sincerity. The argument seemed to go like this: The Cell Cleaner couldn't be proved safe without a decade—at least—of tests on real, whole human beings. (I decided not to look up "partial-being studies." I didn't really want to know.) It was, however, inhumane to subject real human beings to such risks. There was therefore no way to prove the Cell Cleaner safe. And if it was unsafe, the potential for widespread disaster was spectacular.

Including, in the curious phrasing of the printout, "tremendous functional upset, including death."

Therefore, the opposition would recommend that the Cell Cleaner not be licensed, not be approved for further study within the United States, and be placed on the Banned List of the International Genetic Modification Advisory Council.

Apparently we had already left the fact-finding stage and were well into the political-recommendation stage. Washington is Washington. Facts are political; politics is a fact.

It was a quarter to twelve when Dr. Lee finished. Moderator Yongers leaned over her bench. "Ms. Sharifi, it's nearly time to break for lunch. Would you prefer to postpone your opening statement until this afternoon?"

"No, Madame Moderator. I'll be brief." Why hadn't Leisha Camden told Miranda to leave off the red hair ribbon? It gave her an Alice-in-Wonderland youthfulness that was a liability. Her voice was calm and dispassionate.

"The patent you are considering today is the greatest life-saving medical development since the discovery of antibiotics. Dr. Lee speaks of the dangers to the body if the Cell Cleaner nanomachinery fails, or is inaccurately programmed, or produces unknown side effects. He does not mention the people who will die premature or painful deaths *without* this innovation. You would rather keep one person from dying with the Cell Cleaner than have hundreds of thousands die without it. That is morally wrong.

"*You* are morally wrong, all of you. The whole purpose of this so-called scientific Forum is to protect drug company profits at the expense of the sick and dying. You are moral Fascists, using the strength of government to harm those already weak and powerless, in order to keep them powerless and so keep yourselves in power. And I except none of you from these charges, not even the scientists, who conspire with profit and power and so deliver science to them.

"With the Cell Cleaner, Huevos Verdes offers you life. Even though you do not deserve to live. But Huevos Verdes does not distinguish between the deserving and the undeserving when it offers a product. *You* do, every time your regulations stifle genetic or nanotech research, every time that lost research deprives someone of life. You are killers, all of you. Political and economic mercenaries, no better at judging true science than the jungle animals whose morality you emulate. Nonetheless, Huevos Verdes Corporation offers you the Cell Cleaner, and I will prove to you here its essential safety, even though I'm not sure any of you has the capacity to understand the science I will explain."

And Miranda Sharifi sat down.

The panel looked stunned, as well they might. More interestingly, Leisha Camden also looked stunned. Evidently this was not what she'd expected to hear her protégée say. She whispered frantically into Miranda's ear.

"I have never heard such unprofessional bullshit!" Martin Davis Exford, Nobel laureate in molecular physics, on his feet behind the panelists' table. His powerful voice outshouted everyone else. Maroon veins pulsed below the surface of his neck.

"I deeply resent, Ms. Sharifi, your perversion of this Forum. We're here to determine scientific fact, not indulge in ad hominem attacks!"

A journalist in fashionable yellow stripes yelled from the front row of the press box, "Ms. Sharifi—are you *trying* to lose this case?"

Slowly I turned my head in his direction.

"Hey, Miranda, look this way!" a Liver-channel reporter, his robocam floating beside him. "Smile pretty!"

"Order, please! Order!" Moderator Yongers, her glasses gone, banging her metal water pitcher since she had no gavel because of course this wasn't really a court.

"Smile, Miranda!"

"—an outrage to professional discourse and—"

"Please sit down," said several seats, "others may have trouble seeing over you. Please sit—"

"I will have order in this Forum!"

But the pandemonium grew. A man broke from the public section and charged down the inclined aisle toward the Forum floor.

I had a clear view of his face. It twisted with the terrible rigidity of hate, a rigidity that no amount of reason can relax and that takes years to calcify. Miranda Sharifi's insults today hadn't created that face. The man ran toward her, pulling something from his jacket. Seventeen robocams and three security 'bots zoomed toward him.

He hit the invisible Y-energy shield in front of the participants' tables, and spread-eagled against it with an audible crack of skull or other bone. Dazed, the man slid down the shield exactly as down a brick wall. A security 'bot dragged him away.

"—restore *order* to these proceedings *now*—"

"A smile, Miranda! Just one smile!"

"—unwarranted assumption of moral superiority, and contempt for United States law, when in reality—"

"—and it looks, newsgrid viewers, as if the fracas were deliberately created by Miranda Sharifi for hidden Huevos Verdes motives about which we can only—"

Miranda Sharifi never moved.

Eventually Moderator Yongers, having no real choice, recessed for lunch.

I pushed my way to the front of the chaotic Forum chamber, trying to shadow Miranda Sharifi, which was of course impossible. The Y-shield stood between us, and spectacularly built bodyguards muscled her and Leisha Camden out a rear door. I caught sight of them again on the roof, having knocked over four people to get there. They climbed into an aircar. Several other cars followed in close pursuit, but I was convinced it wasn't going to do any of them—reporters, GSEA, FBI, rogue geneticists, whoever—any good. They weren't going to learn any more than I had.

What had I learned?

The journalist in yellow stripes was right. Miranda Sharifi's performance had just ensured that Case 1892-A was dead. She had insulted not only the intellectual and technical competence of eight scientists, but their characters as well. I had cursorily researched three of those scientists, the Nobel laureates, and I knew they were not venial sellouts but people of integrity. Miranda must know that, too. So—why?

Maybe, despite any research she'd done, she genuinely believed all Sleepers were corrupt. Her grandmother, a brilliant woman, had believed it. But somehow I didn't think Miranda did.

Maybe she believed the five non-laureate scientists, mediocrities with good political connections, would inevitably outvote the impartial laureates. But if so, why alienate her three potential allies? And why agree to seating the five mediocrities in the first place? All panelists had been agreed upon by both sides.

No. Miranda Sharifi *wanted* to lose this case. She wanted a decision against the Cell Cleaner.

But maybe I was being too anthropomorphic. Miranda Sharifi was, after all, completely different from me. Her mental processes were different, which included her motives. Maybe she'd alienated the panel to . . . what? To make it harder to obtain official approval for the patent. Maybe she only valued victory if it was hard won. Maybe making everything as difficult as possible was part of some Sleepless Code of Honor, built upon the fact that things came so easily to them. How the fuck would I know?

All this ratiocination translated itself into self-disgust. Despite the heat, it was a gorgeous day in Washington, one of those clear-blue-sky-and-golden-light afternoons that seem to have blown in from some more favored city. I walked along the mall, attracting attention: the crazy donkey dressed like a gone-native Liver. Drug dealers and lovers and gravboarding teenagers left me alone, which was just as well. I was having one of those brief, sharp self-questionings that leave you both enervated and embarrassed afterwards. What was I *doing* skulking around in these silly plastic clothes, trying to manufacture some difficult personal meaningfulness out of following around people who were clearly my superiors?

For the Sleepless were my superiors, and in more than intelligence. In discipline, in sheer sweep of vision. In the enviable certainty that accompanies purpose, even if I didn't know what that purpose was, whereas all I had was an aimless, drifting alarm about where my country was headed. An alarm set off by a semi-sentient pink dog hurling over a terrace railing. When I thought of that now, it sounded silly.

I couldn't even define where I thought my country ought to head. I could only impede, not propel, and I wasn't even sure what I was impeding. It was sure as hell more than Case 1892-A.

I didn't know what the Sleepless were trying to do. Nobody knew. So what made me so damn sure I should be stopping them from doing it?

On the other hand, nothing I had done so far, or seemed likely to do in the near future, had had the slightest effect on Miranda Sharifi's plans. I had not reported on her to the GSEA, not kept her under constant surveillance, not even reached a coherent conclusion about her in the private and unsought-after recesses of my mind. I was completely irrelevant. So there was nothing for me to regret, nothing to agonize over doing or not doing, nothing to change. Zero, whatever you multiply or divide it by, is still zero. Somehow this failed to cheer me up.

The next four days were a letdown. People primed for scientific theater—I include myself—instead received hours of incomprehensible graphs, tables, equations, explanations, and holomodels of cells and enzymes and such. Much time was given to the tertiary and quaternary structure of proteins. There was a spirited and incomprehensible debate on Worthington's transference equations as applied to redundant RNA coding. I fell asleep during this. I was not alone. Fewer people showed up each day. Of those who did, only the scientists looked rapt.

It didn't seem fair, somehow. Miranda Sharifi had told us we were looking at the greatest medical breakthrough in two hundred years, and to most of us it looked like alchemy. THE PEOPLE MUST CONTROL SCIENCE AND TECHNOLOGY. Yes, right. How do churls make decisions about wizardry we can't understand?

In the end, they rejected it.

Two of the Nobel laureates wrote dissenting opinions, Barbara Poluikis and Martin Exford. They favored allowing beta testing on human volunteers, and didn't rule out possible future licensing. They wanted the scientific knowledge. You could see, even through the formal wording of their brief, joint opinion, that they panted for it. I saw Miranda Sharifi watching them carefully.

The majority opinon did everything but print copies of itself on the American flag. Safety of United States citizens, sacred trust, preservation of the identity of the human genome, blah blah blah. Everything, in fact, that had led me to join the GSEA the day Katous hurled himself off my balcony.

At some deep level, I still believed the majority opinion was right. Unregulated biotech held the potential for incredible disaster. And nobody could really regulate Huevos Verdes biotech because nobody could really understand it. SuperSleepless intelligence and American patent protection combined to ensure that. And if you can't regulate it, better to keep it out of the country entirely.

Nonetheless, I left the courtroom profoundly depressed. And immediately learned that my ignorance about cellular biology was not my only, or worst, ignorance. I'd thought I was a cynic. But cynicism is like money: somebody else always has more of it than you do.

I sat on the steps of the Science Court, my back to a Doric column the thickness of a small redwood. A light wind blew. Two men paused in the shelter of the column to light sunshine pipes; I'd noticed that Easterners like it smoked. In California, we preferred to drink it. The men were genemod handsome, dressed in the severe sleeveless black suits fashionable on the Hill. Both ignored me. Livers noticed instantly that I wasn't one of them, but donkeys seldom looked past the jacks and soda-can jewelry. Sufficient grounds for dismissal.

"So how long do you think?" one man said.

"Three months to market, maybe. My guess is either Germany or Brazil."

"What if Huevos Verdes doesn't do it?"

"John, why *wouldn't* they? There's a fortune to be made, and that Sharifi woman is no fool. I'm going to be watching the investment trends very carefully."

"You know, I don't even really care about the investment factor?" John's voice was wistful. "I just want it for Jana and me and the girls. Jana's had these growths on and off for years . . . what we've got now only restrains them so far."

The other man put a hand on John's arm. "Watch Brazil. That's my best guess. It'll be quick, quicker than if we'd licensed it here. And without all the complications of every blighted Liver town clamoring for it for their medunit, at some undoable cost."

Pipes lighted, they left.

I sat there, marveling at my own stupidity. Of course. Turn down the Cell Cleaner for American development, make huge political capital from your "protection" of Livers, save a staggering amount of credits from not offering it to your political constituency, and then buy the medical breakthrough for yourself and your loved ones overseas. Of course.

The people must control science and technology.

Maybe Dr. Lee Chang was right. Maybe the Cell Cleaner would run amok and kill them all. All but the Livers. Who would then rise up to establish a just and humane state.

Yes. Right. Desdemona's mommy and the other Livers I'd seen

on the train controlling biotech that could eventually alter the human race into something else. The blind splicing genes, blindly. Right.

Inertia, first cousin to depression, seized me. I sat there, getting colder, until the sky darkened and my ass hurt from the hard marble. The portico was long since deserted. Slowly, stiffly, I got my body to its feet—and had my first piece of luck in weeks.

Miranda Sharifi walked down the wide steps, keeping to the shadows. The face wasn't hers, and the brown jacks weren't hers, and I had seen her and Leisha Camden climb into an aircar, which took off two hours ago, pursued by half of Washington. This Liver had pale skin and a large nose and short dirty-blonde hair. So why was I so sure this was Miranda? The big head, and the tip of red ribbon that I, zoom-lensed, saw peeking from her back hip pocket. Or maybe it was just that I needed it to be her, and the "Miranda" who took off with Leisha Camden to be a decoy.

I groped in my pocket for the mid-range infrared sensor Colin Kowalski had given me and surreptitiously aimed it at her. It went off the scale. Miranda or no, this person had the revved metabolism of a SuperSleepless. And no GSEA agents in sight.

Not, of course, that I would see them.

But I refused to give in to negativity. Miranda was mine. I followed her to the gravrail station, pleased at how easily all my old training returned. We boarded a local train traveling north. We settled into a crowded, malodorous car with so many children it seemed the Livers must be breeding right there on the uncleaned floor.

We stopped every twenty minutes or so at some benighted Liver town. I didn't dare sleep; Miranda might get off someplace without me. What if the trip lasted days? By morning I had trained myself to nap between stops, my unconscious set like an edgy guard dog to nip me awake each time the train slowed and lurched. This produced very strange dreams. Once it was David I was following; he kept shedding his clothes as he danced away from me, an unreachable succubus. Once I dreamed I'd lost Miranda and the Science Court had me on trial for uselessness against the state. The worst was the dream in which I was injected with the Cell Cleaner and realized it was in fact chemically identical with the industrial-strength cleaner used by the household 'bot in my

San Francisco enclave, and every cell in my body was painfully dissolving in bleach and ammonia. I woke gasping for air, my face distorted in the black glass of the window.

After that I stayed awake. I watched Miranda Sharifi as the grav train, miraculously not malfunctioning, slid through the mountains of Pennsylvania and into New York State.

Seven

There was a latticework in my head. I couldn't make it go
away.

Its shape floated there all the time now, looking a little like
the lattices that roses grow on. It was the dark purple color that
objects take on in late twilight when it's hard to see what color
anything really is. Miri once told me that nothing "really" is any
color—it was all a matter of "circumstantial reflected wave-
lengths." I didn't understand what she meant. To me, colors are
too important to be circumstantial.

The lattice bent around and met itself to form a circle. I
couldn't see what was inside the circle, even though the lattice
had diamond-shaped holes. Whatever was inside remained completely hidden.

I didn't know what this graphic was. It suggested nothing to
me. I couldn't will it to suggest anything, or to change form, or
to go away. This hadn't ever happened to me before. I was the
Lucid Dreamer. The shapes that came from my deep unconscious
were always meaningful, always universal, always malleable. I
shaped them. I brought them outward, to the conscious world.
They didn't shape me. I was the Lucid Dreamer.

I watched Miri's final day in Science Court on hologrid in a hotel
room in Seattle, where I was scheduled to give the revised "The
Warrior" concert tomorrow afternoon. The robocams zoomed in
close on Leisha and Sara as they climbed into their aircar on the
Forum roof. Sara looked exactly like Miri. The holomask over her

face, the wig, the red ribbon. She even walked like Miri. Leisha's eyes had the pinched look that meant she was furious. Had she already discovered the switch? Or maybe that would come in the car. Leisha wouldn't take it well. Nothing frustrated her more than being lied to, maybe because she was so truthful herself. I was glad I wasn't there.

Spiky red shapes, taut with anxiety, sped around the purple latticework that never went away.

Sara/Miri closed the car door. The windows, of course, were opaqued. I turned off the newsgrid. It might be months before I saw Miri again. She could slip in and out of East Oleanta—she had, in fact, come to Washington from there—but Drew Arlen, the Lucid Dreamer in his state-of-the-art powerchair, followed everywhere by the GSEA, could not. And even if I went to Huevos Verdes, Nikos Demetrios or Toshio Ohmura or Terry Mwakambe might decide a shielded link with East Oleanta was too great a risk for just personal communication. I might not even talk with Miri for months.

The spiky red shapes eased a little.

I poured myself another scotch. That slowed down the anxiety-shapes sometimes. But I tried to be careful with the stuff. I did try. I could remember my old man, in the stinking Delta town where I grew up:

Don't you lip me, boy! You ain't nothing, you, but a shit-bottomed baby!

I ain't no baby, me! I'm seven years old!

You're a shit-bottomed teatsucker, you, who ain't never gonna own nothing, so shut up and hand me that beer.

I'm gonna own Sanctuary, me, someday.

You! A stupid bayou rat! Laughter. Then, after thinking it over, the smack. *Whap.* Then more laughter.

I downed the scotch in a single gulp. Leisha would have hated that. The comlink shrilled in two short bursts. Twice meant the caller wasn't on the approved list but Kevin Baker's comlink program had nonetheless decided it was somebody I might want to see. I didn't know how it decided that. "Fuzzy logic," Kevin said, which made no shapes in my mind.

I think I would have talked to anybody just then. But I left off the visual.

"Mr. Arlen? Are you there? This is Dr. Elias Maleck. I know

it's very late, but I'd like a few minutes of your time, please. It's extremely urgent. I'd rather not leave a message."

He looked tired; it was three in the morning in Washington. I poured myself another scotch. "Visual on. I'm here, Dr. Maleck."

"Thank you. I want to say right away this is a shielded call, and it's not being recorded. Nobody can hear it but us two."

I doubted that. Maleck didn't understand what Terry Mwakambe or Toshio Ohmura could do. Even if Maleck's Nobel had been in physics and not medicine, he wouldn't have understood. Maleck was a big man, maybe sixty-five, not genemod for appearance. Thinning gray hair and tired brown eyes. His skin fell in jowls on either side of his face but his shoulders were square. I felt him as a series of solid navy cubes, unbreakable and clean. The cubes hovered in front of the unmoving lattice.

"I'm not sure exactly where to begin, Mr. Arlen." He ran his hand through his hair and the navy cubes took on a reddish tinge. Maleck was very tense. I sipped my drink.

"As you undoubtedly know by now, I voted against allowing further development of the Huevos Verdes patent claim in the Federal Forum for Science and Technology. The reasons for my vote are stated clearly in the majority opinion. But there are things that a public document can't contain, things I want permission to inform *you* about."

"Why?"

Maleck was blunt. "Because I—we—have no way to talk to Huevos Verdes. They accept messages but not two-way communication. You represent the only path by which I can convey information directly to Ms. Sharifi about genetic research."

The shapes in my mind rippled and twisted.

I said, "How did you leave any messages for Huevos Verdes? How'd you get the access code to leave any messages?"

"That's part of what I want to tell you, Mr. Arlen. In five minutes two men will request access to your suite. They want to show you something approximately half an hour from Seattle by plane. The purpose of my call is to urge you to go with them." He hesitated. "They're from the government. GSEA."

"No."

"I understand, Mr. Arlen. That's the purpose of my call—to tell you this isn't a trap, or a kidnapping, or any of the other atrocities you and I both know the government is capable of. The

GSEA agents will take you outside the city, keep you about an hour, and return you safely, without implants or truth drugs or anything else. I know these men personally—*personally*—and I'm willing to stake my entire professional reputation on this. I'm sure you're recording my call on your end. Send copies to anyone you like before you so much as open your hotel door. You have my word you will return safe and unaltered. Please consider what that's worth to me."

I considered. The man filled me with shapes I hadn't felt in a long time: light, clean shapes, without any hidden agenda. Nothing like the shapes at Huevos Verdes.

Of course, Maleck might be completely sincere and still be used.

Somehow the glass of scotch, my fourth, was empty.

Maleck said, "If you want to take extra time to call Huevos Verdes for instructions—"

"*No.*" I lowered my voice. "No. I'll go."

Maleck's face changed, opened, growing years younger and hours less tired. (A light cleansing rain falling on the navy cubes.)

"*Thank you,*" he said. "You won't regret it. You have my word, Mr. Arlen."

I would bet anything that he, an eminent donkey, had never seen any of my concerts.

I cut off the link, sent off copies of the call to Leisha, to Kevin Baker, to a donkey friend I trusted in Wichita. The link shrilled. Once. Even before I answered it Nikos Demetrios appeared on visual. He wasted no words, him.

"Don't go with them, Drew."

There was another glass of scotch in my hand. It was half empty. "That was a shielded call, Nick. Private."

He ignored this. "It could be a trap, despite what Maleck says. They could be using him. You should know that!"

Impatience had crept into his voice, despite himself: the stupid Sleeper had overlooked the obvious once again. I saw him as a dark shape with a thousand shades of gray, undulating in subtle patterns I would never understand.

"Nick, suppose—just suppose—that I wanted, me, to talk to somebody private, somebody who I don't want you listening to, somebody who isn't, them, no part of Huevos Verdes? Somebody *else?*"

Nick stared. I heard then, me, how I was talking. Liver talk. My glass was empty again. The hotel system said politely, "Excuse me, sir. There are two men requesting access to your suite. Would you like visuals?"

"Nah," I said. "Send the men in, them."

"*Drew*—" Nick began. I blanked him. It didn't work. Some sort of SuperSleepless override. Wasn't there anything they couldn't do, them?

"Drew! Listen, you can't just—" I disconnected the terminal from the Y-energy power unit.

The GSEA agents didn't look like GSEA agents. I guess they never do, them. Mid-forties. Donkey handsome. Donkey polite. Probably donkey smart. But if they thought, them, in donkey words, at least the words would come one at a time, not in bunches and clusters and libraries of strings.

Snow fell on the purple lattice, cool and blank.

"You guys like a drink, you?"

"Yes," one said, a little too fast. Going along with me. But he felt, him, almost as solid, almost as clean, as Maleck. That confused me. They were GSEA, them. How could they feel unhidden?

"Changed my mind," I said. "Let's go now, us, wherever you're taking me." I powered my chair toward the door. It hit the jamb, it, and hurt my legs.

But on the hotel roof, the cold sobered me. Some, anyway. Cars landed, bringing home early party-goers; it was just a little after midnight. Seattle was built on hills and the hotel was on top of a big one. I could see way beyond the enclave: the dark waters of Puget Sound to the west, Mount Rainier white in the moonlight. Cold stars above, cold lights below. Liver neighborhoods at the bases of the hills, except along the Sound, which was waterfront land too good for Livers.

The GSEA aircar, armored and shielded, took off to the east. Pretty soon there were no more lights. Nobody spoke. I might have slept, me. I hope not.

Don't bother your Daddy, Drew. He's asleep.

He's drunk, him.

Drew!

Drew! Nick said on the comlink. Huevos Verdes said. Miranda Sharifi said. Drew, do this. Give this concert. Spread this subconscious idea. Drew—

The lattice curled in my mind, floating like swamp gas in the bayou where my Daddy finally drowned, him, dead drunk. Some kids found him, long after. They thought the thing in the water was a rotten log.

"We're here, Mr. Arlen. Please wake up."

We had landed on a pad somewhere in wild, dark country, dense and wooded, with huge outcroppings of rock that I slowly realized were parts of mountains. My head pounded. One of the agents turned on a portable Y-lamp and cut the car's lights. We got out. I realized for the first time I didn't know their names.

"Where are we?"

"Cascade Range."

"But where *are* we?"

"Just another few minutes, Mr. Arlen."

They looked away while I pulled myself into my chair. It floated on its gravunit six inches above a narrow dirt track that led from the landing pad into thick woods. I followed the agents, who carried the lamp. The blackness on either side of the track, under the trees, was like a solid wall, except for rustlings and distant, deep hoots. I smelled pine needles and leaf mold.

The track ended at a low foamcast building hidden by trees, a building too small to be important. No windows. An agent had his retina scanned and spoke a code to the door and it opened. The inside lit up. An elevator filled the interior, and that too had retinal scanner and a code. We went underground.

The elevator opened on a large laboratory crowded with equipment, none of it running. The lights were low. A woman in a white lab coat hurried through one of many side doors. "Is that him?"

"Yes," an agent said, and I caught his quick involuntary glance to see if the Lucid Dreamer minded not being recognized. I smiled.

"Welcome, Mr. Arlen," the woman said gravely. "I'm Dr. Carmela Clemente-Rice. Thank you for coming."

She was the most beautiful woman I had ever seen, even lovelier than Leisha. Hair so black it looked blue, enormous eyes of a clear navy, flawless skin. She looked about thirty but, of course, might have been much older. Donkey genemods. She was wreathed with the wispy shapes of sorrow.

She held her hands lightly clasped in front of her. "You're wondering why we brought you here. This isn't a GSEA installation, Mr. Arlen. It's an outlaw gene facility we discovered and captured. Setting up the law-enforcement operation took an entire year. The trial of the scientists and technicians working here took another year. They're all in prison now. Ordinarily the GSEA would dismantle an outlaw lab completely, but there are reasons we couldn't dismantle this one. As you'll see in a minute."

She unclasped her hands and made a curious gesture, as if she were pulling me toward her. Or pulling my mind toward her. The navy-blue donkey eyes never left my face.

"The . . . beasts working here were creating illegal genemods for the underground market. One of the underground markets. These facilities exist across the United States, Mr. Arlen, although fortunately most of them aren't as successful as this one. The GSEA expends a lot of money, time, manpower, and legal talent putting them out of business. Follow me, please."

Carmela Clemente-Rice led the way back through the same side door. We followed. A long white corridor—how big was this underground place?—was lined with doors. She led me through the first one and stepped aside.

There were two of them, male and female, both naked. They had the dreamy, unfocused expressions of heavy users, but somehow I knew they didn't exist on drugs. They just existed. Both of them were masturbating with a dreamy nonurgency that matched their expressions. The woman had one hand in the vagina between her legs, the other in the one between her breasts. But her other vaginas, between her eyes and on each palm, had also gone labile, their tissues swollen and flushed. The man fondled both his gigantic erect penis and his vagina, and I saw that he had pushed what looked like a food utensil of some kind up one asshole.

"For the sex trade," Carmela Clemente-Rice said quietly behind me. "Underground genetic embryonic engineering. There's no way we can undo it, no way we can raise their IQs, which are about 60. All we can do is keep them comfortable, and out of the market they were designed for."

I powered my chair out of the room. "You're not showing me anything I don't already know about, lady," I said, more harshly than I intended. The sex slaves made bruised, painful shapes in my mind. "This stuff has been around for years, long before Huevos Verdes existed. Huevos Verdes doesn't quarrel with the GSEA outlawing it and shutting it down. Nobody sane argues in favor of this kind of genetic engineering."

She didn't answer, just led me down the corridor to another door.

Four of them this time, in a much larger room, with the same dreamy expressions. These weren't naked, although their clothes were odd: jacks clumsily hand-sewn to fit around the extra limbs and the deformities. One had eight arms, one four legs, another three pairs of breasts. Judging from its body shape, the extra organs on the fourth must have been internal. Pancreases, or livers, or hearts? Could the genes be programmed to grow extra hearts?

"For the transplant market," Carmela said. "But then, you probably already knew about that, too?"

I had, but didn't say so.

"These are luckier," she continued. "We can remove the extra limbs and return them to normal bodies. In fact, Jessie is scheduled for surgery on Tuesday."

I didn't ask her which one was Jessie. The scotch made nauseous burbles in my stomach.

In the next room the two people looked normal. Dressed in pajamas, they lay asleep on a bed covered with a pretty chintz spread. Carmela didn't lower her voice.

"They're not sleeping, Mr. Arlen. They're drugged, heavily, and will be for most of the rest of their lives. When they're not, they're in intense and constant pain. It's caused by a tiny genomod virus designed to stimulate nerve tissue to an unbearable degree. The virus is injected and then replicates in the body—sort of like the Huevos Verdes Cell Cleaner. The pain is excruciating, but there's no actual tissue damage, so theoretically it could continue for years. Decades. It was designed for the international torture market, and there was supposed to be an antidote to be administered. Or withheld. Unfortunately, the gene engineers working here had gotten only as far as the nanotorturer, not the antidote."

One of the drugged pair—I saw now that it was a girl, barely past puberty—stirred uneasily and moaned.

"Dreaming," Carmela said briefly. "We don't know what. We don't know who she is. Mexican maybe, kidnapped, or sold on the black market."

"If you think that the research at Huevos Verdes is anything like—"

"No, it's not. We know that. But the—"

"Everything researched and created from nanotechnology at Huevos Verdes is done with only the pubic benefit in mind. *Everything*. Like the Cell Cleaner."

"I believe that," Dr. Clemente-Rice said. She kept her voice low and controlled; I could feel the effort that cost her. "The Huevos Verdes applications are completely different. But the basic science, the breakthroughs, are similar. Only Huevos Verdes has gone much further, much faster. But others could close that gap if they had, for instance, the Cell Cleaner to dismantle and study."

I stared at the sleeping girl. Her eyelids were puckered. My mother's eyelids had done that, at the end of her life, when the bone cancer finally got her.

I said, "I've seen enough."

"One more, Mr. Arlen. Please. I wouldn't ask if it weren't so urgent."

I turned my chair to study her. She was a series of sharp pale ovals in my mind, with the same clean truthfulness as Maleck and the GSEA agents. Probably they had all been picked for just that quality. Then I suddenly realized who Carmela reminded me of: Leisha Camden. A weird pain shot through me, like a very thin lance.

I followed her through the last door in the corridor.

There were no genomod people in this room. Three heavy-duty shields shimmered from floor to ceiling, the kind that can keep out anything not nuclear. Behind them grew tall grass.

Carmela said softly, "You said that Huevos Verdes works only on genemods and nanotechs that are designed for the public benefit. So was this. It was commissioned by a Third World nation with terrible recurrent famines. The grass blades are edible. Unlike most plants, their cell walls are constructed not of cellulose but of an engineered substance that the human system can convert to monosaccharides. The grass is also amazingly hardy, fast-growing, self-seeding, and efficient in using nutrients from poor soils and water from arid ones. The engineers who developed it estimated that it could furnish six times the food of the most concentrated current farming."

"Furnish food," I repeated, idiotically. "Food . . ."

"We planted it in a controlled and shielded ecosphere of fifty ecologically diverse acres," Carmela continued, her hands jammed into the pockets of her lab coat, "and within three months it had wiped out every other plant in the ecosphere. It's so well fitted to thrive that it outcompeted everything else. Humans and some mammals can digest it; other animals cannot. The other plant eaters all starved, including so many larval insects that the insect population disappeared. The amphibian, reptile, and bird populations went with them, then the carnivorous mammals. Our computers figure that, given the right wind conditions, this grass would take about eighteen months to be the only thing left on Earth, give or take a few huge trees with extensive root systems that weren't quite done dying."

The grass rustled softly behind its triple shield. I felt something on my shoulders. Carmela's hands. She turned my chair to face her, then immediately lifted her hands.

"You see, Mr. Arlen, we don't think Huevos Verdes is evil. Not at all. We know Ms. Sharifi and her fellow SuperSleepless believe not only in the good of their research but in the good of the rest of us. We know she believes in the United States, as defined in the Constitution, as the best possible political arrangement in an imperfect world. Just as Leisha Camden did before her. I've always been a great admirer of Ms. Camden. But the Constitution works because it has so many checks and balances to restrain power."

She licked her lips. The gesture wasn't sexual; she was in such deadly earnest that I could feel her whole body dry and tense with strain.

"Checks and balances to restrain power. Yes. But there *are* no checks on Huevos Verdes. No restraints. No balances, because the rest of us simply can't do what SuperSleepless can do. Unless they do it first. Then some of us could copy some of the tech, maybe, and adapt it. Some of us like the people who worked *here*."

I said nothing. The deadly, food-rich grass rustled.

"I can't tell what you're thinking, Mr. Arlen. And I can't tell you what to think. But I—we—just wanted you to see all sides of the situation, with the hope you'll think about what you've seen, and talk about it with Huevos Verdes. That's all. The agents will take you back to Seattle now."

I said, "What will happen to this grass?"

"We'll destroy it with radiation. Tomorrow. Not so much as a strand of DNA will be left, and none of the records, either. It only existed this long so we could show it to Ms. Sharifi, or, failing that, to you."

She led me back to the elevator, and I watched her body, taut with unhappiness and hope, walk gracefully between the narrow white walls.

Just before the elevator door opened I said to her, or maybe to all three of them, "You can't stop technological progress. You can slow it down, but it always comes anyway."

Carmela Clemente-Rice said, "Only two nuclear bombs have ever been dropped on Earth as an act of wartime aggression. The science was there, but the applications were left unused. By co-operation or restraint or fear or force—the applications were stopped." She held out her hand. It was damp and clammy, but something electric ran from her touch to mine. The navy-blue eyes beseeched me.

Just as if *I* held actual power over what Huevos Verdes did.

"Good-bye, Mr. Arlen."

"Good-bye, Dr. Clemente-Rice."

The agents, good as their word, returned me to my hotel room in Seattle. I sat down to wait to see who would arrive from Huevos Verdes, and how long it would take.

It was Jonathan Markowitz, at five in the morning. I'd had three hours' sleep. Jonathan was perfect. His tone was civil and interested. He asked about everything I'd seen, and I described everything to him. He asked a lot of other questions: Did I experience any temperature changes, no matter how slight, at any point in the corridor? Did I ever smell anything like cinnamon? Did the light have a greenish tinge? Did anyone ever touch me? He didn't argue against anything Carmela Rice-Clemente had told me. He treated me like a member of the team whose loyalty was unquestioned, but who might have been tampered with in ways I couldn't understand. He was perfect.

And all the while I could feel the shapes he made in my mind, and the picture: a man lifting heavy rocks, the rocks mindless and sullen gray.

As Jonathan left, I said brutally, "They should have sent Nick. Not you. Nick doesn't bother to hide it."

Jonathan looked at me steadily. For a minute he said nothing, and I wondered what impossibly complex and subtle strings formed in that Super brain. Then he smiled wearily. "I know. But Nick was busy."

"When can I see Miranda? Has she left Washington yet for East Oleanta?"

"I don't know, Drew," he said, and the shapes in my mind exploded, spattering the lattice with red.

"You don't know if she's left, or you don't know when I can see her? Why not, Jon? Because I'm tainted now? Because you don't know what Carmela Rice-Clemente might have done to me when she put her palms on my shoulders, or when I shook her hand? Or because you can't control what I'm really thinking about the project?"

Jonathan said quietly, "It was my impression you'd accepted not seeing Miri. Without too much regret."

That stopped me.

Jonathan went on, "You have an important role, Drew. We need you. We don't . . . The computer projects a steeply rising curve in the general social breakdown, due to the unexpected duragem situation. We have to accelerate the project. Kevorkel's equations. Mitochondrial regression. DiLazial urban engineering."

And that was how my anger ended. In a bunch of words from SuperSleepless shorthand. I didn't understand the words, and didn't understand how they went together, and didn't understand why I was being told them. I couldn't answer, and so I stood there, mute and bleary-eyed from lack of sleep, while Jonathan quietly left.

Did he say words from his string because he thought they were so basic that even the Liver Sleeper Drew, him, would understand? Or did they just slip out because Jonathan was upset, too? Or did he say them because he *knew* I wouldn't understand, and what better way to put me in my place?

I'm going to own Sanctuary, me, someday.

You! A stupid bayou rat! Whap.

I had to sleep. My concert was in less than five hours. I rolled into bed, still in my clothes, and tried to sleep.

* * *

On the way to the Seattle KingDome, the aircar broke down.

We had left the enclave and were above the Liver city, which from the air looked like a lot of small Liver towns, organized in blocks around cafés and warehouses and lodge buildings. The Senator Gilbert Tory Bridewell KingDome was twenty years old; somebody had told me it was named for some historical site. It sat well outside the enclave, of course, a huge foamcast hemisphere with a shielded landing pad that now we might not reach.

The car bucked, back to front, and listed to the left. An ocean liner rolling, a toxic dump swelling in sickly pink bubbles. My stomach rose.

"Jesus H. Christ," the driver said, and began punching in override codes. I didn't know how much he could actually do; aircars are robomachinery. But maybe he did know about it. He was a donkey.

The car rolled, and I fell against the left door. My powerchair, folded into traveling size, slammed against me. The car gave a little buck and I thought *I'm going to die.*

Warm blood-red shapes filled my mind. And the lattice disappeared.

"Christ Christ Christ," the driver said, punching frantically. The car bucked again, then righted. I closed my eyes. The lattice in my mind disappeared. *It wasn't there.*

"Okay okay okay," the driver said in a different voice, and the car limped down onto the landing pad.

We sat there, safe, while figures rushed toward us from the KingDome. And the lattice reappeared in my mind. It had disappeared when I thought I was going to die, and now it was back, still closed tightly around whatever was hidden inside.

"It's the lousy gravunits," the driver said, in the same pleading voice he'd said *okay okay okay.* He twisted in his seat to look directly into my eyes. "They cut costs on materials. They cut costs on robotesting. They cut costs on maintenance because those lousy robounits break. The whole franchise's going under. Two crashes in California last week, and the newsgrids paid to keep them quiet. I'm never riding in one of these things again. You hear me? Never again." All said in the same low, pleading voice.

In my mind he was a crouching, black, squashed shape in front of the purple lattice.

"Mr. Arlen!" a woman cried, throwing open the aircar door. "Are y'all okay in there?" Her Southern accent was thick. Sallie Edith Gardiner, freshman congresswoman from Washington State, who was paying for this concert for her Liver constituents. Why did a congresswoman from Washington State sound like Mississippi?

"Fine," I said. "No damage."

"Well, it's just shockin', is what it is. Has it really come to that? That we can't even make a decent aircar any more? Do you want to postpone the concert a bit?"

"No, no, I'm fine," I said. The accent wasn't Mississippi after all; it was fake Mississippi. She was all flaking gilded hoops in my mind. I thought suddenly of Carmela Clemente-Rice, clean pale ovals.

Why had the lattice in my mind disappeared when I thought I was going to die?

"Well, the truth is, Mr. Arlen," Congresswoman Gardiner said, chewing on her perfect bottom lip, "a tiny delay for you might be a good idea anyway. There's a little problem with the gravrail comin' in from South Seattle. And just a tiny problem with the security 'bot system. We have techs workin' on it now, naturally. So if you come this way we'll go to a place you can wait . . ."

"My system was installed onstage yesterday," I said, "if you can't guarantee security for it—"

"Oh, of *course* we can!" she cried, and I saw she was lying. The aircar driver climbed out and leaned against the car, muttering under his breath. His prayerful pleading had finally turned to anger. I caught *falling apart* and *fucking societal breakdown* and *can't support so many fucking people* before Congresswoman Gardiner threw him a look that would rot plastisynth. She hadn't asked if he was hurt. He was a tech.

"Your wonderful equipment will be just *fine*," Congresswoman Gardiner said. *Fahn.* "And we're all lookin' forward so much to your performance. You come this way, please."

I powered my chair after her. She wouldn't watch the performance. She'd leave after she introduced me and the grid cameras had their fill of her. Donkeys always left then.

But it didn't happen that way.

I sat in my chair in an anteroom of the KingDome for two hours. I might have slept. People came and went, all telling me everything was fine. The lattice in my mind snaked in long slow undulations. Finally the congresswoman came in.

"Mr. Arlen, "I'm afraid we have an unpleasant complication. There's been a just *terrible* accident."

"An accident?"

"A gravrail crashed comin' from Portland. There are . . . a number of Livers dead. The crowd heard about it, and they're upset. Naturally." *Natchally.* Her voice sounded upset, but her eyes were resentful. The first big event she'd sponsored since her election, and a lot of inconsiderate Livers had to go die and ruin it. *An unpleasant complication.* I would have bet a quarter million credits against her reelection.

"We're goin' to go ahead with the concert anyway, unless you object. I'm goin' to introduce you in about five minutes."

"Try drawing out your vowels slightly less," I said. "It would be at least a little more authentic."

I had underestimated her. Her smile didn't waver. "Then five minutes is all right with you?"

"Whatever you say." The lattice in my head was shaking now, as if in a high wind.

They had built a floating gravplatform at one end of the arena, with a wide catwalk to the upper room where I waited. The gravtrain had crashed; the aircar had faltered. I knew that gravdevices didn't really manipulate gravity, but magnetism; I didn't understand how. What were the odds of three magnetic devices failing me in an evening? Jonathan Markowitz would know, to the twentieth decimal.

"—one of the premier artists of our times—" Congresswoman Gardiner broadcast from the stage. *Tahms.*

Of course, it might not have been the gravunit itself that failed in the train. A gravrail might have hundreds of different moving parts, thousands, for all I knew. What were they all made of?

"—with deep gratitude for the opportunity to bring y'all the Lucid Dreamer, I—"

I. I. I. The donkeys' favorite word. In Huevos Verdes, at least they said *we.* And meant more than just the SuperSleepless.

Pale green grass rippled in front of the purple lattice. Grew over it, through it, around it. Took it over. Took over the world.

I clasped my hands hard in front of me. I had to perform in two minutes. I had to control the images in my mind. I was the Lucid Dreamer.

"—understandably grieved about the tragedy, but grief is one of the emotions the Lucid Dreamer—"

"What the fuck do you know about grief, you?" someone unseen screamed, so loud I jumped. Somebody in the audience had a voice magnifier as powerful as my own sound system. From where I sat I couldn't see the audience, only Congresswoman Gardiner. But I heard a low rumble, almost like the Delta in flood.

"—pleased to introduce—"

"Get off, you bitch!" The same magnified voice.

I powered my chair forward. Halfway across the catwalk the congresswoman passed me, her head high, her lips smiling, her eyes burning with anger. There was no applause.

I powered my chair to the center of the floating platform and put my lenses on zoom. The KingDome was only half full. People stared at me, some sullen, some uncertain, some wide-eyed, but nobody smiling. I hadn't ever faced anything like this. They were balanced on an edge, right between an audience and a mob.

"That a donkey chair you sit in, Arlen, you?" the magnified voice shrieked, and I identified its owner when several people turned to him. A man pushed him, hard; another glared; a third moved protectively in front of the heckler and stared hard-eyed at the platform. Somebody down front called faintly, unmagnified, "The Lucid Dreamer ain't no donkey, him. You shut up!"

I said, so softly that everyone had to quiet to hear, "I'm no donkey, me."

Another rumble went up from the audience, and in my mind I saw water flooding the Delta where I was born, the water not fast but relentless, unstoppable, rising as steeply as any Huevos Verdes curve of social breakdown.

"People are dead, them, in the lousy donkey trains nobody bothers to keep up!" the magnified voice cried. "Dead!"

"I know," I said, still softly, and the lattice stopped shaking as my mind filled with slow, large shapes, moving with stately grace, the color of wet earth. I pressed the button on my chair and the concert machinery began to dim the stage lights.

I was supposed to give "The Warrior," designed and redesigned and redesigned again to encourage independent risk taking, action, self-reliance. Stored in the concert machinery were also the tapes and holos and subliminals for "Heaven," the most popular of my concerts. It led people to a calm place inside their own minds, the place all of us could reach as children, where the world is in perfect balance and we with it, and the warm sunlight not only falls on our skin but goes all the way through to the soul and draws us in to blessed peace. It was a concert of reconciliation, of repose, of acceptance. I could give that. In ten minutes the mob would be a yielding pillow.

I began "The Warrior."

"Once there was a man of great hope and no power. When he was young he wanted everything . . ."

The words quieted them. But the words were the least of it, were unimportant, really. The shapes were what counted, and the way the shapes moved, and the corridors the shapes opened to the hidden places in the mind, different for each person. And I was the only one in the world who could program those shapes, working off my own mind, whose neural pathways to the unconscious had been opened by a freak illegal operation. I was the Lucid Dreamer.

"He wanted strength, him, that would make all other men respect him."

No one at Huevos Verdes could do this: seize the minds and souls of eighty percent of the people. Lead them, if only deeper into themselves. Shape them. No—give them their own shapes.

"Do you understand what it is you do to other people's minds?" Miri had asked me in her slightly-too-slow speech, shortly after we met. I had braced myself—even then—for equations and Lawson conversion formulas and convoluted diagrams. But she had surprised me. "You take people into the otherness."

"The—"

"Otherness. The reality under the reality. You pierce the world of relativities, so that the mind glimpses that a truer absolute lies behind the fragile structures of everyday life. Only glimpses it, of course. That's all even science can really give us: a glimpse. But you take people there who couldn't ever be scientists."

I had stared at her, strangely frightened. This wasn't the Miri I usually saw. She brushed her unruly hair away from her face, and I saw that her dark eyes looked soft and far away. "You really do that, Drew. For us Supers, as well as the Livers. You hold aside the veil for just a glimpse into what else we are."

My fright deepened. She wasn't like this.

"Of course," she added, "unlike science, lucid dreaming isn't under anybody's control. Not even yours. It lacks the cardinal quality of replicability."

Miri saw my face, then, and realized her last words were a mistake. She had ranked what I do second . . . again. But her stubborn truthfulness wouldn't let her back down from what she did in fact actually believe. Lucid dreaming lacked cardinal quality. She looked away.

We had never spoken of the otherness again.

Now the Liver faces turned up to me, open. Old men with deep lines and bent shoulders. Young men with jaws clenched even as their eyes widened like the children they had so recently been. Women with babies in their arms, the tiredness fading from their faces when their lips curved faintly, dreaming. Ugly faces and natural beauties and angry faces and grieving faces and the bewildered faces of people who thought they'd been running their lives and were just now discovering they weren't even on the Board of Directors.

"He wanted sex, him, that would make his bones melt with satisfaction. He wanted love."

Miri was probably already in the underground facility at East Oleanta, and I was too cowardly to admit that I was glad. Well, I'd admit it now. She was safer there than at Huevos Verdes, and I didn't have to see her. Eden. The carefully programmed subliminals on the café HTs throughout New York's Adirondack Mountains called it "Eden." Not that the Livers knew what this new Eden meant. I didn't either, not really. I knew what the project was supposed to *do*—but not what it would ultimately mean. I'd been too cowardly to admit my questions. Or admit that even SuperSleepless confidence might not add up to automatic rightness.

Pale, deadly grass waved in my mind.

"Aaaaaaahhh," a man sighed, somewhere close enough that I could hear him over the low music.

"He wanted excitement, him."

A man in the sixth or seventh row wasn't watching me. He

glanced around at everybody else's rapt face. He was first puzzled, then uneasy. A natural immune to hypnosis—there were always a few. Huevos Verdes had isolated the brain chemical necessary to respond to lucid dreaming, only it wasn't a single brain chemical but a combination of what Sara Cerelli called "necessary prerequisite conditions," some of which depended on enzymes triggered by other conditions . . . I didn't really understand. But I didn't need to. I was the Lucid Dreamer.

The unaffected man shuffled restlessly. Then settled down to listen anyway. Afterwards, I knew, he wouldn't say much to his friends. It was too uncomfortable, being left out.

I knew all about that. My concerts counted on it.

"He wanted every day to be filled with challenges only he could meet."

Miri loved me in a way I could never love her back. It burned, that love, as hard as her intelligence. It was the love, not the intelligence, that had made me never say to her directly, "Should we go ahead with the project? What proof do we have that this is the right thing to do?" She would tell me, of course, that proof was impossible, and her explanation of why not would contain so many things—equations and precedents and conditions—that I wouldn't understand it.

But that wasn't the real reason I'd never pushed my doubts. The real reason was that she loved me in a way I could never love her, and I had wanted Sanctuary since I was six years old and discovered that my grandfather died building it, a grunt worker before Livers were taken care of by a vote-hungry government. That was why I had turned my mind, so much weaker than hers, over to Huevos Verdes.

But now there was the pale grass, growing over the lattices in my mind, growing over the world.

"He wanted—"

He wanted to belong to himself again.

The shapes slid around my chair; the subliminals flickered in and out of my audience's consciousness. Their faces were completely unguarded now, oblivious to each other and even to me, as the private doors of their minds swung briefly open. To the desires and fearlessness and confidence that had been buried there for decades, under the world that needed order and conformity and predictability to function. This was my best concert of "The Warrior" yet. I could feel it.

At the end, almost an hour later, I raised my hands. I felt the usual outpouring of holy affection for all of them. "Like a pope or a lama?" Miri had asked, but it wasn't like that. "Like a brother," I'd answered, and watched her dark eyes deepen with pain. Her own brother had been killed on Sanctuary. I'd known my answer would hurt her. That was a kind of power, too, and now I felt ashamed of it.

But it was also the turth. In a moment, when the concert ended, these Livers would go back to being the same whining, complaining, ineffectual, ignorant people they'd been before. But for this instant before the concert ended, I did feel a brotherhood that had nothing to do with likeness.

And they wouldn't go completely back to what they had been. Not completely. Huevos Verdes's computer programs had verified that.

" . . . back to his kingdom."

The music ended. The shapes stopped. The lights came up. Slowly the faces around me dissolved into themselves, first blinking wide-eyed, then laughing and crying and hugging. The applause started.

I looked for the man with the voice magnifier. He wasn't standing in his same place in the crowd. But I didn't have to wait long to find him.

"Let's go, us, to that gravtrain crash—it's only a half-mile away. There's still folks hurt there, them, more than there are medunits—I saw, me! And not enough blankets! We can help, us, to bring the injured here. . . . Us!"

Us. Us. Us.

There was confusion in the crowd. But a surprising number of Livers followed the new leader, burning to do something. To be heroes, which is the true hidden driver of the human mind. Some people started organizing a hospital corner. Others left, but from behind the now-opaqued shield that let me watch them without being seen, I observed even the departing Livers donating spare jackets and shirts and blankets for the aid of the wounded. Congresswoman Sallie Edith Gardiner bustled over the catwalk toward me.

"Well, Mr. Arlen, that was just marvelous—" *Mahvelous.*

"You didn't watch it."

She wasn't listening. She stared at the activity in the King-Dome. "What's all *this* now?"

I said, "They're getting ready to help the survivors of the gravrail crash."

"Them? Help how?"

I didn't answer. All of a sudden I was very tired. I'd had only a few hours' sleep, and I'd spent the previous night viewing man-made horrors.

Like this woman.

"Well, they can all just stop this nonsense right now!" *Raht now.*

She bustled away. I watched a little longer, then went to find my driver—who had, of course, vowed to never drive an aircar again. But that was before the gravrail crash showed that nothing else was any better. Still, I'd find some way back to Seattle. And to the airport. And to Huevos Verdes. And from there to East Oleanta. There were things I had to ask Miranda, critical things, things I should have asked a long time ago. And I was going to say them. I, Drew Arlen. Who had been the Lucid Dreamer long before I met Miranda Sharifi.

Eight

The floor of the State Representative Anita Clara Taguchi Hotel was covered in leaves. It was late August—no leaves falling yet, them. That meant these leaves were left over from last year, blowing into the hotel last October and November and lying around ever since, without no 'bot to clean them out. I hadn't been nowhere near the hotel, me, all those months. But I was now.

The funny thing was that for a few days I didn't even notice the leaves, me. I didn't notice nothing. My head was a fog, it, and I stumbled toward the hotel HT on its red counter and didn't see nothing else. Lizzie was too sick.

The HT turned on when I come near, like it'd been doing for the past four days. "May I help you?"

I put both hands, me, on the counter. Like that would help. "I need the medunit, me. An emergency."

"I'm sorry, sir, the County Legislator Thomas Scott Drinkwater Medical Unit is temporarily out of service. Albany has been notified, and a technician will shortly—"

"I don't want Albany, me! I want a medunit! My little girl's sick bad!"

"I'm sorry, sir, the County Legislator Thomas Scott Drinkwater Medical Unit is temporarily out of service. Albany has been—"

"Then get me another medunit, you! It's an emergency! Lizzie's coughing her guts up, her!"

"I'm sorry, sir, there's no medunit immediately available, due to the temporary inoperability of the Senator Walker Vance

Morehouse Magnetic Railway. As soon as the railway is repaired, another medical unit can be rushed in from—"

"The gravrail ain't inaccessible, it's busted!" I screamed at the HT. I would of busted it with my bare hands if it'd helped. "Let me talk to a human being!"

"I'm sorry, your elected officials are temporarily unavailable. If you wish to leave a message, please specify whether it's intended for United States Senator Mard Todd Ingalls, United States Senator Walker Vance—"

"Off! Turn the hell off!"

Lizzie'd been sick, her, for three days. The gravrail had been down for five. The medunit had been out for who knows how long—nobody'd got sick, them, since Doug Kane's heart attack. The politicians had been assholes as long as anybody could remember.

Lizzie was sick bad. Oh sweet Jesus Lizzie was sick bad.

I squeezed my eyes shut, me, and my head swung down, and when I opened my eyes what did I see? Leaves, that no cleaning 'bot had swept out in nearly a year, and that nobody else didn't bother with neither. Dead leaves, brittle as my old bones.

"There's a HT with override at the café," a voice said. "The mayor can contact your county legislator directly."

"You think, you, I ain't tried that? Do I look that stupid?" I was relieved, me, to yell at somebody, I didn't care who. Then I saw it was the donkey girl dressed like a Liver, the one who got off the train a week ago. She was the only person, her, staying in the State Representative Anita Clara Taguchi Hotel. Since the gravrail breakdowns got worse, there ain't much traveling. Nobody knew why this donkey was in East Oleanta, and nobody knew why she dressed like a Liver. Some people didn't like it, them.

I didn't have no time to talk to a crazy donkey. Lizzie was sick bad. I shuffled back through the leaves to the door, only where was I supposed to go, me? Without no medunit . . .

"Wait," the donkey said. "I heard you, me. You said—"

"Don't try to talk like no Liver when you ain't one! You hear me, you!" I don't know where I got the anger to yell at her like that. Yes, I do. Lizzie was sick bad, and the donkey was just there, her.

"You're quite right. No point in unnecessary subterfuge, is there? My name is Victoria Turner."

I didn't care, me, what her name was, although I remembered her telling somebody else it was Darla Jones. I'd left Lizzie gasping and clawing for breath, her little face hot as a bonfire. I broke into a run, me. The leaves under my boots whispered like ghosts.

"Maybe I can help," the donkey said.

"Go to hell!" I said, but then I stopped, me, and looked at her. She was a donkey, after all. She must be here, her, for something, just like that other girl in the woods last summer, the one that saved Doug Kane's life, must of been there for something. I couldn't guess for what, but I wasn't no donkey. Still, sometimes donkeys could do things, them, that you didn't expect.

The girl stood. Her yellow jacks had a tear in them, like everybody's since the warehouse just stopped opening up for distrib, but they was clean. Jacks don't get dirty or creased—dirt don't stick to them somehow, or it washes off easy. But the girl wasn't really no girl, her. When I looked closer I saw she was a woman, maybe as old as Annie. It was the genemod violet eyes and that body that made me think, me, that she was a girl.

I said, "How can *you* help?"

"I won't know till I see the patient, will I?" she said, crisp and no nonsense. That made sense, at least. I led her, me, to Annie's apartment on Jay Street.

Annie opened the door. I could hear Lizzie coughing, her, a sound that pretty near tore my own guts out. Annie pushed her big body out into the hall and pulled the door closed behind her.

"Who's this? What are you bringing her here for, Billy Washington? You, get lost! We already seen, us, how much help you donkeys are when everything's going wrong!"

I never saw Annie so mad. Her lips pressed together like they'd been mortared, and her fingers curled into claws like she was going to rake this Victoria Turner across her genemod donkey face. Victoria Turner looked at Annie coolly, her, and didn't step back an inch.

"He brought me because I may be able to help the sick child. Are you her mother? Please step back so I can try."

I stepped back, but then forward again because it hurt me, Annie's face. It was furious and scared and exhausted. Annie hadn't left Lizzie, her, to sleep or wash, not in two days. But Annie was used to letting donkeys solve her problems, and that was on her face, too. Along with just the start of hope. Annie wanted something to hit and something to trust, her, and I thought I was both of those things, but here was this Victoria Turner and she was better, her, for both.

Annie reached behind herself and opened the door.

Lizzie lay on the couch where I usually sleep. She was burning up, her, but Annie tried to keep a blanket on her. Lizzie kept kicking it off. There was water and food from the café, but Lizzie hadn't taken any, her. She tossed and cried out, and sometimes her cries didn't make no sense. She threw up just once, but she coughed all the time, great racking coughs that tore my heart.

Victoria Turner put her hand on Lizzie's forehead, and her violet eyes widened. Lizzie didn't seem to know, her, that anybody was there. She gave another cough, a small one, and started moaning. I felt despair start in my bowels, the kind you feel when there's no hope and you don't see how you can bear it. I hadn't felt that kind of despair, me, since my wife Rosie died, twelve years ago. I never thought I'd have to feel it again.

Victoria Turner took a scarf out of her pocket and knelt by Lizzie. She didn't seem at all afraid, her. One of the thoughts I'd had in the night, God forgive me, was: Is this sickness catching? Could Annie get it, her, and die too? Annie . . .

"Cough for me, sweetheart," Victoria Turner said. "Come on, cough into the scarf."

In a few minutes, Lizzie did, her, though not because she was asked. Big slimy gobs of stuff from her tortured lungs, greenish gray. Victoria Turner caught it, her, in the scarf and looked at it closely. Me, I had to look away. That was Lizzie's lungs coming up, Lizzie's lungs rotting themselves away.

"Excellent," Victoria Turner said, "green. It's bacterial. Now we know. You're in luck, Lizzie."

Luck! I saw Annie curve her claws again, her, and I even saw what for: This donkey was *enjoying* this, her. It was some kind of exciting. Like a holovid story.

"Bacterial is good," Victoria Turner said, looking up at me, "because the medication can be far less specific. You have to tailor antivirals, at least grossly. But wide-spectrum antibiotics are easy."

Annie said roughly, "What's Lizzie got, her?"

"I haven't the faintest idea. But this will almost surely take care of it." From another pocket she drew a flat piece of plastic, tore it open, and slapped a round blue patch on Lizzie's neck.

"But you should force more water down her. You don't want to risk dehydration."

Annie stared, her, at the blue patch on Lizzie's neck. It looked like the ones the medunit put on, but how did we really know, us, what was in it? We didn't really know nothing.

Lizzie sighed and quieted. Nobody said nothing. After a few minutes, Lizzie was asleep.

"Best thing for her," Victoria Turner said crisply. I saw again, me, that she liked this. "Not even Miranda Sharifi herself could equal the benefits of sleep."

I remembered, me, hearing that name, but I couldn't think where.

Annie was a different woman, her. She gazed at Lizzie, sleeping peacefully, and at the patch, and Annie seemed to shrink and calm down, both, like a sail collapsing. She looked at the floor, her. "Thank you, doctor. I didn't realize, me."

Dr. Turner looked surprised, her, then she smiled. Like something was funny. "You're welcome. And maybe in return you can do something for me."

Annie looked wary, her. Donkeys don't ask Livers to do favors, them. Donkeys pay taxes to us; we give votes to them. But we don't tell each other, us, more than we got to, and we don't ask things of each other. That ain't the way it's done.

But, then, donkey doctors don't go wandering around East Oleanta dressed in torn yellow jacks neither. We ain't even seen a doctor in East Oleanta, us, since a new plague broke out four years ago and a doctor came from Albany to vaccinate everybody with some new stuff the medunit didn't have.

"I'm looking for someone," Dr. Turner said. "Someone I was supposed to meet here, but we apparently got our data confused. A woman, a girl really, about this tall, dark hair, a slightly large head."

I thought, me, of the girl in the woods, and quick tried to look like I wasn't thinking of nothing at all. That girl came from Eden, I was sure of it, me—and Eden don't got nothing to do with donkeys. It's about *Livers*. Dr. Turner was watching close, her. Annie shook her head, cool as ice, even though I knew she probably remembered that other girl, the big-headed one she said she saw at the town meeting when Jack Sawicki called the district supervisor about them rabid racoons. Or maybe it was the same big-headed girl—I hadn't thought, me, about that before, me. How many big-headed maybe-donkey girls did we have running around the woods near East Oleanta? Why did we have any?

Annie said, polite but not very, "How'd you miss your friend? Don't she know, her, where you are?"

"I fell asleep," Dr. Turner said, which explained nothing. She said it funny, too. "I fell asleep on the gravrail. But I think she might be around here someplace."

"I never saw nobody like that, me," Annie said firmly.

"How about you, Billy?" Dr. Turner said. She probably knew my name, her, even before Annie said it. She'd been in East Oleanta for a week, her, eating at the café, talking to whoever would talk to her, which wasn't many.

"I never saw nobody like that, me," I said. She stared at me hard. She didn't believe me, her.

"Then let me just ask something else. Does the name 'Eden' mean anything to you?"

A gust of wind could of blown me over.

But Annie said cool as January, "It's in the Bible. Where Adam and Eve lived, them."

"Right," Dr. Turner said. "Before the Fall." She stood up and stretched. Her body under the jacks was too skinny, at least by me. A woman should have some softness on her bones.

"I'll come back to look in on Lizzie tomorrow," Dr. Turner said, and I saw, me, that Annie didn't want her to come back, and then that Annie did. This was a doctor. Lizzie slept peaceful, her. Even from by the door, she looked cooler to me.

When the doctor left, Annie and I looked at each other, us. Then Annie's face broke up. Just went from solid flesh creased with worry to a mess of lines that didn't have nothing to do with one another, and she started to cry, her. Before I even thought about it I put my arms around her. Annie clung back, hard, and at the feel of her soft breasts against my chest, I went a little crazy. I didn't think, me. I just raised her face to mine and kissed her.

And Annie Francy kissed me back.

None of your grateful-daughter crap, neither. She cried and pointed to Lizzie and kissed me with her soft berry lips and pushed her breasts against me. Annie Francy. I kissed her back, my mind not even working, it—the words only came later—and then it was like we just met instead of knowing each other for years, instead of me being sixty-eight and Annie thirty-five, instead of everything breaking down and East Oleanta coming apart like it was. Annie Francy kissed me like I was a young man, me—and I was. I ran my hands, me, over her body, and I led her into the bedroom, leaving Lizzie sleeping peaceful as an angel, and I closed the door. Annie was laughing and weeping, the way I forgot, me, that women can do, and she lay her big beautiful body on the bed with me like I was thirty-five, too.

Annie Francy.

If that donkey doctor in yellow jacks had come back then and asked me again where Eden was—if she'd of done that, I could of told her, me. In this room. On this bed. With Annie Francy. Here.

We slept till morning, us. I woke up before Annie. The light was pale gray, thin. For a long time I just sat, me, on the edge of the bed, looking at Annie. I knew this was a one-time thing. I could feel it, even before she fell alseep, in that little space of time when we held each other afterwards. I could feel it, me, in her arms, and in the set of her neck, and in her breathing. What I needed, me, was the words to tell her that it was all right. That this was more than I expected, me, although less than I dreamed. I wasn't going to tell her that part. You always dream more.

But Annie didn't wake, her, and so instead I went to check on Lizzie. She was sitting up, her, looking woozy. "Billy—I'm hungry, me."

"That's a good sign, Lizzie. What you want to eat, you?"

"Something hot. I'm cold, me. Something hot from the café." Her voice was whiny and she smelled awful but I didn't care, me. I was too glad to her her cold, when just yesterday she'd been burning up, her, with fever. That donkey doctor really was as good as a medunit.

"Don't go waking your mother, you. Just sit there until I get your food. Where's your meal chip, Lizzie?"

"I don't know, me. I'm hungry."

Annie must of taken Lizzie's meal chip, her. I could get enough food on mine. I don't eat all that much anymore, me, and this morning I felt I could live on air.

There wasn't nobody in the café, them, except for Dr. Turner.

She sat eating her breakfast and watching a donkey channel on the hologrid. She looked tired, her.

"Up early, you," I said. I got myself a cup of coffee and a bun, and Lizzie some eggs and juice and milk and another bun. Annie or I could reheat the eggs on the Y-energy unit, us. I sat down, me, next to Dr. Turner, just to be sociable for a minute. Or maybe to think what to say to Annie. Dr. Turner stared at the eggs like they was a three-day-dead woodchuck.

"Can you actually eat those, Billy?"

"The eggs?"

" 'Eggs.' Soysynth stamped out and dyed, like all the rest of it. Haven't you ever tasted a real, natural egg?"

And the weird thing was, the minute she said that, her, I remembered what a real egg tasted like. Fresh from the chicken, cooked by my grandmama two minutes and served with strips of hot toast with real butter. You dipped the toast into the egg and the yellow yolk coated it, and then you ate them together, hot. All those years and at that minute I remembered it, me, and not before. My mouth filled with sweet water.

"Look at that," Dr. Turner said, and I thought she still meant the egg but she didn't, her, she'd turned back to the hologrid. A handsome donkey sat at a big wood desk, talking, like they always do. I didn't understand all the words:

"—if even a possibility of an escaped self-replicating dissembler . . . not verified . . . duragem . . . government should put the facts before us . . . emphasize restricted to certain molecular bonds and these are nonorganic . . . very important distinction . . . duragem . . . GSEA . . . underground facility . . . understaffed in current difficult economic climate . . . duragem . . . ."

I said, "Sounds like the same old stuff to me."

Dr. Turner made a sound, her, in the back of her throat, a sound so strange and so unexpected I stopped eating, me, with my plastisynth fork halfway to my mouth. I must have looked a moron. She made the sound again, and then she laughed, her, and then she covered her face with her hand, and then she laughed again. I ain't never seen no donkey behave like that before, me. Never.

"No, Billy—this isn't the same old stuff. It's definitely not. But it might all too easily get to be the same new stuff, in which case we should all worry."

"About what?" I ate faster, me, to bring Lizzie her food still hot. Lizzie was hungry, her. A good sign.

"What the hell is *this* shit?" a stomp kid asked, the second he stepped through the café door. "Who's playing this donkey crap, them?" He saw Dr. Turner, him—and he looked away. I could of sworn he didn't want no part of her, which was so weird— stomps don't back off shoving nobody, them. I stopped eating, me, for the second time and just stared. The stomp said loudly, "Channel 17," and the hologrid switched to some sports channel, but still the stomp didn't look at Dr. Turner. He got his food, him, off the belt and went to sit at a far table in the corner.

Dr. Turner smiled a little. "I tangled with him two nights ago. He got grabby. He doesn't want it to happen again."

"You *armed,* you?"

"Not like you think. Come on, let's go see how Lizzie is doing this morning."

"She's doing just fine, her," I said, but Dr. Turner was already standing up, and it was clear she was going with me. I couldn't think of no reason she shouldn't, except that I still didn't know, me, what words I was going to say to Annie about what happened last night. A little cold lump was growing in me that maybe Annie would think, her, that I shouldn't come around no more. Because of being embarrassed—her or me or us. If that happened, I wouldn't have no more reason to go on dragging around this old body with its old-fool head.

Lizzie was sitting up on the couch, her, playing with a doll. "Mama went to get water to wash me," she said. "She said I can't go to the baths yet, me. What did you bring me to eat, Billy?"

"Eggs and bun and juice. Now don't you overdo, you."

"Who's this?" The black eyes were bright again, them, but Lizzie's face still looked thin and drawn. I got scared all over again, me.

"I'm Dr. Turner. But you can call me Vicki. I gave you some medicine last night."

Lizzie studied the situation, her. I could see that smart little mind going. "You from Albany, you?"

"No. San Francisco."

"On the Pacific Ocean?"

Dr. Turner looked surprised, her. "Yes. How do you know where it is?"

"Lizzie goes to school a lot," I said, fast in case Annie came in and heard, "but her mother ain't crazy about that."

"I worked, me, through all the high school software. It wasn't hard."

"Probably not," Dr. Turner said dryly. "And so now what? College software? With the location of the Indian Ocean?"

I said, "Her mama don't—"

"There ain't no college software in East Oleanta," Lizzie said, "but I already know, me, where the Indian Ocean is."

"Her mama really don't—"

"Can you get me some college software?" Lizzie said, her, soft but not scared, just like it was an everyday thing to ask donkeys for work they're supposed to do for our benefit. Or something. Lately I wasn't so sure, me, that I knew who was studying and working for who.

"Maybe," Dr. Turner said. Her voice had changed, her, and she looked at Lizzie real hard. "How are you feeling this morning?"

"Better." But I could see Lizzie was tiring, her.

I said, "You eat, and then lie down again. You been very sick, you. If that medicine—" The door opened behind me and Annie came in.

I couldn't see her, me, but I could *feel* her. She was warm and soft and big in my arms. Only that wasn't ever going to happen again. Dr. Turner was watching, her, with that sharp donkey stare. I fixed my face and turned around. "Morning, Annie. Let me help you with them buckets."

Annie looked at me, and then at Lizzie, and then at Dr. Turner. I could see she didn't know, her, who to get stiff with first. She chose Lizzie. "You eat that food and lie down, Lizzie. You been sick.

"I'm better now," Lizzie said, sulky.

"She's better now, her," Annie said to Dr. Turner. "You can leave." It wasn't like Annie to be so rude, her. She was the one believed even donkeys have their place.

"Not just yet," Dr. Turner said. "I'm going to talk to Lizzie first."

"This is my home!" Annie said, between pressed-together lips.

I wanted to say to Dr. Turner, *She ain't mad at you, her, she's confused at me,* but there ain't no way to say that to a donkey doctor dressed in torn yellow jacks standing in a living room that ain't even yours and that you're afraid you're about to get tossed out of yourself for loving in the wrong way. No way to say that.

Lizzie said, "Please let Vicki stay, Mama. Please. I feel better, me, when she's here."

Annie set down the two buckets of water she carried. She looked ready to explode, her. But then Dr. Turner said, "I do need to examine her, Annie. To make sure the medication is the right one. You know that if the medunit were working it would check her every day and sometimes change the dosage. A live doctor isn't any different."

Annie looked ready to cry. But all she said was, "She got to get washed first, her. Billy, bring this water into Lizzie's bedroom."

Annie dragged up Lizzie and half carried her to the bedroom, ignoring Lizzie's squawk: "I can walk, me!" I followed with the water, set it down, and came back out. Dr. Turner had picked up Lizzie's doll. It was plastisynth, from the warehouse, with black curls and green eyes and a genemod face, but Annie had sewn it jacks from a pair she ripped up, and Lizzie had made it soda-can jewelry.

"Annie doesn't want me here."

"Well," I said, "we don't get many donkeys, us."

"No, I imagine not."

We stood in silence. I didn't have nothing to say to her, or her to me. Except one thing. "Dr. Turner—"

"Call me Vicki."

I knew, me, that I wasn't going to do that. "What you watched, you, on that donkey channel, the stuff you said wasn't more of the same old government shit—what was it? What's happening?"

She looked up from the doll, then, more sharp than before. "What do you think it meant?"

"I don't know, me. I don't know those words. It sounded like just more worry over the economy, more excuses why the government can't get things working right, them."

"This time it's not an excuse. Maybe. Do you know what a dissembler is?"

"No."

"A molecule?"

"No."

"An atom?"

"No."

Dr. Turner shook Lizzie's doll. "This is made of atoms. Every-thing is made of atoms. They're very tiny pieces of matter. Atoms clump together into molecules like . . . like snow sticking together into a snowball. Only there's all kinds of atoms, and they stick together in different ways, so you get different kinds of matter. Wood or skin or plastic."

She looked at me hard, her, trying to see if I understood. I nodded.

"What holds molecules together are molecular bonds. Sort of a . . . an electrical glue. Well, dissemblers take those bonds apart. Different kinds of dissemblers take different kinds of molecular bonds apart. Enzymes in your stomach, for instance, break the bonds on food so you can digest it."

I heard Lizzie laugh, her, behind the bedroom door. It was a tired kind of laugh, and the worry about her started up in my gut again. And in another few minutes Annie would come out. I didn't know, me, what to say to Annie. But I knew what Dr. Turner was saying was important—I could see it on her donkey face—and I tried, me, to listen. To understand.

"We can make dissemblers, and have for years. We use them for all kinds of things: disposing of toxic waste, recycling, cleaning. The dissemblers we make are pretty simple, and each one can only break one kind of bond. They're made out of viruses, mostly—that means they're genemod."

"Could a . . . dissembler break bonds, it, that cause rabies?"

"Rabies? No, that's a complex organic condition that—why do you ask, Billy?" Her look was sharp again.

"No reason."

"No reason?"

"No." I stared her down, me.

"Anyway," she said, "the making of dissemblers is very care-fully controlled by the GSEA. The Genetic Standards Enforce-ment Agency. Naturally they have to control anything that can go around dissembling things. But the GSEA is constantly ferreting out and busting illegal genemod operations, run outside the law for profit or even pure research, creating things without proper controls. Including dissemblers. A lot of them are self-replicating, that means they can reproduce themselves like small animals—"

"Animals? Sex?" I could feel, me, the surprise on my face.

She smiled. "No. Like . . . algae on a pond. But GSEA-approved dissemblers have built-in clocking mechanisms for control. After a certain number of replications, they stop reproducing. Illegal ones sometimes don't. Now there are rumors—still just rumors—that an ilegal replicator without a clocking mechanism is loose. It attacks the molecular bonds of an alloy called duragem that's used in many machines. *Many* machines. It—"

I suddenly saw. "It's causing all these breakdowns, it. The gravrail and the foodbelt and the warden 'bot and the medunit. My God, some crazy donkey germ is breaking everything!"

"Not exactly. Nobody knows yet. But maybe."

"You people are doing it to us again!"

She stared at me, her. I said, "You take everything, you, away from us and call it aristo Living, and then you wreck the what's left!"

"*Not* me," she said, hard. "*Not* the government. The government is what kept all of you alive after you became utterly unnecessary to the economy. Rather than just eliminate seventy percent of the population the way they did in Kenya and Chile. Donkey genemod science could do that, too. But we didn't."

The bedroom door opened and Lizzie came out, cleaned up, leaning on Annie. Lizzie laid on the couch and said, "Tell me something, Vicki."

"Tell you what?" Dr. Turner said. She was still mad, her.

"Anything. Anything I don't know, me. Anything new."

Dr. Turner's expression changed again. For a second she almost looked afraid, her. Annie said, "Can I see you a minute, Billy?"

This was it, then. Annie was ready, her, to send me away. I followed her into Lizzie's bedroom. She shut the door.

"Billy, what we did, us, last night . . ." She didn't look at me. I couldn't help her, me, even if I'd of wanted to. My throat was too closed up. And I didn't want to.

"Billy, I'm sorry. I behaved, me, like a fool. It just been too long. I didn't mean to make you . . . I can't . . . Can we just go back, us, to the way we was before? Friends? Partners, sort of, but not . . ." She raised her beautiful chocolate eyes to me.

I felt light, me, filled with light, like I might float off the floor. She wasn't going to send me away. I could stay, me, with her and Lizzie. Just like we were before.

"Sure, Annie. I understand, me. We won't never talk about it again."

She let out a long sigh, her, like she'd been holding it in since last night. Maybe she was. "Thank you, Billy. You're a good friend, you."

We went back out to Lizzie, who was listening hard to Dr. Turner talk donkey talk. Here was more trouble.

". . . isn't like that, Lizzie. The basic principle of the computer is binary, which just means 'two.' Tiny switches, too small to see, with two positions: on and off. They make a code."

"Like base two in math," Lizzie said eagerly, but underneath her eagerness she was tired so deep, her, she could hardly keep her eyes open.

Annie said sharply, "She has to sleep now, her. Is the examination done, Doctor?"

"Yes," Dr. Turner said, standing up. She looked bewildered, her; I didn't see no reason why. "But I'll come back this afternoon."

"Medunit don't see people twice a day," Annie said.

"No," Dr. Turner said, still looking bewildered. She stared at Lizzie, who was already asleep, her. "That's a remarkable child."

"Bye, doctor," Annie said.

Dr. Turner ignored her. She stood quiet, her, but tensed up inside, like she was making some kind of important decision. "Billy—listen to what I'm going to tell you. Stockpile whatever you can from the food line here in this apartment. And if the warehouse reopens, stockpile blankets and jacks and—oh—toilet paper and soap and whatever else occurs to you. And buckets for water—lots of buckets. Do it." She said it like nobody else but her could of thought of all that. Like *I* couldn't of thought of it.

Annie said, "Folks start stockpiling, them, there ain't going to be enough for everybody else."

Dr. Turner stared at Annie bleakly. "I know, Annie."

"Ain't right."

The doctor said softly, "A lot of things ain't right."

"So you telling us, you, to make it more not right?"

Dr. Turner didn't answer. I had the weird feeling, me, that she didn't *have* an answer. A donkey without an answer.

With a last look at Lizzie, Dr. Turner left. Annie said, "I don't want *her* around here no more! She can just leave Lizzie alone!"

I could of told Annie, me, that wasn't going to happen. Not from the look in Lizzie's tired, sick eyes when the donkey doctor was telling her about that computer code. This was what Lizzie'd been looking for, her, all her life. Looking in the school software that Dr. Turner talked down, and in the East Oleanta library when we still had one, and in taking apart the apple peeler 'bot in the Congresswoman Janet Carol Land Café kitchen. This. Somebody who could tell her, them, what that smart little throwback mind wanted to know. And Annie wasn't going to be able to stop it. Annie didn't know that, her, but I did. Lizzie was already nearly twelve years old, her, and ain't nobody been able to really stop her from anything since she was eight.

But I didn't say nothing, me, to Annie. Not then. Annie watched Lizzie sleep with her whole heart in her eyes, and I couldn't say nothing, because I was too busy, me, watching them both.

That afternoon, though, I did hunt up Jack Sawicki, me, and ask him for a terminal password. He gave it to me, him, without asking too many questions. We go back a long way, Jack and me, and besides he had his hands full. A technician actually arrived, her, from Albany to fix the medunit. And there was supposed to be a big all-lodge dance that night in the café. Three lodges combined, them, to give the party. There was a dance jam, and betting games, and some kind of bare-breasted beauty contest, and most of the young people in town were going, which meant testing all the security 'bots. Especially since the gravrail was running again, it, and word of the dance might of traveled to other towns. Jack didn't even ask, him, why I wanted the password.

I walked, me, to the hotel. Dr. Turner wasn't around. It had turned cool for August; maybe she went for another walk in the woods, looking for Eden. She wasn't going to find it. I had looked, me, and there wasn't nothing nowhere near where Doug Kane had keeled over beside that rabid raccoon. No place that big-headed girl could of come from.

I said to the hotel HT, "Newsgrid mode. Password Thomas Alva Edison." Jack don't want the whole town knowing the hotel HT can go newsgrid; you'd have every Tom, Dick, and Harry in here, them, who want to watch a different channel than the HT at the café or the lodge houses.

"Newsgrid mode," the HT said cheerfully. It's always cheerful, it. "What channel, please?"

"Some donkey channel."

"What channel, please?"

I tried different numbers, me, until I found a donkey newsgrid. Then I sat and watched, me, for an hour, trying to remember the words Dr. Turner explained. Molecular bonds. Dissemblers. Alloy. Duragem. Only the newsgrid didn't use those words, it, except for "duragem." Instead it used words like "proposed epicenter" and "replication rate equations" and "Stoddard equations for field failure curves" and "manual replacement efforts falling behind incident rate." I watched anyway, me. After an hour I got up and said, "Information mode."

I went home, me, and got Lizzie's and Annie's meal chips. When nobody in the café was near the foodbelt, I took everything the chips would give me and put it all in a clean covered bucket and carried it home. Lizzie was still asleep, her, holding her doll. I went to the warehouse, which was opened again after a new shipment came on the gravrail, and got two more buckets, three blankets, and three sets of jacks on all our chips. Plus a new door lock, flowerpots, and a suitcase. The tech there looked at me funny, him, but didn't say nothing. I filled all the buckets with clean water, one at a time, and lugged them, me up the stairs to Annie's apartment. At the end my back ached and I was panting like the old fool I was.

But I didn't stop, me. I rested for ten minutes and then borrowed Annie's broom. I took it down to the hotel. People were carrying plasticloth banners into the café to decorate for the dance. They laughed and joked, them; a young girl flashed her breasts. Getting ready for tonight's contest. A few strangers checked themselves into the hotel on their New York State chips. They chattered on about the dance. Dr. Turner was still gone, her.

I took Annie's broom, me, and swept all the dead leaves out of the hotel lobby, all the leaves left by the broken cleaning 'bot that wasn't never going to get fixed now because it wasn't all that important compared to other breakdowns, all the leaves that had died, them, since last year, before all the breakdowns started and the rabid coons first come to East Oleanta.

Nine

DREW ARLEN: FLORIDA

When I left Seattle for Huevos Verdes, it was on a plane from Kevin Baker's corporate fleet. Kevin's reasons for not following the rest of the Sleepless to Sanctuary, unlike Leisha's, were not idealistic. He was Sanctuary's financial liaison with the rest of the planet. I figured that a Sleepless plane was the least likely in the world to crash from duragem dissembler damage. The plane would have been checked and rechecked compulsively; the Sleepless do safety very well. "Because we've had so little of it," Kevin said somberly when I phoned him and begged the use of plane and pilot. I was not interested at that moment in the social problems of the Sleepless. Kevin had never liked me, and I'd never asked him for any favors before. But I did now. I was going to force a showdown at Huevos Verdes, learn some important answers. Maybe Kevin knew that. You never know how much they know.

The unceasing lattice, closed tight, swayed in my mind.

"There's just one thing, Drew," Kevin said, and I thought I saw the shades and shapes of apology flit across his face on the vidscreen. Like all his generation of Sleepless, he looks a handsome thirty-five. "Leisha insists on going with you."

"How did Leisha even know I was going to Huevos Verdes? As far as she knows, I'm on a concert tour!"

"I don't know," Kevin said, which may or may not have been true. Maybe Leisha had her own electronic spies in my hotel room, or at the Seattle concert. Although it was hard to imagine she and Kevin could do that without Huevos Verdes knowing. Maybe the Supers did know, and tolerated Leisha's information system.

Maybe Leisha just knew me so well that she guessed what I was feeling. Maybe she had some kind of probability program predicting what I would do, what any Norm would do. You never know what they know.

"And if I say no to Leisha?" I said.

"Then no plane," Kevin said. He didn't meet my eyes. I saw that he felt he owed her this, for old debts, things that had happened before I was born. I saw, too, that there was just the slightest sign of puffiness along his jaw, the very beginning of a sag to his handsomeness. He was 110 years old. Flat, low shapes slid through my mind, the color of tarnished silver. Kevin was not going to change his mind.

Before Huevos Verdes, the plane went to Atlanta, to drop off something very secret and very industrial, in which I was not interested at all. Before that, it landed in Chicago to pick up Leisha. There were no reporters. The GSEA agents must have been there, of course, somewhere, but I didn't see them. Leisha climbed on board with a lawyerly briefcase and a small green overnight case, her golden hair blowing in the brisk wind off Lake Michigan. She wore white pants, sandals, and a thin yellow shirt. I stared straight ahead.

"I have to go with you, Drew," Leisha said with no hint of apology. This was her straight-forward, reasonable voice. It made me feel like a kid again, being chided for flunking out of the expensive donkey schools she'd sent me to. Schools no Liver could have succeeded in—or so I'd told myself at the time. "I love Miranda, too, you know. And I have to know what you and she and the other Supers are up to. Because if it's what I think it is . . ."

A hint of anger had crept into her voice. Leisha would feel entitled to anger, just for being excluded from knowledge. I didn't answer her.

Miri once told me that there were only four important questions you could ask about any human being: How does he fill up his time? How does he feel about how he fills up his time? What does he love? How does he react to those he perceives as either inferior or superior to him?

"If you make people feel inferior, even unintentionally," she had said, her dark eyes intense, "they will be uncomfortable around you. In that situation, some people will attack. Some will ridicule, to 'cut you down to size.' But some will admire, and learn from you. If you make people feel superior, some will react by dismissing you. Some by wielding power—just because they can—in greater or lesser ways. But some will be moved to protect and help. All this is just as true of a junior lodge clique as of a group of governments."

I had wondered how she could possibly know anything about junior lodge cliques. But, admiring her and wanting to learn, I hadn't said anything.

"I only want to protect you and Miranda, Drew," Leisha said, "and to help any way I can."

I looked out the plane window, at the sunlight reflected blindingly on the metal wings, until the shapes behind my eyelids blotted out the ones in my mind.

The plane, which had been so carefully checked for duragem-dissembler contamination in Seattle, must have become contaminated in Atlanta. It went down over upcountry Georgia.

It was the KingDome all over again, except that this pilot didn't pray or curse or moan, and we were flying at twenty thousand feet. The sky was a hazy blue, with clouds below that blocked any view of the ground. The plane listed to the left, just slightly, and I saw the flesh on the back of the pilot's neck change from light brown to a mottled maroon. Leisha looked up from her briefcase. Then the plane righted and I could feel my mind, which had clenched into a tight hard shape like constipation, open again.

But the next moment the plane lurched again, and began to shudder. The pilot spoke to his console in low, urgent orders, simultaneously punching in manual commands. The plane nose-dived.

The pilot pulled it up so hard I was thrown against Leisha. Her bright hair filled my mouth. Her briefcase hurled forward, against the back of the front seat. The briefcase said, "For maximum utility, please hold this unit steady." A long, thin, thread spun itself in my mind.

Leisha grabbed the back of the front seat and pulled herself off me. "Drew! Are you all right?"

The plane dropped. The pilot stayed with it, issuing orders in a monotonous voice controlled as machinery, manipulating the manual. Leisha's briefcase said, "This unit is deactivating," in a clear high voice like a trained soprano. Leisha's hand groped to check my restraints. "Drew!"

"I'm all right," I said, thinking, *This is not all right*. The thread spun itself out, stretching tauter and tauter.

We plunged through the clouds. There was a shrieking high in the air, almost sounding above us, as if it were coming from some entirely different machinery. Then the plane hit flat on its belly on marshy ground. I felt the hit in my teeth, in my bones. Leisha, thrown once more against me, said something very low, a single word; it might have been "Daddy."

The second the plane smashed into the ground, the sides lifted. But it couldn't have been the same second, I thought later, because nobody would design crash equipment that way. But it seemed only a second until the sides lifted and the passenger restraints sprang free. Leisha pushed me out of the plane, the same moment I caught the acrid smell of smoke.

I dropped on my belly into four inches of water covering mucky ground. Leisha splashed down beside me, falling to her knees. Without my powerchair I felt myself flailing, a desperate fish, holding myself above water on my elbows. I crawled forward, pulling myself with my upper arms through the muck and away from the plane dragging my useless legs behind.

Leisha staggered to her feet and tried to lift me. "No, run!" I screamed, as if the smoke billowing out from the plane blocked sound and not sight. "Not without you," she said. I could feel the plane behind me, a bomb. I screamed, "I can go faster on my own!" Maybe it was true.

She kept on tugging at my body, though I was far too heavy for her. The smoke thickened. I didn't hear the pilot climb out— was he hurt? My left palm slipped in the mud and I fell face first into it. Frantically I tried to get back up on my hands and drag myself forward. "Run!" I screamed again at Leisha, who wouldn't leave. Hopeless, hopeless. She wasn't strong enough to carry me, and the plane was going to blow.

The thread snapped. The lattice in my mind, as in Seattle, disappeared.

Someone ran toward Leisha from the other side of the plane. The pilot? But it wasn't. The man tackled Leisha and she fell on top of me. Once more my face was pushed into the mud. Then I heard a faint pop. When I fought my eyes free of the mud, I saw the air around the three of us shimmering. A force shield. Y-energy. How strong was it? Could it withstand—

The plane exploded in light and heat and blinding color.

I fell back into the muck, pinned under Leisha. The world rocked and I saw a tiny black water snake, terrified at the intrusions into its swamp, dart forward and bite me on the cheek. The snake started as a thin thread, then became a blur of close motion, and then the world went black as its shiny scales and I didn't know if the thread held or not.

He was a GSEA agent. When I came to, three of them stood around me in a circle, like the ring of doctors around my bed decades ago, when I was crippled. I lay on my back on a patch of relatively dry, spongy ground at the edge of the shallow lake. Leisha sat a little way off, her back against a custard-apple tree, her head bent forward on her knees. Across the swamp, Kevin Baker's plane burned, its smoke rising in billowy clouds.

"Leisha?" I heard myself croak. My voice sounded as alien as everything else. Only it wasn't alien at all. I recognized the heaviness of the muggy air, the whine of insects, the scummy pools and waxy-white ghost orchids. And over everything, the gray dripping beards of Spanish moss. I had been raised in upcountry Louisiana. This was—had to be—Georgia, but much of the swampy country is the same. It was I who had become the alien.

"Ms. Camden will be all right in a moment," an agent answered. "Probably just a concussion. There's help on the way. We're GSEA, Mr. Arlen. Lie still—your leg is broken."

Again. But this time I felt no pain. There were no nerves left to feel pain. I raised my chin slightly, feeling the pull in my stomach muscles. My left leg lay bent at a sharp, unnatural angle. I lowered my chin.

The shapes slithering through my mind were gray and indistinct on the outside, spiked within. They had a voice. *Can't do anything right, can you, boy? Who d'you think you are—some goddamn donkey?*

I said aloud, like a little boy, "A snake bit my cheek."

A second man bent to squint at my face. It was covered with mud. He said, not harshly, "There's a doctor on the way. We're not going to move you until she gets here. Just lie still and don't think."

Don't think. Don't dream. But I was the Lucid Dreamer. I was. I had to be.

Leisha's voice said thickly behind me, "Are we under arrest? On what charges?"

"No, of course not, Ms. Camden. We're happy to be able to assist you," said the man who had squinted at my cheek. The other two agents stood blank-faced, although I saw one of them blink. You can convey contempt with a blink. Leisha and I consorted with, assisted, Huevos Verdes. Gene manipulators. Destroyers of the human genome.

I saw Carmela Clemente-Rice standing beside the lattice in my mind, a clean cool shape, vibrating softly.

"You *are* Genetic Standards Enforcement Agency," Leisha said. It wasn't a question. But she was a lawyer: she waited for an answer.

"Yes, ma'am. Agent Thackeray."

"Mr. Arlen and I are grateful for your assistance. But by what right—"

I never found out what legal point Leisha had been going to make.

Men dressed in rags burst from behind trees, through tangled vines, from the mucky ground itself. One moment they weren't there, the next they were—that's how it felt. They hollered and shrieked and whooped. Agent Thackeray and his two comtemptuous deputies didn't even have time to draw their guns. Lying flat on my back, I saw the ragged men foreshortened as they raised pistols and fired at what seemed like, but couldn't have been, point-blank range. Thackeray and the two agents went down, the bodies twitching. I heard somebody say, "Hail, *yes,* she's an abomination, that there's Leisha Camden," and a gun fired again: once, twice. The first time, Leisha screamed.

I jerked my head toward her. She still sat with her back against the custard-apple tree, but now her upper body leaned forward, gracefully, as if she had fallen asleep. There were two red spots on her forehead, one below the other, the higher spot matting a strand of bright blonde hair that had somehow escaped the mud. I heard a long low moan and I thought "She's alive!"—the thought a desperate bright bubble—until I realized the moan was mine.

The man who had said "Hail, *yes*" leaned over me. His breath blew in my face; it smelled of mint and tobacco. "Don't you worry none, Mr. Arlen. We know *you* ain't no abomination against nature. You're safe as houses."

"Jimmy," a woman's voice said sharply, "Here they come!"

"Well, Abigail, y'all are ready for 'em, ain't you?" Jimmy said in a reasonable voice. I tried to crawl toward Leisha. She was dead. Leisha was dead.

A plane droned overhead. The medical team. They could help Leisha. But Leisha was dead. But Leisha was a Sleepless. Sleepless didn't die. They lived, on and on, Kevin Baker was 110. Leisha couldn't be *dead*—

The woman called Abigail stepped off the high ground into the swamp. She wore hip-high waders and tattered pants and shirt, and she carried a shoulder-mounted rocket launcher, ancient in design but gleaming with spit and polish. The medical plane folded its wings for a grav-powered landing. Abigail aimed, fired, and blew it into a second torch in the swamp.

"Okay," Jimmy said cheerfully. "That's it. Come on y'all, make tracks, they'll be all over here in no time. Mr. Arlen, I'm sorry this is going to be a rough ride for y'all, sir."

"No! I can't leave Leisha!" I didn't know what I was saying. I didn't know—

"Sure you can," Jimmy said. "She ain't going to get no deader. And you ain't none of her kind anyways. You're with James Francis Marion Hubbley now. Campbell? Where you at? Carry him."

"No! Leisha! Leisha!"

"Have a little dignity, son. You ain't no child bawlin' after its mama."

A huge man, fully seven feet high, picked me up and swung me over his shoulder. There was no pain in my leg but as soon as my body struck his, red fire darted up my spine to my neck and I screamed. The fire filled my mind, and the last view I ever had of Leisha Camden was of her slumped gracefully against the custard-apple tree, enveloped in the red fire of my mind, looking as if she had just fallen quietly asleep.

I woke in a small, windowless room with smooth walls. Too smooth—not a nanodeviance from the smooth, the perpendicular, the unblemished. I didn't realize at the time that I noticed this.

My mind filled with grief, welling up in spurts, geysers, rivers of hot lava the color of the two spots on Leisha's forehead.

She really was dead. She really was.

I closed my eyes. The hot lava was still there. I beat on the ground with my fists, and cursed my useless body. If I could have moved to shield her, to put myself between her and the ragged gunmen . . .

Not even trained GSEA agents had been able to shield her. Or themselves.

I couldn't hold back my tears, which embarrassed me. The lava had swamped the furled lattice in my mind, buried it, as it was burying me. *Leisha* . . .

"Now, y'all stop that, son. Keep a little dignity. Ain't no woman sired by man worth that kind of carryin' on."

The voice was kind. I opened my eyes, and hatred replaced the hot lava. I was glad. Hatred was a better shape: sharp, and cold, and very compact. That shape would not bury me. I looked at the concerned face of James Francis Marion Hubbley looming over me, and I let the cold compact shapes slide through me, and I knew that I was going to stay alive, and stay alert, and stay in control of myself, because otherwise I might not be able to kill him. And I knew I was going to kill him. Even if that meant his was the last face I ever saw.

"That's better," Hubbley said genially, and sat down on a tree stump, hands on his knees, nodding encouragingly.

It really was a tree stump. The walls snapped into sharp focus, then, and I knew what kind of place I was in. I had seen the same kind of walls with Carmela Clemente-Rice, and at Huevos Verdes. This was an underground bunker, dug out of the earth by the tiny precise machines of nanotechnology, plastered over with alloy by other tiny precise machines. Eating dirt and laying down a thin layer of alloy were not hard, Miri had told me once. Any competent nanoscientist could create nonorganic mechanisms to do that. Corporations did it all the time, despite government regulations. It was only organic-based replicating nanotechnology that was hard. Anyone could dig a hole, but only Huevos Verdes could build an island.

But Hubbley didn't look like a scientist. He leaned forward and smiled at me. His teeth were rotten. Wisps of graying hair hung on either side of a long, bony face with deeply sunburned skin and pale blue eyes. An odd lump under the skin disfigured the right side of his neck. He might have been forty, or sixty. He wore cloth rags, not jacks, of a streaky dull brown, but his boots, whole and high, were almost certainly from some goods warehouse someplace. I had never seen him before, but I recognized him. He belonged to the backwater South.

In most of the country, the donkey-run District Supervisor This Warehouse or Congressman That Café had forced out all independent businesses. Livers could get everything they needed for free, so why pay for it? But in the rural South, and sometimes in the West, you still found hardscrabble businesses, weedy motels and chicken farms and whorehouses, getting poorer and poorer over forty years but hanging on, because damn it the gov'mint don't have no business runnin' our lives, them. Such people didn't mind much being poor. They were used to being poor. It was better than being owned by the donkeys. They took handicrafts or chickens or beans or other services in trade. They disdained jacks and medunits and school software. And wherever these pathetic business held on, so did criminals like Hubbley. Stealing, too, was outside the gov'mint, and so a mark of pride.

Hubbley and his band would rob warehouses, apartment blocks, even gravrails, for what they absolutely needed. They would hunt in the deep swamps, and fish, and maybe grow a little of this and that. There would be a still someplace. Oh, I knew Jimmy Hubbley, all right. I'd known him all my life, before Leisha took me in. My daddy was a Jimmy Hubbley without the independence to break free from the system he cursed until the day free government whiskey—not even home-distilled—killed him.

And this was the man that had killed Leisha Camden.

The shapes of hatred have great energy, like robotic knives.

I said, "This is an illegal genemod lab."

Hubbley's face creased into a huge grin. "That's exactly right! Y'all are sharp, boy. Only this is just a bitty little outstation, where Abigail can see to her equipment and we can pick up supplies. And this place ain't used by the gene abominators no more. Y'all are visitin' the Francis Marion Freedom Outpost, Mr. Arlen. And let me say we're honored to have y'all. We all seen all your concerts. You're a Liver, all right. Livin' with the donkeys and the Sleepless ain't harmed you at all. But then that's the way with the true blood, ain't it?"

There was something wrong with his speech. I fumbled, then got it. He didn't talk like a Liver—none of what Miri called "intensifying reflexive pronouns"—but he didn't talk like a donkey, either. There was something artificial about his sentences. And I'd heard this kind of speech before, but I couldn't remember where.

I said, to keep him talking, "The Francis Marion Freedom Outpost? Who was Francis Marion?"

Hubbley squinted at me. He rubbed the lump on the side of his neck. "Y'all never heard of Francis Marion, Mr. Arlen? Really? An educated man like you? He was a hero, maybe the biggest hero this here country ever had. Y'all really never heard of him, sir?"

I shook my head. It didn't hurt. I realized then that my leg had been set. I was on painkillers. A doctor must have seen me, or at least a medunit.

"Now I don't want to make y'all feel bad," Hubbley said earnestly. His long bony face radiated regret. "Y'all's our guest, and it ain't right to make a guest feel bad about his ignorance. Especially ignorance he cain't help. It's the school system, a sorry disgrace for a democracy, that's entirely to blame here. *Entirely.* So don't you fret, sir, about ignorance that just ain't your fault."

He had killed Leisha. He had killed the GSEA agents. He had kidnapped me. And he sat there concerned about my feeling bad over not knowing who Francis Marion was.

For the first time, I realized I might be dealing with a madman.

"Francis Marion was a great hero of the American Revolution, son. The enemy called him the 'Swamp Fox.' He'd hide in the swamps of South Carolina and Georgia and just swoop down on them British, hit 'em when they was least expectin' it, and then melt back into the swamp. Couldn't never catch him. He was fightin' for freedom and justice, and he was usin' nature to help him. Not hinder."

I had his speech now.

Once Leisha and I had spent a whole night watching ancient movies about a civil rights movement. Not civil rights for Sleepless but a movement before that—a hundred years earlier?—about blacks or women. Or maybe Asians. I was never too good at history. But I had to do a paper for one of the schools Leisha kept trying to get me through. I don't remember the history, but I remember that Leisha searched for old movies adapted for decent technology because she thought I wouldn't read through the assigned books. She was right, and I resented that. I was sixteen years old. But I liked the movies. I sat in my powerchair, pleased because it was 3:00 A.M. and I wasn't sleepy, I was keeping up with Leisha. I still thought, at sixteen, that I could.

All night we watched sheriffs in groundcars busting up places where voters registered in person—this was even before computers. We watched old women sit at the backs of buses. We watched black Livers denied seats in cafés, even though they had meal chips. They all talked like James Francis Marion Hubbley. Or, rather, he talked like them. His speech was a deliberate creation, a reenactment of an earlier time: history as far back as it was electronically available. Maybe he thought they talked like that in the American Revolution. Maybe he knew better. Either way, it was disciplined and deliberate.

He was an artist.

Hubbley said, "Marion was puny, and none too firm in his education, and bad-tempered, and given to black moods. His knees were made wrong, right from the day his mother bore him. The British burned his plantation, his men deserted him whenever they got a hankerin' after their families, and his own commandin' officer, Major General Nathanael Greene, wasn't none too fond of him. But none of that slowed down Francis Marion. He did his duty by his country, his duty as he saw it, whether all hail busted out or not."

I said, forcing the words out, "And what are you imagining is *your* duty by your country?"

Hubbley's eyes gleamed. "I said y'all was sharp, son, and you are. Y'all got it right off. We're doin' our same duty as the Swamp Fox, which is to fight off foreign oppressors."

"And this time the foreign oppressors are anybody genemod."

"Y'all got that right, Mr. Arlen. Livers are the true people of this country, just like Marion's army was. They had the will to decide for themselves what kind of country they wanted to live in, and we got the will to decide for ourselves, too. We got the will, and we got the idea of what this glorious nation ought to look like, even if it don't look like it right now. We. Livers. And y'all don't believe it, hail, just look at the mess the donkeys made of this great country. Debt to foreign nations, entanglin' alliances that sap us dry, the infrastructure crumblin' in our faces, the technology misused. Just like the British misused the cannons and guns of their day."

My hip began to throb, distantly. The painkiller wasn't quite strong enough. I had heard all this before. It was nothing more than anti-research hatred, dressed up as patriotism. They had gotten Leisha after all, the haters. I couldn't stand to look at Hubbley, and I turned my head away.

"Course," he said, "you cain't stop genetic engineering. And nobody should stop it. We sure aren't, or we wouldn't have let go this here duragem dissembler."

I turned my head slowly to stare at him. He grinned. His pale blue eyes gleamed in his sunburned face.

"Don't look like that, son. I don't mean me personally, Jimmy Hubbley. Or even this brigade. But y'all didn't think this duragem dissembler got loose by accident, did you?"

That's when I noticed the walls, nanotech perfect. And I saw again Miri's printouts, unable to pinpoint a single source for the dissembler leak.

Hubbley said, serious again, "There's a lot of us. Y'all need a lot of people to make a revolution. We got the will to decide what kind of country we want to live in, and we got the idea. The technology."

I choked out, "What technology?"

"All of it. Well, maybe not all. But a lot. Some nonorganic nano, some low-level organic nano."

"The duragem dissembler . . . How did you . . . ."

"Now, y'all will learn that in good time. For today, just know that we did. And it's going to bring down the false government, same as the Revolution brought down the British. We capture the technology we need, like Marion captured guns right from the enemy. Why, in 1781, right on the Santee River—"

"But you killed the GSEA agents—"

"Genemod," Hubbley said briefly. "Abominations against nature. Hail, using nanotech to fight the good fight—that ain't no different than using the cannon of General Marion's time. But to use it on human beings—that's a whole different war, son. That ain't right. People ain't things, and shouldn't be treated like things, with their parts altered and retrofitted and realigned. They ain't vehicles, nor factories, nor robots. The donkeys done been treating people like things way too long in this country. Liver people."

"But you can't just allow organic genetic engineering on microorganisms and expect that it won't happen on people, too. If you allow one—"

"Hail, no." Hubbley stood and flexed his legs. "It ain't the same thing at all. It's all right to kill germs, ain't it? Even to kill animals to eat? But it ain't all right to kill human beings. We make that distinction just fine in our laws about killin', don't we? What in hail thinks we cain't make them in our laws about genemod engineering?"

I said, before I knew I was going to, "You can't hide from the GSEA!"

Hubbley gazed at me mildly from those watery blue eyes. "Huevos Verdes does, don't it?"

"That's different. They're Supers—"

"They ain't gods. Or even angels." He stretched his back. "Fact is, Mr. Arlen, we been hidin' from the GSEA for nearly five years now. Oh, not all of us. The enemy has killed quite a few good soldiers so far. And we inflicted our casualties, too. But we're still here. And the duragem dissembler's out there bringin' the whole war to a hastier conclusion."

"But you can't hide from Huevos Verdes!"

"Well, that's tougher to call. But the fact is, I suspect we're not. I suspect Huevos Verdes knows a whole lot more about us than the GSEA. Stands to reason."

Miranda had never said. Not to me. Jonathan had never said, nor Christy, nor Nikos. Not to me. Not to me.

"Up till now, we ain't been strong enough to take on Huevos Verdes as well, so it's been a good thing they've kind of ignored us. But it's all different now. Not even Huevos Verdes can stop the way this government's losing control, now that the duragem dissembler is beyond stopping."

"But—"

That's enough for now," Hubbley said, not unkindly. "We got to get movin' now. Those agents' deaths'll cause all hail to bust loose. The company ought to be just about ready to go, and y'all are goin' with us. But don't y'all worry none, Mr. Arlen—they'll be plenty of time for you and me to talk. I know all this is new to you, because y'all *did* have a faulty education. And y'all been spendin' time with Sleepless, who ain't even human no more. But y'all will learn better. Cain't help it, once you see the real war up close. And we owe you that. You been a real help to us."

I only stared at him. A sickening flood of shapes swept to the edge of my mind, a wave poised to flow over me, swamp me.

"I've been—"

"Well, of course," Hubbley said, in what felt like genuine astonishment. "Didn't you already guess that? Your last concert, 'The Warrior,' has been leavin' people feelin' far more independent and ready to fight with will and idea. Y'all done that, Mr. Arlen. It probably warn't what y'all intended, but that's what's been happenin'. Since y'all began giving 'The Warrior,' our recruitment's up three hundred percent."

I couldn't speak. A door opened and Campbell loomed over me.

"Hail," Hubbley said, "two months ago we even got a cell of genemod scientists who joined us voluntarily, without no torture or nothing. You been making all the difference in the world, son.

"And now, we really got to move out. Campbell will carry you. If that hip starts to hurtin' too much, y'all be sure to holler. We got more painkillers, and where we're going, there's a doctor. We sure don't want you to suffer, not with all the help you been givin' us, Mr. Arlen, sir. You been on the right side. It just takes some folk a little longer than others to know it.

"Handle him careful, Campbell . . . there. Here we go."

Campbell carried me across the swamp for about two hours, as near as I could tell. It's hard to be certain about the time because I kept blacking out. He had slung me over his shoulder like a sack of soy, but I could tell he was trying to be gentle. It didn't help.

We walked single file, about ten of us, led by Jimmy Hubbley. Hubbley knew the swamps. His people sometimes walked on narrow ridges of semi-firm land with mucky pools on either side, the kind of quicksand that as a child I had seen swallow a man in less than three minutes. Other times we sloshed through brackish water alive with turtles and snakes. Everybody wore hip-high waders. They kept close to dense tangles of vines, under gray moss dripping from trees. That wouldn't make any difference, of course, as soon as the GSEA brought in a tracking 'bot, which does ten times better than the best hound at picking up pheromones, not only following their trail but analyzing their content. I expected to be back with the GSEA in two hours.

Then I saw that the last person in line was the woman, Abigail, who had blown up the rescue plane with a rocket launcher. She had left that at the outstation. Instead she carried a curved, dull-colored machine like a metal bow, holding it above her head, parallel to the ground. I knew what it was: a Harrison Pheromone Obliterator. It released molecules that homed in on any molecular traces of humans and neutralized them. It was classified military equipment, which I happened to know about only through Huevos Verdes, and there was no way the Francis Marion Freedom Outpost could have one. But they did.

For the first time, I began to believe Jimmy Hubbley that his movement was not made up of isolated fanatics.

Abigail was pregnant. With her arms raised above her head, I could clearly see the curve of her belly under her jacks, maybe five months along. As she walked she hummed to herself, a happy tuneless little song. Her thoughts looked miles and landscapes away.

The swamp got thicker and hotter. Branches scratched my face where I hung, helpless, over Campbell's shoulder. Snakes as thick as a man's wrist slithered into shallow pools. A log heaved up, slid beneath black water, and disappeared in a row of hissing bubbles. Alligator.

I closed my eyes. The humid air was thick with the waxy-white scent of ghost orchids, growing on the trunks of pop-ash trees. They weren't parasites. They lived on air.

Insects sang and stung, a constant cloud.

"Well, here we are," Jimmy Hubbley said. "Mr. Arlen, sir, how are y'all faring?"

I didn't answer. Every time I looked at him, my mind filled with the shapes of hatred, cold and rotating like knives. Leisha was dead. Jimmy Hubbley had killed Leisha Camden. She was dead. I was going to destroy him.

He didn't seem to care that I didn't answer. We had halted under an enormous bay tree hung with gray moss. Other trees crowded close. An ancient fallen cypress had half crumbled into pulp, covered with the sucking tendrils of a strangler fig. In the murky half-light I saw a striped lizard scuttle down a vine. On the other side of the bay tree was a dark-green expanse of moss, soft and even as an enclave lawn. The place smelled heavily of jungle rot.

"Now, son, this next part might look a little disconcertin' to y'all. It's real important that y'all remember you're in no danger. That, and to take a real deep breath, close your mouth, and hold your nose. And I'll tell you what—I'll go first, just to reassure y'all. In the ordinary way, Abby would go first, but this time I will. At least in part out of deference to the bride."

He grinned at Abigail, flashing his broken teeth. She smiled back and lowered her eyes, but a minute later I caught her shoot a hooded glance at one of the other men, hard and meaningful as a grenade. Jimmy Hubbley didn't see it. He gave a rebel yell and jumped into the expanse of moss.

I gasped, which sent unexpected pain through my left side. Jimmy sank immediately to his waist in black, jellylike muck that lay beneath the moss. His only hope now was to stay absolutely still and let Campbell pull him out. But instead he gave a jaunty little wiggle of his upper shoulders, one hand holding his nose, the other nonchalantly clamped to his side. He stayed motionless for maybe ten seconds, and then something sucked him down into the muck. His chest disappeared, and then his shoulders, and then his head. The moss, lightly spattered with muck, closed over him.

My heart hammered against my lungs.

Abigail went next. She shoved her Harrison Pheromone Obliterator into a plastisynth pouch and sealed it. Then she jumped onto the moss and dissappeared.

"Hold your nose, you," Campbell said—the first words he had spoken.

"Wait. *Wait.* I—"

"Hold your nose, you." He threw me out over the muck.

My left side screamed. My feet hit the moss first, but there was no feeling there, had been no feeling there for decades. It wasn't until I'd sunk to my waist that I felt the clammy muck, sucking against me like feces, cool after the hot air. It smelled of rot, of death. Black shapes flooded my mind and I struggled, even while a part of me knew I must hold absolutely still, there was no help unless I held absolutely still, *Leisha* . . . Somebody chuckled.

Then something grabbed me from below, something incorporeal but powerful, like a wind. It sucked me down. The muck rose above my shoulders, and then to my mouth. It covered my eyes, filling the world with the same fecal shapes as my mind. I went under.

For the third time, as I expected death, the purple lattice disappeared.

And then I was lying on the floor of an underground room, while gloved hands seized me and dragged my mucky body. Pain spasmed my left side. Someone wiped my face. The hands stripped my clothes from me and thrust me naked into a sonar shower, and the muck dropped from my head and clothing in dry, scaly flakes that were in turn sucked into a vacuum at the shower's floor. Someone slapped a medpatch on my spine, and the pain disappeared.

"Y'all can have a real shower, too, if y'all want," Jimmy Hubbley said kindly. "Some folks need one. Or think they do." He stood before me already dressed in clean jacks, not at all raggedy, indistinguishable from any other Liver except by his uncared-for teeth.

Abigail emerged from the water shower, unself-consciously naked, drying her hair. Her pregnant belly waggled slightly from side to side. A bell rang, high and sweet, and Campbell was sucked down onto the landing stage, which I saw now extended only a few feet under a low overhang. Two men immediately pulled Campbell off the stage, wiping his eyes and nose. Campbell stood, covered with the shiny muck, and lumbered into the sonar shower.

"Take off them gloves, boys, and help Mr. Arlen, here. Joncey, y'all just have to take your eyes off your lovely bride."

One of the two men reddened slightly. Hubbley seemed to think this was funny, breaking into a guffaw, but I felt in my mind the shapes of Joncey's anger. He said nothing. Abigail went on coolly drying her hair, her face expressionless. Joncey and the other man seized me under the armpits, carried me between them out of the sonar shower, and set me down in the middle of the room. Joncey handed me a set of clean jacks.

"What size boots you wear, you?" He was younger than Abigail, with black hair and blue eyes, handsome in a rough way that had nothing to do with genetic egnineering.

I said, "I'd like my own boots back." They were Italian leather. Leisha had given them to me. "Put them in the sonar shower."

"Better you wear our boots, you. What size?"

"Ten and a half."

He left the room. I dressed. The lattice was back in my head, closed tight as one of Leisha's exotic flowers.

She was really dead.

Joncey returned, with a pair of boots and a wheelchair. It wasn't even grav-powered; it had actual wheels that apparently you turned by hand.

"An antique," Jimmy Hubbley said. "Sorry, Mr. Arlen, sir, that here thing is the best we can do on such short notice. But y'all just give us a little time."

He beamed at me, obviously expecting some surprise that this underground bunker was well enough equipped that an unexpected crippled captive could be provided with a wheelchair. I didn't react. A faint disappointment shimmered over his face.

I had his shape, then. He wanted to be admired. James Francis Marion Hubbley. And he didn't even know that at least two of his followers, Abigail and Joncey, already resented him.

How much?

I would find out.

Joncey and the other man lifted me into the wheelchair. I pulled on the Liver boots. Dressed, seated instead of flopping on the floor like a fish, I felt less hopeless. Leisha was dead. But I was going to destroy the bastards who'd killed her.

I studied the room. It was low, no more than six and a half feet high; Campbell had to stoop. Corridors radiated off in five directions. The walls were nanotech smooth. I knew from Miranda that the weak point of any shielded underground bunker is the entrance. That's what's most likely to be detected by GSEA experts. The lab in East Oleanta had an elaborate entrance shield created by Terry Mwakambe; no chance the GSEA would get through that. But these people were not Supers. They would have no more advanced technology than the government did. I guessed, however, that the swamp-pool entrance was a use of technology that the government hadn't yet thought of, adapted by some crazy scientist who'd grown up in swamp country, and that it was virtually undetectable. So far.

How far did the underground tunnel system extend? With nanodiggers, additional construction could be going on even now, miles from here, without much disturbance on the surface. Hubbley had said his "revolution" had been in progress for over five years.

And these people had loosed the duragem dissembler on the country. Without the GSEA ever figuring out that it was not Huevos Verdes.

Or did the GSEA know that, and nonetheless leak to the press that the Supers were responsible? Because it was all right to blame Sleepless, but embarrassing to admit you couldn't catch a bunch of Livers with captured or renegade nanoscientists on their side.

I didn't know. But I did know that in a war this advanced, these tunnels would contain terminals. Miri had made me memorize override codes for most standard programming. And even if the programming wasn't standard, Jonathan Markowitz had made me memorize, over and over, access tricks that would get through to Huevos Verdes. And Huevos Verdes monitored everything. There had to be a way to reach them. All I needed was a terminal.

If Huevos Verdes monitored everything, wouldn't they know about the underground movement?

They must know. I remembered Miranda bending over printouts at Huevos Verdes: "We can't locate the epicenter of the duragem problem." But the Supers must have at least been aware that the dissembler was being released by some nationwide, organized group. Their intelligence was too good not to know it.

And Miranda hadn't told me.

"Are you hungry, you?" Joncey said. He spoke to Abigail, now dressed in green jacks, but Hubbley answered.

"Hail, yes. Let's have at it, boys."

He pushed my chair himself. I let him, passive, feeling the shapes in my mind hard as carbon-fiber rods. We all went down the left-hand tunnel, passing several closed doors. Eventually everyone else went through one door, Hubbley and I through another. A small white room was furnished with wood—not plastisynth—table and chairs. On the wall hung a large holo portrait of a big-nosed, dark-eyed soldier in some sort of antique uniform.

"Brigadier General Francis Marion himself," Hubbley said, with satisfaction. "I always eat separate from the troops, Mr. Arlen. It makes for better morale. Did y'all know, sir, that General Marion was a fanatic on cleanliness? God's own truth. He dry-shaved any soldier who didn't appear neat and clean on parade, and he himself drank vinegar and water every day of his life, pretty near, for his health. Drink of the Roman soldiers. Did you know that, sir?"

"I didn't know that," I said. My hatred for him burned cold, sleek shapes in my mind. The room held no terminal.

"As early as 1775 one British general wrote, 'Our army will be destroyed by damned driblets'—and Francis Marion was the damndest driblet those poor redcoats ever saw. Just like this war will be won by damned driblets, sir." Hubbley laughed, exposing his brown teeth. His pale eyes crinkled. He never took them off me.

"Will and idea, son. We got them both. Will and idea. You know what makes the Constitution so great?"

"No," I said. A young boy entered, dressed in turquoise jacks, his long hair tied back with a ribbon. He carried bowls of hot stew. Hubbley paid him as much attention as a 'bot.

"What makes the Constitution so great is it brought the common man into the decision-making process. It let *us* decide what kind of country we want. Us, the common man. Our will, and our idea."

Leisha had always said that what made the Constitution so great was its checks and balances.

She was dead. She was really dead.

"That's why, sir," Hubbley continued, "it's so all-fired necessary that we take back this great country from the donkey masters who would enslave us. By driblets, if necessary. Yes, by God, by driblets." He attacked his stew with gusto.

"In fact, preferably by driblets," I said. "You wouldn't like this war nearly as much if you fought it aboveground, in the courts."

I had expected to make him angry. Instead he laid down his spoon and squinted thoughtfully.

"Yes, I do believe y'all are right, Mr. Arlen. I do believe y'all are right. We each have our God-given temperament, and mine is for fighting in driblets. Just like General Marion. Now, that's a real interesting insight." He went back to spooning stew.

I tasted mine. Standard Liver soy base, but with chunks of real meat added, gamy and a little tough. Squirrel? Rabbit? It had been decades since I'd had to eat either.

"Not that the Constitution don't have its own limits," Hubbley continued. "Now y'all take Abigail and Joncey. They understand exactly what those limits need to be. They're manipulatin' gene combinations in the right way: through human procreation." He dragged out the last two words, savoring each syllable. "Some of Joncey's genes, some of Abby's, and the final shuffle in God's hands. They respect the clear line in the Constitution between what is God's and what is man's to manipulate."

I needed to know everything I could about him, no matter how nutty, because I didn't know yet what I would need to kill him. "Where in the Constitution does it draw that line?"

"Ah, son, don't they teach you nothin' in them fancy schools? It oughtn't be allowed, no, it ought not. Why, right there in the Preamble, it announces clear as daylight that 'We the People' are writin' the thing 'in Order to form a more perfect Union, establish Justice, insure domestic Tranquility, provide for the common defence,' and et cetera. What's a perfect union about letting donkeys control the human genome? It just drives people farther apart. What's Justice about not letting Joncey and Abby's babe start life on an equal footin' with a donkey child? How does that make for domestic tranquility? Hail, it makes for envy and resentment, that's what it makes for. And what on God's green earth is the 'common defence' if it ain't the defence of the common people, the Livers, to have their kids count just as much as a genemod babe? Abby and Joncey are fightin' for their own, just like natural parents everywhere, and the Constitution gives 'em the right to do that right there in its first sacred paragraph."

I had never heard anyone use the word 'babe' before. He sat there spooning his wretched stew, Jimmy Hubbley, as artificial and as sincere as anyone I had ever met.

Intellectual arguments confuse me. They always have. I felt the helpless feeling rise in me, the one I'd always had arguing with Leisha, with Miranda, with Jonathan and Terry and Christy. The best I could answer, out of confusion and hatred, was, "What gives *you* the right to decide what's right for 175 million people?"

He squinted at me again. His apologetic voice returned. "Why, son—ain't that what your Huevos Verdes was doin'?"

I stared at him.

"Sure it is. Only they cain't decide for common people, 'cause *they* ain't. Clearly. Not like us. Not like *him*." He waved his spoon at the portrait of Francis Marion. Stew dribbled off the spoon onto the table.

"But—"

"Y'all need to examine your premises, son," he said very gently. "Will and idea." He went back to eating.

The boy returned, carrying two mugs. Still-brewed whiskey. I left mine untouched, but I made myself eat the stew. I might need my strength. Hatred shone in me like suns.

Hubbley talked more about Francis Marion. His courage, his military strategy, his ways of living off the land. "Why, he wrote to General Horatio Gates to send him supplies because 'we are all poor Continentals without money.' Poor Continentals! Ain't that a great one? Poor Continentals! And so we are." He drained his whiskey. So much for vinegar and water.

I choked out, "The GSEA will stop you. Or Huevos Verdes will."

He grinned. "You know what the Lieutenant Colonel Banastre Tarleton of His Majesty's army said about Francis Marion? 'But as for this damned old fox, the Devil himself could not catch him.' "

I said, "Hubbley—*you aren't Francis Marion.*"

Immediately he grew serious. "Well, of course not, son. Anybody can see that, so clear it don't hardly need commentin' on, does it, except by somebody crazy. Clear as day I'm not Francis Marion. I'm Jimmy Hubbley. What's wrong with you, Mr. Arlen? You feelin' all right?"

He leaned across the table, his bony face creased with concern.

I could feel my heart thud in my chest. He was impenetrable, as impenetrable as Huevos Verdes. After a moment he patted my arm.

"That's all right, Mr. Arlen, sir, y'all just a little shocked by events is all. Y'all will be fine in the mornin'. It's just real upsettin', discoverin' the truth after all this time of believin' falsehoods. Perfectly natural. Now don't you worry none; y'all be fine in the mornin'. You just sleep, and please excuse me, I got a council of war to attend to."

He patted my arm again, smiled, and left. The boy wheeled my chair to a bedroom with a single bed, a chemical toilet, and a deadbolt on the door that could only be unlocked from the outside.

In the morning the doctor came to check me. He turned out to be the small man who had helped Joncey at the landing stage.

Joncey was with him. I saw that Joncey was guarding him; apparently the doctor was not here of his own Will and Idea. But he was allowed to roam the underground compound, which meant he probably knew where the terminals were.

"Leg looks good," he said. "Any pain in your neck?"

"No." Joncey leaned against the doorjamb, smiling. The smile deepened and I glimpsed Abigail pass by in the corridor. Joncey stepped away from the door. Giggles and a tussle.

I said, quickly and very low, "Doctor—I can get us out of here, if you can get me to a terminal. I know ways to call for help that will override anything they can possibly have—"

His small face wrinkled in alarm. Too late I realized that, of course, he was monitored. Hubbley's people would overhear everything he heard or said.

Joncey came back and the doctor hurried off by his side, interested only in staying alive.

The lattice in my mind had circled tighter than ever, a huddled closed shape, hiding whatever was inside. Even the diamond patterns on its outer surface looked smaller. Angry, ineffective shapes flopped sluggishly around it, like beached fish.

Hubbley left me to my sour shapes until midmorning. When he opened my door he looked stern. "Mr. Arlen, sir, I understand y'all want to get to a terminal and set your friends at Huevos Verdes on us."

I stared at him with open hatred, sitting in my antique wheelchair.

He sighed and sat on the edge of my cot, hands on his long knees, body bent earnestly forward. "It's important that y'all *understand,* son. Contactin' the enemy in wartime is treason. Now I know y'all ain't a regular soldier, leastways not yet, y'all are more like a prisoner of war, but just the same—"

"You know Francis Marion never talked like that, don't you?" I said brutally. "That kind of speech only dates from maybe a hundred fifty years ago, from movies. It's phony. As phony as your whole war."

He didn't change expression. "Why, of course General Marion didn't talk this way, Mr. Arlen. Y'all think I don't know that? But it's different from how my troops talk, it's old-fashioned, and it ain't neither donkey nor Liver. That's enough. It don't matter how truth gets expressed, long as it does."

He gazed at me with kindly, patient eyes.

I said, "Let me wheel my chair around the compound. I'm not going to learn your truths locked in this room. Give me a guard, like the doctor has."

Hubbley rubbed the lump on his neck. "Well—could do, I suppose. It ain't like y'all are going to overpower anyone, sittin' in that chair."

The shapes in my mind abruptly changed. Dark red, shot with silver. Hubbley's people didn't do very deep background checks. He didn't realize I'd trained my upper body with the best martial arts masters Leisha's money could buy. She'd wanted to give me an outlet for my adolescent anger.

What else didn't he know? Leisha, unable to alter my non-Sleepless DNA, had nonetheless done what she could for me. My eyes had implanted corneas with bifocal/zoom magnification; my arm muscles had been augmented. Probably these things counted as abominations, crimes against the common humanity in the Constitution.

I tried to look wistful. "Can I have Abigail for my guard?"

Hubbley laughed. "Won't do y'all no good, son. Abby's goin' to marry Joncey in a couple of months. Give that baby a real daddy. Abby's got a whole lot of lace around here someplace, for a weddin' dress."

I saw Abigail in her waders and torn shirt, firing a rocket launcher at the rescue plane. I couldn't picture her in a wedding gown. Then it came to me that I couldn't picture Miranda in one either.

Miranda. I had hardly thought of her since Leisha's death.

"But I'll tell you what," Hubbley said, "seein' as y'all are so starved for feminine company, I'll assign a woman to guard you. But, Mr. Arlen, sir—"

"Yes?"

His eyes looked grayer, harder. "Keep in mind that this *is* a war, sir. And grateful as we are for the help your concerts gave us, y'all are expendable. Just keep that in mind."

I didn't answer. In another hour the door opened again and a woman entered. She was, must have been, Campbell's twin. Nearly seven feet tall, nearly as muscled as he was. Her short shit-brown hair was plastered flat around a sullen face with Campbell's heavy jaw.

"I'm the guard, me." Her voice was high and bored.

"Hello. I'm Drew Arlen. You're . . ."

"Peg. Just behave, you." She stared at me with flat dislike.

"Right," I said. "And what natural combination of genes produced *you?*"

Her dislike didn't deepen, didn't waver. I saw her in my mind as a solid monolith, granite, like a headstone.

"Take me to whatever your café is, Peg."

She grasped the wheelchair and pushed it roughly. Beneath her green jacks, her thigh muscles rippled. She outweighed me by maybe thirty pounds; her reach was longer; she was in superb shape.

I saw Leisha's body, light and slim, slumped against the custard-apple tree, two red holes in her forehead.

The café was a large room where several tunnels converged. There were tables, chairs, a holoterminal of the simplest, receive-only kind. It showed a scooter race. No foodbelt, but several people were eating bowls of soystew. They stared frankly when Peg wheeled me in. At least half a dozen faces were openly hostile.

Abigail and Joncey sat at a far table. She was actually sewing panels of lace together—by hand. It was like watching someone make candles, or dig a hole with a shovel. Abigail glanced at me once, then ignored me.

Peg shoved my chair against a table, brought me a bowl of stew, and settled down to watch the scooter race. Her huge body dwarfed the standard-issue plastisynth chair.

I watched the race, while observing everything through the zoom area of my corneas. Abby's lace was covered with a complex design of small oblongs, no two the same, like snowflakes. She snipped out an oblong and presented it, laughing, to Joncey. Three men played cards; the one whose hand I could see held a pair of kings. After a while I said to Peg, "Is this how you spend all your days? Contributing to the revolution?"

"Shut up, you."

"I want to see more of the compound. Hubbley said I could if you take me."

"Say 'Colonel Hubbley,' you!"

"Colonel Hubbley, then."

She seized my chair hard enough to rattle my teeth and shoved it along the nearest corridor. "Hey! Slow down!"

She slowed to an insolent crawl. I didn't argue. I tried to memorize everything.

It wasn't easy. The tunnels all looked the same: featureless white, nanoperfect, lined with dirt-resistant alloy and identical white, unmarked doors. I tried to memorize tiny bits of dropped food, boot scuffs. Once I saw a small oblong bit of lace half caught under a door, and I knew Abigail must have come that way. Peg pushed me like a 'bot, impassive and tireless. I was losing track of what I'd tried to memorize.

After three hours, we passed a cleaning 'bot, whirling up the things I had used as markers.

In the whole tour, I saw only two open doors. One was to a common bath. The other was only opened for a moment, then closed, allowing the fastest glimpse of high-security cannisters, rows and rows of them. Duragem dissemblers? Or some other nonhuman-genome destruction that Jimmy Hubbley thought ought to be unleashed on his enemies?

"What was that?" I said to Peg.

"Shut up, you."

An hour later, we returned to the commons area. Lunch was still in progress. Peg shoved me to an empty table and plunked another bowl of stew in front of me. I wasn't hungry.

A few minutes later Jimmy Hubbley sat down with me. "Well, son, I hope y'all are satisfied with your tour."

"Oh, it was great," I said. "I saw all kinds of contributions to the revolution."

He laughed. "Oh, it's happenin', all right. But y'all ain't goin' to provoke me into showing y'all before I'm ready. Time enough, time enough."

"Aren't you afraid your troops will get restless, doing nothing like this? What did General Marion do with his men between battles?" I put down my spoon; I hated him too much to even pretend to eat in his presence. God, I wanted a drink.

He seemed surprised. "Why, Mr. Arlen, sir, they don't ordinarily do nothin'. This here's Sunday, the Sabbath. Come tomorrow, we go back to regular drill. General Marion knew the value of a day for rest and recuperation of the human spirit."

He looked around with satisfaction at the desultory gambling, scooter watching, slumped figures probably on sunshine. Only three faces in the whole damn room showed any real animation.

Joncey and Abigail, smiling at each other, Abby still sewing on billowing patterned lace. And Peg.

"Eat your stew, son," Hubbley said kindly. "Y'all will need food to keep your strength up."

I left my spoon where it lay. "No," I said. "I won't."

Of course he didn't understand that. But Peg, with animal alertness, caught something in my tone. She looked at me hard, before she went back to watching Jimmy Hubbley, her sullen face transformed by awe and respect and the hopeless, longing love of an ordinary person for one clearly as far above her as a god.

III

OCTOBER 2114

The test of our progress is not whether we
add more to the abundance of those who
have much; it is whether we provide enough
for those who have too little.

**—Franklin Delano Roosevelt,
Second Inaugural Address**

Ten

The most remarkable thing about being in an off-line dump like East Oleanta was my realization that the GSEA didn't know where Miranda Sharifi was. They were a sophisticated and determined agency, but apparently they didn't know where I was either. I wasn't using any of the identities that Colin Kowalski had issued me, and I had changed personae three times on the way to East Oleanta. "Victoria Turner" had credentials with the IRS, the state of Texas, the bank where her family trust was stashed, educational software franchises, the National Health Care Institute, grocery stores . . . My larcenous friend was good at what he did. Good enough to convince Huevos Verdes . . . who knew? But I felt confident the GSEA didn't.

The second most remarkable thing was that I didn't call up the GSEA and tell them where I was and what I suspected. I put this down to hubris. I wanted to be able to say, "Here is Miranda Sharifi, lattitude 43°45′16″ longitude 74°50′86″, it's an illegal genemod lab, go get her, boys," instead of saying, "Well, I think she's here *someplace* nearby, possibly, although I have no proof." If I were a regular agent, my silence would have been intolerable. But I wasn't a regular agent. I wasn't a regular anything. And I wanted, once in my ineffectual life, to succeed at something by myself. I wanted that very badly.

Of course, like the GSEA, I didn't exactly know where Miranda was, either, although I suspected she was underground somewhere in the wooded Adirondack Mountains near East Oleanta. But I didn't have the faintest idea how to actually find her.

Until Lizzie Francy.

* * *

I went back to see Lizzie Francy the same evening I first told her about simple computer operations, the day after I'd put a medpatch on her. I'd seen how Billy Washington changed color when I'd asked about Eden. That old man was the worst liar I'd ever seen. He knew something about Eden; he was hopelessly in love with the much tougher and more conventional Annie; Lizzie could do anything with him she chose. Poor Billy.

Lizzie still sat on the spectacularly ugly plastisynth sofa, dressed in a pink nightshirt, her hair in sixteen braids tied with pink ribbon. Electronic parts lay scattered over her blanket. I viewed her around Billy, who opened the door but didn't want to let me in.

"Lizzie's asleep, her."

"No, she isn't, Billy. She's right there."

"Vicki!" Lizzie cried in her little-girl voice, and something unexpected turned over in my chest. "You're here!"

"She's sick, her, too sick for no company."

"I'm *fine*, me," Lizzie said. "Let Vicki in, Billy. Pleeeaasse?"

He did, unhappily. Annie wasn't around. I said, "What have you got there, Lizzie?"

"The apple peeler 'bot from the café kitchen," she said promptly, and without guilt. Billy winced. "It broke and I took it apart, me, to see if I can fix it."

"And can you?"

"No. Can you?" She looked at me with hungry brown eyes. Billy left the apartment.

"Probably not," I said. I'm not a 'bot tech. But let me see."

"I'll show you, me."

She did. She put together the pieces of the peeler 'bot, which had a simple standard Kellor chip powered by Y-energy. I went to school with Alison Kellor, who always professed a world-weary disdain for the electronic empire she would inherit. Lizzie assembled the 'bot in about two minutes and showed me how it wouldn't work despite an active chip. "See this little teeny bit here, Vicki? Where the peeler arm fits onto the 'bot? It's sort of melted, it."

I said, "What do you think did that?"

The big brown eyes looked at me. "I don't know, me."

"I do." The destroyed joint was duragem. *Had been* duragem, until attacked by the renegade replicating dissembler.

"What melted it, Vicki?"

I turned the 'bot over in my hands, looking for other duragem joints. They were there, between the less durable but cheaper nonmoving plastics. The others weren't "sort of melted, them." But neither were a few of the duragem parts.

"What melted it, Vicki? Vicki?" I felt a hand on my arm.

Why hadn't the other duragem joints been attacked? Because the dissembler was clocked. It had self-destructed after a certain time, and had also stopped replicating after making a certain number of copies of itself. Much—maybe even most—nanotech had this safety feature.

Lizzie shook my arm. "*What* melted it, Vicki? What?"

"A tiny little machine. Too small to see."

"The duragem dissembler? The one I saw, me, on the newsgrid?"

Then I did look up. "You watch the donkey newsgrids?"

She gave me a long, serious look. I could see this was an important decision for her: to trust me or not. Finally she said, as if it were an answer, "I'm almost twelve, me. My mama, she still thinks I'm six."

"Ah," I said. "So how does a twelve-year-old see donkey newsgrids? They're never on at the café."

"Nothing's on in the middle of the night. Some nights. I go there, me, and watch."

"You sneak out?"

She nodded solemnly, sure that this admission would bring down the world. She was right. I had never imagined a Liver kid with that much ambition or curiosity or intelligence or guts. Lizzie Francy was not supposed to exist. She was as much a wild card as the duragem dissembler, and as unwelcome. To both Livers and donkeys.

And then I saw a way to use her difference.

"Lizzie, how'd you like to make a bargain with me?"

She looked wary.

"If you tell me what I want to know, I'll help you learn as much as I can about how machines work."

Lizzie's face changed. She leapt on my words like the promising little piranha she was.

"You promised, you. Vicki, I heard you, me, and that was a promise. You say you'll help me find out everything about how machines work!"

"I said, 'as much as I can.' Not everything."

"But you *promised*, you."

"Yes, yes, I promised. But in return you have to answer all the questions *I* have."

She considered this, her head cocked to one side, the sixteen pink-tied braids all sticking out in different directions. She didn't see any major trap. "All right."

"Lizzie, have you ever heard of Eden?"

"In the Bible?"

"No. Here, near East Oleanta."

Despite our agreement, she hesitated. I said, "You promised, too."

"I heard, me, Billy and Mama talking about it. Mama said Eden don't never exist except in the Bible. Billy, he said he wasn't so sure, him. He said maybe it was a place in the mountains or the woods that donkeys don't know about, and Livers might work there, them. They thought I was asleep."

A place donkeys don't know about. Meaning, to East Oleanta, government donkeys, practically the only kind a town like this ever saw.

"Does Billy ever go off alone into the woods? Without your mama?"

"Oh, yeah, he likes it, him. Mama wouldn't never go off in the woods. She's too fat." Lizzie said this matter-of-factly; for some reason I thought suddenly of Desdemona, seizing my soda-can bracelet without guilt or evasion.

"How often does he go? How long does he stay?"

"Every couple of months, him. For five or six days. Only now he's getting too old, him, Mama says."

"Does that mean he won't go any more?"

"No, he's going next week, him. He told her he got to, unless something important breaks down and he's afraid, him, to leave us alone. But we got the food." She pointed to the pathetic piles of tasteless synthetic food rotting in buckets in the corners.

"When next week?"

"Tuesday."

Lizzie knew everything. But more to the point—what did Billy know? Did he know where Miranda Sharifi was?

"What time does Billy leave when he goes to the woods?"

"Real early in the morning. Vicki, how are you going to teach me, you, everything about machines? When do we start, us?"

"Tomorrow."

"Today."

"You're still recovering. You had pneumonia, you know. Do you know what that is?"

She shook her head. The silly pink ribbons bobbed. If this were my kid, I'd tie up her braids with microfilaments.

If this were *my* kid? Jesus.

"Pneumonia is a disease caused by bacteria, which is itself a tiny little living machine, which got destroyed in your body by another tiny living machine engineered to do that. And that's where we'll start tomorrow. If you have the right codes there are programs you can access on the hotel terminal, where people hardly ever go . . ." For the first time it occurred to me that Annie would object vigorously to this tutorial program. I might be educating Lizzie in the middle of the night.

"What codes?" Her eyes were bright and sharp as carbon-rod needles.

"I'll show you tomorrow."

"I already reprogrammed, me, the servoentrance door at the café to let me and Mama in. I can understand about the hotel terminal. Just say, you, a little bit *how* . . ."

"Good-bye, Lizzie."

"Just say how—"

"Good-bye."

As I closed the door, she was once more taking apart the peeler 'bot.

In the next six weeks, Lizzie spent all her free time at the hotel terminal, accessing education software in the vast donkey public library system. She appeared at the hotel at odd times, in the early morning with her hair wet from the baths, or at twilight, times I suspected Annie thought she was playing with her friends Carlena and Susie, a pair of dumb chirps. Lizzie disappeared just as abruptly, an outlaw running from the scene of the scholastic crime to report for dinner or for church. I don't know if she accessed in the middle of the night or not; I was, sensibly, asleep. She learned at a frightening rate, once she had something substantial to learn. I didn't control what she accessed, and I only commented when she had questions. After the first day she zeroed in on computer systems, both theory and applications.

Within a week she showed me how she'd reprogrammed a still-functional cleaning 'bot to dance, by combining, speeding up, and sequencing its normal movements. The thing jigged around my dismal hotel room as if it had a metallic seizure. Lizzie laughed so hard she fell off the bed and lay helplessly shrieking on the floor, her arms wrapped around her negligible middle, and again that unwelcome something turned over, blood warm, in my chest.

Within a month she had worked through the first two years of the American Education Association–accredited secondary school software for computer science.

After six weeks she showed me, gleefully, how she'd broken in to the Haller Corporation data banks. I peered over her shoulder, wondering if the Haller security software would trace the intrusion to East Oleanta, where there should not have existed anyone capable of data bank intrusion. Did the GSEA monitor corporate break-ins?

I was being paranoid. There must be a quarter million teenage net busters snooping around in corporate data banks just to count technological coup.

But those kids were donkeys.

"Lizzie," I said, "no more net busting. I'm sorry, honey, but it's dangerous."

She pressed her lips together, a suspicious little Annie. "Dangerous how?"

"They could trace you, come here, and arrest you. And send you to jail."

Her black eyes widened. She had some respect for authority, or at least for power. A cowardly little Annie.

"Promise," I said, relentless.

"I promise, me!"

"And I'll tell you what. Tomorrow I'll go to Albany on the gravrail"—it was working again, briefly—"and buy you a handheld computer and crystal library. It has far more on it than you can access here. You won't believe what you'll learn to do." And a free-held unit couldn't be traced. I could use the "Darla Jones" account, which the high cost of a crystal library and compatible unit would just about empty. Maybe I'd better go farther than Albany to buy it. Maybe New York.

Lizzie stared at me, for once speechless. Her pink mouth made a little "O." Then she was hugging me, smelling of warehouse distrib soap, her voice muffled against my neck.

"Vicki . . . a crystal library . . . oh, Vicki . . ."

For you. I didn't say more. I couldn't.

Anthony, who came before Russell and after Paul, once told me that there was no such thing as a maternal instinct, nor a paternal one either. It was all intellectual propaganda designed to urge humans toward a responsibility they didn't really want, but couldn't admit not wanting. It was a PR tour de force without genuine biological force.

I used to love some very stupid men.

Three days after I brought Lizzie her crystal library, I was up by 4:00 A.M., ready to follow Billy yet again into the deep woods.

This was my third trip in six weeks. Lizzie kept me informed, per our bargain, of Billy's plans. She told me he used to go every few months, but now he went far more often. Maybe he had even made a few short trips Lizzie and I missed. Something was stepping up his scouting schedule, and I hoped it would lead me to "Eden," careful hints about which were increasing on the local Liver channels. Broadcast from where? By whom? I'd bet anything they weren't part of the regularly organized broadcasting from Albany.

This morning it was snowing in a desultory, nonserious way, even though it was only mid-October. In San Francisco, I hadn't paid much attention to the "coming mini-ice age" stuff. In the Adirondacks, however, there wasn't much choice. Everyone went around bundled in winter jacks, which were surprisingly warm, although no more tastefully dyed than summer jacks. Marigold, crimson, electric blue, poison green. And for the conservative, a dun the color of cow piles.

Which was what Billy wore when he emerged from his apartment building at 4:45 A.M. He carried a plasticloth sack. It was still dark out. He walked toward the river, which flowed by the edge of the village, only five or six blocks from what passed as downtown. I followed him unseen while there were buildings for cover. When there weren't, I let him get out of sight and then followed his footprints in the light snow. After a mile the footsteps stopped.

I stood under a pine whose branches started ten feet up the trunk, pondering my choices. From behind me Billy said quietly, "You ain't gotten any better, you, in the woods. Not since your first time."

I turned. "How did you do that?"

"Don't matter how *I* did it, me. The question is what *you* think you're doing here."

"Following you. Again."

"Why?"

He had never asked before. The other times I'd followed him, he'd refused to talk to me at all. He looked unusually impressive, standing there in the bleak landscape with his wrinkled face stern and judgmental: a Liver Moses. I said, "Billy, where is Eden?"

"That what you after, you? I don't know where it is, me, and if I did I wouldn't take you there."

This was promising; when someone has reasons not to do something, he has at least conceived that it's possible to do it. From possibility to agreement isn't nearly as large a leap as from denial to possibility. "Why not?"

"Why not what?"

"Why wouldn't you take me to Eden if you knew where it was?"

"Because it ain't no donkey place, it."

"Is it a Liver place?"

But he seemed to realize he'd said too much. Deliberately he put down his sack, brushed the snow off a fallen tree, and sat down with the air of a man who wasn't going to move until I left. I would have to prod him by offering more.

"It's not a Liver place, either, is it, Billy? It's a Sleepless place. You've seen a SuperSleepless from Huevos Verdes, or more than one, in these woods. They have larger heads than normal, and they talk like they're slowing down their speech, because they are. They think so much faster and more complexly than we do—you or me—that it's an effort for them to choose a few simple-enough words for us to understand. You saw one, didn't you, Billy? A man or a woman?"

He stared at me, a wrinkled somber face against the gray and white woods.

"When was this, Billy? In the summer? Or longer ago than that?"

He said, with transparent effort and equally transparent mendacity, "I never saw nobody, me."

I walked toward him and put my hand firmly on his shoulder. "Yes, you did, you. When was it?"

He stared at the snowy ground, angry but unwilling, or unable, to show it.

"Okay, Billy," I sighed. "If you won't tell me, you won't. And you're right—I can't follow you unseen through the woods because I don't know what I'm doing. And I'm already cold."

Still he said nothing. I trudged back to town. Lizzie's computer and crystal library wasn't all that Darla Jones had bought in New York. The homing device I'd stuck on the back of his plastisynth jacket, behind the shoulder and below the neck where he wouldn't see it until he removed the jacket, registered as a motionless dot on my handheld monitor. It stayed a motionless dot for over an hour. Wasn't he cold?

Russell, who came before David and after Anthony, had a theory about body temperature. He said that we donkeys, who are used to having instant adjustments in anything that happens to distress us, have lost the ability to ignore slight fluctuations in body temperatures. Constant environmental pampering had softened us. Russell saw this as a positive, because it made very easy identification of the successful and the genetically highly tuned (who naturally were one and the same). Watch a person pull on a sweater for a one-degree temperature drop and you know you're looking at a superior person. I lacked the strength of will to avoid responding to this. Sort of a Princess and the Centigrade Pea, I said, but whimsey was wasted on Russell. We parted shortly afterwards when I accused him of inventing even more artificial social gradations than the ridiculous number that already existed, and he accused me of being jealous of his superior genemod leftbrain logic. The last I heard, he was running for congressional representative from San Diego, which has possibly the most monotonous climate in the country.

Maybe Billy Washington made a fire; the monitor wouldn't show that. After an hour, as I sat in warmth in my East Oleanta hotel room, the Billy-dot moved. He walked several more miles over the course of the day, in easy stages, in various directions.

A man looking for something. At no point did the dot disappear, which would have meant he'd disappeared behind a Y-energy security shield. The same thing happened for three more days and nights. Then he came home.

Incredibly, he didn't confront me about the homer. Either he never found it, even after he took his jacket off (hard to believe), or he did but had no idea what it was and decided not to wonder. Or—and this only occurred to me later—he saw it but thought someone else had put it there, maybe while he was sleeping, and wanted it left alone. Someone out in the woods. Someone he wanted to please.

Or maybe that wasn't it at all. What did I know about how a Liver thought? What, in fact, did I know about how anybody thought? Would somebody who had the ability to discern that knowledge on short acquaintance have actually spent eighteen months with Russell?

Two days after Billy's return from the woods, Annie said, "The gravrail's broke again, it." She didn't say it to me. I sat in her apartment, visiting Lizzie, but Annie had yet to acknowledge directly that I was there. She didn't look at my face, she didn't speak to me, she maneuvered her considerable bulk around the space I occupied as if it were an inexplicable and inconvenient black hole. Probably Billy had let me in only because I'd brought a double armful of food and warehouse goods, obtained on "Victoria Turner's" chip, to contribute to the growing stockpiles along the walls. The place smelled vaguely like a landfill where the waste-eating microorganisms had fallen behind.

"Where's it at?" Billy said. He meant the actual train, sitting somewhere along its magnetic track.

"Right here," Annie said. "About a quarter mile outside town, that's what Celie Kane said, her. Some of them are mad enough to burn it."

Lizzie looked up with interest from the handheld terminal with her precious crystal library. I hadn't witnessed Annie's reaction to my gift, but Lizzie had told me about it. The only reason Lizzie still owned the thing was that she'd threatened to run away on a gravrail otherwise. She was twelve, she'd told her mother—a lot of kids left home at twelve. I suppose Liver kids did, coming and going with their portable meal chips. That was when Annie had stopped speaking to me.

Lizzie said, "Can trains burn, them?"

"No," Billy said shortly. "And it's against the law to do hurt to them anyway."

Lizzie digested this. "But if nobody can't come, them, from Albany on the train to punish people who break the law—"

"They can come, them, on a plane, can't they?" Annie snapped. "Don't you be thinking about breaking no laws, young lady!"

"I ain't thinking about it, me. Celie Kane is," Lizzie said reasonably. "Besides, ain't nobody going to come, them, to East Oleanta on a plane anymore from Albany. All those donkeys got bigger problems than us, them."

"Out of the mouths of babes," I said, but naturally no one answered.

Outside, in the hall, someone shouted. Feet ran past our door, came back, pounded once. Billy and Annie looked at each other. Then Billy opened the door a crack and stuck his head out. "What's wrong?"

"The warehouse ain't opened again, it! Second week in a row! We're going smash that fucking building—I need another blanket and some boots, me!"

"Oh," Billy said, and shut the door.

"Billy," I said carefully, "who else knows you have food and warehouse goods hoarded here?"

"Nobody but us four," he said, not meeting my eyes. He was ashamed.

"Don't tell anyone. No matter how much they say they need this stuff."

Billy looked helplessly at Annie. I knew he was on my side. East Oleanta, I had discovered, had a healthy barter economy existing side-by-side with the official donkey one. Skinned rabbits, good roasted over an open fire, were traded for spectacularly hideous handmade wall hangings or embroidered jacks. Nuts for toys, sunshine for food. Services, everything from babysitting to sex, for music decks or homemade wooden furniture from trees in the forest. I could see Billy trading some of our stockpiled stuff, but not risking it all by letting anyone know we had it. Not when there was a chance Lizzie might need it.

Annie was another story. She would die for Lizzie, but she

had in her the sharing and fairness and unthinking conformity that create a sense of community.

I stretched. "I think I'll go witness the liberation of the District Supervisor Aaron Simon Samuelson Goods Distribution Center."

Annie gave a sour look without actually looking at me. Billy, who knew that I was equipped with both a personal shield and stun weaponry, nonetheless said unhappily, "Be careful." Lizzie jumped up. "I'm going too, me!"

"You shut up, child! You ain't going no place, you, that dangerous!" Annie, of course. The broken gravrail temporarily invalidated Lizzie's leverage: her threat to leave.

Lizzie pressed her lips together so tightly they all but disappeared. I had never seen her do that before. She was still Annie's child. "I am too going, me."

"No, you're not," I said. "It's too dangerous. I'll tell you what happens." Lizzie subsided, grumbling.

Annie was not grateful.

A small crowd, twenty or so, battered on the foamcast door of the warehouse, using a sofa as battering ram. I knew this was hopeless; if the Bastille had been made of foamcast, Marie Antoinette would have gone on needing wigs. I lounged across the street, leaning against a turquoise apartment building, and watched.

The door gave way.

Twenty people gave a collective shout and rushed inside. Then twenty people gave another shout, this one furious. I examined the door hinges. They had been duragem, taken apart atom by atom by dissemblers.

"There's nothing in here!"

"They cheated us, them!"

"Fucking bastards—"

I peered inside. The first small room held a counter and terminal. A second door led to the depository, which was lined with empty shelves, empty bins, empty overhead hooks where jacks and vases and music chips and chairs and cleaning 'bots and hand tools should go. I felt a chill prickle over me from neck to groin, an actual frisson complexly made of fear and fascination. It was true then. The economy, the political structure, the duragem crisis, were acutally this bad. For the first time in over a hundred years, since Kenzo Yagai invented cheap energy and remade the world, there really was not enough to go around. The politicians were conserving production for the cities, where larger numbers of voters resided, and writing off less populous or less easily reached areas with fewer votes. East Oleanta had been written off.

No one was going to come to fix the gravrail.

The crowd howled and cursed: "Fucking donkeys! Fuck them all, us!" I heard the sound of shelves ripping from the walls; maybe they'd had duragem bolts.

I walked rapidly but calmly back outside. Twenty people is enough to be a mob. A stun gun only fires in one direction at a time, and a personal shield, although unbreachable, does not prevent its wearer from being held in one place without food or water.

The hotel or Annie's? Whichever I chose, I might be there semipermanently.

The hotel had a networked terminal I could use to call for help, if I chose my moment well. Annie's apartment was on the edge of town, which suddenly seemed safer than dead center. It also had food, doors whose hinges were not duragem, and an owner already hostile to me. And Lizzie.

I walked quickly to Annie's.

Halfway there, Billy rounded the corner of a building, carrying a baseball bat. "Quick, doctor! Come this way, you!"

I stopped cold. All my fear, which had been a kind of heightened excitement, vanished. "You came to protect *me?*"

"This way!" He was breathing hard, and his old legs trembled. I put a hand on his elbow to steady him.

"Billy . . . lean against this wall. You came to protect *me?*"

He grabbed my hand and pulled me down an alley, the same one the stomps used for creative loitering when the weather had been warm. I heard it, then—the shouts from the opposite end of the street from the warehouse. More angry people, screaming about donkey politicians.

Billy led me through the alley, behind a few buildings, on our hands and knees through what seemed to be a mini-junkyard of scrapped scooters, chunks of plastisynth, mattresses, and other large unlovely discards. At the back of the café he did something to the servoentrance used by delivery 'bots; it opened. We crawled into the automated kitchen, which was busily preparing soysynth to look like everything else.

"How—"

"Lizzie," he gasped, "before she even . . . learned nothing . . . from you," and even through his incipient heart attack I
heard his pride. He slid down the wall and concentrated on breathing more slowly. His hectic color subsided.

I looked around. In one corner was a second, smaller stockpile
of food, blankets, and necessities. My eyes prickled.

"Billy . . ."

He was still catching his breath. "Don't nobody know . . . about
this, so they won't think, them . . . to look for you here."

Whereas they might have in Annie's apartment. People had
seen me with Lizzie. He wasn't protecting me; he was protecting
Lizzie from being associated with me.

I said, "Will the whole town go Bastille now?"

"Huh?"

I said, "Will the whole town riot and smash things and look
for somebody to blame and hurt?"

He seemed astounded by the idea. "Everybody? No, of course
not, them. What you hear now is just the hotheads that don't never
know, them, how to act when something's different. They'll calm
down, them. And the good people like Jack Sawicki, he'll get them
organized to seeing about getting useful things done."

"Like what?"

"Oh," he waved a hand vaguely. His breathing was almost
normal again. "Putting by blankets for anybody who really needs
one. Sharing stuff that ain't going to be coming in. We had a
shipment of soysynth, us, just last week—the kitchen won't run
out for a while, though there won't be no extras. Jack will make
sure, him, that people know that."

Unless the kitchen broke, of course. Neither of us said it.

I said quietly, "Billy, will they look for me at Annie's?"

He looked at the opposite wall. "Might."

"They'll see the stockpiled stuff."

"Most of it's here. What you saw is mostly empty buckets,
them. Annie, she's putting them in the recycler now."

I digested this. "You didn't trust me to know about this place.
You were hoping I'd leave before I had to know."

He went on staring at the wall. Conveyer belts carried bowls
of soysynth "soup" toward the flash heater. I looked again at the
stockpile; it was smaller than I'd thought at first. And if the kitchen
did break, then of course it would be only a matter of time before

the homegrown mob remembered the untreated soysynth that must be behind their foodbelt somewhere. Billy must have other piles. In the woods? Maybe.

"Will anybody bother you or Annie or Lizzie because I used to be with you, even if I'm not now?"

He shook his head. "Folks ain't like that."

I doubted this. "Wouldn't it be better to bring Lizzie here?"

His furrowed face turned stubborn. "Only if I have to, me. Better I bring food and stuff out."

"At least make her hide that terminal and crystal library I gave her."

He nodded and stood. His knees weren't trembling anymore. He picked up his baseball bat and I hugged him, a long hard hug that surprised him so much he actually staggered. Or maybe I pushed him slightly.

"Thank you, Billy."

"You're welcome, Doctor Turner."

He gave me the code to the servoentrance door, then crawled cautiously out. I made a blanket nest on the floor and sat in it. From my jacks I pulled out the handheld monitor. The homer I'd fastened firmly inside his deepest pocket when he staggered off balance showed Billy walking back to Annie's. He wouldn't go anywhere else today, maybe for several days. When he did, I wanted to know about it.

Rex, who came before Paul and after Eugene, once told me something interesting about organizations. There are essentially only two types in the entire world, Rex had said. When people in the first type of organization either don't follow the organization's rules or otherwise become too great a pain in the ass, they can be kicked out. After that they cease to be part of the organization. These organizations include sports teams, corporations, private schools, country clubs, religions, cooperative enclaves, marriages, and the Stock Exchange.

But when people in the second type of organization don't follow the rules, they can't be kicked out because there isn't any place to send them. No matter how useless or aggravating or dangerous are the unwanted members, the organization is stuck with them. These organizations include maximum-security prisons, families with impossible nine-year-olds, nursing homes for the terminally ill, and countries.

Had I just seen my country kick out an unwanted and aggravating town of voters who had been following the rules?

Most donkeys were not cruel. But desperate people—and most especially desperate politicians—had been known to act in ways they might not usually act.

I settled my back against the wall and watched the automated kitchen turn soysynth into chocolate chip cookies.

Eleven

T he day after East Oleanta wrecked the warehouse, them, food started coming in by air.

Like I told Dr. Turner, it wasn't all of us in East Oleanta. Only some stomps, plus the people like Celie Kane who was always angry anyway, plus a few good people who just couldn't take it no more, them, and went temporary crazy. They all calmed down when the plane started coming every day, without no warehouse goods but with plenty of food. The tech who ran the delivery 'bots smiled wide, her, and said, "Compliments of Congresswoman Janet Carol Land." But she had three security 'bots with her, and a bluish shimmer that Dr. Turner said was a military-strength personal shield.

Dr. Turner moved, her, out of the space behind the kitchen just an hour before the delivery 'bots started marching in. She just barely didn't get caught, her. "All of Rome meets in the Forum," she said, which didn't make no sense. She moved back to the State Representative Anita Clara Taguchi Hotel.

Then the women's shower in the baths broke. A security 'bot broke. The streetlights broke, or something that controlled the streetlights. We got a cold stretch of Arctic air, and the snow wouldn't stop, it.

"Damn snow," Jack Sawicki grumbled every time I saw him. The same words, them, every time, like the snow was the problem. Jack had lost weight. I think he didn't like being mayor no more.

"It's the donkeys doing it to us," Celie Kane shrilled. "They're using the fucking weather, them, to kill us all!"

"Now, Celie," her father said, reasonable, "can't nobody control the weather."

"How do *you* know what they can do, them? You're just a dumb old man!" And Doug Kane went back to eating his soup, staring at the holoterminal show of a Lucid Dreamer concert.

At home, Lizzie said to me, "You know, Billy, Mr. Kane is right. Nobody *can* control the weather. It's a chaotic system."

I didn't know what that meant. Lizzie said a lot of things I didn't know, me, since she'd been doing software every day with Dr. Turner. She could even talk like a donkey now. But not around her mother. Lizzie was too smart, her, for that. I heard her say to Annie, "Nobody can't control the weather, them." And Annie, counting sticky buns and soyburgers rotting in a corner of the apartment, nodded without listening and said, "Bed time. Lizzie."

"But I'm in the middle of—"

"*Bed time.*"

In the middle of the night somebody pounded on the apartment door.

"B-B-Billy! Annie! L-L-Let me in!"

I sat up on the sofa where I slept, me. For a minute I thought I was dreaming. The room was dark as death.

"L-Let m-m-me in!"

Dr. Turner. I stumbled, me, off the sofa. The bedroom door opened and Annie came out in her white nightdress, Lizzie stuck behind her like a tail wind.

"Don't you open that door, Billy Washington," Annie said. "Don't you open it, you!"

"It's Dr. Turner," I said. I couldn't stand up straight, me, so fuddled with dreaming. I staggered and grabbed the corner of the sofa. "She don't mean no harm, her."

"Nobody comes in here! We won't understand none of it, us!"

Then I saw she was fuddled with dreaming, too. I opened the door.

Dr. Turner stumbled in, her, carrying a suitcase but wearing a nightdress, covered with snow. Her beautiful donkey face was white and her teeth chattered. "L-L-Lock the d-door!"

Annie demanded, "You got people hunting you, them?"

"No. N-N-No . . . j-just let me g-g-get warm . . ."

It hit me then. From the hotel to our apartment wasn't all that far, even if it was freezing out. Dr. Turner shouldn't be that cold, her. I grabbed her shoulders. "What happened at the hotel, doctor?"

"H-H-Heating unit qu-quit."

"Heating unit can't quit, it," I said. I sounded like Doug Kane trying to talk to Celie. "It's Y-energy."

"N-N-Not the circulating equipment. It m-m-must have dura-gem p-parts." She stood by our unit, rubbing her hands together, her face still the same white-gray as all the snow piled in the streets.

Lizzie said suddenly, "I hear screaming!"

"Th-they're b-burning the hotel."

"*Burning* it?" Annie said. "Foamcast don't burn!"

Dr. Turner smiled, her, one of those twisted donkey smiles that said Livers just now caught on to what donkeys already knew. "They're trying anyway. I told them it won't eradicate the duragem dissembler, and somebody will likely get hurt."

"*You* told 'em," Annie said, one hand on her wide hip. "And then you come here, you, with a *mob* following you—"

"No one's following me. They're far too busy trying to contravene the laws of physics. And Annie, I'm freezing. Where else would I go? The tech reprogrammed the entrance codes for the kitchen, and anyway it's still full of delivery 'bots whenever that unpredictable plane comes."

Annie looked at her, and she looked at Annie, and I could see, me, that there was something wrong with Dr. Turner's speech. It wasn't no plea for help, even if the words said that. And it wasn't trying to sound reasonable, either. Dr. Turner really was asking *Where else would I go? Can you tell me some other place I ain't mentioned?* Only it wasn't Annie she was asking, her. It was me.

And I wasn't about to tell her, me, that finally I knew. After all my looking, I knew where Eden was.

"You can stay here with us," Lizzie said, and her big brown eyes looked at her mother. I felt my back muscles knot, them. This was it, the big Armaggedon between Annie and Dr. Turner. Only it wasn't. Not yet. Maybe because Annie was afraid, her, of whose side Lizzie would take.

"All right," Annie said, "but only because I can't stand, me, to see nobody freeze to death, or get tore apart by them damn stomps. But I don't like it, me."

Like anybody ever thought she did. I was careful, me, not to meet nobody's eyes.

Annie gave Dr. Turner a few blankets off the stockpile along the west wall. We had everything there, us, crowding out the space: blankets and jacks and chairs and ribbons and rotting food and I don't know what else. I wondered, me, if I should give Dr. Turner the sofa, but she spread her blankets in a nest on the floor, her, and I figured that she might be company but she was also thirty years younger than me. Or twenty, or forty—with donkeys you can't never really tell.

We all got back to sleep, us, somehow, but the shouts outside went on a long time. And in the morning the State Representative Anita Clara Taguchi Hotel was wrecked. Still standing, because Dr. Turner was right and foamcast don't burn, but the doors and windows were tore off the hinges, and the furniture was all broke up, and even the terminal was a twisted pile of junk in the street. Jack Sawicki looked serious, him, about that. Now all he had to talk to Albany on was the café terminal. Besides, them things are expensive. State Representative Taguchi was going to be mad as hell, her.

Snow blew in the hotel windows and drifted on the floor, and you'd of thought the place had been deserted for years, the way it looked. It kind of twisted my chest to see it. We were losing more and more, us.

That afternoon the plane didn't come, it, and by dinner the next day the café was out of food.

There's a place upriver, about a half mile from town, where deer go, them. When we had a warden 'bot, it put out pellets for the deer in the winter. The pellets had some kind of drug inside, so the deer couldn't never breed, them, more than the woods can feed. The warden wasn't never replaced, it, since before them rabid raccoons in the summer. But the deer still come to the clearing. They just do what they always did, them, because they don't know no better.

Or maybe they do, them. Here the river flowed fast enough that it didn't freeze completely through unless the temperature got down in the single numbers. The snow blew across the clearing, it, and piled up against the wooded hill beyond, so plants were easy to uncover. You could usually spot two or three deer without waiting very long.

When I went there, me, with Doug Kane's old rifle, somebody else had already got there first. The snow was bloody and a mangled carcass laid by the creek. Most of the meat was spoiled, it, by somebody too lazy or too stupid to butcher it right. Bastards didn't even bother to drag the carcass away from the water.

I walked, me, a little ways more. It was snowing, but not hard. The ground crunched under my feet and my breath smoked. My back hurt and my knees ached and I didn't even try, me, to walk without any noise. "Don't go alone, you," Annie'd said, but I didn't want Annie to leave Lizzie by herself. And I sure as hell wasn't going to take Dr. Turner. She'd moved in with us, her, and that was probably good because donkeys got all kinds of things you don't never suspect until you need them, like medicine for Lizzie last summer. But Dr. Turner was a city woman, her, and she scared away the game, crashing through the brush like an elephant or dragon or one of them other old-time monsters. I needed to kill something today. We needed the meat, us.

In a week, all out stockpiled food had gotten eaten up. One lousy week.

No more came, by rail or air or gravsled, from Albany. People tore into the café, them, to the kitchen where Annie used to cook apple pudding for the foodbelt, but there wasn't nothing left there.

I walked farther upstream. When I was a young boy, me, I used to love being in the woods in winter. But then I wasn't scared out of my skull. Then I wasn't an old fool with a back that hurts and who can't see nothing in his mind but Lizzie's big dark eyes looking hungry. I can't stand that, me. Never.

Lizzie. Hungry . . .

When I left town, the rifle under my coat, people were hurrying to the café. Something was going on, I didn't know what. I didn't want to know. I just wanted, me, to keep Lizzie from going hungry.

I could only think, me, of two ways to do that. One was to hunt for food in the woods. The other was to take Lizzie and Annie to Eden. I'd found it, me, just before the gravrail quit this last time. I found that big-headed girl in the woods, and I followed her, me, and she let me follow her. I watched a door in the mountain open up, where there couldn't be no door, and her go inside, and the door close up again like it was never there in the first place. But just before it closed, the Sleepless girl turned, her, right toward me. "Don't bring anyone else here, Mr. Washington, unless you absolutely must. We're not quite ready for you yet."

Those were the scariest words, me, I ever heard.

Ready for us for *what?*

But I'd bring Lizzie and Annie there if I had to, me. If they got too hungry. If there wasn't no other way for me to feed them.

I came to a place where dogtooth violets used to grow, them, back in June. I dropped to my knees. They sang out in pain, them, but I didn't care. I dug up all the dogtooth violet bulbs I could find and stuffed them into my pockets. You can roast them. My jacks already held acorns, to pound into flour—wearying work, it—and some hickory twigs to boil for salt.

Then I settled down, me, on a rock, to wait. I held as quiet as I could. My knees hurt like hell. I waited, me.

A snowshoe rabbit came out of the brush, him, on the opposite bank, like he was right at home. Casual, easy. A rabbit ain't much food to use up a bullet. But I was cold enough, me, so I knew I'd start shivering soon, and then I wouldn't never be able to hit nothing.

Bullet or rabbit? Old fool, make up your mind.

I saw Lizzie's hungry eyes.

Slowly, slowly, I raised the gun, me, and squeezed off the shot. The rabbit never heard it. He flew up in the air and come down again, clean. I waded across the creek and got him.

One good thing—he fit under my coat, him. A deer wouldn't of fit. I didn't want nobody hungry to see my rabbit, and I didn't want to stay around, me, near where the gun fired. An old man is just too easy to take things away from.

But nobody tried, until Dr. Turner.

"You're going to *skin it?*" she said, her voice going up at the end. I could of laughed, me, at the look on her face, if anything could of been funny.

"You want to eat it, you, with the skin on?"

She didn't say nothing, her. Annie snorted. Lizzie put down her terminal and edged in close to watch.

Annie said, "How we going to cook it, Billy? The Y-unit don't get hot enough for that."

"I'll cook it. Tonight, by the river. I can make an almost smoke-less fire, me. And I'll roast the violet bulbs in the coals." It made me feel good to see how Annie looked at me then.

Lizzie said, "But if you—where are you going, Vicki?"

"To the café."

I looked up. Blood smeared my hands. It felt good. "Why you going there, Doctor? It ain't safe for you." The stomps still gather at the café, them. The foodbelt's empty but the HT works.

She laughed. "Oh, don't worry about me, Billy. Nobody bothers me. But there's something going on down there, and I want to know what."

"Hunger's what," Annie said. "And it don't look any different at the café than it does here. Can't you leave those poor people alone, you?"

"I'm one of those 'poor people,' as you put it," Dr. Turner said, still smiling without nothing being funny. "I'm just as hungry as they are, Annie. Or you are. And I'm going to the café."

"Huh," Annie snorted. She didn't believe, her, that Dr. Turner wasn't eating some donkey food somehow, and nobody could convince her any different. With Annie, you never can.

I finished skinning the rabbit, me, and showed Annie and Lizzie how to pound the acorns into flour. You have to cook a bit of ash with it, to take away the bite. It was late afternoon, already dark. I wrapped the rabbit meat in a pair of summer jacks, which pretty much kept the smell inside unless you were a dog. I put a small Y-lighter in my pocket, and set out for the river, me, to make a fire.

Only I didn't go to the river.

More and more people were walking to the café. Not just stomps, but regular people. In the winter dark they hurried, them, hunched over but fast, like something was chasing every last one of them. Well, something was chasing me, too. I sniffed hard to make sure nobody really couldn't smell the fresh rabbit meat, and then I walked into the café.

Everybody was watching the Lucid Dreamer concert, "The Warrior."

I had the feeling that people'd been watching all day, them. More and more, coming and going but even the goers coming back for more. I guess, me, that if your belly's empty, it helps to have your mind feel good. The concert was just ending when I come in, and people were rubbing their eyes and crying and looking dazed, like you do after lucid dreaming. But I saw right away that Dr. Turner was right, her. Something else was going on here.

Jack Sawicki stepped in front of the holoterminal and turned it off. The Lucid Dreamer, in his powerchair, with that smile that always feels like warm sunlight, disappeared.

"People of East Oleanta," Jack said, and stopped. He must of realized, him, that he sounded like some donkey politician. "Listen, everybody. We're in a river of shit here. But can do things, us, to help ourselves!"

"Like what?" somebody said, but it wasn't nasty. He really wanted to know. I tried to see, me, who it was, but the crowd was too packed in.

"The food's gone," Jack said. "The gravrail don't work. Nobody in Albany answers, them, on the official terminal. But we got *us*. It's what—eight miles?—to Coganville. Maybe they got food, them. They're on a spur of the gravrail franchise, plus they're a state line, so they got two chances for trains to be running, them. Or maybe their congressman or supervisor or somebody arranged for food to come in by air, like ours, only it didn't stop. They're in a different congressional district. We don't *know*, us. But we could walk there, some of us, and see. We could get help."

"Eight miles over mountains in winter?" Celie Kane yelled. "You're as crazy as I always thought, Jack Sawicki! We got a crazy man, us, for a mayor!"

But nobody yelled along with Celie. I stepped up onto a chair, me, along the back wall, just to see this more clearly. The feeling you get after a Lucid Dreamer concert still filled them. Or maybe not. Maybe the concert had got down *inside* them, from watching it so much. Anyway, they weren't raging, them, about the donkey politicians that got them into this mess, except for Celie and a few like her. There's always them people. But most of the faces I could see, me, looked thoughtful, and people talked in low voices. Something moved inside my belly that I didn't never know was there.

"I'll go, me," Jack said. "We can follow the gravrail line."

"It'll be drifted in bad," Paulie Cenverno said. "No trains for two weeks to blast the snow loose."

"Take a Y-unit," a woman's voice said suddenly. "Turn it on high, it, and melt what you can!"

"I'll go, me," Jim Swikehardt said.

"If you make a travois, you," Krystal Mandor called, "you can bring back more food."

"If they got food, them, we could set up a regular schedule—"

People started to argue, them, but not to fight. Ten men walked up near Jack, plus Judy Farrell, who's six foot high, her, and can beat Jack arm-wrestling.

I climbed down off my chair, me. One knee creaked. I shoved my way through the crowd and stood next to Jack. "Me, too, Jack. I'm going."

Somebody laughed, hard and nasty. It wasn't Celie. But then they stopped, all at once.

"Billy . . ." Jack said, his voice kind. But I didn't let him finish. I spoke real low and fast, me, so nobody could hear but Jack and, standing next to him, Ben Radisson.

"You going to stop me, Jack? If you men go, you going to stop me from walking along behind you? You going to knock me down, you, so's I can't follow? Lizzie's hungry. Annie don't have nobody else but me. If there ain't enough food brought back from Coganville, you telling me Lizzie and Annie, them, are going to get a fair share? With Dr. Turner staying with us?"

Jack didn't say nothing. Ben Radisson nodded, him, real slow, looking right at me. He's a good man. That's why I let him hear.

The rabbit meat squished against my chest, inside my coat. Nobody could smell it. Nobody could see the bulge, them, because it was after all just a small piece of meat, a measly rabbit, pathetic as dirt. Lizzie was hungry. Annie was a big woman. I was going, me, to Coganville.

But I wasn't going to tell Annie. She'd kill me, her, before I even got the chance to save her.

We started out, us, at first light, twelve people. More might scare the people of Coganville. We didn't want, us, what they needed for themselves. Just the extra.

No, that ain't true. We wanted, us, whatever we needed.

I got up from the sofa too quiet to wake Annie or Lizzie in the bedrooms. But Dr. Turner, on her pile of blankets in the corner, she heard me, damn her. A man can't never have no privacy from donkeys.

"What is it, Billy? Where are you going?" she whispered.

"Not to no Eden," I said. "Lay back down, damn it, and leave me alone."

"They're going to another town for food, aren't they?"

I remembered, me, that she'd said last night she was going down to the café. But I didn't see her there, me. But they know things, donkeys. Somehow. You never know how much they know.

"Listen, Billy," she said, real careful, but then she stopped like she didn't know what I should listen to. I pulled on three pairs of socks before she got it.

"There's a novel, written a long time ago—"

"A what?" I said, and then cursed myself, me. I shouldn't never ask her nothing, me. She can out-talk me every time.

"A story. About a small worldful of people who believed in sharing everything in common. Until a famine struck, and people on a broken train needed food from the nearby town. The passengers hadn't eaten in two days. But the townspeople didn't have much food themselves, and what they did have they wouldn't share." The whisper in the dark room was flat, her.

I couldn't help asking, me. I like stories. "What happened to the people on the gravrail?"

"The gravrail got fixed in the nick of time."

"Lucky them," I said. Wasn't nobody going to fix *our* gravrail or café kitchen. Not this time. Dr. Turner knew that, her.

"It was a fairy tale, Billy. Brave and inspiring and sweet, but a fairy tale. You're in a real United States. So take this with you."

She didn't say not to go, her. Instead she gave me a little black box that she pushed onto my belt and it stuck there. I got a funny flutter in my chest, me. I knew what it was, even though I never wore one before, me, and never expected to. It was a personal energy shield.

"Touch it *here*," Dr. Turner said, "to activate. And the same place to deactivate. It'll withstand damn near any attack that isn't nuclear."

Turned on, it didn't feel like nothing. Just a little tingle, and that might have been my imagination. But I could see a faint shimmer around me.

"But, Billy, don't lose it," Dr. Turner said. "I need it. I might need it badly."

"Then why you giving it to me, you?" I flashed at her, but I already knew, me. It was because of Lizzie. Everything was because of Lizzie. Just like it should be.

Anyway, Dr. Turner probably had another one, her. Donkeys

don't give away nothing unless they already got another one for themselves.

"Thank you," I said, rougher than I meant, me, but she didn't seem to mind.

The morning was cold and clear, with that kind of pink and gold sunrise that turns clean snow to glory. There wasn't no wind, thank God. Wind would of bit deep. We tramped, us, along the gravrail track to Coganville. Nobody talked much, them. Once Jim Swikehardt said, "Pretty," about the sunrise, but nobody answered.

At first the snow wasn't too deep because the woods crowding the tracks on either side held the snow from blowing. Later it did get deep. Stan Mendoza and Bob Gleason carried Y-energy units, them, that they'd ripped out of some building, and they aimed them at the worst places and melted the snow. The units were heavy, them, and the men puffed hard. It was slow going, part uphill, but we did it. I walked last, me.

After two miles my heart pounded and my knees ached. I didn't say nothing, me, to the others. I was doing this for Lizzie.

About noon clouds blew in and a wind started. I lost track, me, of how far we might of come. The wind blew straight at our faces. Stan and Bob turned the heating units around, them, whenever they could, and then we walked in warmer air that the wind whipped away as fast as it could.

I got to thinking, me, stumbling through the snow. "Why couldn't . . . couldn't . . ."

"You need to rest, Billy?" Jack said. I could see tiny ice crystals on his nose hairs. "This too much for you?"

"No, I'm fine," I said, never mind that it was a lie. But I had to say, me, what I started. "Why couldn't . . . the donkeys make lots of . . . lots of little heat units for us all to . . . c-carry—"

"Easy, Billy."

"—c-carry around in our gloves and b-boots and jackets . . . in the winter? If Y-energy is really so . . . cheap?"

Nobody answered, them. We came to a big drift, and they turned the heat units on it. It melted real slow. Finally we just slogged, us, through what was left, snow to the waist, wetter and more sticky than it would of been if we hadn't tried to melt it. Jack stumbled, him. Stan pulled him up. Judy Farrell turned her back to the wind to get a moment's rest, and her cheeks were the red-white that is going to hurt like hell when it finally warms up.

Finally Jim Swikehardt said, real low, "Because we never *asked*, us, for lots of tiny heaters, and they only give us enough of what we ask for to keep our votes." After that nobody said nothing.

I don't know, me, what time it was when we got to Coganville. The sun was completely hid behind clouds. It wasn't twilight yet. The town was quiet and peaceful, it, with nobody in the streets. Lights blazed in all the windows. We walked, us, up the main street to the Congressman Joseph Nicholls Capiello Café, and we could hear music. A holosign flashed blue and purple on the roof: THANK YOU FOR ELECTING DISTRICT SUPERVISOR HELEN ROSE TOWNS-END! It was like the world here was still normal, and only us was wrong.

But I didn't believe that no more, me.

We went in to the café. It must of been too late for lunch, too early for dinner, but the café was full of people. They were hanging plastisynth banners and bows, them, for a scooter race betting night. Tables were pushed around to make booths and a dance floor. The smell of food from the belt hit us all the same time the warmth did, and I swear I saw tears, me, in Stan Mendoza's eyes.

Everybody got real quiet, them, when we came in.

Jack said, "Who's the mayor here?"

"I am," a woman said. "Jeanette Harloff." She was about fifty, her, skinny, with silver hair and big blue eyes. The kind of Liver who gets kidded about having secret genemods, even though you know she don't. It's just something people say, them. People can be damn stupid. But maybe that's why this woman was mayor, her. Nobody wouldn't just let her be one thing or the other.

Jack explained, him, who we were and what we wanted. Everybody in the café listened. Somebody had turned the holoterminal off. You could of heard a mouse walk.

Jeanette Harloff studied us, her, real careful. The big blue eyes looked cold. But finally she said, "The main gravrail's busted, it, but we got a spur and it works. There's another kitchen shipment coming in tomorrow. And our congressman can really be trusted, him. We'll always have food, us. Take what you need."

And Jack Sawicki looked down at the ground, him, like he was ashamed. We all were, us. I don't know of what. We were Liver citizens, after all.

The mayor and two men helped, them, to load the two travoises with everything we could from the food line. Jeanette Harloff wanted us to stay the night in the hotel, but we all said no, us. The same thing was in all our minds. Folks were sitting home hungry, them, in East Oleanta: kids and wives and mothers and brothers and friends, with their bellies rumbling and hurting and that pinched look around their eyes. We'd rather walk back now, us, even after it got dark, than hear those bellies and look at them faces in our minds. We stuffed food off the belt into our mouths while we loaded the travoises, stuffed it into our jackets and hats and gloves. We bulged like pregnant women, us. The Coganville people watched in silence. A few left the café, them, their eyes on the floor.

I wanted to say: We trusted our congresswoman, too, us. Once.

There was only so much food prepared for the line. The travoises would hold more. When it ran out, we had to stop, us, and wait for the kitchen 'bots to make more. And all that whole time nobody except Jeanette Harloff spoke to us. Nobody.

When we left, us, we carried huge amounts of food. Looking at it, I knew it wouldn't be huge when there was all the hungry people of East Oleanta to feed. We'd be back tomorrow, or somebody else would. Nobody said that to Jeanette Harloff. I couldn't tell, me, if she knew.

The sky had that feel that says the most part of the day is over. Stan Mendoza and Scotty Flye, the youngest and strongest, dragged the travoises first, them. The runners were curved plastifoam, smoother than any wood could be. They slid easily over the snow. This time, at least, we had the wind at our backs.

After half an hour Judy Farrell said, "We can't even talk, us, to the next town, with the terminal. We can talk to Albany, us, or to any donkey politician, and we can get information easy, but we can't talk to the next town to tell them we're out of food."

Jim Swikehardt said, "We never asked to, us. More fun to just hop the gravrail. Gives you something to do."

"And keeps people separate, us," Ben Radisson said, but not angry, just like he never thought of it before. "We should have asked, us." After that, nobody said nothing.

After dark, the cold got sharp as pain. I could feel, me, the hollow place in my chest where the wind whistled through. It made a noise inside me that I could hear in my ears. The Y-lights made the tracks bright as day, but the cold was a dark thing, it, circling us like something rabid. My bones felt, them, like icicles, and just as like to snap.

But we were almost there. No more than a mile left to go. And then there was the crack of a rifle, and young Scotty Flye fell over dead.

In another minute they were on us, them. I recognized most of them, me, although I only had names to go with two of them: Clete Andrews and Ned Zalewski. Stomps. Ten or twelve of them, from East Oleanta and Pilotburg and Carter's Falls, come in before the gravrail busted, and then stuck here. They whooped and hollered, them, like this was a game. They jumped Jack and Stan and Bob and I saw all three go down, even though Stan was a big man and Bob was a fighter, him. The stomps didn't waste no more bullets, them. They had knives.

I pushed the little black box on my belt.

The tingle was there, it, and the shimmer. A stomp jumped me and I heard him hit solid metal. That's what it sounded like. I could hear everything, me. Judy Farrell screamed and Jack Sawicki moaned. The stomp's eyes under his ski mask got wide.

"Shit! The old fart's got a shield, him!"

Three of them pounded on me. Only it wasn't me, it was a thin hard layer an inch from me, like I was a turtle in an uncrackable shell. They couldn't touch me, them, only push and pull the shell. Finally the first stomp yelled something with no words, him, and shoved the shell so hard I went over the edge of the track and down a little embankment, picking up snow like the snowmen Lizzie used to roll, her. Something in one knee cracked.

By the time I staggered, me, back up to the gravrail track, the stomps were disappearing into the woods, dragging the travoises.

Only Scotty was dead. The others were in bad shape, them, especially Stan and Jack. Stab wounds and broken heads and I couldn't tell, me, what else. Nobody could walk. I staggered the last mile through the snow, me, afraid to carry one of the lights, feeling for the track every time I fell down. Some men from East Oleanta met me part way, them, just when I didn't think I could go no further. They'd heard the rifle shot.

They went out to get the others. Somebody, I don't know who, carried me to Annie's. He didn't say nothing about me wearing a donkey personal shield. Or maybe it was turned off by then. I can't remember, me. All I remember is me saying over and over again, "Don't crush them, you! Don't crush them, you!" There were six sandwiches in my jacket pocket. For Lizzie and Annie and Dr. Turner.

Everything didn't all go black, the way Annie said later. It went red, it, with flashes of light in my knee, so bright I thought they would kill me.

But of course they didn't. When the red went away it was the next day, and I laid, me, on Annie's bed, with her asleep next to me. Lizzie was there, too, on the other side of Annie. Dr. Turner bent over me, doing something to my knee.

I croaked, "Did they eat?"

"For now," Dr. Turner said. Her voice was grim. What she said next didn't make no sense to me. "So much for community solidarity in the face of adversity."

I said, "I brought Annie and Lizzie food, me." It seemed a miracle. Annie and Lizzie had something to eat. I did it, me. I didn't even think, then, that two sandwiches wouldn't keep them long. It didn't even occur to me. I must of been on some of them painkillers, me, that cloud your mind.

Dr. Turner's face changed. She looked startled, her, like what I said was some kind of good answer to what she said, although it wasn't, because I didn't even understand her big words. But I didn't care, me. Annie and LIzzie had something to eat. I did it, me.

"Ah, Billy," Dr. Turner said, her voice was low and sad, mournful, like somebody died. Or something. What?

But that wasn't my problem. I slept, me, and in all my dreams Lizzie and Annie smiled at me in a sunshine green and gold as summer on the mountain, where it turned out, I learned later, that Stan and Scotty and Jack and Dr. Turner's something had all really died after all.

Twelve

After they brought Billy back to Annie Francy's, his poor heart laboring like an antique factory and his hands shaking so much he couldn't even turn off the personal shield, I realized what an ass I'd been not to call the GSEA earlier.

But it wasn't Billy who made me realize this. It was—again, always—Lizzie.

I knew that Billy wasn't badly hurt, and I suppose I should have been more concerned about the other Livers, especially the three dead. But the fact was, I wasn't. I had changed my mind about Livers since I came to East Oleanta, and Jack Sawicki in particular seemed a good man, but there it was. I just didn't really care that Liver stomps had turned on other Liver non-stomps and destroyed them. We donkeys had never expected anything else. The Livers were always a potentially dangerous force, kept at bay only by sufficient bread and circuses, and now the bread was running short and the big tops folded. Bastille time.

But I cared—against all odds—about Lizzie. Who was going hungry. If I called the GSEA, they would come storming in and East Oleanta would no longer be the Forgotten Country. With them would come food, medicine, transport, all the things Livers had come to expect from the labor of others. Which meant Lizzie and Annie would get fed.

On the other hand, Congresswoman Janet Carol Land might resume her planeloads of food any minute. Or the gravrail might be fixed again. That had happened many times already. And if it did, I would lose my chance to cover myself with glory by handing over Miranda Sharifi, lock, stock and illegal organic nanotech, to the GSEA. Also, the moment I called the GSEA, Eden might very well pick up my signal, in which case Ms. Sharifi might have been moved out before the GSEA even got here.

While I wrestled with this three-horned dilemma of altruism, vanity, and practicality, Lizzie blew the whole argument to terrifying smithereens.

"Vicki, look at this."

"What is it?"

"Just look."

We sat on the plastisynth sofa in Annie's apartment. In the bedroom Annie moved around, tending Billy. The medunit had treated his cuts, bruises, and heart rate, and he should probably have been sleeping, which he probably couldn't do with Annie fussing around him. I doubt he minded. The bedroom door was closed. Lizzie held her terminal, frowning at the screen. Billy's pathetic squashed sandwiches had temporarily returned the color to her thin cheeks. On the screen was a multicolor holo.

"Very pretty. What is it?"

"A Lederer probability pattern."

Well, of course it was. It's been a while since my school days. To save face, I said authoritatively, "Some variable has a seventy-eight percent chance of significantly preceding some other variable in chronological time."

"Yes," Lizzie said, almost inaudibly.

"So what are the variables?"

Instead of answering, Lizzie said, "You remember that apple peeler 'bot I used to play with, when I was a kid?"

Two months ago. But compared to the intellectual leaps she'd made since, last summer probably did feel like lost childhood to her.

"I remember," I said, careful not to smile.

"It first broke in June. I remember because the apples then were Kia Beauties."

Genemod apples ripened on a staggered schedule, to create seasonal variety. "So?" I said.

"And the gravrail broke down before that. In April, I think. And a couple of toilets before that."

I didn't get it. "And so . . . ?"

Lizzie wrinkled her small face. "But the first things to break down in East Oleanta were way back over a year ago. In the spring of 2113."

And I got it. My throat went dry. "In spring, 2113? Lots of things breaking, Lizzie, or just a few? Such as might happen from normal wear combined with reduced maintenance?"

"Lots of things. Too many things."

"Lizzie," I said slowly, "are those two variables in your Lederer pattern the East Oleanta breakdowns, as you personally remember them, and the newsgrid mentions from the crystal library of any similar breakdown patterns elsewhere?"

"Yes. They are, them. I wanted, me . . ." She broke off, aware of how her language had reverted. She went on staring at the screen. She knew what she was looking at. "It started here, Vicki, didn't it? That duragem dissembler got released here first. Because it got made at Eden. We were a test place. And that means that whoever runs Eden . . ." Again she trailed off.

Huevos Verdes ran Eden. Miranda Sharifi ran Eden.

And so my decision was made for me, as simply as that. The duragem dissembler could not be part of any save-Diana-through-a-personal-success-*finally* strategy. It was too concretely, urgently, majorly malevolent. I had no right to sit around playing semi-amateur agent when I suspected that somewhere in these very same mountains that were torturing us with winter was a Huevos Verdes franchise, dispensing molecular destruction. Every decent feeling required that I tell my disdainful bosses, despite their disdain, what I knew.

Everybody has her own definition of decency.

"Vicki," Lizzie whispered, "what are we going to do, us?"

"We're going to give up," I said.

I made the call from a secluded place down by the river, away from Annie's suspicious eyes. I had forbidden Lizzie to follow me, but of course she did anyway. The air was cold but the sun shone. I wriggled my butt into a depression in the snow on the riverbank and cut the transmitter from my leg.

It was an implant, of course: that was the only way to be positive it couldn't be stolen from me, except by people who knew what they were doing. After the GSEA had it installed, I'd gone to some people I knew and had detached and taken out the automatic homing-signal part of it, which of course was there. You needed professionals for that. You didn't need professionals to remove the transmitter itself for use. That could be done with a little knowledge, a local anesthetic, and a keen-edged knife, and in a pinch you could do without either the anesthetic or the keen edge.

I didn't have to. I slid the implant from under the skin of my thigh, sealed the small incision, and wiped the blood off the transmitter wrapping. I unsealed it. Lizzie's black eyes were enormous in her thin face.

I said, "I told you not to come. Are you going to faint now?"

"Blood don't make me faint!"

"Good." The transmitter was a flat black wafer on my palm. Lizzie regarded it with interest.

"That uses Malkovitch wave transformers, doesn't it?" And then, in a different voice, "You're going to call the government to come help us."

"Yes."

"You could have called before. Any time."

"Yes."

The black eyes stayed steady. "Then why didn't you?"

"The situation wasn't desperate enough."

Lizzie considered this. But she was a child, still, under the frightening intelligence and the borrowed language and the pseudo-technical sophistication I had taught her. And she had been through a terrifying two weeks. Abruptly she pounded on my knees, soft ineffectual blows from cold mittened hands. "You could of got us help before! And Billy wouldn't of got hurt and Mr. Sawicki wouldn't of died and I wouldn't of had to be so very very very hungry! You could of! You could of!"

I activated the transmitter by touch code and said clearly, "Special Agent Diana Covington, 6084 slash A, to Colin Kowalski, 83 slash H. Emergency One priority: sixteen forty-two. Repeat, sixteen forty-two. Send large task force."

"I'm so *hungry*," Lizzie sobbed against my knees.

I put the transmitter in my pocket and pulled her onto my lap. She buried her head in my neck; her nose felt cold. I looked at the river choked with ice, at the blood from the wrapper on the dirty snow, at the uncharacteristically blue sky. It would take the GSEA maybe a few hours to arrive from New York. But the

SuperSleepless, at their hidden Eden, were already here. And of course there was no way they would not have picked up my message. They picked up everything. Or so I had been told.

I held Lizzie and made pointless maternal noises. Her cold nose dribbled into my neck.

"Lizzie, did I ever tell you about a dog I saw once? A genemod pink dog that should never have existed, poor thing?"

But she only went on sobbing, cold and hungry and betrayed. It was actually just as well. The story about Stephanie Brunell's dog seemed, at this point, lame even to me, something I had once believed in, probably still did, but could no longer clearly recall.

Like so much else.

The GSEA showed up within the hour, which I have to admit impressed me. First came the planes, then the aircars, and by nightfall, the gravrail was up, roaring into East Oleanta with a complement of thirty calm-eyed agents, some techs, and a lot of food. Government types work best on a full stomach. The techs went around town repairing things. The GSEA commandeered the Congresswoman Janet Carol Land Café, threw a Y-shield around the half of it farthest from the techs stocking the foodbelt, and ordered everybody else to stay out, which the good citizens were happy to do because food was being dispensed from the ruins of the warehouse. God knows how they were cooking it. Maybe they were eating soysynth raw.

"Ms. Covington? I'm Charlotte Prescott. I'm in temporary command here, until the arrival of Colin Kowalski from the West Coast. Come with me, please."

She was tall, flame-haired, absolutely beautiful. Expensive genes. She had the accent that goes with the monied Northeast, and eyes like the Petrified Forest. I went with her, but not without a patented little Diana-protest: spirited but essentially ineffectual.

"I don't want to talk until I'm sure that two people are getting fed. Three actually. An old man and a little girl and the girl's mother . . . they might not be able to handle being part of that mob outside . . ." What was I saying? Annie Francy could handle being part of Custer's Last Stand, protesting all the while that the Indians weren't behaving properly.

Charlotte Prescott said, "Lizzie Francy and Billy Washington are being seen to. The guard at the apartment will procure them food."

And she had only been in East Oleanta ten minutes.

Charlotte Prescott and I sat opposite each other in two plastisynth café chairs and I told her everything I knew. That I had followed Miranda Sharifi from Washington to East Oleanta, after which she had disappeared. That I'd been searching the woods for her. That some of the locals half believed there was a place in the mountains they called Eden, probably a shielded underground illegal genemod lab, and that I believed that was where Huevos Verdes was releasing the duragem dissembler. That I'd followed various locals into the woods in the hopes of discovering Eden, but had never seen anything, and was now convinced nobody knew where, or if, this mythical place existed.

This last wasn't strictly true. I still suspected Billy Washington knew something. But I wanted to tell that directly to Colin Kowalski, whom I halfway trusted, rather than to Charlotte Prescott, whom I trusted not at all. She reminded me of Stephanie Brunell. Billy was an ignorant and exasperating old man, but he was not a pink dog with four ears and overly big eyes, and I was not going to watch him go over any metaphorical terrace railing.

Prescott said, "Why didn't you report your whereabouts, and Miranda Sharifi's suspected whereabouts, as soon as you reached East Oleanta? Or even en route?"

"I was fairly sure that the SuperSleepless outpost would be able to monitor any technology I used."

This was a fair hit; not even the GSEA flattered itself that it could outinvent Supers. Prescott showed no reaction.

"You were in violation of every Agency procedure."

"I'm not a regular agent. I run wild-card for Colin Kowalski, under informant status. You wouldn't even know about me now if he hadn't told you."

Still no reaction. She had the ability, like some reptiles, to just draw a nicitating membrane between herself and any blowing insinuating sand. I saw this about her: her limitations, her rigidity born of the automatic assumption of superiority. Yet I still couldn't help feeling unworthy beside her, in a way I hadn't felt unworthy in months. Me in my rumpled turquoise jacks and untrimmed hair, she looking like something off a holovid ad for the Central Park East Enclave. Even her fingernails were perfect, genemod rose so they never had to be painted.

The questions went on. I was as honest as I could be, except for Billy. It didn't help my mood, which was middling lousy. I was doing what I should, what I needed to do, what was right and patriotic for my country three cheers and "Hail to the Chief." No, I don't mean that cynicism—it *was* right. So why did I feel so terrible?

Colin Kowalski arrived about 9:00 P.M. I was still under house arrest, or whatever, but Charlotte Prescott had apparently run out of questions. The foodbelt was working, serving an insatiable line of the hungry, who peered curiously at the Y-shield cramping them into half their café but could see nothing because the outer layer had been one-way opaqued.

"Colin. I'm glad you're here."

He was angry, not hiding it, but keeping it under control. I gave him points for all three.

"You should have contacted me in August, Diana. Maybe we could have stopped release of the duragem dissembler sooner."

"Can you stop it *now?*" I said, but he didn't answer. I wasn't having any of that. I grabbed both his lapels—or what passes for lapels in the new fall fashions—and said, slowly and with great distinctness, "You've found something. Already. Colin, you have to tell me what you've found so far. You have to. I got you all this far, and besides there's no earthly reason not to tell me. You know damn well you've got reporters all over every place out there by now."

He stepped back a pace and pulled his lapels free. Billy and Doug Kane and Jack Sawicki and Annie and Krystal Mandor had been all over each other constantly. I was a little shocked at how quickly I'd forgotten the donkey intolerance for being touched.

But I was not going to give up. Maybe it wouldn't be necessary to involve Billy more than he already was by having taken me into Annie's apartment for the last month. "What have your agents found, Colin?"

"Diana—"

"*What?*"

He told me, not because of my persistence but because there really wasn't any reason not to. He even gave me the lattitude and longitude, to the minutes and seconds. Proud of himself. And yet, somehow, not. I listened harder.

"Just what you suspected, Diana, an underground lab. Shielded. We broke the shield half an hour ago, once we knew the general area to look. The Supers had fled, but the duragem dissembler originated there, all right. Bastards didn't even bother to destroy the evidence. The dangerous recombinant and nanotech stuff in that lab . . ."

I had never seen words fail Colin Kowalski before. He didn't sputter, or twitch. Instead his mouth just clamped shut on the last word with a small audible pop! as if naming these words had hurt his lip and he was protecting it. I felt sick inside. *The dangerous recombinant and nanotech stuff* . . . "What else have they got cooked up for us?"

"Nothing that's going to get out," he said, and looked straight at me. Too straight. I couldn't tell what the look meant.

And then I could.

"Colin, no, if you don't examine it all minutely—"

The explosion rocked the café, even though we were probably miles away and undoubtedly the GSEA had thrown a blast shield around the area first. But a blast shield only contains flying debris, and anyway nothing really muffles a nuclear blast. People at the foodbelt screamed and clutched their bowls of soysynth soup and soysnth steak. The holoterminal, which was in the food-line half of the café and which someone had turned to the National Scooter Championships, flickered momentarily.

Colin said stiffly, "It was too dangerous to examine minutely. Anything could have escaped from there. Anything they were working on."

I stood up unsteadily. There was no reason for the unsteadiness. I kept my voice level. "Colin—was the lab really empty? Did Miranda Sharifi and the other Supers really get out before you got there? *Before you blew it up,* I wanted to say.

"Yes, they were gone," Colin said, and met my eyes so steadily, so guilessly, that I immediately knew he was lying.

"Colin—"

"Your service with the GSEA is terminated, Diana. We appreciate your help. Six months' pay will be deposited to your credit account, and a discreet and nonspecific letter of commendation provided if you ever want one. You are, of course, constrained from selling your story to the media in any form whatsoever. Should you break this prohibition, you could be subject to severe penalties up to and including imprisonment. Please accept the Department's warmest thanks for your assistance."

"*Colin—*"

For just a second there was a flash of a real person on his face. "You're done, Diana. It's over."

But, of course, it wasn't.

I slipped through the general street pandemonium—reporters, townspeople, agents, even the first sightseers on the newly fixed gravrail—without notice. In my rumpled winter jacks, a scarf over the bottom half of my face, my hair as dirty as everyone else's in East Oleanta, I looked like just one more confused Liver. This might have pleased me, if I had been capable of being pleased by anything just then. Something was terribly wrong, wrong in my head, and I didn't know what. I had gotten what I wanted: Huevos Verdes was stopped from releasing destruction such as the dur-agem dissembler. The country, unchanged economic problems notwithstanding, now stood at least a chance of recovery, once the clocking mechanism on all the released dissemblers ran through its set number of replications. Twelve-year-old girls could eat; old men would not have to trudge through the snow along disabled rail tracks, attacked for food. I had gotten what I wanted.

Something was very wrong.

The guards were just leaving Annie's apartment. I passed them in the hall. Neither one gave me a second glance. Billy lay on the sofa, with Annie seated on a chair at his head, her lips pressed together tightly enough to create a vacuum. Lizzie sat on the floor, gnawing on something that was probably supposed to be a chicken leg.

"You. Get out," Annie said.

I ignored her, drawing up a second chair beside Billy. It was the same kind of plastisynth chair I'd sat in opposite Charlotte Prescott of the perfect nails, the only kind of chair I'd ever sat on in East Oleanta. Only this one was poison green. "Billy. You know what happened?"

He said, so quietly I had to lean forward to hear him, "I heard, me. They blew up Eden."

Annie said, "And how'd they know, them, there was anything to blow up? *You* told them, Dr, Turner! You brought them government men to East Oleanta!"

"And if I hadn't, you'd still all be starving," I snapped. Annie always brought out the worst in me. She never doubted herself.

Annie subsided, fuming. Billy said, "It's really gone, it? They really blew it up?"

"Yes." My throat felt thick. God knows why. "Billy, that's where they were making the duragem dissembler. The thing that was causing so many breakdowns. Of all kinds of machinery."

He didn't answer for a long time. I thought he'd fallen asleep. His wrinkled eyelids were at half mast, and the sag of his jowls hurt my chest.

Finally he said, almost in a whisper, "She saved old Doug Kane's life, her . . . And they were going to save ours, too . . ."

I said sharply, "How do you know that?"

He answered simply, with a guileness so different from Colin Kowalski's that English should have different words for it. "I don't know, me. But I saw her. She was kind to us, her, even though we ain't got no more in common with her than . . . than with beetles. They knew things, them people. If you say she made the duragem dissembler, well, then maybe she did, her. But it's hard to believe. And even if they did make it, them, by mistake, say . . ."

"Yes? Yes, Billy?"

"If Eden's all blown up, it, how we ever going to find out how to unmake it?"

"I don't know. But there were other dangerous nanotechnology projects under way in . . . in Eden, Billy. Stuff that if it had gotten loose, could have caused even more destruction."

He considered this. "But Doctor Turner—"

I said wearily, "I'm not a doctor, Billy. I'm not anything."

"If the government just goes around, them, blowing up all the illegal Edens, then don't we lose the good things, us, as well as the bad ones? There was them rabid raccoons—"

I said impatiently, "You have to have controls of genetic and nanotech research, Billy. Or any lunatic will go around inventing things like dissemblers."

"Seems to me some lunatic *was*," he said, more tartly than I'd ever heard him. "And look what happened. The real scientists can't invent no way to stop it, because they ain't allowed, them, to do no experiments themselves!"

No permitted antidotal research. It wasn't a new argument. I'd heard it before. Never, however, from such a person, in such a situation. Billy had glimpsed Eden, and he thought the gods there were not only omnipotent but benevolent. Capable of antidotes to the evil they themselves had caused. Maybe I had thought so fleetingly, too, at the patent hearing for Miranda Sharifi's Cell Cleaner. But SuperSleepless didn't make mistakes, at least not on this order. If Huevos Verdes had released the duragem dissembler, it must have been deliberate, in order to destroy the culture that hated them. I couldn't imagine any other reason. And Huevos Verdes had almost succeeded.

"Go to sleep, Billy," I said, and rose to leave. But the old man was disposed to talk.

"I *know*, me, they weren't bad. That girl, the day she saved Doug Kane's life . . . and now it's gone. Eden's really gone, it. I ain't never going to go down that mountain trail, me, and splash across that creek, me, and see that door in the hill open and go inside with her . . ."

He was maundering. Of course: The agents had given him a truth drug. Whatever he had been asked, he'd answered. A talking jag was one of the side effects when those pharmaceuticals wore off.

"Good-bye, Billy. Annie." I moved to the door.

Lizzie heard something in my voice. She scuttled over to me, "chicken bone" in her hand, all big eyes and thin hands. But already she looked healthier. Children respond quickly to good food.

"Vicki, we'll have our lesson in the morning? Vicki?"

I looked at her, and suddenly I had the completely insane sensation that I understood Miranda Sharifi.

There exists a kind of desire I had never experienced, and never expected to experience. I have read about it. I have even seen it, in other people, although not many other people. It is desire so piercing, so pointed, so specific, that there is no stopping it, any more than you could stop a lance hurtled unerringly at your belly. The lance propels your whole body forward, according to the laws of physics. It changes the way your blood flows. You can die from it.

Mothers are said to feel that raw agony of longing to save their infants from deadly harm. I have never been a mother. Lovers are said to feel it for each other. I never loved like that, despite shoddy imitations with Claude-Eugene-Rex-Paul-Anthony-Russell-David. Artists and scientists are said to feel it for their work. This last was true of Miranda Sharifi.

What *I* had felt about Miranda Sharifi, ever since Washington, had been envy. And I hadn't even known it.

But not now. Looking at Lizzie, knowing I would leave East Oleanta in the morning, seeing from the corner of my eye the way Annie's bulk shifted in her chair as she watched us, the lance changed the way my blood flowed and I put both hands convulsively over my belly. "Sure, Lizzie," I gasped, and Colin Kowalski was in my voice, guileless with donkey superiority, lying like the pigs we are.

But sometime near dawn, five or six in the morning, I woke abruptly from a blotchy sleep. Billy's voice filled my mind: *and now it's gone. Eden's really gone, it. I ain't never going to go down that mountain trail, me, and splash across that creek, me, and see that door in the hill open and go inside with her . . .*

I crept out of my room in the hastily repaired hotel. A new terminal sat on the counter, but that was far too risky. I went down to the café. People were there, queuing at the foodbelt, a donkey newsgrid playing animatedly on the holoterminal. Liver channels almost never ran news. If East Oleanta wanted to see itself on a grid, it would have to be a donkey grid.

I crouched in a corner, unobtrusively, and watched. Eventually the explosion came on, the sensational tracking of the duragem dissembler source that had so plagued the country, close-ups of Charlotte Prescott and of Kenneth Emile Koehler, GSEA director, in Washington. Then the explosion again. I wanted to freeze-frame the HT, but didn't dare. Instead, I listened carefully.

A gravrail left at 7 A.M. By eight I was in Albany. There was a public library terminal at the station, for the use of Livers who were fuzzy about their destinations and wanted to look up such vital information about them as the average mean rainfall, location of public scooter tracks, or longitude and lattitude. A sign said THE ANNA NAOMI COLDWELL PUBLIC LIBRARY. Cobwebs draped the sign. Few Livers were fuzzy about their destinations, or at least about what they wanted to know about them.

I slipped in one of the credit chips the GSEA didn't know I had. Maybe didn't know. The terminal said, "Working. What town, city, county, or state are you interested in?"

"Collins County, New York." My voice was slightly unsteady.

"Go ahead with your request, please."

"Display a map of the whole county, with natural features and political units."

When the map appeared, I asked to have sections of it enlarged, then enlarged again. The hypertext gave it to me. The map displayed lattitude and longitude.

The explosion destroying the illegal lab had not been at the base of a hill, nor anywhere near a creek.

. . . and now it's gone. Eden's really gone, it. I ain't never going to go down that mountain trail, me, and splash across that creek, me, and see that door in the hill open, and go inside with her . . .

I believed that the GSEA had destroyed an illegal genemod lab. I believed that it was the lab that had released the duragem dissemblers. But whatever, and whoever, that lab was, it wasn't Billy Washington's Eden. Not the Eden at the base of a mountain and beside a creek, the Eden that had permitted Billy to see its door opening, the Eden of the big-headed savior of old men who collapse in the woods. That Eden was still there.

Which meant that whoever had released the duragem dissembler, it hadn't been Huevos Verdes.

So who had? And was Huevos Verdes with them or against them?

On the one hand, the duragem destruction *had* started in East Oleanta, right around the corner from Eden. Coincidence? I doubted it. And yet Miranda Sharifi had done nothing to stop the dissembler release.

On the other hand, if the Supers were interested in destruction, why had one of them allowed Billy Washington to see the entrance to their Adirondack outpost, and to walk away with that knowledge? Why hadn't they killed him? And why had Miranda Sharifi tried to gain legal clearance for the Cell Cleaner, a clear boon to us ordinary mortals? The Sleepless already had that biological protection, and they sure the hell didn't need the money.

And what about the fact—Billy was right about this—that if

some illegal lab did come up with something even worse than a duragem dissembler—a retrovirus that made us all zombies, say—only Huevos Verdes had the brainpower to design a counter-microorganism fast enough to prevent a whole country of ambulatory idiots.

But *would* they?

Was Huevos Verdes my country's enemy, or its covert friend?

These weren't the sort of questions a field agent was supposed to ask. A field agent was supposed to do what she was told and report any significant new developments up the chain of command. A field agent in my position should immediately call the GSEA. Again.

But if I did that, the questions would never get answered. Because Colin Kowalski already thought he knew the answer: Bomb anything too unfamiliar.

I must have stood, motionless, for fifteen minutes in front of the Anna Naomi Coldwell Public Library. Livers rushed by, hurrying to make their trains. A cleaning 'bot ambled along, scrubbing the floor. A sunshine dealer glanced at me, then away. A tech, genemod handsome, spoke into his terminal as he strode the platform.

I have never felt so alone.

I got back on the gravrail and returned to East Oleanta.

IV

OCTOBER–DECEMBER 2114

The personal is political, and the political
is always personal.

—American folk saying

Thirteen

I was underground with the Francis Marion Freedom Outpost
for two months, throughout September and October.
I wouldn't have believed it was possible to hide for days, weeks,
months, from the GSEA. The Outpost was a bunch of nuts; what
possible chance could they have of evading the government after
killing three GSEA agents, murdering Leisha Camden, and blowing up an agency rescue plane? None. Nada. It wasn't possible.
That's what I would have believed.

Nor did I believe it was possible to hide from Huevos Verdes.
Daily, hourly, I expected them to come for me.

The shapes in my head were thin and fragile, like nervous
membranes. Vulnerable. Uncertain. These shapes swam around
the immobile green lattice like spooked fish. Sometimes they had
faces, or the sketches of faces, on the uncertain shapes. Sometimes
the faces were mine.

At 5:00 A.M. of my second day underground an alarm had sounded.
My heart had leapt: their defenses were breached. But it was
reveille.

Peg slouched in, sullen. She wheeled me to a common bath,
dumped me in, pulled me out. I didn't reveal that I could easily
have done this for myself. She wheeled me to commons, jammed
with people hastily eating, so many people that some gulped their
food standing up. Then she pulled a piece of paper from her pocket
and thrust it at me angrily.

"Here. Yours."

It was a printout of a schedule, headed ARLEN, DREW, TEM-PORARY ASSIGNMENT COMPANY 5. "I'm assigned to Company 5. Is that your group, Peg?"

She snorted in derision and wheeled me around so hard I nearly tumbled out of the chair.

Company 5 assembled in a huge barren underground room: a parade ground. I didn't see Joncey, Abigail, or anyone else I recognized. For two hours twenty people did calisthenics. I did intentionally feeble imitations in my chair. Peg grunted and sweated.

Next came two hours of holo instruction on weapons—propellant, laser, biological, grav—I was amazed Hubbley let me see this, and then I wasn't. He didn't expect me to ever have the chance to tell anyone.

As the holo explained weapon charging, care, and use, the twenty members of Company 5 practiced with the real thing. I was ten feet away from wresting a gun from Peg and shooting her dead. She didn't seem bothered by this, although I saw a few others glance at me, hard-eyed. Probably Peg didn't object because these were Hubbley's orders. Perhaps this was the way that Francis Marion had converted his prisoners of war.

Lunch, then more physical training, then a holo on living off the land. Incredibly, it came from the Government Document Office. I fell asleep.

Peg kicked my chair. "Political Truth, you."

She pushed me closer into the company, who sat on the floor in a semicircle, facing the holostage. Everyone sat straight. I could feel taut shapes grow tauter in my mind. The atmosphere prickled and thickened. We were in for something more interesting than the Government Document Office.

Jimmy Hubbley came in and sat with the company. Nobody addressed him. Another holo began.

It had the deliberately grainy texture reserved for real-time unedited filming. There's no way to alter any part of it without destroying the whole thing. It's the same holo-creation technique I use in my concerts, although my equipment compensates for the graininess with deliberately softened edges, like a dream. But it's important to people to see a real-life concert, not some patched together and edited version afterwards. They need to know it's really me.

This holo had really happened.

It showed the underground, including James Hubbley, capturing the duragem dissembler in an outlaw lab. The captured inventors were then forced to manufacture dissemblers in huge quantities, which were stored in small canisters completely dissolvable once opened. None had been released until the canisters had been stockpiled all over the United States. Then the clocked dissembler had been released simultaneously everywhere, so no source could be traced. I was looking at information the GSEA would give its collective life to know.

The original outlaw lab had been located in Upstate New York, in the Adirondack Mountains, near a small town called East Oleanta.

I sat quietly, letting the shapes in my mind overwhelm me. There was no use fighting them. Miranda had always said East Oleanta had been chosen at random for the Huevos Verdes project, picked by a computer-generated random program to avoid the GSEA deductive-locale programs. That's what she had told me.

You're a necessary part of the project, Drew. A full member.

"Okay," Jimmy Hubbley said, when the holo had finished, "now who can tell me why we all see this here holo over and over again like this, pretty near every damn day?"

A young girl said fervently, "Because we share knowledge, us, equally. Not like the donkeys."

"That's fine, Ida." Hubbley smiled at her.

A man said in a deep, upcountry voice, "We need, us, to know the facts so's we can make good decisions about our country. The idea of an America for real human Americans. The will to get us there."

"That's fine," Hubbley said. "Don't it sound fine, soldiers?"

Someone said hesitantly, "But don't that mean, it, that we should ask everybody in the whole country what they think? For a vote?"

There was a little stir in the room.

"If they had all the knowledge we do, Bobby, then it sure would mean that," Hubbley said earnestly. Light shone in his pale eyes. "But they don't know all the things we do. They ain't had the privilege of fightin' for freedom on the front lines. Specifically, they ain't seen the holo of the captured lab. They don't know what weapons we got on our side now. They might think this here revolution is hopeless, not knowing that. But we know better. So we got the obligation to decide for them, and to act in the best will of all our fellow Americans."

Heads nodded. I could see how special they felt, Ida and Bobby and Peg, deciding so selflessly in the best interests of all Americans. Just as Francis Marion had done.

I heard Miranda's voice in my head: *They can't possibly understand the biological and societal consequences of the project, Drew, any more than people of Kenzo Yagai's time could foresee the social consequences of cheap ubiquitous energy. He had to go forward and develop it on the basis of his best informed projections. And so do we. They can't really understand until it happens.*

Because they were norms. Like Drew Arlen.

There was a long silence. People shifted from ham to ham or sat preternaturally still. Eyes darted at each other, then away. I could feel my own back straighten. All this tension was not over some holo they had seen "pretty near every damn day."

Hubbley said, "I said they don't know what we got, and I *meant* they don't know what we got. But they're sure the hail going to find out. Campbell, bring him in."

Campbell entered from one of the many corridors, half dragging a naked, handcuffed Liver. The man was a sorry sight, barely five and a half feet to Campbell's seven and looking even shorter as he futiley resisted being dragged. He was hunched over, his bare heels scraping the floor. He didn't make a sound.

Hubbley said, "Is the robocam ready?"

Someone behind him said, "I just turned it on, Jimmy."

"Good. Now, y'all know this film is the kind that cain't be edited without self-destructin'. And you watchers out there, y'all know it too. Son, look at me when I'm talkin'."

The captive raised his head. He made no effort to cover his genitals. I saw with a shock that his lack of height wasn't due to bad Liver genes; he was a boy. Thirteen, maybe fourteen, and genemod. It was there in the bright green eyes, the sharp handsome line of his jaw. But he wasn't donkey. He was a tech, those offspring of borderline families who can't afford full genetic modification, including the expensive IQ boosters, but who aspire to be more than Livers. They buy their children the appearance mods only, and the kids grow up—early—to provide those services halfway between robots and donkey brains. My roadies were techs. At Huevos Verdes, you could argue, Kevin Baker's grandson Jason, a Sleepless, was nonetheless a tech.

The boy looked terrified.

Hubbley said, not to the boy, "What did General Francis Marion's young lieutenant call him?"

Peg answered fervently, " 'An ugly, cross, knock-kneed, hook-nosed son of a bitch'!"

"Y'all see, son," Hubbley explained kindly to the boy, "General Marion warn't genemod. He was just the way his Lord made him. And he became the greatest hero this country ever had. Curtis, what did General Marion say was his policy when he was too outnumbered to attack the enemy directly?"

A man to my left said promptly, " 'Yet I pushed them so hard as in a great measure to break them up.' "

"Absolutely right. 'Pushed them so hard as to break them up.' And that's just what we're doin', you watchers out there. Pushin' y'all. This here man is a captured enemy, a worker in a genemod clinic. Parents take their innocent unborn babies to this place and *turn them into something that ain't human.* Their own children. To some of us this is damn near inconceivable."

I wanted to say that *in vitro* genetic modification happened before there was a 'babe,' that it was done to the fertilized egg in artificial biostasis. But my tongue was stuck to the roof of my mouth. The tech boy stared straight ahead, seeing nothing, like a rabbit caught in bright lights.

"Now, y'all might think that this boy is too young to be held accountable for his actions. But he's fifteen years old. Junie, how old was Francis Marion's nephew Gabriel Marion when he was killed fightin' the enemy at Mount Pleasant Plantation?"

"Fourteen," a female voice answered. From my chair, I couldn't see her face.

Hubbley's voice grew confidential. He leaned forward slightly, "Y'all out there see, don't y'all? This is war. We mean it. We got the Idea what kind of country we want to live in, and we got the Will to get there. No matter what the personal cost. Earl, tell all our watchers out there at the GSEA about Mrs. Rebecca Motte."

A man dressed in purple jacks stood awkwardly, his arms dangling loose at his side. "On May 11—"

"May 10," Hubbley said, with a brief frown. He didn't want any inaccuracies in his uneditable tape. Earl, rattled, took a deep breath.

"On May *10* General Marion and his men attacked Mount Pleasant Plantation, them, 'cause the British had took it for a headquarters. They made the lady and her kids move, her, into a log cabin. Her name was Mrs. Rebecca Motte. The house was too well fortified for direct attack, it, and so the general decided, him, to shoot flaming arrows and set it on fire. But they didn't have no good bow and arrows. Lighthorse Harry Lee, who was working with General Marion, he went, him, to tell Mrs. Motte they had to burn her house down. And she went into the cabin and come out with beautiful bow and arrows, real donkey stuff. And she said, her, about her house, 'If it were a palace, it should go.' " Earl sat down.

Hubbley nodded. "Genuine sacrifice. A genuine patriot, Mrs. Rebecca Motte. You hear that, son?"

The tech didn't appear to hear anything. Was he drugged?

Leisha had always warned me against believing history's more colorful stories.

"We cain't never stop resistin' all you enemies of America. And you watchers are the worst, just like traitors and spies is always the worst in any revolution. They pretend to be on one side while plottin' and workin' for the other. GSEA agents are all traitors, pretendin' to safeguard the purity of human beings while actually permittin' all kinds of abominations. And then handin' over this great country to those same abominations, the donkeys, just like we Livers didn't realize y'all would let us starve if you could. And in fact y'all *are.* Joncey, what did General Marion say in his speech to the men before they attacked Doyle at Lynche's Creek?"

Joncey's voice, so much stronger and at ease than Earl's, recited, " 'But, my friends, if we shall be ruined for bravely resisting our tyrants, what will be done to us if we tamely lie down and submit to them?' "

I turned around. The room was full of people, all the "revolutionaries" from other "companies." Staring at the young tech, I hadn't even heard them come in. Neither, I was convinced, had he.

Hubbley said, "This here boy is a traitor. Workin' in a genemod clinic. He's goin' to die like a traitor, and y'all out there remember that he ain't the only one today, or tomorrow, or the day after that. Abby?"

Abigail came out of the crowd. She carried a featureless gray canister, no bigger than her closed fist.

"Abby," Hubbley said, "what did General Marion do with goods confiscated from the enemy?"

She turned to speak directly to the robocam. "Every metal saw the brigade could find, them, they hammered into a sword."

"That's exactly right. And this here—" he hoisted the canister high above his head "—is a saw. It ain't even been concocted in some illegal gene lab. This here comes straight from the biggest traitor of all: the so-called United States government." He turned the canister around. I saw stamped on it PROPERTY OF U. S. ARMY. CLASSIFIED. DANGER.

I didn't believe it. Hubbley had painted the words on. I didn't believe it, and I didn't even know as yet what the canister held. This ragtag bag of so-called revolutionaries had delusions, dreams, pathetic wishes . . . I didn't believe it.

The lattice in my mind sighed, as if wind soughed through.

"Okay, Abby," Hubbley said, "do it."

Abby, her back to me, did something I couldn't see. The shimmer of a heavy-duty Y-energy shield appeared around the naked tech, a domed and floored hemisphere six feet in diameter. The canister was inside the shimmer.

The boy wasn't drugged after all. Immediately he started screaming. The sound couldn't carry through the shield, which was the kind nothing got through, not even air. The boy beat his fists against the inside and screamed, his open mouth a pink cave, his eyes round with terror. There was faint down on his upper lip, like a fledgling bird, and scarcely more on his groin.

Jimmy Hubbley looked disgusted. "He lives causin' death and then cain't even die like a man . . . do it, Abby."

Whatever Abby did, I couldn't see. The canister glowed briefly, then dissolved into a gray puddle.

"This here is your metal saw you made to cut us up with," Hubbley said, "but we made it a sword. Live by the sword, die by the sword. Matthew 26:52. Y'all already know what this stuff does.

But for them that don't—" he looked directly at me "—I'll repeat it. This here's one of your own genemod abominations. It takes apart cell walls, cells of livin' human beings. Like this."

The boy had stopped beating against the shield. He was still screaming, but his mouth was changing shape. He was dissolving. It wasn't the same as when someone had acid poured on him—I had seen that once, in the days before Leisha took me in. Acid burns away the flesh. The boy's flesh wasn't burning, it was breaking up, like ice in springtime. Bits of skin fell to the dome floor, exposing red flesh, and then bits of that fell. He went on screaming, screaming, screaming. I felt my stomach heave, and the shapes in my mind heaved, too, around the ever-closed lattice.

It took the boy almost three minutes to die.

Hubbley said, very softly, "General Marion ended his Lynche's Creek speech this way: 'As God is my judge this day, that I would die a thousand deaths, most gladly would I die them all, rather than see my dear country in such a state of degradation and wretchedness.' As God is my judge, watchers." His pale eyes in their bony, sunburned face looked directly outward, filled with light.

Then everyone moved. The robocam must have been turned off. The shapes in my mind were tarry, foul. I had done nothing to save the boy. I hadn't even tried to speak up. I had not tried to get myself on the uneditable tape, to provide the watchers some clue about where this abomination was taking place . . . I had done nothing.

"That's a wrap," Jimmy Hubbley said, clearly pleased with himself. "That's old-time movie talk, it means the filmin' is done. Y'all are dismissed. And Mr. Arlen, sir, I think Peg better take y'all to your room. Y'all look a little peaked. If it ain't too great an impertinence in me to tell you so."

It went on like that for weeks.

Physical training, holos about the state of society (where were they made?), political drill. It was the worst of being in school, all over again. I kept finding small lace oblongs from Abigail's wedding gown, and Peg never pushed my chair anywhere in spitting distance of a terminal.

There were no more executions.

I badly wanted a drink. Hubbley said no. He allowed sunshine, because it didn't dull reaction time. I wanted a drink, because it dulled reaction time.

Hubbley had allowed me a handheld dumb terminal, the kind kids use for schoolwork, and a standard encyclopedia library. I said to him once, because I couldn't bite back the words, "Francis Marion discouraged the killing of prisoners. He even spirited a Tory, Jeff Butler, out of his own camp when it looked like Marion's men might butcher him."

Hubbley laughed with delight and rubbed the lump on his neck. "Damn, you been studyin', son, hail if you haven't! I'm damn proud of you!"

My teeth hurt from clenching them. "Hubbley—"

"But it don't make no never mind, Mr. Arlen, sir. No, it really don't. General Marion showed compassion to Tories because they were his own kind, his neighbors, living off the land same as he did. He didn't show that same compassion to British soldiers, now, did he? Donkeys ain't our kind. They ain't our neighbors in their snooty enclaves. And they sure don't live like we do, deprived of education and personal property and real power. No, donkeys are the British, Mr. Arlen. Not Jeff Butler—but Captain James Lewis of His Majesty's Forces, who was killed by a fourteen-year-old patriot named Gwynn. That's natural law, son. Protect your own."

"Marion didn't—"

"You say 'General Marion,' you!" Peg yelled. She glanced at Hubbley, like a dog hoping for a pat on the head. Hubbley smiled, showing his broken teeth.

These were the people who had loosened the duragem dissembler on the country, wrecking civilization. These.

And it *was* wrecked. The HT in commons received donkey newsgrids. There was scarcely a gravrail running a steady schedule, especially outside the cities. Most technicians had been diverted to major population areas, where the votes were. And the danger of rioting. Security had been tripled at most enclaves. Few planes flew, which meant the country was being run mostly by teleconferencing, at a distance. Medunits malfunctioned regularly. They didn't dispense wrong diagnoses; they just stopped diagnosing.

A viral plague was spreading in southern California. Nobody knew if it was a natural mutation, or bioengineered.

A Liver messiah in East Texas had proclaimed this the Time

of the End. He was quoting Revelations on the four horsemen, with a twist: The horseman of war must be loosed by the Livers. Now. When the state security squad tried to arrest him, he and his followers blew away thirty-three people with illegal Mexican weapons. The governor, said the newsgrid with concern, was virtually certain to fail reelection.

In Kansas, a soysynth factory owned by the D'Angelo franchise was ripped apart by hoarders, who carried off the treated and untreated soy. They also wrecked three million dollars of robotic machinery.

The lieutenant-governor of South Dakota was somehow knifed to death in his sleep, within a protected enclave.

Livers in San Diego broke into the world-famous zoo there, killed a lion and two elehippos, and ate them, following a report that animals could not get the new plague.

The northeast had been hit by early winter. Small towns were isolated without gravrails, starving without food. People starved. Small towns like East Oleanta.

Where was Miranda? And what was she waiting for? Unless something had gone wrong in the last steps of the project. Unless the GSEA had discovered Eden, traced it back from the carefully disseminated rumors in the little isolated Liver towns.

Unless there was even more that she, and Huevos Verdes, hadn't told me.

For the first time, I wondered if she wasn't coming for me at all.

"The greatness of the Constitution is in its Will to the common people," Jimmy Hubbley said, his pale eyes bright.

"The greatness of the Constitution is in its checks and balances," Leisha had always said. Leisha. Who. Was. Dead.

The dark lattice in my mind was furled tight as an umbrella, impenetrable, a thin sharp line that cut me inside.

Where were the checks and balances on Huevos Verdes?

"Take me around the compound again," I said to Peg.

She was slumped in a chair in commons, watching a scooter race someplace in California. A part of California without plague. "I don't want, me, to take you again. You seen everything you're gonna see."

"Fine. I'll go alone." I wheeled the chair away from her. I didn't dare exercise my upper body, not even after she'd locked me in at night. I couldn't see the surveillance monitors but I knew they had to be there. I settled for furtively hoisting myself a few inches above the arms of my chair several times a day, lifting my useless legs, careful to choose different locations each day.

"Wait, you." Peg sighed and heaved herself up. Roughly she shoved the chair forward.

A white corridor with the featureless doors locked.

Another white corridor with the featureless doors locked.

And another white corridor with the featureless doors locked.

The landing stage, guarded by Campbell, who was asleep but not very. Another white corridor with . . .

A piece of Abby's wedding dress lay snagged on a rough spot in the wall.

"Damn!" Peg said, with more energy than I'd ever heard her say anything. "That bitch can't keep nothing tidy, her! This stupid stuff's everywhere!" She snatched it up savagely and tore the small oblong into even smaller pieces. Her face was a mottled, angry red. There were tears in her eyes.

Why was there a rough place on a nanosmooth wall to snag a piece of dropped lace?

"Stupid bitch!" Peg said. Her voice caught.

"Why, Peg," I said. "You're jealous."

"You shut up, you!"

Through the zoom portion of my corneas, the rough place on the wall had an added-on look. Not a mistake in the nanoprogramming, but a bump built later, with another clocked nanoassembler, manually. Why?

To snag an oblong of lace?

Every oblong was different. The lace had been programmed that way. To make a unique pattern on an old-fashioned wedding gown.

To make a code.

Peg had recovered herself. Blank-faced once more, but with red eyes, she shoved the torn bit of lace in the pocket of her hideously unbecoming turquoise jacks. Her mouth twitched in pain. No sympathetic shapes slid through my mind. Peg didn't know what pain was. Peg hadn't seen Leisha die, mud caked on her thin yellow shirt, two small red dots on her forehead.

"Let's go, you," she said impatiently, as if I were the one who'd delayed her.

A code. The bits of lace were a code, in a place where every word, every action, every chance encounter was monitored. And everyone was encouraged to be "tidy" and pick up litter, because Brigadier General Francis Marion had been the tidiest son-of-a-bitch to ever attack the British army.

How many people were involved? Abigail and Joncey, most certainly. Who did they have with them against Hubbley? Did they have anyone on the outside?

I saw again the gray canister. PROPERTY OF U.S. ARMY. CLASSIFIED. DANGER.

"See," Peg snarled when we got back to commons, "you seen everything, you! Now can we stay put?"

"I get bored staying put," I said. "Let's do it again." And I wheeled away my primitive chair, hearing her curse behind me.

Three days later, three days of ceaseless wheeling, the door to Jimmy Hubbley's private quarters opened and he and Abigail came out. When Abigail saw Peg, she lowered her eyes, smiled, and pretended to finish zipping the pants to her jacks.

Peg was behind me, where I couldn't see her face, but I could see her hands, large and rough on the handles of my chair. In the stiffening of her hands—controlled, habitual—I saw that she already knew about Abigail and Hubbley. Of course. Everyone would know; you couldn't hide it in a place like this. Joncey must accept it. Maybe it advanced his and Abby's plans for the counterrevolution. Maybe he thought Hubbley was just spreading his genes in the allowable natural way to strengthen the human genome. Maybe Hubbley even thought he was spreading Francis Marion's, to every pretty soldier with a duty to Will and Idea.

"Evenin', Peg," Hubbley said. She choked out some reply. Abigail smiled demurely. She made a shape in my mind: flowers with tiny, deadly teeth in their sunny yellow centers.

"Evenin', Major Hubbley," Peg choked out. I didn't even know he'd been promoted.

But now I had him.

At dinner the commons was full. Abigail sat with her friends, laughing, sewing on her white lace wedding dress. Her face was flushed and giddy. Above, in the world I now knew only from the

HT, it turned November. Sixty-seven days underground, and Miranda had not come.

Joncey stood with a group watching a pair of gamblers play Devil. The twelve-sided dice, made of some shiny metal, flashed as they were thrown overhead. Everyone shrieked and laughed. Peg sat slumped, blank-faced, in her chair, her rough hands slack on her knees. I'd asked her for paper and pen, which made her first suspicious and then disgusted.

"What for? You got your library terminal, you."

"I want to write something."

"You can speak, you, to the terminal anything you want saved."

"I want to write it. On paper."

Her suspicion deepened. "You can write?"

"Yes."

"I thought Major Hubbley said, him, that you wasn't no donkey, you."

"I've been to donkey schools. I can write. Can't you read?"

"Course I can read, me!"

She probably could, at least a little. Liver children usually learned to read basic words, if not to write them. You needed to read names on packages at the warehouse, on street signs, on scooter bet sheets. I hoped to hell she could read.

An unseen monitor watched me, of course. I bent over the paper Peg brought me, coarse pale sheets probably meant to wrap something in. I couldn't remember the last time I'd written anything. I was never very good at it. The pen felt heavy in my hand.

Drew, hold it like this.

What for, Leisha? I can speak, me, to the terminal anything I want it to know.

What if someday there aren't any terminals?

In your nose hairs! There will always be terminals, them!

Slowly I printed A HISTERY OF THE SECUND AMERICAN REVALUTION.

Three hours later, after much crumpling up and tearing of paper and fidgeting in my chair, I had three crossed-out pages. They described James Francis Marion Hubbley's philosophy, activities, and goals. Hubbley himself strode across the room, looming over me. I wondered what had taken him so long.

"Now, Mr. Arlen, sir, I'm glad as Sundays that y'all are

interested enough in our revolution to write it down. But naturally I want to check what y'all are sayin,' for accuracy. Y'all can understand that, son."

"Does that mean y'all think anybody's going to actually see it?" I said, handing over the papers. But baiting him had no effect. His face, always bony, looked gaunt and drawn. The skin around the eyes bunched in thick ridges. He hardly glanced at my "histery."

"Hail, that's fine, son. Only y'all need more on Colonel Marion. Inspiration is the heart of action, we always say down here."

"I haven't ever heard any of you say that."

"Ummm," he said, not really listening. He gazed distractedly around the room. Abigail was still laughing brilliantly with her friends, sewing on her everlasting wedding gown; she'd been at it for three solid hours. She was now around seven months pregnant, and the white lace cascaded over the bulge of her belly. Joncey had disappeared. So had Campbell and the doctor. Peg, awake beside me, gazed at Hubbley as if at the sun. Something was happening, something I didn't understand.

The shapes in my mind were tight and hard, as closed as the dusky lattice. I was running out of time.

Bracing my hands on the arms of the wheelchair, I lifted my torso inches off the seat. Then I shifted my weight to the left hand, until the chair—not anywhere as stable as a powerchair—toppled. I fell on top of Peg, who instantly had her hands around my throat, squeezing. I fought with myself not to respond. Every fiber in my arms screamed to slug her, but I kept myself still, eyes wide, choking to death. The room wavered, dimmed. It was eternity before Jimmy Hubbley pulled her off me.

"There now, Peg, let go, the man ain't fightin', he just fell . . . Peg! Let go!"

She did, instantly. Air rushed back into my lungs, burning and painful as acid. I gasped and wheezed.

Hubbley stood restraining Peg, although she topped him by ten inches and was undoubtedly stronger than he. He kept one arm around her waist. With the other he hauled my chair upside down. Spectators had gathered.

"C'mon, y'all, this ain't nothin'. Mr. Arlen's chair tipped—see how this metal thing is bent underneath here? Calm down, Peg. Shoot, he ain't even armed. You hurt, Mr. Arlen, sir?"

"N-n-no."

"Wail, these things happen. Starrett, lift Mr. Arlen into this here chair. Where's Bobby? There you are. Bobby, this is your department, straighten out this metal so his wheelchair don't tip again on him. That's downright dangerous. Now, y'all, it's gettin' close to lights out, so just move on to your quarters."

I was lifted into a commons chair. Bobby took a power brace from his pocket and straightened the metal strut on the underside of the chair in fifteen seconds. Lacking a power brace, it had taken me half an hour and every ounce of strength I possessed to bend it that afternoon.

Hubbley took his arm away from Peg, who shivered. He left the room. I picked up my "histery" and let Peg wheel me to bed and lock me in. She was rough, upset at herself for overreacting, wondering if anyone else had seen how desperately she had protected Jimmy Hubbley. She really didn't know that everyone else saw, and mocked, her hopeless passion. Poor Peg. Stupid Peg. I was counting on her stupidity.

In my room I humped up the blanket on the pallet, trying to make it look as if I were underneath. This wasn't easy; the blanket was thin. I left the wheelchair conspicuously empty, to my right, visible as soon as the door was partially open. I positioned myself behind the door, propped against the wall, my useless legs tucked under me.

How long would it take Peg to undress? Did she go through her pockets? Of course she did. She was a professional. But a stupid professional. And sick with passion.

Stupid and sick enough? If not, I was as dead as Leisha.

I was sitting in almost the same position Leisha had when she died. But Leisha had never known what hit her. I would know. The shapes in my mind were taut and swift, silver sharks circling the closed green lattice.

The note in Peg's pocket was written with the same pencil as my histery—it might have been the only pencil in the entire bunker—but not on thick pale wrapping paper. It was written on a piece of lace from Abigail's wedding gown, an oblong discarded oh-so-carelessly along a corridor, an oblong with fewer lacy perforations than normal and so room to scrawl, in a hand as different from my histery as I could make it. Of course, a handwriting expert would know the writing was the same person's. But Peg was not a handwriting expert. Peg could barely read. Peg was stupid. Peg was sick with passion, and jealousy, and protectiveness for her crazy leader.

The note said: *She is traitor. Plan with me. Arlens room safest.* I had written it amidst all the crumpling and tearing and fidgeting of my histery, and it had not been hard to slip it into Peg's pocket. Not for someone who had once picked the pocket of the governor of New Mexico, Leisha's guest, because the governor was an important donkey and I was a sullen crippled teenager who had just been kicked out of the third school Leisha's donkey money had tried to keep me in.

Leisha . . .

The silver sharks moved faster through my mind. Could Peg puzzle out the word "traitor"? Maybe I should have stayed with words of one syllable. Maybe she was more professional than lovesick, or less stupid than jealous. Maybe—

The lock glowed. The door opened. The second she was inside I slammed her in the face with the wheelchair, swinging it upward with every bit of strength in my augmented arm muscles. She fell back against the door, closing it. She was only stunned a moment, but I only needed a moment. I swung the chair again, this time aiming the arm rest, which I had bent out at an angle, directly into her stomach. If she had been a man I could have gone for her balls. Patiently I'd removed the padding on the armrest and worked the metal back and forth, sweat streaming down my face, until it broke off jagged, and then I replaced the armrest. This had taken days, finding the odd moments when I could plausibly bend over the armrest to hide my work from both the monitors and Peg. It took only seconds for the sharp jagged metal to pierce Peg's abdomen and impale her.

She screamed, clutched the metal, and fell to her knees, stopped by the bulk of the chair. But she was strong; in a moment she had the jagged armrest out of her flesh. Blood streamed from her belly over the twisted metal of the chair, but not as much as I'd hoped. She turned toward me, and I knew that in all my concerts, all my work with subconscious shapes in the mind, I'd never created anything as savage as Peg's face looked that moment.

But she was on her knees now, on my level. She was strong, and trained, and bigger than I was, but I was augmented, as her philosophy—Hubbley's philosophy—could never let her be. And

I was trained, too. We grappled, and I got both my hands around her neck and squeezed the fingers Leisha had paid to have strengthened. In case I would ever, in my bodily weakness, need them.

Peg struck at me viciously. Pain exploded in my head, a hot geyser, spraying the dark lattice. I hung on. Pain drowned us both, drowned everything.

For the third time, the purple lattice disappeared. Then so did everything else.

Slowly, slowly, I became aware that objects in the room had shapes of their own, shapes outside my head. They were solid, and sharp-edged, and real. My body had shapes: legs crumpled under me, my head lying on top of the metal wheelchair, my balls screaming with hurt. My hands had shape. They clenched, locked into shape, around Peg's neck. Her face was purple, the tongue poking out swollen between her lips. She was dead.

It hurt to unclench my hands.

I looked at her. I had never killed anybody before. I looked at every inch of her. The note scrawled on lace was locked in her rigid fingers.

As quickly as I could I righted the wheelchair, stuck the padding back on the jagged armrest, and hauled my hurting body into it. Peg had a gun in her jacks; I took that. I didn't know how sophisticated the room's surveillance program was. Peg was presumably allowed to enter at will. Could the surveillance program interpret what it recorded, making judgment calls about sounding an alarm? Or did someone have to be actively watching? *Was* someone actively watching?

Francis Marion, Hubbley had told me, was meticulous about pickets and sentries.

I opened the door and wheeled myself into the corridor. The wheels left a thin line of blood on the perfect nanobuilt floor. There was nothing I could do about it.

I had watched, through all the wheeled trips around the bunker, who went in and out of which doors. I had listened, trying to figure out who were the most trusted lieutenants, who seemed smart enough for computer work. I had guessed which doors might have terminals behind them.

Nobody had come for me. It had been five minutes since I left my room. Eight. Ten. No alarms had sounded. Something was wrong.

I came to a door I hoped held a terminal; it was of course locked. I spoke the override tricks Jonathan and Miranda had taught me, the tricks I didn't understand, and the lock glowed. I opened the door.

It was a storage room, full of more small metal canisters, stacked to the ceiling. None of the canisters were labeled. There were no terminals.

Footsteps ran down the hall. Quickly I closed the door from the inside. The footsteps ceased; the room was sound shielded. I opened the door again a few inches. Now people were shouting farther down the corridor.

"Goddamn it, where is he, him? Goddamn it to hell!" Campbell, whom I had never heard even speak. They were looking for me. But the surveillance program should show clearly where I was . . .

Another voice, a woman's, low and deadly, said, "Try Abby's room."

"Abby! Fuck, she's in on it! Her and Joncey! They already got the terminal room—"

The voices disappeared. I closed the door. The shapes in my mind suddenly ballooned, crowding out thought. I pushed them down. This was it, then. It had started. They weren't looking for me, they were looking for Hubbley. The revolution against the revolution had started.

I sat thinking as fast as I could. Leisha. If Leisha were here—

Leisha was no plotter. No killer. She'd believed in trusting the eventual outcome of any clash between good and evil, in trusting the basic similarities among human beings, in trusting their ability to compromise and live together. Humans might need checks and balances, but they didn't need imposed force, nor defensive isolation, nor crushing retribution. Leisha, unlike Miranda, believed in the rule of law. That's why she was dead.

I opened the door the rest of the way and wheeled my chair, bent as it was, into the corridor. The padding fell off the armrest. I blocked the corridor, gun drawn, and waited for someone to round the corner. Eventually someone did. It was Joncey. I shot him in the groin.

He screamed and fell against the wall. There was a lot more blood than there had been with Peg. I raced my chair up to him and pulled him across my lap, holding his wrists with one of my augmented hands and the gun with the other. Another man rounded the corner, Abigail waddling after him. Abigail made a moaning sound, more like wind than people.

"Oohhhhhhhh . . . ."

"Don't come close or I'll kill him. He'll live, Abby, with medical attention, if I let him have it soon. But if you don't do what I ask, I'll kill him. Even if you draw a gun and shoot me, I'll kill him first."

The other man said, "Shoot the crippled bastard, you!"

"No," Abby said. She'd regained control of herself immediately; her eyes darted like trapped rabbits, but she was in control. She was a better natural leader than most, maybe better than Hubbley. But I held Joncey in my arms, and she wasn't leader enough for that sacrifice.

"What do you want, Arlen?" She licked her lips, watching the blood pour out of Joncey's groin. He'd fainted, and I shifted him to free my other hand.

"You're leaving, aren't you? The ones of you left alive. Did you kill Hubbley?"

She nodded. Her eyes never moved from Joncey. He was still on my lap. The almost forgotten shapes of childhood prayer whipped through my mind: *Please don't let him die yet.* I saw the same shapes in Abigail's eyes.

"Leave me here," I said. "Just that. Here, and alive. Somebody will come eventually."

"He'll call, him, for help," the other man said.

"Shut up," Abby said. "You know nobody can't use them terminals but Hubbley and Carlos and O'Dealian, and they're all dead, them."

"But, Abby—"

"Shut up, you!" She was thinking hard. I couldn't feel Joncey's heart.

A woman raced into the corridor. "Abby, what's the matter, you? The submarine's off the coast—" She stopped dead.

The *submarine.* All of a sudden I saw how the underground revolution had evaded the GSEA for so long. A sub meant military help. There were agencies inside the government involved, or at least people within agencies. PROPERTY OF U.S. GOVERNMENT. CLASSIFIED. DANGER.

For a long moment I thought I was dead.

"All right!" Abby said. "Give him to me and lock yourself in that there storage room, you!"

"Don't come close," I said. I backed into the room with the canisters, still carrying Joncey. At the last minute I dumped him onto the floor and slammed the door. It could be locked from the inside, but I had no doubt she could override it. I held onto the urgency in the second woman's voice, the panic: *Abby, the submarine's off the coast!* Let the sub be ready to go. Let Abby want Joncey alive, safely tucked inside a medunit, more than she wanted me dead. Let the canisters all around me not contain deadly viruses, and let them not be able to be released by remote . . .

I sat, heart pounding. The shapes in my mind were red and black and spiky, painful as cactuses.

Nothing happened.

Minutes dragged by.

Finally a small section of the wall beside me brightened. It was a holoscreen, and I hadn't even realized it. A dumb terminal. Abby's face filled it. It was smeared with blood, twisted with hate.

"Listen, Arlen, you. You're going to die there, underground. I done sealed it off. And the terminals are frozen, them, all of them. In another hour the life support will cut out automatically. I could kill you now, me, but I want you to think about it first . . . You hear me? You're dead, you—dead dead DEAD." With each word her voice rose, until it was a shriek. She whipped her head from side to side, her hair seething and foaming, caked with blood. I knew Joncey was dead.

Someone pulled her away from the screen, and it went blank.

I edged open the door of the storage room. My wheelchair was so bent I could hardly wheel it along the corridors. My vision kept fading in and out, until I wasn't sure what shapes were in front of me and what were in my head, except for the dark lattice. That was in my head. It stirred, and for the first time began to open, and every inch of its opening pushed against my mind like pain.

I found Jimmy Hubbley. They had killed him clean, as near as I could tell. A bullet through the head. Francis Marion, I remembered, had died quietly in bed, of an infection.

Campbell must have fought. His huge body blocked a corridor, bloody and torn, as if by repeated blows. He lay sprawled across the captured doctor. The doctor's face looked both terrified and indignant; this was not supposed to be his war. His blood slid down the nanosmooth walls, which had been designed to shed stains.

Two bodies lay on the terminal room floor, when I had finally opened enough doors to find it. A woman named Junie, and a man I'd never heard called anything but "Alligator." They, too, had died clean, of bullets through the forehead. Abigail's bid for power hadn't been sadistic. She just wanted to control things. To be in charge. To know what was best for 175 million Americans, give or take a few million donkeys.

I sat in front of the main terminal and said, "Terminal on." It answered, "YES, SIR!"

Francis Marion had believed in military discipline.

It took me fifteen minutes to try everything Jonathan Markowitz had taught me. I spoke each step, or coded it in manually, not understanding what any of them meant. Even if Jonathan had explained, I wouldn't have understood. And he had not explained. The shapes in my mind darted quickly, palpitating, sharp as talons.

"READY FOR OUTSIDE TRANSMISSION, SIR!"

I didn't move.

If Abigail had been telling the truth, I had thirty-seven minutes of life support left in the underground bunker.

Huevos Verdes, off the Mexican coast, could be here in fifteen. But would they be? Miranda had not come for me before now.

"SIR? READY FOR OUTSIDE TRANSMISSION, SIR!"

The dark lattice in my mind was, finally, opening.

It started to unfurl like an umbrella, or a rosebud. They have rosebuds now, genemod, that will unfurl completely in five minutes, with the right stimuli, for use in various ceremonies. They're pretty to watch. The opaque diamond-shaped panes on the lattice lightened and widened, both at the same time. The lattice itself expanded, larger and larger, until it had opened completely.

Inside was a ten-year-old boy, dirty and confident, his eyes bright.

I hadn't seen him, me, in decades. Not his sureness about what he wanted, his straight-line going after it. That boy had been his own man. He made his own decisions, undaunted by what the rest of the world said he should do. I hadn't seen him since the day he arrived at Leisha Camden's compound in New Mexico, and met his first Sleepless, and gave his mind to their superior ones. Not since I'd become the Lucid Dreamer. Not since I'd met Miranda.

And here he was again, that solitary grinning boy, released from the stone lattice that had encased him. A bright glowing shape in my mind.

"SIR? DO YOU WISH TO CANCEL TRANSMISSION, SIR?"

There were thirty-one minutes left.

"No," I said, and spoke the emergency override code, the one I'd been urged to memorize carefully and not forget, as Drew Arlen common Liver might easily forget, in case of emergency.

She herself answered. "Drew? Where are you?"

I gave her the exact longitude and lattitude, obtained from the terminal, and told her how to get the rescue force through the mucky pool. My voice was completely steady. "It's an illegal underground lab. Part of the revolution that already released the duragem dissemblers. But you know all about that, don't you?"

Her eyes didn't flicker. "Yes. I'm sorry we couldn't tell you."

"I understand." And I did. I hadn't understood before, but I did now. Since Jimmy Hubbley. Since Abigail. Since Jontcey. I said, "There's a lot I have to tell _you_."

She said, "We'll be there in twenty minutes. There are people already close by . . . just wait twenty minutes, Drew."

I nodded, watching her face on the screen. She didn't smile at me; this was too important. I liked that. The shapes in my mind left no room for smiles. The crying boy, the people—all the people in the world—inside the dark lattice. Inside my mind, inside my unwilling responsibility.

"Just twenty minutes," Carmela Clemente-Rice said in her warm voice. "Meanwhile, tell us how the—" and then the screen went dead as Huevos Verdes picked up the signal, overrode it, and cut off my communication with the GSEA.

Fourteen

The morning the President declared martial law, him, was the same morning I found the dead genemod rabbit by the river. It was a week after we walked to Coganville and the government people came, them, to East Oleanta to blow up Eden. Only when Annie finally let me out of bed, I listened hard, me, to what everybody in the café said about the place that got blown up. Some people even hiked out, them, to look at it. And soon as they described it, I knew, me, that the government didn't blow up the place my big-headed girl went underground. Not my Eden.

And I was the only person in the world, me, that knew that.

Still, I wanted, me, to go see for myself. I *had* to go.

"Where you going, Billy?" Annie said, breathing hard. She'd just lugged in a bucket of river water for washing. The government techs fixed everything, them, but two days later stuff started to break again. That's when a lot of people left East Oleanta on the gravrail, before *it* could break. The women's bath wasn't working. Lizzie was right behind Annie, her, lugging another bucket. It broke my heart, nearly, with my own uselessness. The medunit said, it, that I wasn't supposed to lift nothing.

"Down to the café," I lied.

Annie pressed her lips together. "You don't want, you, to go down to the café again. Where you really going, Billy? I don't want you, me, taking no more walks in them woods. It's too dangerous. You might fall again."

"I'm going to the café," I said, and that was two lies.

"Billy," Annie said, and I knew from her bottom lip that she was going to say it again, "We could leave, us. Now. Before more duragem gets eat away on that train."

"I ain't leaving East Oleanta, me," I said. It scared me to tell her no. Each time it scared me, each and every single time. What if Annie left anyway, her, without me? My life would end. What if Annie took Lizzie and just left?

But I had to stay, me. I *had* to. I was the only person who knew, me, that the government didn't blow up Eden. Dr. Turner was the one that called the government to come to East Oleanta. Lizzie told me, her. Annie didn't know. I had to stay and make sure Dr. Turner didn't find that Eden still existed and call the government to come back and finish the job. I didn't know, me, how I could stop Dr. Turner unless I killed her, and I didn't think I could do that. Maybe I could. But I couldn't go off, neither, and leave the dark-haired big-headed girl who'd deliberately let me know where Eden was in case I ever really needed it again. I owed that girl, me.

Only it wasn't only that.

So I said to Annie, "Get off my back, woman. I'm going, me, down to the café, and I'm going alone!"

Then I held my breath, me, the sick fear churning inside me.

But Annie only sighed, her, and took off her parka and picked up a washrag. That was the wonderful thing about Annie. She knew there was things a person was just going to do, them, and she didn't waste her breath arguing about it, unless of course the person was Lizzie. Actually, the next person I expected trouble from, me, was Lizzie. But Lizzie sat on the sofa with her library terminal, doing her everlasting studying, her, and glancing up at the door for Dr. Turner, ready to ask the doctor questions nineteen to the dozen.

That was another reason for taking my walk now. Dr. Turner wasn't around, her. For a change.

I zipped my parka, me, and picked up the walking stick Lizzie brought me. It's a good stick. I'd use it even if it wasn't, because Lizzie brought it to me, but it *is* good. The right height and thickness. Lizzie's got an eye, her. When she takes it off her library terminal and Dr. Turner.

Annie said, more gentle, "You be careful, Billy Washington. We don't want, us, anything to happen to you," just like she knew I wasn't going to the café after all, just like we didn't have no bitter fights over leaving East Oleanta. And she put her arms around me. For a minute I held Annie Francy, me, against my chest, her head resting just under my chin, and closed my eyes.

"You," I said, which was stupid enough, but then it was all right because Annie smiled. I could feel her smiling, her, against my neck. So I said it again. "You."

"You yourself," she said, pulling away. Her chocolate brown eyes had a tender look, them. I walked out that door like I was walking on sky. And I didn't feel too weak, me, neither. My legs worked better than I expected. I got all the way, me, down to the river without my heart racing. Only my mind, it.

Why wouldn't I leave East Oleanta? Annie really wanted, her, to go someplace better for Lizzie. She was only staying for me.

And why was I staying, me? Because a big-headed Sleepless girl, who was probably Miranda Sharifi herself, might need me. Me, Billy Washington, who couldn't even help carry water or trap rabbits or move Y-energy heat cones to places where they was needed. It was funny when you thought about it. Miranda Sharifi, from Huevos Verdes and Eden, needing Billy Washington.

Only it wasn't funny.

I poked the end of my stick, me, in the soft mud and leaned on it to ease my old fool's body down the riverbank. I was kidding myself. The truth was, it was me that needed Eden. In my head anyway. And I didn't really know why.

I picked my way, me, over the rocks along the river. We'd got a thaw the last few days, and the river mud was thick as soup dotted with patches of snow. The sun was shining, it, and the water ran high, green and cold, rushing along like a gravrail. I saw something dark, me, lying in some snow, and I stumped along for a closer look.

It was a rabbit. With long, clawed paws. It laid on its side, him, on the white snow, its guts torn out. Fox prints dotted the mud, them. The rabbit was reddish brown.

Somebody climbed down the bank behind me. I poked my stick, me, into the rabbit and turned it over. The rabbit was brown.

"Ugh," Dr. Turner said. "What killed it?"

"Fox."

"Well, why are you looking so funereal about it? Surely this must happen all the time out here in God's country. Were you thinking we could eat it?"

"No. Not this rabbit, him."

"Well, if you can get your mind off the local wildlife, I have news. The President's declared martial law."

She sounded upset, her. I didn't say nothing.

"Congress has backed him up. Good old Article 1 Section 8. That big fuck-up on Wall Street yesterday, and enough state budgets have run out of money so they can't afford to pay jurors, which means that even where there aren't food riots the judiciary has stopped functioning in just enough states for ol' Commander-in-Chief Bonny Profile to declare civil authority inadequate to—you don't know what the hell I'm talking about, do you, Billy? Do you know what martial law is?"

"No, Dr. Turner."

"The President has put the army in control. To keep peace where there's rioting. No matter what they have to do to keep it."

"Yes, Dr. Turner."

She looked at me, her, sideways. I ain't never been any good, me, at hiding things. "What is it, Billy? What's wrong with that rabbit?"

I said, slower than I meant, "It's brown."

"So? We've seen lots of brown rabbits. Lizzie told me she even had a brown rabbit for a pet, last summer."

"It ain't summer."

She went on, her, looking at me, and I saw she really didn't understand. Sometimes donkeys don't know the most simple things.

"This here rabbit's a snowshoe rabbit. It should of changed its coat, him, by now. Reddish brown in the summer, white in the winter, and here it is the start of November. It should have changed, him."

"Always, Billy?"

"Always."

"Genemod." Dr. Turner kneeled in the snow, her, and studied the rabbit hard. There wasn't nothing to see, except that reddish brown coat. Almost the same color as the little hairs escaping from her hat onto the back of her neck where she kneeled down, her, in front of me. I could of killed her right then, me, bashed her neck with my stick, if I was the killing kind. And if I'd of thought, me, that it would of done anybody any good.

"Billy—are you *positive* the coat shouldn't still be brown?"

I didn't even answer, me.

She sat back on her feet, thinking hard. Then she looked up at me, her, with the damnedest look I ever saw on anybody's face. I didn't have no idea, me, what it meant, except it reminded me of Jack Sawicki when he played chess. When he was alive, him, to play chess. People used to snicker, them, at Jack for liking chess. It wasn't no game for a Liver.

Then Dr. Turner smiled, her. She said, " 'Oh, my ears and whiskers, how late it's getting!' " which didn't even make no sense. "Billy, you have to take me to Eden."

I leaned on my stick. The end of it was mucky from poking at the rabbit. "There ain't no Eden, Dr. Turner. The government blew it up, them."

" 'There *is* no rabbit,' " she said, smiling, her, in that same voice that didn't make no sense. "Down the rabbit hole, Billy. Off with their heads. You and I both know they didn't blow it up. They missed."

I looked, me, again at the dead rabbit. The fox had done a job on it. "What makes you say, you, that they missed?"

"It doesn't matter. What matters is that they *did* miss, and that there are things I need to know. And I've decided that the only way left to discover them is to go to Eden and ask. Nicely direct, don't you think? Will you take me there?"

I picked, me, a place in the river, and stared at it. Then I stared at it some more. I wasn't going, me, to get into no argument with no donkey. There ain't never any way to win those arguments. But I wasn't going to take her to Eden, neither. She had called the government once, her, to blow up Eden, and she could do it again. She wasn't going to learn nothing from me.

After a few minutes Dr. Turner stood up, her, wiping mud off the knees of her jacks. Her voice was serious again. "All right, Billy. Not yet. But you will, I know, when something happens. And something will. The SuperSleepless aren't releasing genemod rabbits that everyone can see are genemod rabbits for no reason at all. This is a message. Pretty soon the meaning will come clear, and then we'll discuss this again."

"Ain't nothing to discuss," I said, me, and I meant it. Not with her. No matter how many genemod rabbits turned up.

The sun was lower now, it, and the air was getting cold. And my walk was pretty much ruined anyway. I climbed the riverbank, me, taking my time. Dr. Turner knew better than to try and help me.

Lizzie was dancing around the apartment, clean from a bath, waving her study terminal. "Godel's proof!" she sang, her, like it was a song. "Godel's proof, Billy!"

She was as bad as Dr. Turner with her looking glasses and rabbit holes. Still, I was glad to see Lizzie so happy.

"Look, Vicki, look what happens if you take this formula and just kind of sneak up on these numbers . . ."

"Let me get my coat off, Mr. Godel," Dr. Turner said, which didn't make no more sense than her talk at the river. But she was smiling, her, at Lizzie.

Lizzie couldn't hardly stay still, her. Whatever she had on that library terminal must of been pretty exciting. She grabbed my stick, her, and started dancing around with it like it was a partner. Then she stuck it under her and rode it like a hobbyhorse. Then she raised it up over her head like a flag. I knew from all this, me, that Annie wasn't home.

"All right, let's see Godel's proof," Dr. Turner said. "Did you access Sven Bjorklind's variations?"

"Course I did, me," Lizzie said, with scorn. I couldn't take my eyes off her. She was like a light, her. A sun. My Lizzie.

By the next morning she was so sick she couldn't move.

It didn't look like no sickness I ever saw, certainly not like the fever she'd had last August. Lizzie was shitting bad, her, with blood in it. Annie kept emptying the bucket and cleaning her up, but the apartment still smelled awful. And Lizzie couldn't move her legs or head without it hurting her. Annie and me were up with her, us, all night. By dawn she wasn't even crying no more, just laying there, her eyes open but not seeing nothing. I was scared, me. She just laid there.

I said to Annie, "I'm going, me, to get Dr. Turner. She's down at the café, her, watching the news about martial—"

"I know, me, where she is!" Annie snapped, because she was so worried, her, about Lizzie, and so exhausted. "She's been there all night, ain't she? But Lizzie don't need no donkey doctor, her. This time our medunit's working."

I didn't say, me, that donkeys invented the medunit. I was too scared myself. Lizzie groaned and shit in the bed.

"You go ahead, you, and wake up Paulie. I'll bring her as soon as she's cleaned up."

Paulie Cenverno's been mayor, him, since Jack Sawicki was killed. Paulie keeps the code to the clinic. I grabbed my stick, me, and set off as fast as I could go to Paulie's apartment building.

Outside was cold and gray but sweet-smelling, which somehow made me feel even scareder for Lizzie. Halfway down the street I met Dr. Turner. She looked, her, so tired and upset that her genemod face was almost plain.

"Billy? What is it?" She grabbed my arm hard, her. "Your face . . . Lizzie? Is it Lizzie?"

"She's sick really bad, her. It got worse so fast . . . she's going to die!" It just came out. I thought I'd faint, me. *Lizzie* . . .

"Get Paulie to unlock the clinic. I'll help Annie." She was gone, her, running like I could of, once.

Paulie got up right away, him. By the time we got to the clinic Annie and Dr. Turner were there. Dr. Turner carried Lizzie. Lizzie was crying, her. Her poor legs dangled like broke branches.

It felt like hot coals burned in my stomach, I was so scared. No normal kid sickness should get that bad that fast.

The clinic ain't nothing but a locked foamcast shed, no windows, big enough to hold the medunit and four or five other people who might be standing around. Paulie said, "Put her there, her . . . right there . . ." Paulie didn't really know nothing, him. He was as scared as we were.

Dr. Turner laid Lizzie on the medunit couch, strapped her down, and slid the couch inside the unit. We could see Lizzie, us, through the plasticlear windows. The needles came out and went into Lizzie, but she didn't cry out, her. It was like she didn't feel nothing that was happening.

A few minutes went by. Lizzie didn't move, her. She looked almost asleep. Maybe the medunit gave her something, it, to sleep. Finally the medunit said, "This unit is inadequate to make a diagnosis. Viral configuration is not on file. Administering wide-spectrum anti-virals and secondary antibiotics . . ." There was more. Nobody never listens to a medunit, them. You just let it fix you.

But Dr. Turner jumped like she was shot. She shoved Paulie aside, her, and talked at the medunit.

"Additional information! What class is the viral configuration?"

"You have exceeded this unit's capabilities. This unit responds only manually to specific medical requests."

"Cheap politicians." Dr. Turner spoke again, her, to the medunit and a panel opened on the side, where I never noticed no panel. Inside was a screen and keyboard. Dr. Turner typed hard, her. She studied the screen.

"What is it?" Annie said. "What's Lizzie got, her?" Annie's voice was tiny and thin. It didn't sound nothing like Annie.

This time Dr. Turner didn't have the chess-playing look. This time she looked, her, like my stomach felt. The bones in her cheeks stood out like somebody drew them on her skin.

"Billy . . . did Lizzie touch the end of your walking stick? The end you poked the brown rabbit with?"

I saw Lizzie, me, dancing around the apartment with my stick, riding it, waving it by one end, singing about them Godel's proofs. Something inside my belly dropped, it, and I thought I was going to throw up.

"Yes. She was playing, her . . ."

Dr. Turner slumped, her, against the wall. Her voice was thick. "Not Eden. Eden didn't engineer that rabbit. The other ones did, the illegal lab that released the dissembler . . . oh my sweet Jesus in hell . . ."

"Don't blaspheme, you," Annie said, her, but there wasn't no fire in it. Her eyes were big as Lizzie's. Lizzie, who I saw was going to die.

Paulie said, "Eden? What about Eden, it?" His face looked tight and small.

Dr. Turner looked at me, her. Her eyes, all genemod violet and as unnatural as a brown snowshoe rabbit in a hard November, didn't see me. I could tell, me. She saw something else, her, and her words didn't make no sense. "A pink poodle. A pink poodle with four ears and hyperlarge eyes . . ."

"What?" Paulie Cenverno said, bewildered. "What about a poodle?"

"A pink poodle. Sentient. Disposable."

"Easy there, easy," I said, because she was out of her head, maybe, and I just realized, me, that I was going to need her. Need her sensible. To carry Lizzie. No, Annie could do it. But Annie wasn't in no shape to carry Lizzie. Paulie, then. But Paulie was already backing out of the clinic, him. There was something strange going on here, and he didn't like it, and when Paulie don't like something, him, he gets away from it. He ain't no Mayor Jack Sawicki.

Besides, I couldn't think, me, of no way to keep Dr. Turner from following us, short of killing her, and I didn't have no way to do that. Even if I could of made myself do it. And if Dr. Turner was carrying Lizzie, then Dr. Turner couldn't fire no gun, her, when the door to Eden opened.

Dr. Turner's eyes cleared. She saw me again, her. And she nodded.

I looked again through the medunit window. Lizzie was getting some kind of medicine patch, her, even though the unit said it wasn't the right medicine. Probably the best it could do, it. It was only a fancy 'bot.

The big-headed girl who had saved Doug Kane's life and killed the rabid raccoon wasn't no 'bot.

I was going to do what I swore, me, I'd never do. I was going to take Dr. Turner with me to Eden.

The sun was just coming up when we left town. I walked first, me, leaning on a different stick that Dr. Turner tore off a maple tree. She carried Lizzie, her, wrapped in blankets. Lizzie was still asleep from whatever the medunit gave her. Her skin looked like wax. Annie came last, her, stumbling through the woods, where Annie didn't never go. I think she was crying, her. I couldn't look, because it might be that hopeless kind of crying women do at the very end, and I couldn't of stood it. It wasn't the very end yet. We were going, us, to Eden.

The sky turned all the colors of a pine-knot fire.

I tried to lead them, me, where the snow wasn't too deep. A few times I guessed wrong and fell into a hollow packed with snow, sinking up to my knees. But it was okay because only me fell. I stayed enough ahead, me, for that. Still, each time I fell, me, I could feel my heart go a little faster, and my bones ache a little more.

The thaw we'd been having, it helped. A lot of snow had

melted, especially in the sunny places. Without that thaw I don't know, me, if we could of made it through the mountains.

Lizzie moaned, her, but she didn't wake up.

"Just a . . . minute, Billy," Dr. Turner said, after about an hour. She stopped in a sunny patch, her, and sank to her knees, Lizzie laid across her lap. I was surprised, me, that she'd kept going that long—Lizzie ain't as light as she was even a year ago. Dr. Turner must be stronger than she looked, her. Genemod.

"We don't have any extra minutes, us!" Annie cried, but Dr. Turner didn't pay her no attention, not even to scowl at her. Maybe Dr. Turner was just too tired, her, to scowl. She'd been up all night, watching the newsgrids about the President's martial law. But I think she knew, her, how scared to death Annie was.

"How . . . much farther?"

"Another hour," I said, even though it was more. We weren't making good time, us. "Can you make it?"

"Of . . . course." Dr. Turner stood up, her, struggling with Lizzie, who hung like a sack. For just a minute I thought, me, that I saw Annie put her hand on Dr. Turner's arm, real gentle. But maybe Annie was just steadying herself.

The woods never seemed so big to me.

After a while the ache just started to live in my bones, like some little animal. It chewed away, it, at my legs and knees and the shoulder of the arm holding my stick. And then it started to chew away near my heart.

I couldn't stop, me. Lizzie was dying.

Now we climbed higher, us, up the wooded side of the mountain. The brush and trees got thicker, them. There wasn't no sunny patches. I wasn't taking them, me, the way Doug Kane and I had gone last fall—too much snow. This way was harder, and longer, but we'd get there.

It took us nearly until noon. Dr. Turner made us stop and eat from the food Annie carried. It tasted like mud. Dr. Turner watched, her, to make sure I ate all my share. Lizzie couldn't take nothing, her. She still didn't move, not even her eyes. But she was still breathing. I melted a little clean snow, me, with Dr. Turner's Y-energy lamp and poured it over Lizzie's lips. They were blue.

"Our Father, who art in Heaven, give us this day our daily bread . . ." Dr. Turner stared at Annie in disbelief. I thought she was going to say something sharp about who gave Livers their daily bread, like I'd heard others donkeys say. Donkeys ain't religious, them. But she didn't.

"How much farther, Billy?"

"Soon now."

"You've been saying 'soon now' for two hours!"

"Soon. Now."

We started off again, us.

When we headed back down the trail to the little creek, I thought, me, for a panicky minute that I was in the wrong place. It didn't look the same. The trail was a slick of mud, it, and the creek ran fast but was clogged with ice chunks and fallen branches, which made it wider than I remembered. We slipped and slided, us, down the steep trail. Dr. Turner held Lizzie over her shoulder with one hand, the other clutching tree after tree to keep from falling. We waded careful, us, across the creek. There was a flat, mostly clear ledge of ground, with just one birch, and one oak with last year's leaves rattling in the wind. They were my landmarks, them. We were there, and there wasn't nothing there.

Nothing to see. Nothing different. Creek, mud, rock shelf, the side of the mountain. Nothing.

"Billy?" Annie said, so soft I hardly heard her, me. "Billy?"

"What do we do now?" Dr. Turner said. She sank to the ground, her, trailing Lizzie in the mud, too tired to even notice.

I looked around. Creek, mud, rock shelf, the side of the mountain. Nothing.

Why would the SuperSleepless let in two muddy Livers, a turncoat donkey, and a dying child? Why should they, them?

That was the minute I knew, me, what Annie meant when she talked about Hell.

"Billy?"

I sank down on a rock, me. My legs wouldn't hold me up no more. The door had been right here. Creek, mud, rock shelf, the side of the mountain. Nothing.

Dr. Turner shoved Lizzie onto her mother. Then she jumped up, her, and started screaming like some crazy thing, like somebody wild person who ain't just carried a heavy child for hours and hours through the snow.

"Miranda Sharifi! Do you hear me? There's a dying child here, a victim of an illegal genemod virus transmittable by wildlife! Some illegal lab engineered it, some demented bastards who can wipe out entire communities in days, and probably want to! Do you hear me? It's genemod, and it's lethal! You people are responsible for this, you're supposed to be the big experts on genemod tailoring, not us! You're responsible, you Sleepless bastards, whether you made it or not, because you're the only ones who can cure it! You're the big brains we all kowtow to, you're the ones we're supposed to look up to—Miranda Sharifi! We need that Cell Cleaner that was trampled on in Washington! We need it now! You baited us with that, you bitch—you damn well owe it to us!"

I couldn't believe it, me. She sounded like Celie Kane screaming about donkeys. I whispered, "You can't boss around a *SuperSleepless*, you!"

She didn't pay me no attention, her. I might of not even been there. "Miranda Sharifi! Do you hear me, you bitch? In the name of a common humanity . . . what the hell am I doing?"

She stood looking dazed, her, like she wasn't never going to move again. Then Dr. Turner started to cry.

Dr. Turner. Started to cry.

I didn't know, me, what to do. It's one thing when Annie cries, Annie's a normal woman. But a donkey crying, sobbing and carrying on like she was the bottom of the apple bin, her, instead of the top . . . I didn't know what to do. And even I had known, I couldn't do it. The aching animal was gnawing, it, at my chest too bad, and not even for Lizzie could I of got my body up off the ground.

"Please . . ." Dr. Turner whispered.

And the door in the mountain opened. No, it didn't open, it— that's not how it works. There was a kind of hard shimmer, some kind of shield, and then the earth sort of vanished, mud and dead oak leaves and moss-covered rocks and everything, and there was a solid plasticlear square at our feet, only it wasn't really plasticlear, about three feet by three feet. And then that vanished and there was stairs.

Dr. Turner went down first, her, and reached up for Lizzie. Annie handed her down. Then Annie eased herself down the stairs. I went last, me, because even though my chest hurt so bad my eyesight squiggled, I wanted to see what happened after we were all under the square. It might be the last thing I ever saw, me, and I wanted to see it.

What happened was the shimmer came again, it, and the plasticlear-that-wasn't-plasticlear came back over my head. I reached up, me, and touched it. It was hard as diamonds. It tingled. On the other side dirt and rocks started to grow—they *grew*— and the dirt wasn't loose but hard-packed, joined to all the other dirt. I could see, me, that in a few minutes there wouldn't be no signs anything had happened, except maybe our footprints in the mud. But I wouldn't bet, me, on any footprints being left.

We stood, us, in a small room, all white and bright, with nothing in it. The walls were perfect—not a nick or a scratch or nothing. I never seen such walls, me. We stood there a long time, it seemed, though it probably wasn't. I wrapped my arms across my chest, me, to keep the pain from gnawing straight through. Dr. Turner turned to me and her face changed. "Why, Billy . . ." And then a door opened where there hadn't been no door, and she stood there, my big-headed dark-haired girl from the woods, not smiling, and I had just enough time, me, to see her before the animal in my chest reared back and sank its teeth into my heart and everything disappeared.

Fifteen

I had completely lost my composure, my rationality, and my common sense, and then the door to Eden opened.

This bothered me. I stood there with a dying child and an old man whom I had—against all odds—come to love, at the threshold of the technological sanctum my entire government had been seeking for God knows how long, facing the single most powerful woman in the entire world—and I was bothered that it was my irrational class-based screaming that had caused the gates of Eden to swing wide. Only it wasn't that, of course. I *knew* it wasn't that. I wasn't quite that many standard deviations along the irrationality curve. But the feeling persisted, because nothing was normal and when nothing's normal, nothing seems any more abnormal than anything else. The measuring scales break down. Miranda Sharifi did that to things.

Up close, she looked even plainer than she had in Washington. Big, slightly misshapen head, wild clouds of black hair, body too short and too heavy to be a donkey yet clearly not a Liver. She wore white pants and shirt, generic looking but not jacks, and her face was pale. The only spot of color was a red ribbon in her hair. I remembered what I'd thought on the steps of Science Court— that she was too old for hair ribbons—and I felt obscurely ashamed. It was difficult to keep my mind on serious subjects. We had too many of them. Or maybe it was just the nature of my mind.

I couldn't think of anything to say. I stood staring at the red hair ribbon.

She was everything I was not.

Annie fell to her knees. The hem of her muddy parka pooled ungracefully on the shining floor and her eyes turned upwards as if to an angel. Maybe that's what she thought Miranda was.

"Ma'am, you have to help us, you. My Lizzie's dying, her, with some disease, Billy says she's dying, Dr. Turner says it ain't natural, this disease, it's *genemod,* it . . . and Billy, he's been so good to us, him, and he ain't hardly even got nothing out of it—but Lizzie, my little girl—" She started to cry.

At the words "Dr. Turner," Miranda's eyes moved to me for a moment, then back to Annie. It was like having a laser sweep over you. I felt she suddenly knew everything there was to know about me: my aliases, my supposedly secret and pathetically marginal GSEA affiliation, the entire history of my residences, pseudo-jobs, pseudo-loves. I felt naked, clear to the cellular level. I told myself to stop it immediately. She wasn't a psychic; she was a human being, a woman with awesome technology behind her and a super-heightened brain and thoughts I would never have and would not understand if they were explained to me . . .

This was how Livers felt about donkeys like me.

Annie said, through her tears and still kneeling, "Please." Just that word. In that place, it had a surprising dignity.

A door appeared in the wall behind Miranda, a door that a moment before had not existed even in outline, and a man stuck his head through. "Miri, they're on the way—"

"You go, Jon," she said. They were the first words she'd spoken. Jon had the same misshapen head as Miranda but handsome features, a bizarre and dissettling combination, like a manticore with the face of a domestic collie. His mouth tightened.

"Miri, you *can't*—"

"That's already settled!" she snapped, and for the first time I saw she was under tremendous tension. But then she turned to him and uttered a few words I didn't catch, so rapidly did she speak. Despite her speed, the words had the curious feel of being separate, each a discreet communication rather than part of a grammatical flow . . . I was only guessing. Miranda wore a single ring, a slim gold band set with rubies, on the ring finger of her left hand.

Jon withdrew, and the "door" disappeared. There was no sign it had ever existed.

Miranda put her hand on Annie's shoulder. The hand trembled.

"Don't cry. I can help them both, I think. Certainly your daughter."

But it was Billy she knelt next to first. She held a small box to his heart and studied its miniature screen; she put the box against his neck and studied the screen again; she fastened a medicine patch on his neck. Watching, I was obscurely reassured. This was known. She was treating Billy for his heart attack, if that was what it was.

He started to breathe more easily, and moaned.

Miranda turned to Lizzie. From her pocket she drew a long, thin black syringe, opaque. Very little medication is given by syringe rather than patch. Something turned over in my chest.

I said, "She's already had wide-spectrum antibiotic and antiviral from a K-model medunit. The unit said this was an unknown virus, outside the cofiguration of any known tailored microorganism, you'd have to build it fresh if you can—"

I was babbling. Miranda didn't look up. "This is the Cell Cleaner, Dr. Turner. But I think you already guessed that." There was something deliberate about her speech, as if the words were chosen carefully, and yet she felt they were completely inadequate to whatever she wanted to say. I hadn't noticed that in Washington, where her speeches to the Science Court must have all been carefully prepared in advance. The slowness was in marked contrast to the way she'd spoken to "Jon."

Annie watched the needle disappear into Lizzie's neck. Annie was completely still, kneeling on the hem of her muddy parka, smearing dead leaves across the featureless white floor.

The moment was surreal. Miranda hadn't even hesitated. I choked out, "Aren't you even going to *explain* it to them give them a *choice* . . ."

Miranda didn't answer. Instead she pulled a second syringe from her pocket and injected Billy.

I thought crazily of all the fatty deposits in the arteries of his heart, all the lethal viral copies that can lie in wait for years in lymph nodes until the body weakens, all the toxic mismultiplications of normal DNA over the sixty-eight years of Billy's bone and flesh and blood . . . I couldn't speak.

Miranda pulled out a third syringe and turned to Annie, who put out a warding-off hand. "No, ma'am, please, I ain't sick—"

"You will be," Miranda said, "without this. Soon." She waited.

Annie bowed her head. It looked to me like prayer, which

suddenly enraged me for no reason I could understand. Miranda injected Annie.

Then she turned to me.

"How toxic is the mutated vir—"

"Fatal. Within twenty-four hours. And easily transmitted. You will become infected."

"How do you know? Did your people engineer and release the virus? *Did* you?"

"No," she said, as calmly as if I'd asked her if it was raining. But a pulse beat in her throat, and she was taut as harpstrings, and as ready to vibrate at a touch. I just didn't know whose. I stared at the syringe in her hand: long, thin, black, the fluid hidden inside. What color was it? That fluid had already gone into Lizzie, into Billy, into Annie.

I whispered, before I knew I was going to, "But I'm a *donkey*—"

Miranda said, "I have already been injected myself. Months ago. This is not an untested procedure."

She had missed completely what I had meant. It lay outside her range of vision. Apparently, then, some things did. I said, "You're so—" without knowing how I was going to finish the sentence.

"We don't have much time. Lower your head, please, Dr. Turner."

I blurted out—this is to my everlasting shame, it was so inane, and at such a moment—"I'm not really a licensed doctor!"

For the first time, she smiled. "Neither am I, Diana."

"Why don't we have much time? What's going to happen? I'm not sick yet, you're going to alter my entire biochemistry, let me at least think a moment—"

A screen suddenly appeared on the wall. Even though this—unlike the door—was certainly a normal technology, I nonetheless jumped as if an angel had appeared with flaming sword. But the angel was in front of me, staring at the screen as if in pain, and the sword trembled in her hand, and I was going to die not because I'd eaten of this particular genetically-engineered apple, but because I didn't.

She didn't give me a choice. The screen showed a plane landing where no plane should have been able to land, a folded thing setting straight down like a rotorless coptor but far more precisely than any coptor, on the same small flat patch of ground between stream and mountain where I had screamed for Eden to open. The same naked birch tree, shivering white. The same tattered oak. I raised my head to stare at the four men climbing out of the unfolded cylinder of the government plane, and Miranda pushed the syringe into my neck. With her other hand on my shoulder, she held me still while the fluid drained.

She was very strong.

Somehow, that one fact cleared my head, which just shows how crazed was the whole situation. I said, almost as if we were coconspirators, "They can't get in, can they? They couldn't even find it before, they blew up the wrong installation. They must have followed us here, Billy and Annie and Lizzie and me—oh, I'm sorry, Miranda—"

She wasn't listening. To my complete shock—it was the weirdest thing that had happened yet, because after all, I'd known about the Cell Cleaner, I'd seen her explain it in Washington—to my utter shock, tears glittered in her eyes. She circled the fingers of her right hand around her left. Covering the ring.

A fifth man was helped out of the plane, and into a powerchair someone else swiftly unfolded. I saw with yet another shock that it was Drew Arlen, the Lucid Dreamer.

He put his hand on the birch tree. I didn't know—and never found out—if it was to steady himself, or if it was part of the entry procedure, an activator or a skin-recognition system or just a failsafe of some unimaginable kind. Then he spoke a series of words, very clear, in that famous voice. The door above our heads opened.

Miranda made no effort to stop him, if she could have. Of course she could have. There must have been shields, countershields, *something*. They were SuperSleepless.

The four GSEA agents came down the stairs as if this were a root cellar in Kansas. They had drawn their guns, which filled me with sudden contempt. Drew Arlen stayed outside.

"Miranda Sharifi, you are under arrest for violations of the Genetic Standards Act, Sections 12 through 34, which state—"

She completely ignored them. She pushed past the four men as if they weren't there, a sudden fire glowing around her that had to be some sort of electrified personal shield. One of the agents reached for her, cried out, and cradled his burned hand, his face distorted by pain. The agent blocking the steps hesitated. I saw him think for half a second about firing, and then change his mind. I could almost see the report later: "Civilians were present, making it inadvisable to—" Or maybe they realized that whoever officially killed Miranda Sharifi was dead himself careerwise, forever, a scapegoat. The agent moved off the steps.

Miranda ascended them slowly, heavily, the tears sparkling in her dark eyes. Three of the agents followed. After a stunned moment I bolted after them.

Drew Arlen sat in the cold November woods in a powerchair. Miranda faced him. A slight wind shook the oak tree, and the dead leaves rattled. A few fell.

"Why, Drew?"

"Miri—you don't have the right to choose for 175 million people. Not in a democracy. Not without any checks and balances. Leisha said—"

"Kenzo Yagai did. He chose. He created cheap energy, and changed the world for the better."

"You could have stopped the duragem dissembler. And didn't. People died, Miranda!"

"Not as many as if we had stopped it. Not in the long run."

"That wasn't your reason! You just wanted control of the situation! You Supers, who don't ever have to die!"

There was a noise behind me. I didn't turn around. What I was looking at was more important than any noise. The questions Drew and Miranda hurled at each other were the same public question I had struggled with ever since I'd seen the Cell Cleaner in Washington: Who should control radical technology? Only they were making of it a private weapon, as lovers can make private weapons of anything. *Who should control technology . . .*

And—make no mistake—technology is Darwinian. It spreads. It evolves. It adapts. The most dangerous wipes out the less fit.

The GSEA had hoped to keep radical tech from falling into the wrong hands. But Huevos Verdes was the *right* hands: the hands that used nanotech to strengthen human beings, not destroy them. That was what the GSEA could not admit. It wasn't their place to judge, they claimed; they only carried out the law. Maybe they were right.

But somebody, somewhere, sometime, had to judge, or we'd end up with pure Darwinian jungle, red in byte and assembler.

Huevos Verdes had judged. And I, by not summoning the

GSEA a second time, along with them. And there was no clear way to know whether either of us was right.

All this I realized, with that peculiar clarity that comes in bodily crisis, as I watched Drew Arlen and Miranda Sharifi tear each other apart in the cold woods.

He said, "You don't have the right to carry out this project. You never did. No more than Jimmy Hubbley—"

She said, "It was supposed to be 'we,' not 'you.' You were part of this."

"Not any more."

"Because you fell into the hands of some scientific crazies. God, Drew, to equate Jimmy Hubbley with *us*—"

"So you did know about him. And left me there all these months."

"No! We knew about the counterrevolution, but not specifically where you were—"

"I don't believe you. You could have found me. You Supers can do anything, can't you?"

"You think I'm lying to you—"

"Yes," Drew said. "I think you're lying."

"But I'm *not*. Drew—" It was a cry of pure anguish. I couldn't look at her face.

"You could have stopped the duragem dissembler, too, couldn't you? You knew it came from the underground. But you let it encourage social breakdown because that prepared the way better for the project. For *your* plans. Isn't that true, Miranda?"

"Yes. We could have stopped the dissembler."

"And you didn't tell me."

"We were afraid—" She stopped.

"Afraid of what? That I'd tell Leisha? The newsgrids? The GSEA?"

She said, more quietly, "Which is just what you did. The first chance you got. We did look for you, Drew, but we're not omnipotent. There was no way of knowing which bunker, where . . . And meanwhile you did exactly what Jon and Nick and Christy said you would—betray the project to the GSEA."

"Because I started to think for myself. Again. Finally. And that's not what Supers want, is it? You want to think for all of us, and us to obey you, without question. Because you always know best, don't you? God, Miranda, aren't you ever *wrong?*"

"Yes," she said. "I was wrong about you."

"That won't be a problem for you any longer."

She cried, "You said you loved me!"

"Not any more."

They went on looking at each other. Drew's face I couldn't read. Miranda's had turned stony, her tears gone. Her eyes were lasers.

She said, "I loved *you*. And you couldn't stand being inferior. That's what your betrayal to the GSEA is really about. Jon was right. You can't ever really understand. Anything."

Drew didn't answer. The wind picked up, smelling of cold water. More leaves blew off the oak. The birch tree shuddered. There was more noise behind me. I didn't turn around.

A GSEA agent said, "I arrest you, Miranda Sharifi, for violations of the—"

She cried out, just as if the agent hadn't spoken, "I can't help it that I know more and think better than you, Drew! I can't help what I am!"

He said, his voice unsteady but angry, the way men are when they know they look weak, "Who should control the technology—"

"Shit!" someone called. I turned. Billy sat dazed on the ground, holding his chest. The noise had been him and Annie, pulling the unconscious Lizzie up from the underground bunker, which they didn't understand and must have feared. Or maybe Annie had pulled Lizzie up the steps, and the agent with the burned hand had helped Billy. The agent stood there beside the old man, looking dazed. But there was nothing dazed about Billy. He sat in the frozen mud, an old man with a body about to be the most biologically efficient machine on the planet, and I saw that he, too, knew what he was looking at. Billy Washington, the Liver. His wrinkled old-man's gaze moved from Drew to Miranda—the latter, I saw, with adoration—then back to Drew again, then to Miranda. "Shit," he said again, and there were layers and layers in his tone, unsortable.

"You're fighting, you, about who should control this technology—but don't you see, it don't matter who *should* control it, them? It only matters who *can?*" And he put his gnarled, grateful, hand on the crumpled sleeping form of Lizzie, lying in the mud, her small face peaceful and cool and damp as her lethal fever broke.

Sixteen

T here was nothing to confiscate for evidence. More planes came, and Drew used the codes that made the door appear in the far wall of the bunker. I contrived to be present for this. Security was chaotic, except for Miranda Sharifi, electro-cuffed to the birch tree, whom agents watched as if they expected an anti-grav heavenly ascension, tree and all. Maybe they did. But Miranda allowed herself to be captured. And everybody under-stood that's what happened: she allowed it.

But nobody, including me, understood why.

Behind the bunker door lay nothing. Even the sterile, fortifying walls that had probably been there were self-consuming by the same nanotechnology that had built them. There were only a series of earth-packed tunnels and caves extending back into the moun-tain, dangerous to explore without proper equipment because the dirt walls crumbled and threatened to cave in. It was impossible to tell how extensive the caves/tunnels were. It was impossible to tell what had been nano-destroyed in them, or removed from them before their collapse. *Miri, they're on the way— Miri, you can't—*

I looked for the slim black syringes that had injected the four of us, but all I saw was smudges of melted black, like metallic candle wax, on the floor at the bottom of the steps where Lizzie and Billy had lain.

There was more. And it happened, incredibly, almost as an afterthought.

But first one of the agents arrested me. "Diana Arlene Covington, you are under arrest for violations of the United States Code, Title 18, Sections 1510, 2381, and 2383."

Obstruction of criminal investigations. Assisting rebellion or insurrection. Treason. I was, after all, supposed to be a GSEA agent.

Miranda watched me intently from her birch tree. Too intently. Drew had gone into the plane. We awaited a second plane, either for more space or more security. With a sudden feint that surprised the agent, I ducked around him and sprinted toward Miranda.

"Hey!"

She had time to say to me only, "More in the syringe—" before the outraged agent had me again and dragged me grimly into the plane. His grip bruised my arms.

I barely noticed. *More in the syringe—*

The whole extent of the project, she had said to Drew Arlen.

So not just the Cell Cleaner, which was staggering enough. Not just that. Something else.

Some other biological technology: radical, unexpected. Unimaginable.

Something more.

Huevos Verdes had not needed to set up this elaborate underground lab to perfect or test the Cell Cleaner. They had already done that, openly, before the Science Court hearing last fall.

Huevos Verdes had expected to lose their case in front of the Science Court. That had been clear at the time, to nearly everybody. What had not been clear was why they were presenting the case at all, given the foregone conclusion. It was because Miranda wanted the moral reassurance that all legitimate paths for this larger project were closed, before she completed her stroll down illegitimate paths at East Oleanta.

How much did the agent know? The GSEA top brass, of course, would know everything. Arlen would have told them.

This intellectual speculation lasted only a moment. It was replaced almost instantly with a freezing fear, the kind that doesn't melt your bones but stiffens them, so it seems you won't ever move, or breathe, again.

Whatever bioengineering project Huevos Verdes had been built for, the charade of the Science Court had been staged for, Drew Arlen had performed concerts for, the duragem dissembler had not been stopped for—whatever bioengineering project had occupied all of the SuperSleepless's unfathomable energies—whatever that bioengineering project was, I had been injected with it. It was in my body. In me. Becoming me.

You don't have the right to choose for 175 million people. Not in a democracy. Not without any checks and balances—

Kenzo Yagai did.

I swayed against the metal bulkhead, then caught myself. My fingers were faintly blue with cold. The nail on the middle finger had broken. The flesh was smooth except for one tiny cut on the index finger. Mud, now dried, made a long arc from wrist to nails. My hand. Alien.

I said aloud to Miranda, *"What was it?"*

In my mind she turned her misshapen head to look at me. Tears, which still didn't fall, brightened her eyes. She said, "Only for your good."

"By whose definition!"

Her expression didn't change. "Mine."

I went on staring at her. Then she dissolved, because of course she was an illusion, born of shock. She wasn't really inside my head. She couldn't ever be inside my head. It was way too small.

The plane lifted, and I was transported to Albany to be arraigned in a court of law.

Billy, Annie, Lizzie, and I were taken to the Jonas Salk United States Research Hospital in Albany, a heavily shielded edifice conspicuous for security 'bots. I was led down a different corridor. I craned my neck to keep Lizzie's gurney in sight as long as I could.

In a windowless room Colin Kowalski waited for me, with a man I recognized instantly. Kenneth Emile Koehler, director, Genetic Standards Enforcement Agency. Colin said nothing. I saw that he never would; he was too outranked, included only because he had had the bad judgment to hire me, the wildcat agent who could have led the GSEA to Miranda Sharifi before Drew Arlen did, and hence just as much an official quisling. But, of course, for the other side. Colin was in disgrace. Arlen was probably a hero who had belatedly but righteously seen the light. I was under arrest for treason. One loser, one winner, one who doesn't know how to play the game.

"All right, Diana," Kenneth Emile Koehler said: a bad beginning. I'd been reduced to a first name. Like a 'bot. "Tell us what happened."

"Everything?"

"From the beginning."

The recorders were on. Drew Arlen had undoubtedly spilled his brain cells already. And I myself could think of no reason not to tell the truth: *Something bioengineered had been injected into my veins. More in the syringe—*

But I didn't want to start there. I felt instead an overwhelming desire to begin at the beginning, with Stephanie Brunell and her illegal genemod pink poodle hurtling itself over my terrace railing. I needed to tell it all, every last action and decision and intellectual argument that had brought me from disgust at illegal bioengineering to championing it. I wanted to explain clearly to myself as well as to these men exactly what I had done, and why, and what it meant, because that was the only way I would fully understand it myself.

That was the moment I realized the GSEA had already gotten a truth drug into me. Which was, of course, a completely illegal violation of the Fifth Amendment, a fact too insignificant to even comment on. I didn't comment on it. Instead I gazed at Koehler and Kowalski and the others who had suddenly appeared and then, wrapped in the glow of absolute truth and in the tender and selfless desire to share it, I talked on and on and on.

Seventeen

There were human guards, robot guards, guard shields. But it was the human guards I noticed. Techs, mostly, although at least one was donkey. I noticed them because there were so many. Miranda had more human guards than the entire population of Huevos Verdes, even including the Sleepless hangers-on like Kevin Baker's grandchildren. She awaited her trial in a different prison from her grandmother, whose treason conviction was ancient history now. Jennifer probably had fewer guards.

"Put your eye directly up to the 'scope, sir," one of them said. He wore the drab blue prison uniform, cut like jacks but not jacks. I let my retina be scanned. Huevos Verdes had passed this level of identification ten years ago.

"You, too, ma'am."

Carmela Clemente-Rice stepped closer to the scope. When she stepped back, I felt her hand on my shoulder, cool and reassuring. I felt her in my mind as a series of perfectly balanced interlocking ovals.

I felt the prison as hot blue confusion. Mine.

"This way, please. Watch the steps, sir."

They evidently didn't see too many powerchairs here. Inanely, I wondered why. My chair skimmed down the steps.

The warden's office showed no signs of security or surveillance, which meant there was plenty of both. It was a large room, furnished in the currently popular donkey style, simple straight-lined tables of teak or rosewood combined with some fancy antique chairs with cloth seats and carved arms. I didn't know what period they were from.

Miranda would have known.

The warden didn't rise as Carmela and I were shown in. He was donkey to his blond hair roots. Tall, blue-eyed, heavily muscled, a genemod re-creation of a Viking chief by parents with more money than imagination. He spoke directly to Carmela, ignoring me.

"I'm afraid, Dr. Clemente-Rice, that you are unable to see the prisoner after all."

Carmela's voice remained serene, with steel. "You're mistaken, Mr. Castner. Mr. Arlen and I have clearance from the Attorney General herself to see Ms. Sharifi. You've received both terminal and hard copy notification. And I have copies of the paperwork with me."

"I already received this notification from Justice, doctor."

Carmela's expression didn't change. She waited. The warden leaned back in his antique chair, hands laced behind his head, eyes hostile and amused. He waited, too.

Carmela was better at it.

Finally he repeated, "Neither of you can see the prisoner, despite what Justice says."

Carmela said nothing.

Slowly his amused look vanished. She wasn't going to either ask or beg. "You can't see the prisoner because the prisoner doesn't choose to see *you*."

I blurted, despite myself, "At all?"

"At all, Mr. Arlen. She refuses to see either of you." He leaned back in his chair even farther, unlacing his hands, his blue eyes small in his handsome face.

Maybe I should have expected it. I had not. I laid my hands, palms flat, on his desk.

"Tell her . . . tell her just that I . . . tell her . . ."

"Drew," Carmela said softly.

I pulled myself together. I hated that the smirking bastard had seen me stammer. Supercilious donkey prick . . . In that moment I hated him as much as I had hated Jimmy Hubbley, as much as I had hated Peg, that poor ignorant hopeless slob pathetically trying to measure up to Jimmy Hubbley . . . *I can't help it that I know more and think better than you do, Drew! I can't help what I am!*

I turned the powerchair abruptly and moved toward the door.

After a moment I felt Carmela follow me. Warden Castner's voice stopped us both.

"Ms. Sharifi did leave a package for you, Mr. Arlen."

A package. A letter. A chance to write back, to explain to her what I'd done and why I'd done it.

I didn't want to open the package in front of Castner. But I might need to make arrangements to answer her letter, now, here, and the letter might have some clue to that . . . It had taken Carmela three weeks to get us this far. A direct favor from the Attorney General. Besides, Castner had undoubtedly already read whatever Miranda had to say. Hell, entire computer-expert security teams had undoubtedly analyzed her words for code, for hidden nanotech, for symbolic meaning. I turned my back to Castner and ripped open the slightly padded envelope.

What if she'd written words too hard for me to read—

But there were no words. Only the ring I'd given her twelve years ago, a slim gold band set with rubies. I stared at it until the ring blurred and only its image filled my empty mind.

"Is there an answer?" Castner said, his voice smooth. He'd scented blood.

"No," I said. "No answer." I went on looking at the ring.

You said you loved me!

Not any more.

Carmela had her back to me, giving me the illusion of privacy. Castner stared, smiling faintly.

I put the ring in my pocket. We left the federal prison. Now there were no shapes in my mind, nothing. The dark lattice, that had dissolved in Jimmy Hubbley's underground bunker to show me my own hemmed-in isolation, had never reappeared. I was no longer sealed in by Huevos Verdes. But Miranda was gone. Leisha was gone. Carmela was there, but I didn't feel her in my mind, didn't even really see her.

I was alone.

We went back through the security system and out of the prison, into the cold bright Washington sunlight.

Eighteen

I blinked and shut my eyes against the glare of a wall that seemed
excessively white. For a moment I couldn't remember where
I was, or who I was. This information returned. I sat up, too
quickly. Blood rushed from my head and the room swirled.

"Are you all right?"

A pleasant-faced, middle-aged woman, with a thick body and
deep lines from nose to mouth. Minimally genemod, if at all, but
not a Liver. She wore a security uniform. She was armed.

I said, "What day is it?"

"December tenth. You've been here thirty-four days." She
spoke to the wall. "Dr. Hewitt, Ms. Covington is back."

Back. Where had I been? Never mind, I knew. I sat on a white
hospital bed in a white hospital room thick with medical and surveillance equipment. Under the disposable white gown my arms
and legs and abdomen were covered with small clear globs of
blood-clotter. Somebody had been taking many many samples.

"Lizzie? Billy? The Livers who came in with me, there were
three of them . . ."

"Dr. Hewitt will be here in a minute."

"Lizzie, the little girl, was sick, is she—"

"Dr. Hewitt will be here in a minute."

He was, with Kenneth Emile Koehler. Immediately my head
cleared.

"All right, Dr. Hewitt. What did Huevos Verdes do to me?"

My directness seemed expected. Why not? We'd spent thirty-
four days in intimate communion, none of which I could remember. He said, "They injected you with several different kinds of

nanotechnology. Some are built from bioengineered organisms, primarily viruses. Some apparently are completely machines, created one atom at a time, that have lodged in your cells. Most seem self-replicating. Some, we guess, are clocked for replication. We have everything under study, trying to determine the exact nature of—"

"What do the machines *do?* What's been changed in *my body?*"

"We don't know yet."

"You don't *know?*" I heard my own shrillness. I didn't care.

"Not completely."

"Lizzie Francy? Billy Washington? Lizzie was sick—"

"A part of the injection you received is the Cell Cleaner mechanism, as you already know. But the rest . . ." A strange look passed over Hewitt's face, resentful and yearning. I didn't want to pursue this look. I was in a sudden frenzy, the kind that makes you think you can't live through the next five minutes without hearing information that you know you will reject in the five minutes after that.

"Doctor—what do you *think* this fucking injection will *do?*"

His face closed. "We don't know."

"But you must know *something*—"

A 'bot rolled through the door. It was table-shaped, with an unnecessary grille suggesting a smiling face. On its surface was a covered tray. "Lunch for Room 612," the 'bot said pleasantly. I smelled chicken, rice—the real thing, not soysynth, foods I hadn't tasted for months. Suddenly I was ravenous.

Everybody watched me eat. They watched with peculiar intensity. I didn't care. Chicken juices trickled down my chin; rice grains fell from my lips. My teeth tingled with the thick sweetness of ripping meat. Fresh sweet peas, spiced applesauce. I was greedy for food, consumed by what I was consuming. No amount could be enough.

When I had finished, I lay back on the pillows, curiously exhausted. Hewitt and Koehler wore identical expressions, and I couldn't read either of them. There was a long, pregnant silence—pointlessly so, it seemed to me.

I said, "So now what? When am I going to be arraigned?"

"Not necessary," Koehler said. His face was still inscrutable. "You're free to leave."

My sudden exhaustion just as suddenly departed. This was not how the system worked.

"I'm under arrest for obstructing justice, conspiring to over-throw—"

"Charges have been dropped." Hewitt this time. It was as if they'd switched roles. Or as if roles no longer mattered. I lay there, thinking about this.

I said slowly, "Let me have a newsholo."

Koehler repeated Hewitt's line, tonelessly, "You're free to go."

I swung my feet over the sides of the bed. The hospital gown tented shapelessly around me. In big moments, small things matter: the world's way of keeping us petty. I demanded, "Where are my clothes?" Just as if I *wanted* the muddy cheap jacks and parka I'd worn to the hospital.

There would be body monitors, of course. Subepidermal homers, radioactive blood markers, who knew what else. I'd never find them.

A 'bot brought me my clothes. I put them on, not caring that the men watched. The usual rules did not apply.

"Lizzie? Billy?"

"They left two days ago. The child is recovered."

"Where did they go?"

Koehler said, "We do not have that information." He was lying. His information was closed to me. I was off the government net.

I walked out of the room, expecting to be stopped in the corridor, at the elevator, in the lobby. I walked out the front door. There was absolutely nobody around: nobody crossing from the parking lot, nobody hurrying in to visit a brother or wife or business partner. A 'bot groomed the spring grass, which to my East Oleanta eyes looked aggressively genemod green. The air was soft and warm. Spring sunlight slanted over it, making long late-afternoon shadows. A cherry tree bloomed with fragrant pink flowers. My parka was far too heavy; I took it off and dropped it on the sidewalk.

I walked the length of the building, wondering what I was going to do next. I was genuinely curious, in a detached way that should have alerted me to how quietly and numbly crazed I actually was. Reality could only interest me, not surprise me. Even the interest was precarious. The next step would have been catatonia.

I reached the corner of the building and turned it. A shuttle bus sat there, compact, green as the engineered grass. The door was open. I climbed in.

The bus said, "Credit, please."

My hands fumbled in the pocket of my jacks. There was a credit chip there: not a Liver meal chip, but donkey credit. I pushed it into the slot. The shuttle said, "Thank you."

"What name is on that chip?"

"You have exceeded this unit's language capacity. Destination, please? Civic Plaza, Hotel Scheherazade, Ioto Hotel, Central Gravrail Station, or Excelsior Square?"

"Central Gravrail Station."

The shuttle doors closed.

There were people in the station, Livers dressed in bright jacks and a few government donkeys; this was Albany, the state capital. Everybody seemed in a hurry. I walked into the Governor John Thomas Lividini Central Gravrail Café. Three men huddled at a corner table, talking intently. The foodbelt had stopped. The holo-grid showed a scooter race, and none of the men looked up when I changed it to a donkey news channel.

"—continues to spread in the midwestern and southern states. Because the engineered virus can be carried by so many different species of animals and birds, the Centers for Disease Control recommend avoidance of all contact with wildlife. Since the plague is also highly contagious among humans—"

I switched channels.

"—strict embargo on all physical trade, travelers, mail, or other entrance of any object whatsoever into France from North America. As with other nations, French fear of contamination has led to an hysteria that—"

I switched channels.

"—apparently ended. Scientists at Massachusetts Institute of Technology have issued a statement that the duragem dissembler's clocked nanomachanisms have *not* run their programmed course, but rather have failed over time because of faulty understanding of the complex scope of their construction. Department of Engineering Chairman Myron Aaron White spoke with us at his office in the—"

I switched channels.

"—chronic food shortages. The situation, however, is expected to ease now that the so-called duragem dissembler crisis has slowed, apparently due to—"

I watched for an hour. Famine was easing; famine was increasing. The engineered plague was spreading; the engineered plague had been checked. The rest of the world had been infected by American goods and travelers; the rest of the world showed only minor signs of either duragem contamination or the "wildlife plague." There was less breakdown from the duragem dissemblers; there was more breakdown in some areas, but scientists were close to a solution to the problem, which was actually difficult to understand because of the advanced nature of the science, for which experts were on the verge of a major breakthrough. Albany was Albany.

But not once was an underground organization of nanotech saboteurs mentioned. Not once was the overground organization of Huevos Verdes mentioned. The SuperSleepless might not have existed. Nor Miranda Sharifi.

I walked over to the table of men in the corner. They looked up, not smiling. I wore purple jacks and genemod eyes. I didn't even feel to see if there was a personal shield on my belt. There would be. Koehler wanted me alive; I was an expensive walking laboratory.

"You men know, you, where I can get to Eden?"

Two faces remained hostile. On the third, the youngest, the eyes flickered and the mouth softened at the corners. I spoke to him.

"I'm sick, me. I think I got it."

"Harry—she's genemod, her," the oldest man said. Nothing in his voice showed fear of infection.

"She's sick," Harry said. His voice was older than his face.

"You don't know who—"

"You go to the sunshine machine by track twelve, you. A woman's there with a necklace pounded like stars. She'll take you to the Eden, her."

"The" Eden. One of many. Prepared for in advance by Huevos Verdes: technology, distribution, information dissemination, all of it. And the Liver security, if you could call it that, consisted only of Harry's companions' mild discouragement, which meant the government wasn't interfering. I felt dizzy.

On the long walk to track 12, I saw only fourteen people. Two of them were donkey techs. I saw no trains leave the station. A cleaning 'bot sat immobile where it had broken down, but there were no soda cans, half-eaten sandwiches, genemod apple cores, soysynth candy wrappers on the ground. Without them, the station looked donkey, not Liver.

A middle-aged woman sat patiently on the ground by the sunshine machine. She wore blue jacks and a soda-can necklace, each soft metal lid bent and pounded into a crude star. I planted myself in front of her. "I'm sick."

She inspected me carefully. "No, you're not."

"I want to go to Eden."

"Tell Police Chief Randall if he wants, him, to shut us down, to just do it. He don't need no donkeys pretending to be sick, them, when you ain't." The woman said this mildly, without rancor.

"Down the rabbit hole," I said. " 'Eat Me,' 'Drink Me.' " To which she naturally did not respond at all.

I walked to a gravrail monitor and asked it for information about train departures. It was broken. I tried another. On the fourth try, a working monitor answered me.

Track 25 was in another section of the station. There was more activity here, although not more garbage on the ground. Three techs worked on a small train. I sat cross-legged on the ground, not speaking to them, until they'd finished. They repaired only this one train, then left, looking tired. Colin Kowalski and Kenneth Koehler had known where I would go.

I was the only passenger. The train was direct. It was just barely the beginning of sunset when I stepped off onto the deserted main street of East Oleanta.

Annie's apartment on Jay Street was empty, the door ajar. Nothing had been taken. Not the ugly garish wall hanging, not the water buckets, not the plasticloth throw pillows, not Lizzie's discarded doll. I went in and lay down on Lizzie's bed. After a while I walked to the Café.

Nobody was there, either. The foodbelt was stopped and empty, the holoterminal off. The Café hadn't been trashed. It had just been evacuated, like the rest of the town. The government wanted everything extraneous cleared out for a while, which did not include me. I was not extraneous. From their point of view, I was one of the five most important people in the world: four walking biological laboratories and their captured mad scientist. I had the run of the laboratory, and so probably did three of the others. I only had to wait for them to arrive.

Before the light failed, I walked through the snow to the flat, stony riverbank where Billy had poked at the brown snowshoe rabbit with the stick Lizzie had given him. The rabbit was gone. I sat for a long time on the embankment, watching the cold water, until the sun set and the rock chilled my butt.

I spent the night in Annie's apartment, on the sofa. The heat unit still worked. Although I woke often during the night, it was only for brief periods. It wasn't true insomnia. Each time, I listened carefully in the darkness. There was nothing to hear.

Once, from some half-conscious impulse, I fingered my ears. The holes for my earrings had closed. I ran a finger over my thigh, searching for the scar from a childhood accident. The scar was gone.

I spent the next morning watching the holoterminal. Bannock Falls, Ohio, had been wiped out by plague in twenty-four hours. Camera 'bots showed bodies dead where they'd fallen outside the Senator Ellen Piercy Devan Café, sprawled across each other in heavy winter jacks like fourteenth-century victims of bubonic plague.

Jupiter, Texas, had rioted, blowing up their town with nanotech explosives that Livers should not, could not, have obtained. The townspeople promised to move on Austin if 450,000 cubits of food, apparently a biblical measure, was not delivered within twenty-four hours.

The donkey enclave of Chevy Chase, Maryland, had imposed quarantine on itself: nobody in, nobody out.

Most of Europe, South America, and Asia had imposed embargoes on anything coming from North America, violations punishable by death. Half the countries claimed the embargoes were working and their borders were clean; the other half claimed legal vengeance for their failing infrastructures and dying people. Much of Africa made both claims at once.

Washington, D.C., outside of the Federal Protected Enclave, was in flames. It was hard to know how much government remained to answer claims of legal vengeance.

Timonsville, Pennsylvania, had disappeared. The entire town of twenty-three hundred people had just packed up and dispersed. That was the closest any newsgrid came to hinting at vast changes in where people went, or why, or what microorganisms they carried with them in their diaspora.

Nobody mentioned East Oleanta at all.

In the afternoon it started to snow, even though the temperature was just barely above freezing. I'd thought about hiking into the mountains, looking for the place Billy had led us to over a month ago, but the weather made that impossible.

All night I lay awake, listening to the silence.

In the morning I took a shower at the Salvatore John DeSanto Public Baths, which were mysteriously working again. Then I returned to the café. East Oleanta was still deserted. I sat on the edge of a chair, like an attentive donkey schoolgirl, and watched the HT as my country disintegrated into famine, pestilence, death, and war, and the rest of the world mobilized its most advanced technology to seal us within our own borders. If there was other news, the newsgrids weren't reporting it. By 11:00 A.M. only three channels still transmitted.

At noon I felt a sudden, overwhelming urge to sit by the river. This urge struck me with the force of a religious revelation. It was not arguable. I must go sit by the river.

Once there, I took off my clothes, an act as uncharacteristic and as unstoppable as public diarrhea. It was forty degrees and sunny, but I had the feeling it wouldn't have mattered if it were below zero. I *had* to take off my clothes. I did, and stretched full length on an expanse of exposed mud.

I lay on my back in the sun-softened mud, shivering violently, for maybe six or seven minutes. Stones poked into my shoulder blades, the backs of my thighs, the small of my back. The river mud smelled pungent. I was *cold*. I have never been so uncomfortable in my life. I lay there, one arm flung over my face to shield my eyes from the bright noon sun, unwilling to move. Unable to move. And then it was over, and, still shivering, I sat up and dressed again.

It was over.

Eat me, said the vials Alice found at the bottom of the rabbit hole. *Drink me.*

It had been two full days since I'd devoured the chicken and rice and genuine new peas in the Albany government hospital. I hadn't felt hungry: shock, anxiety, depression. All those can arrest appetite. But the body needs fuel. Even when hunger is absent, glucose levels fall. There are hidden storages of starch in the liver and muscles, but eventually these get used up. The blood needs new sources of glucose to send to the body.

Glucose is nothing but atoms. Carbon, oxygen, hydrogen. Arranged one way in food. Arranged another way in mud and water and air. Just as energy exists in one form in chemical bonds, and another in sunlight.

Y-energy rearranged the forms of energy so there would always be a readily available, cheap supply.

Nanotechnology rearranged atoms, which could be found everywhere and anywhere.

Under my clothes, I could feel the mud still caking the backs of my thighs. I tried to remember what those openings were called through which plants took in air, those minute orifices in the epidermis of leaves and stems. The word wouldn't come. My mind was watery.

My body had fed.

I walked carefully, setting my foot down cautiously on each step, transferring my weight slowly from one foot to the other. My arms hovered protectively six inches from my side, to catch myself if I fell. I held my head stiffly. I made very slow progress up the embankment, and it felt excruciating. It seemed to me I had no choice. I moved as if I were something rare and fragile that I myself were carrying, as if I shouldn't jar myself. Nothing must happen to my body. I was the answer to the starving world.

No. Huevos Verdes was the answer.

Once that thought came, I could walk normally. I scrambled up the hill to town. I was not the only one. By now there were hundreds, thousands of us. Eden existed in a gravrail station in Albany, beside the sunshine machine. The entire town of Timonsville, Pennsylvania, had disappeared. Miranda Sharifi had gone public with the Cell Cleaner, the most comprehensible part of her project, over three months ago. And in the last month Huevos Verdes could have stockpiled oceans of serum in forests of slim black syringes. That's what they were doing all over the country, in all those places the plague was *not* killing people. I was not the only one. I had only been the first.

Except for the Sleepless themselves.

My body felt good, which is to say it felt like nothing at all. It disappeared from my consciousness, as healthy and fed bodies do. It was just there, ready to climb or run or work or make love, without depending on the Congresswoman Janet Carol Land Café. Without depending on CanCo Franchise agrobots, on political food distribution systems, on the FDA, on controlling the means of production, on harvesters and combines and the banks you owed them to, on forty acres and a mule, on the threshing floor, on the serfs in the field, on the rains coming this year and the locusts staying away, on Demeter and Indra and the Aztec corn gods. Seven thousand years of civilization built on the need to feed the people.

More in the syringe.

I could still eat normally—I had eaten chicken and rice and peas in the Albany hospital. But I didn't *have* to. From now on, my body could "eat" mud.

I thought wildly of all the food I had consumed in my one single life. Beef Wellington, the pastry flaky around succulent medium-rare roast. Macaroons chewy with fresh-grated coconut. Potatoes Anna, crisp and crunchy. Bittersweet Swiss chocolate. Cassoulet. Alaskan crab as they did it at Fruits de la Mer in Seattle. Deep-dish apple pie . . .

My mouth watered. And then it stopped. A programmed biological counterresponse? I would probably never know.

Biscuits dripping with butter. But I could still have them. Lamb Gaston. Fresh arugula. *If* they were available. Strawberries in cream. But would anybody grow or raise the ingredients without a captive market?

A sudden wave of dizziness overtook me. I must have been in shock, or some kind of quiet hysteria. It was lightheadedness at the sheer *size* of the thing, the audacity. Miranda Sharifi and her twenty-six inhuman Supergeniuses, thinking in ways fundamentally different from ours, aided by technology they themselves built so that each step ahead opened six more pathways, and twenty-seven Superminds added to those branching possibilities . . . Miranda Sharifi and Jonathan Markowitz and Terry Mwakambe and the others whose names I didn't remember from old newsgrids, whom I would never meet, who were not like us and never had been, and yet who had seen what would happen to a society they didn't belong to and had planned a countermeasure. Planned, probably, for years, and carried out the unimaginably complex plans that would change everything for everybody—

And I had once thought that *donkeys* were perpetually dissatisfied and never found anything to be enough.

"How *could* she?" I said aloud, to nobody.

Dazed, I wandered past the station. A train pulled in and Annie and Billy and Lizzie stepped off the otherwise empty gravrail, carrying bundles. Lizzie saw me, shrieked, and ran toward me. I stood watching them, feeling lighter and lighter in the head, my cranium swelling like a balloon. Lizzie hurtled herself into my arms. She was taller, stronger, filled out, all in just a month. Billy's face broke into a huge grin. He loped toward me like a man half his age, Annie trailing.

"Billy," I said. "Billy—"

He went on grinning.

"We're home now, us," Billy said. "We're all home."

Annie sniffed. Lizzie squeezed me tight enough to crush ribs. Under my jacks I felt mud flake off the skin of my thighs.

"Hurry," Annie said. "I want to get to the café, me, before the broadcast."

"What broadcast?" I said.

All three of them looked at me, shocked. Lizzie said, "The *broadcast*, Vicki. From Huevos Verdes. The one all the Liver channels been talking about, them, for days. Everybody's going to watch it!"

"I've been watching only donkey channels." But if it were coming from Huevos Verdes, they could use all channels at once, Liver and donkey. They'd done it once before, thirteen years ago.

"But, Vicki, it's the Huevos Verdes *broadcast*," Lizzie repeated.

"I didn't know," I said, lamely.

"Donkeys," Annie said. "They never know nothing, them."

Nineteen

This is Miranda Serena Sharifi, speaking to you on an unedited holo recorded six weeks ago.

You will want to know what has been done to you.

I am going to explain, as simply as I can. If the explanation is not simple enough, please be patient. This broadcast will play over and over again for weeks, on Channel 35. Perhaps parts of it will become clearer as you hear it more than once. Or perhaps as more technically trained people—donkeys—use the syringes we are making available everywhere, some donkeys will explain to you in easier words. Meanwhile, these are the simplest words I can find for these concepts without losing scientific accuracy.

Your body is made of cells. A cell, any cell, is basically a complex of systems for transforming energy. So is an organism, including a human being.

Humans get their basic energy from plant food, either directly or indirectly, through a process called oxidative phosphorylation. Your bodies break down the bonds of carbon-containing molecules, and a significant portion of the food's potential energy is repackaged into the phosphate bonds of adenosine triphosphate (ATP). When human cells need energy, they get it from ATP.

Plants get their basic energy from sunlight. They use water from the soil and carbon dioxide from the air to form glucose. Glucose can then be repackaged as ATP. Most plants use chlorophyll to carry on this photophosphorylation.

Some bacteria, the halobacteria, can carry on both oxidative phosphorylation and photophosphorylation. They can both ingest nutrients and, under the right conditions, create ATP through a photosynthetic mechanism. In other words, they can get basic energy from either food *or* sunlight.

The halobacteria don't use chlorophyll to do this. Instead, they use retinal, the same pigment that responds to light in the human eye. The retinal exists in conjunction with protein molecules in a complex called bacteriorhodopsin.

Your bodies have been modified to include a radically genetically engineered from of bacteriorhodopsin.

It exists under clear membranes which now exist at the ends of tiny tubules projecting between the dead skin cells of your outer epidermis. The modified bacteriorhodopsin is far more efficient, orders of magnitude more efficient, at capturing photons than are any thylakoids found in nature.

Additional tubules, with active transport capacity, also end in a permeable membrane at the surface of your skin. These can selectively absorb molecules of carbon, plus additional necessary elements, directly from the soil or other organic material. The absorbed molecules are acted upon by genemod enzymes, working in conjunction with your human thylakoids, and with nanomachinery replicating in your cells.

This is not as foreign to you as it may sound. The human embryo, when only a few cells old, develops an outer layer of cells called the trophoblast. The trophoblast possesses the unusual property of being able to digest or liquefy the tissues it comes in contact with. This is how the embryo implants itself in the uterus wall. Your reengineered skin can now liquefy and absorb other kinds of matter.

You have also been injected with genetically engineered nitrogen-fixing microorganisms.

Human tissue consists 96.6 percent of carbon, hydrogen, oxygen, and nitrogen. The nanomachinery now in your cells has been programmed to arrange these plus other less concentrated elements into whatever molecules are needed. These processes are all powered by sunlight, used far more efficiently than in nature. The energy from sunlight is stored as ATP to be used when there is no sunlight. Less than thirty minutes' naked exposure per twenty-four-hour period is sufficient. A surplus can, as with food, be stored as glycogen or fat.

The Cell Cleaner will destroy any cancerous cells engendered as a result of ultraviolet exposure. It will also, of course, destroy any toxic molecules absorbed from the soil, by rearranging their atoms into nontoxic forms.

Nanomachinery will keep your gastrointestinal system capable of operation, even when it is unused for long periods of time. Genemod enzymes are designed to eliminate, through allosteric interactions, any subjective feelings of hunger.

When food is available, you can eat, and store energy from oxidative phosphorylation. When food is not available, you can lie on the soil, in the sunlight, and store energy through photophosphorylation.

Now you understand.

You are now autotrophic.

You are now free.

Summer 2115

Our defense is not in armaments, nor in science, nor in going underground. Our defense is in law and order.

—Albert Einstein, in a letter to Ralph E. Lapp

Twenty

Annie was out in the deep woods when I finally found her, me, after looking for a couple hours. She didn't even tell me that she was going. More and more in the last year she's independent like that, her. I was mad.

"Annie Francy! I been looking, me, all over the woods for you!"

"Well, I been right here, me," Annie said. She sat up. She'd been lying on her back in a little sort of hollow in the leaves, and when she sat up, her, I forgot that I was supposed to be mad. She'd been feeding, her. Her naked chocolate breasts bobbed, them, and her hair had a few leaves stuck in it, and I could see the edge of her ass where it pushed on the soft ground. My pipe swelled. I was next to her, me, in two jumps.

But she pushed me away. I might of forgot, me, that I was mad, but Annie don't ever forget when *she* is. "Not now, Billy. I mean it, you!"

I stopped. It was hard. She tasted so sweet, her, it seemed like I couldn't never get enough of her. Not in the year since we went down into Eden. Not in ten more years, not in hundred. My old pipe was stiff as a hunk of metal.

Annie got up, her, real leisurely, dusting the leaves off her thighs and ass. She knew, her, how I was watching. There was even a little smile in her eyes. But she was still mad.

"Billy—I still don't want, me, for us to go to West Virginia. It ain't going to help nobody."

I eased my pants a little, me. "Lizzie wants to go. She *is* going, her. With or without us."

Annie scowled. Her and Lizzie fight even more now, them, since Lizzie turned thirteen. Annie wants to keep Lizzie a little girl, is what I think, same as for a long time she wanted to keep me an old man, like old men used to be. Before. Annie didn't never like change, her. That's why she don't want to go to West Virginia.

"Lizzie really said that, her? That she'd go without me?"

I nodded. Lizzie would, too. She would go, her, even if Vicki didn't. There ain't no stopping Lizzie these days. You'd of thought it'd be the old and the sick who'd be the most changed since Before, but the truth is, it's the young. There ain't no stopping none of them from doing nothing. Used to be a thirteen-year-old—or twelve, or ten—needed to be taken care of. Fed, nursed through sickness, protected from a rabid raccoon or a bad cut or spoiled food. No more. They don't need us, them.

Just like we don't need the donkeys.

Annie pulled on her dress, her, watching me watch, but without seeming to notice nothing. The dress was longer than the youngest women wear, even in the summer—Annie can't change everything about herself, her, just 'cause there ain't no more endless supplies of jacks or parkas or boots. Her dress was weaved out of some plant thing, not cotton, on the weaving 'bot, just two weeks ago. It didn't have no color, like they don't now. People like their clothes, them, to look natural, which don't make sense because Annie's dress had already started to get eaten by her breasts and hips and ass. There was tiny holes in interesting places. My pants was the same way. I ain't going to wear no dress, me, like the younger men, even if it is easier for feeding. I ain't no young man in my head, me, no matter what my body can do now.

Annie Francy's gorgeous ass disappeared under the drop of her dress.

She tied on her sandals, left over from Before. They were nearly worn out, them. Shoes and boots was supposed to of been on the Council's meeting tonight, until this other thing come up so fast and hard and there ain't going to be no East Oleanta Council meeting tonight. Maybe never again, for all I knew, me.

I held Annie's hand, me, while we walked back to town. I remember when she wouldn't never go into the woods, her. But now not even Annie's afraid in the woods.

In West Virginia—that's something else.

Annie's hand felt smooth and strong. I rubbed my thumb, me, in a little circle over her palm. Annie Francy. Annie. Francy. She was scowling, her, her lips pressed tight together.

"It ain't right to let them vote in Council as young as twelve. It ain't right."

I knew better, me, than to get into *that* again.

"If it wasn't for the kids' votes, we wouldn't be going, us, on this useless trip. And it *is* useless, Billy. What does a thirteen-year-old know, her, about adult voting? She's still a baby, her, even if she don't think so!"

I didn't say nothing. I ain't no fool.

We walked in silence, us. There was pine needles underfoot, and in the sunny places, daisies and Indian paintbrush. The woods was just as pretty, them, and smelled just as sweet, as if the world hadn't of changed for good over a year ago by things too small, them, to even see.

Vicki's tried right along, her, to explain the Cell Cleaner to me. And the nanomachinery. Lizzie seems, her, to understand it, but it still ain't clear to me.

It don't have to be clear. All it has to do, it, is work.

"Annie," I said, just before we got to town, "you don't *know*, you, that we can't do nothing in West Virginia. Maybe somebody's got a plan, them—one of the kids, even!—and by the time we get there—"

She scowled. "Nobody's got no plan."

"Well, maybe by the time we get there, us . . . you got to figure walking will take three, four weeks—"

She turned on me. "Nobody will make no plan! Who knows, them, how to break into that prison and get that girl out? Donkeys? They put her there! That Drew Arlen, her own man? He put her there, too! Her own kind? They'd of done it by now, them, if they knew how! We can't do nothing, Billy. And meantime, we could use the time and brains, us, on things we do need! Better weaving, and more of it! We still only got that one weaving 'bot the kids put together, and it's *slow*, it. And the clothes keep getting eaten. And boots! We still ain't settled, us, about getting boots, and winter will come eventually!"

I gave it up, me. You can't argue with Annie. She's too right, her. Winter *would* come eventually and the weaving 'bot is only one 'bot for the whole town, which might be all right for summer clothes but winter is something different. And we *ain't* settled the boots, us. Annie's still feeding the world, even when there ain't no cooking.

Sometimes it's kind of scary, knowing there ain't nobody to take care of us but us. Sometimes it ain't.

Vicki met us, her, at the edge of town. Her dress was nearly as bad as Lizzie's. I could see pretty near one whole breast, and— old fool that I am—damn if my pipe didn't stir a little, it. But her face was too thin, and she looked unhappy, her, like she done for months now. She was the only one, her, in the whole town who looked so unhappy.

"It's coming apart, Billy. This time, it really is."

"What?" I said. I thought, me, she meant her dress. I really did. Old fool.

"The country. The classes, For good this time. The gap between donkeys and Livers was always held together with baling wire and chewing gum, and now the last semblance is going."

I motioned Annie on, me, with a wave of my hand. She marched off, her, probably to find Lizzie. I sat down on a log and after a minute Vicki sat down too. She can't help, her, being upset about the country. She's a donkey. In East Oleanta that don't matter, everybody left is used to her, but we still get news channels in the café. A few, anyway. Donkeys are having a hard time, them. It's like when Livers found out we don't need donkeys anymore, we got mad, us, that we'd ever needed them. Only that ain't all of it. There's been a lot of killing, and most donkeys are holed up, them, in their city enclaves. Some ain't come out in damn near half a year.

I looked, me, for something to make Vicki feel better. "There ain't no police no more. To punish people who break the law, them, by attacking other people. If we got security 'bots back—"

"Oh, Billy, it's broader than that. There isn't any *law* anymore. There's just the town councils. And where people don't feel like obeying those, there's anarchy."

"I ain't seen, me, nobody get hurt here."

"Not in East Oleanta, no. In East Oleanta the Huevos Verdes plan worked. People made the transition to small, local, cooperative government. To tell you the truth, I give Jack Sawicki, poor dead bastard, credit for that. He had everybody primed for self-responsibility. And other places have worked just as well. But they've killed off donkeys in Albany, they killed off *each other* in Carter's Falls, they've had a rape fest and general lawless might-makes-right in Binghamton, and in other places they've had a witch hunt for "subhuman genemods" worse than any the GSEA ever mounted. And where *is* the GSEA? Where is the FBI? Where is the Urban Housing Authority and the FCC and the Department of Health? The entire network of government has just vanished, while Washington walls itself off, issuing decrees to which the rest of the country pays not the slightest attention!"

"We don't need to, us."

"Precisely. As an entity, the United States no longer exists. It fragmented into classes with no common aims at all. Karl Marx was right."

"Who?" I didn't know, me, nobody with that name.

"Never mind."

"Vicki—" I had to hunt, me, for my words. "Can't you . . . care less, you? Ain't this enough? For the first time, we're free, us. Like Miranda said, her, on her HT broadcast, we're really *free*."

She looked at me. I ain't never seen, me, before or since, such a bleak look. "Free to do what, Billy?"

"Well . . . *live*."

"Look at this." She held out a piece of metal, her. It was twisted and melted.

"So? Duragem. The dissembler got it. But the dissemblers are clocked out, them. And the kids are figuring out all new ways to build stuff without no metals that—"

"This wasn't duragem. And it wasn't attacked by a genemod organism. It was melted by a U-614."

"What's that?"

"A weapon. A very devastating, powerful, government weapon. That was only supposed to be released in case of foreign attack. I found this last week near Coganville. It had been used to blast an isolated summer cottage where, I suspect, there'd been some donkeys hiding months ago. Not even the bodies are there now. Not even the *building* is there."

I looked at her, me. I didn't know she'd walked, her, to Coganville last week.

"Don't you get it, Billy? What Drew Arlen hinted at during Miranda Sharifi's trial is true. He didn't say it outright, and I'll bet that's because somebody decided it was prejudicial to national security. 'National security'! For that you need a real nation!"

I still didn't get it, me. Vicki looked at me, and she put her hand, her, on my arm.

"Billy, somebody's arming Livers with secret government weapons. Somebody's engineering civil war. Do you really think all this violence isn't being deliberately nursed? It's probably the same bastards who released the duragem dissembler in the first place, still out there, trying to get all the donkeys wiped out. And maybe all the Sleepless, too, that aren't holed up in Sanctuary. Somebody wants this country to continue coming apart, and they've got enough underground government support to do it. Civil war, Billy. This last nine months of bioengineered pastoral idyll is only a hiatus. And we people—struggling to create weaving 'bots and rejoicing in our liberation from all the old biological imperatives—are not going to stand a chance. Not without a strong government participation on our side, and I don't see that happening."

"But, Vicki—"

"Oh, why am I talking to you? You don't understand the first thing I'm talking about!"

She got up, her, and walked away.

She was half right. I didn't understand, me, all of it, but I understood some. I thought of Annie not wanting, her, to leave East Oleanta, not even to get Miranda Sharifi free. *We got it good here, Billy. There ain't nothing to be afraid of here . . .*

Vicki came back. "I'm sorry, Billy. I shouldn't take it out on you. It's just . . ."

"What?" I said, me, as gentle as I could.

"It's just that I'm afraid. For Lizzie. For all of us."

"I know." I *did* know, me. That much I knew.

"Do you remember what you said, Billy, that day that Miranda injected us with the syringes, and she and Drew Arlen were arguing about who should control technology?"

I don't remember that day, me, real clear. It was the most important day in my entire life, the day that gave me Annie and Lizzie and my body back, but I don't remember it real clear. My chest hurt, and Lizzie was sick, and too much was happening. But

I remember, me, Drew Arlen's hard face, may he rot in Annie's hell. He testified against her at her trial, and sent his own woman to jail. And I remember the tears in Miranda's eyes. *Who should control technology* . . .

"You said it only matters who *can*. Out of the mouths of the untutored, Billy. And you know what? We can't. Not the syringed Livers or the syringed donkeys in their shielded enclaves. And without some pretty sophisticated technology of our own, any really determined technological attack by the government or by this demented purist underground could wipe us out. And will."

I didn't know, me, what to say. Part of me wanted to hole up with Annie and Lizzie—and Vicki, too—forever in East Oleanta. But I couldn't, me. We had to get Miranda Sharifi free, us. I didn't know how, me, but we had to. She set *us* free, her.

"Maybe," I said, slow, "there ain't no underground stirring up fighting. Maybe this is just a . . . a getting-used-to period, and after a while Livers and donkeys will go back, them, to helping each other live."

Vicki laughed, her. It was an ugly sound. "May God bless the beasts and children," she said, which didn't make no sense. We weren't neither.

"Oh, yes, we are," Vicki said. "Both."

The next week we left, us, to walk to Oak Mountain Maximum Security Federal Prison in West Virginia.

We weren't the only ones, us. It wasn't the East Oleanta Council's original idea. They got it, them, off a man walking south in one of the slow steady lines of people moving along the old gravrail tracks. Feeding in the afternoons in pastures and fields. Leaving the grass torn up to lie in the sweet summer mud. Deciding together where the latrines should be. Making chains of daisies to wear around their necks, until the daisies get slowly fed on and disappear, the same as cloth does from the weaving 'bot. Vicki says, her, that eventually we'll all just go naked all the time. I say, me, not while Annie Francy's got breath in her beautiful body.

Our second day on the road I talked, me, to another old man come along the tracks clear down from someplace near Canada. His grandsons were with him, carrying portable terminals, the way the young ones all do, them. They were moving south before the weather gets cold again. The old man's name was Dean, him. He told me that Before he had soft, rotted bones, him, so bad he couldn't even of sat in a chair without nearly crying. The syringes came to his town in an airdrop, them, at night, the way a lot of towns got them. He said they never even heard the plane. I didn't ask him, me, how he even knew it was a plane.

Instead, I asked him if he knew, him, what the government donkeys were doing about all the Livers on the road moving toward Oak Mountain.

Dean spat. "Who cares? I ain't seen no donkeys, me, and I better not. They're abominations."

"They're what?"

"Abominations. Unnatural. I been talking, me, to some Livers from New York City. They set me straight, them. The donkeys ain't no part of the United States."

I looked at him, me.

"It's true. The United States is for *Livers*. That's what President Washington and President Lincoln and all them other heroes meant, them, for it to be. A government *for* the people, *by* the people. And the real people, the natural people, is us."

"But donkeys—"

"Ain't natural. Ain't people."

"You can't—"

"We got the Will and we got the Idea. We can clean up the country, us. Rid it of abominations."

I said, "Miranda Sharifi's not a Liver."

"You mean you believe, you, that the syringes come from Huevos Verdes? Because of that lying broadcast? Them syringes come, them, from God!"

I looked at him.

"What's the matter, you an abomination lover, you? You harboring one of them donkeys?"

I raised my head, me, real slow.

" 'Cause a few donkey lovers tried, them, to join up with decent Livers. We know how to deal with those kind here, us!"

"Thanks for the information," I said.

All the way back to Vicki, I breathed funny, me. I could feel my chest pound almost the way it used to, Before. But Vicki was all right, her. She sat on a half-busted chair by the gravrail, in the

shade of some old empty building, brooding. The people from
East Oleanta went around her doing what they always do, them,
paying her no attention. They were used to her.

"Vicki," I said, "you got to be careful, you. Don't go away
from us East Oleanta people. Keep your sun hat on, you. A *big*
sun hat. There's people going south, them, that want to kill
donkeys!"

She looked up, her, cross. "Of course there are. What do you
suppose I've been telling you for days and days?"

"But this ain't some big-word argument about the government,
it, this is *you*—"

"Oh, Billy."

"Oh Billy what? Are you listening, you, to what I'm saying?"

"I'm listening. I'll be careful." She looked ready to cry, her.
Or shout.

"Good. We care, us, what happens to you."

"Just not to the government," she said, and went back to staring, her, at nothing.

We walked the tracks, us, for days. At places in the mountains it
was pretty narrow, but we weren't none of us in any particular
hurry. More and more Livers joined us, them. At night people sat
around Y-cones or campfires, them, talking, or knitting. Annie
liked teaching people to knit. She did it a lot, her. People wandered, them, into the woods to feed or to use the latrines we dug
every night. There was ponds and streams for water. It didn't
matter if the water wasn't too clean, it, or even if it was close to
the latrines. The Cell Cleaner took care of any germs that might
of got into us. We wouldn't need no medunit, us, ever again.

The young ones carried their terminals, them. The older ones
carried little tents, mostly made from plasticloth tarps. The tents
were light, they didn't tear, and they didn't get dirty. They didn't
even get that mildewed smell, them, that I remember from tents
when I was a boy, me. I remember, me, a lot more than I used
to. I kind of miss the mildewy smell.

When it rained, we put up the tents, us, and waited it out. We
weren't in no hurry. Getting there would take as long as it took.

But Annie was right. Nobody had no plan, them. Miranda

Sharifi, who gave us back our lives, sat there in Oak Mountain, and nobody had the foggiest idea, them, how we were supposed to get her out.

I never saw, me, other donkeys beside Vicki, who laid pretty low. A few times strangers gave her dirty looks, them, but me and Ben Radisson and Carl Jones from East Oleanta sort of stood up, us, near her, and there wasn't no trouble. Some other people didn't even seem to realize, them, that Vicki was a donkey. Since the syringes, a lot more women got bodies, them, almost good enough to be genemod. Almost. I told Vicki, me, to keep her sun hat pulled low enough to shade them violet genemod eyes.

Then we came, us, to some town with a HT in the café. Vicki insisted, her, on watching one whole afternoon of donkey news-grids. Lizzie sat with her. So did me and Ben and Carl, just to be safe.

That night, around our campfire, Vicki sat slumped over, her, more depressed than before.

There was her, me, Annie, Lizzie, and Brad. Brad was a kid, him, who joined us a week ago. He spent a lot of time, him, bent over a terminal close to Lizzie. Annie didn't like it, her. I didn't like it neither. Lizzie's body was feeding on her dress faster than mine or Annie's, the way the young bodies did, them. Her little breasts were half hanging out, all rosy in the soft firelight. I could see she didn't care, her. I could see Brad did. There wasn't a damn thing Annie or I could do.

Lizzie said, "The Carnegie-Mellon Enclave hasn't lowered its shield once. Not once, in nine months. They have to be out of food completely, which means they have to have used the syringes."

She didn't even talk, her, like us anymore. She talks like her terminal.

Annie said sharply, "So? Donkeys can use syringes. Miranda said so, her. Just so long as they stay, them behind their shields, and leave us alone."

Vicki said sharply, "You didn't want them to leave you alone when they were providing everything you needed. You were the one, in fact, who had the most reverence for authority. 'Give us this day our daily bread . . .' "

"Don't blaspheme, you!"

"Now, Annie," I said, "Vicki don't mean nothing, her. She just wants—"

"She just wants you to stop apologizing for her, Billy," Vicki said coldly. "I can apologize myself for my outworn caste." She got up, her, and walked off into the darkness.

"Can't you stop bothering her?" Lizzie said furiously to her mother. "After all she's done for us!" She jumped up and followed Vicki.

Brad looked helplessly after her, him. He stood up, sat down, half got up again. I took pity, me. "Don't do it, son. They're better off, them, alone for a while."

The boy looked at me gratefully, him, and went back to his everlasting terminal.

"Annie . . ." I said, as gently as I could.

"Something's *wrong* with that woman, her. She's jumpy as a cat."

So was Annie. I didn't say so, me. Their jumpiness wasn't the same kind. Annie was thinking, her, about Lizzie, just like she'd always been. But Vicki was thinking, her, about a whole country. Just like donkeys always did.

And if they didn't, them, who would?

I thought, me, about Livers not needing donkeys no more, and donkeys hiding behind their shields from Livers. I thought about all the fighting and killing we'd watched, us, that afternoon on the newsgrids. I thought about the man who'd called donkeys "abominations" and said the syringes was from God. The man who said he'd got the Will and the Idea.

I got up, me, to go look for Vicki and make sure she was all right.

Twenty-one

They don't understand. None of them. Livers are still Livers, despite the staggering everything that's happened, and there's a limit to what you can expect.

I walked toward West Virginia wearing my new legal name and my rapidly decaying dress, full of health and doom. Where was Heuvos Verdes in all this? Miranda Sharifi had been tried under the most spectacular security known to man, and the press from thirty-four countries had waited breathlessly for the Lancelotian high-tech rescue, the snatching from the legal fire, that had never materialized. Miranda herself had said not one word throughout the trial. Not one, not even on the stand, under oath. She had, of course, been found in contempt, and the crowds of Livers outside—syringed, all—had raised enough un-Liver-like howls to compensate for the silence of ten sacrificial lambs. But not for Huevos Verdes's silence. No rescue. No defense, to speak of. Nada, unless you count syringes raining from the sky, pushing up from the earth, appearing like alchemy out of the very stones and fields and pavements of the country the Supers were utterly, silently, invisibly transforming.

Drew Arlen had testified. He'd described the illegal Huevos Verdes genemod experiments in East Oleanta, in Colorado, in Florida. The last two labs were apparently only backup locations to East Oleanta and Huevos Verdes, but Jesus Christ, there were only *twenty-seven* Supers. How in hell had they staffed four locations?

They weren't like us.

That became clearer and clearer, as the trial progressed. It became clear, too, that Arlen *was* like us: stumbling around in the same swamp of good intentions, moral uncertainties, limited understanding, personal passions, and government restrictions about what he could or could not say on the stand.

"That information is classified," became his monotonous response to Miranda Sharifi's defense attorney, who was surely the most frustrated man on the planet. Arlen sat in his powerchair, his aging Liver face expressionless. "Where were you, Mr. Arlen, between August 28 and November 3?" "That information is classified." "With whom did you discuss the alleged activities of Ms. Sharifi in Upstate New York?" "That information is classified." "Please describe the events that led to your decision to notify the GSEA about Huevos Verdes." "That information is classified."

Just like wartime.

But not *my* war. I had been declared a noncombatant, removed lock and stock and retina print from any but the most public databases, in perpetuity. Three times over the last year I had been picked up, transported to Albany, and knocked out, while biomonitors gave up their secrets to scientists who, most probably, had by now syringed themselves with the same thing. The results of the biomonitoring were not shared with me. I was a government outcast.

So why did I even care that the United States, qua United States, was on the verge of nonexistence, the first nationalistic snuff job brought about by making government itself obsolete? Why should *I* care?

I don't know. But I did. Call me a fool. Call me a romantic. Call me stubborn. Call me a deliberate, self-created anachronism.

Call me a patriot.

"Billy," I said as we trudged along the endless gravrail track in the high rolling hills of Pennsylvania, "are you still an American?"

He gave me a Billy-look, which is to say intelligent without the remotest glimmer of vocabular understanding. "Me? Yes."

"Will you be an American if you are killed by some fanatic last-ditch legalistic donkey defense at Oak Mountain?"

He took a minute to sort this out. "Yes."

"Will you still be an American if you're killed by some attack by a purist Liver-government underground that thinks you've sold out to the genetic enemy?"

"I ain't going, me, to be killed by no other Livers."

"But if you *were*, would you die an American?"

He was losing patience. His old eyes with the young energy roamed over our fellow walkers, looking for Annie. "Yes."

"Would you still be an American if there *is* no America, no central government left and nobody to administer it if there were, the Constitution forgotten, the donkeys wiped out by some fanatic revolutionary underground, and Miranda Sharifi rotting in a prison run exclusively by 'bots?"

"Vicki, you think too much, you," Billy said. He turned his concern on me, that *agápe* concern off which I'd been living, out of caste, for so long. It didn't help. "Think about whether we're going to stay alive, us—that makes sense. But you can't take on the whole damn country, you."

"The human mind, Charles Lamb once remarked, can fall in love with anything. Call me a patriot, Billy. Don't you still believe in patriotism, Billy?"

"I—"

"Besides, I once saw a genemod dog fall to its death off a balcony." But Billy suddenly spotted Annie. He smiled at me and moved off to walk by his beloved, whose dress, despite her best efforts, was being consumed by her big-breasted body. She looked like a pastoral goddess, utterly unaware that the industrial revolution has begun and the looms are clacking like gunfire.

We reached Oak Mountain July 14, which only I found funny, or even notable. There were already ten thousand people there, by generous estimate. They ringed the flat land around the prison and spread up the sides of the surrounding mountains. Brush had been cleared for feeding for miles around, although the trees remained for shade. No one was on solid food; there was little shit. Tents in the wild colors of Before jacks dotted the grounds: turquoise, marigold, crimson, kelly green. At night, there were the usual campfires or Y-energy cones.

World War I lost more soldiers to disease, the result of being messed together in unsanitary conditions, than to guns. At the siege of Dunmar, they had eaten the rats, and then each other. During the Brazilian Action, the damage to the rain forest was greater than the damage to the combatants as high tech destroyed everything it touched. Never again, none of it.

Did history still apply? Human history?

Billy was right. I thought too much. Concentrate on staying alive.

"Put more dirt on your face," Lizzie said, peering at me critically. This seemed superfluous; everyone was constantly covered in dirt, which had become acceptable. Dirt was clean. Dirt was mother's milk. I suspected that Miranda and Company had altered our olfactory sense with her magic brew. People did not seem to smell bad to each other.

"Put more leaves in your hair," Lizzie said, tipping her head critically to study me. Her pretty face was creased with worry. "There are some weird people here, Vicki. They don't understand that donkeys can be human, too."

Can be. On sufferance. If we join the Livers and give up the institutions by which we controlled the world.

Lizzie's lip quivered. "If anything happened to you . . ."

"Nothing's going to happen to me," I said, not believing it for half a minute. Too much already had. But I hugged her, this daughter slipping rapidly away from both Annie and me, who nonetheless fought over her just as if she weren't already a different species. Lizzie was almost completely naked now, her "dress" reduced to a few courtesy rags. Unself-consciously naked. There were thirteen-year-olds in this camp who were just as unself-consciously pregnant. No problem. Their bodies would take care of it. They anticipated no danger in childbirth, had no fears about supporting a baby, counted on plenty of people around all the time to help care for these casual offspring. It was no big deal. The pregnant children were serene.

"Just be careful," Lizzie said.

"You be careful," I retorted, but of course she only smiled at this.

That night the first holo appeared in the sky.

It appeared to be centered above the prison itself. Eighty feet up and at least fifty feet tall—it was hard to judge from the ground— it was clearly visible for miles. The laser lighting was intricate and brilliant. It was around ten o'clock, dark enough even in summer for the holo to dominate even a nearly full moon. It consisted of a red-and-blue double helix bathed in a holy white light, like some biological Caravaggio. Below it letters pulsed and flashed:

DEATH TO NON-HUMANS
WILL AND IDEA

People screamed. In a year, they had apparently forgotten how ubiquitous political holes used to be.

Death to non-humans. Cold seeped along my spine, starting in the small of my back and traveling upwards.

"Who's making that holo, them?" a nearby man called indignantly. There was a frenzied babble of answers: the government, the food franchises nobody needed anymore, the military. The donkeys, the donkeys, the donkeys . . .

I didn't hear anyone say, "The underground, them." Did that mean there were no members of it present, not even informers? There must be informers; every war had them.

Informers would have to fit in, which meant they'd have to be syringed. Did that mean they, too, were non-humans? Who exactly qualified as "non-human"?

I saw Lizzie fighting through the crowd, felt her hands drawing me back into our tent. If she was saying anything, it was lost in the noise. I shrugged off her small insistent hands and stayed where I was.

The holo continued to flash. Then there was a general surge forward, toward the prison. It didn't happen all at once; nobody was in danger of being trampled. But people began to move around tents and campfires toward the prison walls. By the garish pulsing light I could see similar movements down the sides of the distant wooded slopes. The Livers were moving to protect Miranda, their chosen icon.

"Anybody tries, them, to give death to *her* . . ."

"She's as human, her, as anybody with fancy holos!"

"Just let them *try* to get at her . . ."

What on earth did they think they could actually *do* to help her?

Then the chanting started, first closest to the prison walls and quickly spreading outward, drowning out the more random babble of discussion and protest. By the time I reached the edge of the shoulder-to-shoulder crowd, it was strong, rising from thousands of throats: "Free Miranda. Free Miranda. Free Miranda . . ."

Torches appeared. Within a half hour every human being in

miles stood packed by the prison walls, faces grim and yet exalted in that way people get when they're intent on something outside themselves. Firelight turned some of their homely Liver faces rosy; others were striped red and blue from the flashing holo above us. *Free Miranda, Free Miranda, Free Miranda . . .*

There was no response at all from the silent gray walls.

They kept it up for an hour, which was the same length of time the holo flashed its message of death to those like Miranda.

And me.

And the syringed Livers?

When the holo finally disappeared, the chanting did, too, almost as if cut off from above. People blinked and looked at each other, a little dazed. They might have been coming off a Drew Arlen lucid dreaming.

Slowly, without haste, ten thousand people moved away from the prison, back to their tents, spreading out over miles. It took a long time. People moved slowly, subdued, talking softly or not at all. As far as I knew, nobody got pushed or hurt. Once, I would not have believed this possible.

People sat up very late, huddled around common fires, talking.

Brad said, "That holo didn't come from the prison."

I'd never thought it did. But I wanted to hear his reasoning. "How do you know?"

He smiled patiently, the newly fledged techie addressing his illiterate elder. The little prick. I had forgotten more tech than he had yet learned in his belated post-syringe love affair with actual knowledge. He was sixteen. Still, I had no real right to contempt. I hadn't noticed where the holo originated.

"Laser holos have feeds," he said. "You know, those skinny little lines of radiation you can only see kind of sidewise, and only if you're looking—"

"Peripheral vision. Yes, I know, Brad. Where were they coming from, if not the prison?"

"Lizzie and me only studied about them last week." He put a proprietary hand on Lizzie's knee. Annie scowled.

"Where were the feeds coming from, Brad?"

"At first I hardly noticed them at all. Then I remembered the—"

"From where, damn it!"

Startled, he pointed. Horizontally, to the top of a not-very-near mountain I couldn't name. I stared at the mountain, silhouetted in moonlight.

"I don't see why you're yelling at me, you," Brad said, somewhere between a sulk and a sneer. I ignored him. I hoped Lizzie was losing interest in him. He wasn't nearly as bright as she was.

O same new world.

I stared at the dark nameless mountain. That's where they were, then. The Will-and-Idea underground, which Drew Arlen had hinted at, and of which Billy had met a member weeks ago. But that man had been syringed. Did that mean you could be syringed, with all its changes to basic biological machinery, and still be considered human by the underground? Or was the man being used as an informer, who would be dealt with for his turncoat treason once the war was over? Such things were not unknown in history.

This movement had loosed the duragem dissembler. They were killing donkeys. They had successfully hidden Drew Arlen for two months from Huevos Verdes. They armed their soldiers with United States military weapons.

It was dawn before I slept.

The next night, the holo was back, but changed.

The double helix, red and blue in white light, was still there. But this time the flashing letters read:

DON'T TREAD ON ME
WILL AND IDEA

Don't tread on me? What pseudo-revolutionary group could possibly have the demented idea that a bunch of pastoral dirt-feeding chanters were treading on them? Or even interested in them?

I had a sudden insight. It wasn't only that Livers, due to using the syringes, may or may not have become non-human. That alone hadn't provoked the underground's hatred. The Liver's non-interest had. Syringed people not only didn't pay the established government much attention, most of them were equally uninterested in its would-be replacements. They didn't need any replacement, or thought they didn't. And for some people, being hated is preferable to being irrelevant. Any action that provokes response, no matter how irrational, is better than being irrelevant. Even if the response is never enough.

Another thing: These holos were not trying to convert anyone. There were no broadcasts explaining why people should join the underground. There were no simply worded leaflets. There were no cell members furtively reaching out to the susceptible, persuading in hushed voices. The people projecting these holos were not interested in recruitment. They were interested in self-righteous violence.

The Livers gazing upward at the sky responded to this second holo exactly as they had the night before. Orderly, without confusion, without any signal given, they began to move toward the prison. There was no haste. Mothers took the time to wrap up babies against the night chill, to finish breast-feeding, to arrange who would stay with sleeping toddlers. Fires were banked. Knitters did whatever they do at the end of a row of stitches. But within ten minutes every adult in the camp had started to move, ten thousand strong, toward the walls. They moved courteously around the tents and temporary hearths of those camped hard by the prison, careful not to step on anything. As soon as they were shoulder-to-shoulder, they started to chant.

"Free Miranda. Free Miranda. Free Miranda . . ."

The holo pulsed for fifteen minutes, then changed:

LIBERTY OR DEATH
WILL AND IDEA

The white light changed to an American flag, stars and bars superimposed over the double helix.

"Free Miranda. Free Miranda. Free Miranda . . ."

Fifteen minutes later the holo words changed again:

HOPE
WILL AND IDEA

"Free Miranda. Free Miranda. Free Miranda . . ."

The American flag became a rattlesnake, poised to strike. It looked so real that a few children started to cry.

Another fifteen minutes and the snake was replaced by the original double helix and holy white light. This time we got three lines:

DEATH TO ABOMINATIONS
POWER TO TRUE LIVERS
WILL AND IDEA

The double helix rotated slowly. I wondered how many of the chanters even knew what it was.

"*Free Miranda . . .*"

At the end of an hour, it was over. It took another hour for the huge crowd to quietly disperse, which it started to do the moment the holo vanished.

Back in my tent, I borrowed Lizzie's terminal, with its library crystal. "Don't tread on me" was first used on flags in the Colonial South, as relations with Great Britain deteriorated, and later adopted as Revolutionary slogan in much of New England. "Liberty or Death" appeared on flags in Virginia, following Patrick Henry's exhortation to turn on the British masters. "Hope" was the legend on the flag of the Colonial armed schooner *Lee*, the first flag to also feature thirteen stars. I couldn't find a record anywhere of "Will and Idea."

These maniacs considered themselves colonists in their own country, fighting to overthrow a donkey establishment that was largely in passive hiding and, maybe, a syringed Liver population that was essentially defenseless. Unless you count chanting as a weapon.

The government existed, in part, to defend its citizens against this sort of demented civil insurrection. Did we have a government left? Did we have a country left?

The only official representative of that country in sight, Oak Mountain Maximum Security Federal Prison, sat silent and dark. Maybe it was even empty.

I walked back toward the prison walls. This time I went right up to them, borrowing a torch from some obliging camper who asked mildly, without insistence, that I return it when I was done. I walked along the prison walls, inspecting.

A few graffiti, not very many. Few Livers could write. What graffiti there was hadn't been written on the walls themselves, which of course shimmered with a faint Y-energy shield. Instead river boulders had been rolled laboriously against the shield, the earth scraped raw from their passage. On the rocks was painted FREEE MARANDA. WE R PEEPLUL TO. TAK DOWN THEEZ WALLZ.

A pathetic scratching in one rock, a half-inch deep, where some group had begun, symbolically at least, to tak down theez wallz.

The prison door, facing the river, blank and impenetrable. Thirty feet up the security screens, which may or may not have been recording, were dark blank patches.

Above the walls the shimmer, hard to see unless you used your peripheral vision, extended outward a few feet, like eaves. I couldn't imagine why.

Towers loomed at each of the four corners. They had no windows, or else windows holoed to look like they didn't exist.

I walked back to my tent, returning the torch on the way. Annie, Billy, Lizzie, and Brad had already disappeared into their tents, two by two. Clouds were rolling in from the west. I sat outside for a long time, wrapped in a plasticloth tarp, cold even though it was at least seventy degrees out. The prison, too, sat massive and silent, not even flying a holographic flag. Dead.

"Lizzie, I need you to do something for me. Something tremendously important."

She looked up at me. I'd found her deep in the woods, after hours of patiently asking total strangers if they'd seen a thin black girl with pink ribbons tying up her two braids. Lizzie sat on a fallen log, which the backs of her thighs were probably eating. She'd been crying. Brad, of course. I'd kill him. No, I wouldn't. There was no other way for her to learn. Claude-Eugene-Rex-Paul-Anthony-Russell-David.

The timing was good for me. I could make use of these tears.

I said, "There's a message I have to get to Charleston. I can't go myself because the GSEA is monitoring me remotely; I told you that. They'd know. And there's nobody else I can trust. Annie wouldn't do it, and Billy won't leave Annie . . ."

She went on looking at me, not changing expression, her eyes swollen and her nose red.

"It's about Miranda Sharifi," I said. "Lizzie, it's unbelievably important. I need you to walk to Charleston, and I'll time-encode

in your terminal what you need to do after you arrive. In fact,
I've already done that. I know this sounds mysterious, but it's
essential." I put everything I had—or once had—into that last
sentence. The donkey authority. The adult tone of command. The
confidence that this girl loved me.

Lizzie went on gazing at me, expressionless.

I handed her the terminal. "You walk along the gravrail track
until it branches at Ash Falls. Then you—"

"There's no message about Miranda Sharifi," Lizzie said.

"I just told you there was." Donkey authority. Adult command.

"No. There's nothing anybody can do about Miranda. You just
want me out of here because you're afraid that underground will
attack tonight."

"No. It's not that. Why would you think—" *you, who owe me
so much,* my tone said "—that I don't have resources *you* don't
understand? If I say there is a crucial message about Miranda,
there *is* a crucial message about Miranda."

Lizzie stared at me emptily, hopelessly.

"Lizzie—"

"He left me. Brad. For Maura Casey!"

It's wrong to laugh at puppy love. For one thing, it's not that
different from what most adults do. I sat on the log next to her.

"He says . . . he says, him . . . that I'm too smart for my own
good."

"Livers always say that," I said gently. "Brad just hasn't caught
on yet."

"But I am smarter than he is, me." She sounded like the child
she still was. "*Lots* smarter. He's so stupid about so many things!"

I didn't say, *Then why do you want him;* I recognized a hopeless
arena for logic when I saw one. Instead I said, "Most people are
going to look stupid to you, Lizzie. Starting with your mother.
That's just the way you are, and the way the world is going to be
now. For you."

She blew her nose on a leaf. "I hate it, me! I want people to
understand me!"

"Well. Better get used to it."

"He says, him, I try to control him! I don't, me!"

Who should control the technology? Paul's voice said to me, lying
in bed, pleased to be instructing the person he had just fucked.

Pleased to be on top. Lizzie probably did try to control Brad. *Whoever can,* Billy said.

"Lizzie . . . in Charleston . . ."

She jumped up. "I said I'm not going, me, and I'm not! I hope there *is* an attack tonight! I hope I die in it!" She ran off, crashing through the woods, crying.

I took after Lizzie at a dead run. At ten yards, I started gaining. She was fast, but I was more muscled, with longer legs. She was within a yard of my grasp. It was six hours before dark. I could tie her up and physically carry her as far from Oak Mountain, from danger, as I could get in six hours. If I had to, I'd knock her out to let me carry her.

My fingers brushed her back. She spurted forward and leaped over a pile of brush. I leaped, too, and my ankle twisted under me as I fell.

Pain lanced through my leg. I cried out. Lizzie didn't even falter. Maybe she thought I was faking. I tried to call out to her, but a sudden wave of nausea—biological shock—took me. I turned my head just in time to vomit. Lizzie kept running, and disappeared among the trees. I heard her even after I couldn't see her anymore. Then I couldn't hear her either.

Slowly I sat up. My ankle throbbed, already swollen. I couldn't tell if it was sprained or even fractured. If it was, Miranda's nanotech would fix it. But not instantly.

I felt cold, then sweaty. *Don't pass out,* I told myself sternly. Not now, not here. Lizzie . . .

Even if I could find her again, I couldn't carry her anywhere.

When the biologic shock passed, I limped back to camp. Every step was painful, and not just to my ankle. When I reached the outskirts of the camp, some Livers helped me get to my tent. By the time I got there, the pain was already muted. It was also dark. Lizzie wasn't there, and neither was Annie nor Billy. Lizzie's terminal and library crystal were gone from her tent.

I sat huddled in front of my tent, watching the sky. Tonight was cloudy, without stars or moon. The air smelled of rain. I shivered, and hoped I was wrong. Completely, spectacularly, omnisciently wrong. About the underground nobody admitted actually existed, about their targets, about everything.

After all, what did I know?

*   *   *

"*Free* Miranda. *Free* Miranda. *Free* Miranda . . ."

The red-and-blue helix pulsed, overlaid by the red, white, and blue flag. WILL AND IDEA, no other legend. Whose will? What idea? Oak Mountain Prison sat dark and still under the rhythmical light.

"*Free* Miranda. *Free* Miranda. *Free* Miranda . . ."

I still sat in front of my tent, nursing my ankle. Annie had wrapped it tightly in a strip of woven cloth, which my skin was probably consuming. I sat perhaps a quarter mile from the ten thousand chanters. Their chant carried to me clearly.

The sky was dark, overcast. The summer air smelled of rain, of pine, of wildflowers. I realized for the first time that these scents were as strong as ever, whereas the stink of human bodies was muted in my altered olfactory nerves. Miranda & Company knew their business.

The torches held by the chanters mixed with Y-energy cones: wavering primitive light and steady high tech. And above it, the red-and-blue glare. Broad stripes and bright stars.

The first plane came from Brad's nameless mountain, flying without lights, a metallic glint visible only if you were looking for it. They didn't need planes; they could have used long-distance artillery. Somebody wanted to record the action close up. I staggered to my feet, already crying. The plane came in over the top of the prison and swept low, buzzing the chanters. People screamed. It dropped a single impact bomb, which went off in the middle of the crowd. Barely enough to cause fifty deaths, even in that mass of bodies. They were playing.

People started to shove and push, screaming. Those fortunates on the edge of the crowd ran free, toward the distant wooded slopes. I could see figures behind them, distant but separate, stumble over each other. Miranda had left me with 20/20 vision.

A second plane, that I hadn't seen in advance, flew over me from the opposite direction and disappeared over the prison walls. I didn't hear the second bomb, which must have fallen on the other side of the walls. The explosion was drowned out by the screaming.

People started to trample each other.

Billy. Annie. *Lizzie* . . .

The first plane had wheeled and was returning from behind me. This time, I knew, it wouldn't be to play. Too many people from the edges of the crowd were scrambling to safety. Would the bomb take out Oak Mountain itself? Of course. That's where the chief abomination was. I didn't know what kinds of shields the prison had, but if the attack was nuclear . . .

The holo above the prison changed for the last time:

THE WILL OF THE PEOPLE
THE IDEA OF HUMAN PURITY

I thought I saw Lizzie. Insane—it wasn't possible to distinguish individuals at this distance. My mind merely wanted me to die in as much dramatic anguish as possible. And so I thought I saw Lizzie run forward, and be trampled by people panicked to escape what had been inevitable since the creation of the first genemod.

I squeezed my eyes shut to die. And then opened them again.

In time to see the nanosecond in which it happened.

The shield around Oak Mountain glowed brighter than the holo in the sky. One moment the prison was wrapped in silvery light. The next the same silvery light shot out from the prison walls over the crowd below, in grotesquely elongated eaves of pure energy. The bomb, or whatever it was, hit the top of the energy shield and detonated, or ricocheted, or was thrown back. The plane exploded in a light that blinded me, but wasn't quite nuclear. An instant later a second explosion: the other plane. Then dead silence.

People had stopped running, most of them. They looked up at the opaque silver roof protecting them, the roof of manmade high-tech radiation.

I cried out and staggered forward. Immediately my ankle gave way and I fell. I raised myself chest-high off the ground and stared up. The "roof" extended all the way to the lowest slopes of the mountain. I couldn't see through it. But I heard the subsequent explosions, artillery or radiation or something that must have been directed from the top of the distant mountain.

People were screaming again. But the shoving and trampling had stopped. Huddled under this high-energy umbrella was the safest place to be.

I thought: *Huevos Verdes protects their own.*

I lay back down on the ground, my cheek pressed against the hard-packed dirt. It felt as if I had no bones; I literally couldn't move. Small children could have trampled on me. Huevos Verdes had protected their own, incidentally saving the lives of nine or ten thousand Livers while wiping out some other unknown number of Livers. That was who made the laws now: Huevos Verdes. Twenty-seven Sleepless plus their eventual offspring, who did not consider themselves part of my country. Or any other. Not donkeys, not Livers, not the Constitution, which even to donkeys had always been silent in the background but fundamental, like bedrock. No longer.

Who was the statesman whose last, dying words concerned the fate of the United States? Adams? Webster? I'd always thought it was a stupid story. Shouldn't his last words have concerned his wife or his will or the height of his pillow—something concrete and personal? How grandiose to think oneself large enough to match the fate of a whole country—and at such a moment! Pretentious, inflated. Also silly—the man wasn't going to pass any more laws or influence any more policy, he was *dying*. Silly.

Now I understood. And it was still silly. But I understood.

I think I have never felt such desolation.

There was a final explosion that left my ear, the one not pressed to the ground, completely deaf. I struggled to turn my head and look up. The shield had disappeared, and so had the holo and the entire top of the distant mountain. I had never even learned its name.

More screaming. Now, when it was all over. The Livers probably didn't realize that, might never even realize what had been lost. Small bands of roaming, self-sufficient tribes, not needing that quaint entity, "the United States," any more than Huevos Verdes did. Livers.

The first fleeing people ran past me, toward the dark hills. I stumbled to my feet, or rather foot. If I didn't put my full weight on the self-healing ankle, I could hop forward. After a few yards I actually found a dropped torch. I extinguished it and leaned on it like a cane. It wasn't quite long enough, but it would do.

It was slow work being the only person moving toward the prison. People had stopped shoving, and some kind or guilty souls started to carry away the trampled dead. But a crowd that size takes a long time to disperse. The noise from the crying and the shouting was overwhelming, especially after I started pressing my way through the narrow capillaries between people. My ankle throbbed.

It was at least an hour before I reached the prison itself.

I hobbled the length of the wall and turned the corner toward the river. It was somehow astonishing to me that the water continued to flow and murmur, the rocks to sit in their usual dumb fashion. For a second I saw not this river but another, with a dead snowshoe rabbit beside it—which river did I hear murmur in the darkness? There were no people left on this side of the walls, but I thought I saw dead bodies on the ground. They were actually shadows. Even after I realized this, they went on looking like corpses. They went on looking like Lizzie, all of them, at different moments. The pain had spread from my ankle to my whole leg. I wasn't quite sane.

When I reached the prison doors, I looked up at the blank security screens, angled out from the wall much as the silvery shield has been. I said to them, "I want to come in."

Nothing happened.

I said, louder—and even I heard the edge of hysteria in my voice—"I'm coming in now. I am. Now. Coming in."

The river murmured. The screens brightened slightly—or maybe not. After a moment the door swung open.

Just like Eden.

I limped into a small antechamber. The door swung closed behind me. A door opened on the far wall.

I have been in prisons before, as part of my long-ago intelligence training. I knew how they worked. First the computer-run automated doors and biodetectors, all of which passed me through. Then the second set of doors, which are not Y-energy but carbon-alloy barred doors, run only manually because there are always people who can crack any electronic system, including retina prints. It's been done. The second set of doors are controlled by human beings behind Y-energy screens, and if there are no human beings, nobody gets in. Or out. Not without explosives as large as the ones the Will and Idea people had already tried.

I stood in front of the first barred door and peered through the cloudy window to the guard station, a window constructed of plasticlear and not Y-energy, because Y-energy, too, is vulnerable to enough sophisticated electronics. There was a figure there.

Somehow Huevos Verdes must have brought in their own people—when? *How?* And what had they done with the donkey prison officials?

The barred door opened.

Then the next one.

And the next.

There was no one in the prison yard. Recreation and dining halls on the right, administrative and gym on the left. I hobbled toward the cellblocks, at the far end. A solitary small building sat behind them. Solitary. The door opened when I pushed it.

I half expected, when I reached her cell, to find it empty, a rock rolled away from the tomb door. Playing with cultural icons . . .

But the SuperSleepless don't play. She was there, sitting on a sleeping bunk she would never use, in a space ten by five, with a lidless toilet and a single chair. Stacked on the chair were books, actual bound hard copy printouts. They looked old. There was no terminal. She looked up at me, not smiling.

What do you say?

"Miranda? Sharifi?"

She nodded, just once, her slightly too large head. She wore prison jacks, dull gray. There was no red ribbon in her dark hair.

"They . . . your . . . the doors are open."

She nodded again. "I know."

"Are you . . . do you want to come out?" Even to myself I sounded inane. There were no precedents.

"In a minute. Sit down, Diana."

"Vicki," I said. More inanity. "I go by Vicki now."

"Yes." She still didn't smile. She spoke in the slightly hesitant manner I remembered, as if speech were not her natural manner of communication. Or maybe as if she were choosing her words carefully, not from too few but from an unimaginable too many. I moved the books off the chair and sat.

She said the last thing I could have anticipated. "You're troubled."

"I'm . . ."

"Aren't you troubled?"

"I'm *stunned.*" She nodded again, apparently unsurprised. I said, "Aren't you? But no, of course not. You expected this to happen."

"Expected which to happen?" she said in that slow speech, and of course she was right. Too much had happened. I could be referring to any of it: the biological changes since Before, the attack by the Will and Idea underground, the rescue.

But what I said was, "The disintegration of my country." I heard my own faint emphasis on "my" and was instantly ashamed: my country, not yours. This woman had saved my life, all our lives.

But not completely ashamed.

Miranda said, "Temporarily."

"*Temporarily?* Don't you know what you've *done?*"

She went on gazing at me, without answering. I suddenly wondered what it would be like to encounter that gaze day after day, knowing she could figure out anything about you, while you could never understand the first thing she was thinking. Possibly not even if she told you.

All at once, I understood Drew Arlen, and why he had done what he had.

Miranda said—the perfect proof, although of course I didn't think of that until much later—"Huevos Verdes didn't extend that shield."

I gaped at her.

"You thought they did. But we at Huevos Verdes agreed not to defend you against your own kind. We agreed it would be better to let you find your own way. If we do everything, you will just . . . resent . . ." It was the only time I ever felt she was genuinely at a loss for words.

"Then who extended the shield?"

"The Oak Mountain federal authorities. On direct order of the President, who's down but not out." She almost smiled, sadly. "The donkeys protected their own American citizens. That's what you want to hear, isn't it, Vicki?"

"What I want to hear? But is it *true?*"

"It's true."

I stared at her. Then I stood up and hobbled out of the cell. I didn't even say good-bye. I didn't know I was going. I limped so fast across the prison yard that I almost fell. I didn't have to cross the whole yard; they were there, conferring in a huddle. They stopped when they saw me, stared stonily, waited. Two techies in blue uniforms, and a man and a woman in suits. Tall, genemod handsome. With heads of ordinary size. Donkeys.

Federal officials of the United States, protecting citizens under the high-tech shield of the laws and on the subterranean bedrock of the Constitution of the United States. "The right of the people peaceably to assemble, and to petition the Government for a redress of grievances." "The President shall take Care that the Laws be faithfully executed, and shall so Commission all the Officers of the United States." "The United States shall guarantee to every State in this Union a Republican form of Government, and shall protect each of them . . . against domestic Violence." *Each of them.* The donkeys glared at me, clearly unhappy that I was there.

I turned and limped back to Miranda's cell. She didn't seem surprised.

"Why did they let me into the prison? And where were they when I came in?"

"I asked them to let you in, and to let you bring your questions directly to me."

She'd *asked* them. I said, "And why didn't Huevos Verdes . . ." But she had already answered that. *We agreed it would be better to let you find your own way.*

I said quietly, "Like gods. Set above us."

She said, "If you want to think of it that way."

I went on gazing at her. Two eyes, two arms, a mouth, two legs, a body. But not human.

I said—made myself say—"Thank you."

And she smiled. Her whole face changed, opened up, became planes of light. She looked like anyone else.

"Good luck to you, Vicki."

I heard, *To all of you.* Miranda Sharifi would never need luck. When you controlled that much tech, including the tech of your own mind, luck became irrelevant. What happened was what you wanted to happen.

Or maybe not. She had loved Drew Arlen.

"Thank you," I said again, formally, inanely. I left the cell.

They would go back to Sanctuary, I suddenly knew. When they agreed the time was right they would, by some unimaginable technology that would look to us godlike, snatch Miranda out of Oak Mountain and return to their orbital in the sky. They should never have left Sanctuary. Whatever they wanted to do for us, down here, for whatever reasons, they could probably do just as well from Sanctuary. Where they would be safe. Where they belonged.

Not on Earth.

I realized, then, that in my preoccupation with the United States I had failed to ask Miranda about the rest of the world. But it didn't matter. The answer was already clear. The SuperSleepless would supply the rest of the world with syringes, as soon as they had manufactured enough of them. Miranda would not make distinctions among nationalities—not in the face of the much greater distinction between all of us and the twenty-seven of them. And then the rest of the world, like the United States, would undergo the cataclysmic political changes that came from changing the very nature of the species. They would have no choice.

Nobody spoke to me as I made my way back through the barred doors and the automated doors and the biodetectors. That was all right with me; they didn't have to speak. All they had to do was be there, officially there, upholding the laws, keeping law itself in existence. Even when the technology couldn't be controlled, or even understood by most of us. The effort to include all of us humans in the law was what counted. The effort to understand the law, not just follow it. That might save us.

Maybe.

The doors all locked audibly behind me.

Outside it had started to rain. I hobbled through the drizzle, through the dark, toward the Y-lights of the camp. They shone brightly, but my ankle still ached and twice I almost stumbled. Nearly everyone was under cover. From one tent I heard crying, wailing for someone dead in the panic after the air attack. It started to rain harder. The earths beneath my feet, one whole and one temporarily smashed, started to turn to nourishing mud.

I had almost reached my tent when I saw them rushing toward me. Billy in the lead, waving a torch in the rain, his young-old face creased with relief. Annie, whom I didn't like and probably never would. And Lizzie, leaping like a young gazelle, quickly overtaking and passing the other two, shouting and crying my name, so glad that I was here, that I was alive on Earth. My people.

It was enough.

Twenty-two

Oh, Miranda . . . I'm *sorry*.
I never intended . . .
But I would try to stop you again.
And I don't expect you to understand.